1 MONTH OF
FREE
READING

at
www.ForgottenBooks.com

By purchasing this book you are eligible for one month membership to ForgottenBooks.com, giving you unlimited access to our entire collection of over 700,000 titles via our web site and mobile apps.

To claim your free month visit:

www.forgottenbooks.com/free216439

ISBN 978-0-266-21022-1
PIBN 10216439

THE SURGEON'S STORIES.

By Z. TOPELIUS.

THE
SURGEON'S STORIES.

BY

Z. TOPELIUS,

PROFESSOR OF HISTORY, UNIVERSITY OF FINLAND.

A SERIES OF

Swedish Historical Romances,

IN SIX CYCLES.

(EACH CYCLE IN ONE VOLUME. PRICE $1.25.)

NOW PUBLISHED:

FIRST CYCLE—TIMES OF GUSTAF ADOLF.
SECOND CYCLE—TIMES OF BATTLE AND REST.
THIRD CYCLE—TIMES OF CHARLES XII.
FOURTH CYCLE—TIMES OF FREDERICK I.

IN PREPARATION.

FIFTH CYCLE—TIMES OF LINNÆUS.
SIXTH CYCLE—TIMES OF ALCHEMY.

THE SURGEON'S STORIES.

TIMES OF FREDERICK I.

BY

Z. TOPELIUS.

———

TRANSLATED FROM THE ORIGINAL SWEDISH.

———

CHICAGO:
JANSEN, McCLURG, & COMPANY.
1884.

The Surgeon's Stories.

FOURTH CYCLE:

TIMES OF FREDERICK I.

CONTENTS.

PART I.—SPRING IN THE WILDERNESS.

PART II.—THE BURGHER KING.

TIMES OF FREDERICK I.

PART I.—SPRING IN THE WILDERNESS.

INTERLUDE.

ONE winter evening, when the audience was again assembled in the Surgeon's room, and the light-heaped snow covered the window-panes in broad, soft flakes, Captain Svanholm, the postmaster, contrary to all expectation, was pleased to favor the company with his martial presence. The fact is, that after the close of the previous story he had made known, with a very brave oath, that he had now been present at the recital of everything that he cared about hearing, and by no means intended to trouble himself further to listen to any stories about trifling men and matters after the death of Charles XII. The clatter of his heavy iron-heeled boots was nevertheless heard among the first this evening in the attic stairway, and the honest captain, yielding to the force of habit, marched in as usual, as though he had forgotten the rash vow to shine by his absence. It may be also that he lacked the customary amount of contention which he seemed to require every evening, to enable him to sleep upon his laurels, and with which his fretful old housekeeper ordinarily used zealously to furnish him. He entered thus, apparently in the deepest tranquillity, but in reality secretly caged up in advance, like a plucky game-cock which is privately prepared for important scuffles.

9

The Surgeon, with practiced eye, perceived this, and greeted him with a smile. But Magister Svenonius, the schoolmaster, who sat with the assurance of victory depicted in his thin, swarthy face, not being disposed this time to let his old friend and antagonist escape his thrusts, accompanied his salutation with the ironical remark that Brother Svanholm needed to warm himself after that Christmas night on the Norse Alps, A. D. 1718, and ought, therefore, to draw as near the fire as possible.

The captain, who, after his unlucky vow, found a reservation unavoidable, answered, in the beginning as mildly as possible, that if Brother Svenonius wished to roast potatoes by the fire, he was quite welcome to do so, but as he, Svanholm, had come hither to hear something more about the fate of the last Carolins, anything else concerned him very little. He hoped and expected that Brother Bäck might still have a grain of gunpowder left from the great war, enough at least to blacken the noses of the pedants.

The allusion was not elegant, and the schoolmaster perhaps regarded himself as immediately plucked by his black whiskers. He therefore retorted, in his turn, that he was not the one who needed to blacken his moustache (the captain's moustache inclined, as we know, to red,) and as to the gunpowder of Charles XII, that was now fired off, both for his time and for posterity. Brother Svanholm should certainly have an opportunity to smell burnt horn in the next story; but he should also have an opportunity to see how the pedants succeeded by degrees in washing off the vile powder-smoke from the face of time after 1721.

"Yes indeed, seventeen-forty-one and forty-two were finely washed," scornfully interposed the captain. "The writing world showed its exact efficiency there ; and if there was anything potent in all that time, it was that ' shadow of a name,' and those old grenadiers who still haunted the world from the time of Charles XII."

" Seventeen hundred and forty-one was only brag-gadocio in the style of Charles XII," resumed the schoolmaster.

" Yes, after he hàd played out the trump, and only the small cards were left. Shades of heroes ! They had *grande misère ouverte* on hand, and yet undertook to play a game of hearts. One might be beaten on such cards."

" The most remarkable part of the former story to me," continued the schoolmaster, "was Eva Rhenfelt's question to Charles XII, in Christinehamn, in 1718 : ' *What has your majesty done with Finland ?* ' Take notice, Brother Svanholm ; there was no powder in those words, if brother pleases. They were brave words ; I cannot deny that. She might well have add-ed : What has your majesty done with Estonia, with Livonia, with Ingermanland, with half the kingdom, and lastly, with Sweden herself ? But perhaps the one question was enough. Now, if brother had been in the king's place, what answer would brother have made to that question ?"

" I?" repeated Svanholm, flattered and perplexed.

" Yes. Suppose that brother had been Charles XII, what answer would brother have made ?"

" I should have replied, ' Go to ! Have I time now to listen to old women's nonsense ?' "

" Brother remembers, however, that Charles XII did not answer a word, but turned his back to the questioner. Does not brother believe that the question went, like a Cossack pike, straight through his copper-mailed conscience ? And does not brother think that that question alone broke the spell around the career of Charles XII, and around all so-called heroes, who, for their own renown, their own personal glory, have led their people to the butcher's bench ?"

" Shades of heroes ! " ejaculated the captain, utterly amazed and offended at this pedantic tirade against all heroes indiscriminately. But in his martial wrath he was only able to mutter through his moustache an indistinct protest, in which could be distinguished only the words, " Ink-pots, blockheads—people who were not even worthy to brush the coat of Charles XII's shoe-boy, much less domineer over such a Beelzebub as he ! "

The reader may remember that among the younger members of the Surgeon's company, Charles XII had some still more decided adherents, if possible, than the warlike postmaster ; and the captain immediately gained an intrepid ally in Anne Sophie, who repeatedly attacked the enemy in the flank, while little Jonathan harassed him in the rear as importunately as, considering his extraordinary respect for the learned schoolmaster, he dared. An extremely animated discussion consequently arose, during which the pedestal of Charles XII's renown was now stormed and demolished by the assailants, and now retaken and elevated to the very clouds by his defenders. It may be said that the same conflict between conflicting opinions has been going on throughout the entire North for nearly a century and a half, and bids fair to continue so long as " King Orre " and " the Crown Sergeant " contend for the chief place in Swedish history ; so long as the ideal and the real figure are arrayed against each other. In the Surgeon's time, when Tegnèr's " Axel " had just appeared, the contest was decided in favor of those who thought with the poet :

> " Dear is the olden time to me,
> The time of doughty Carolins ;
> For calm as he that hath no sins
> It was, and brave as victory."

A later time is perhaps prone to sanction and approve Fryxell's contribution note for Charles XII's surviving

family; but in that out-of-the way attic, the schoolmaster came very near being thoroughly beaten by the
Carolinian party, especially as two of the great powers
were apparently neutral. The Surgeon purposely now
and then threw in an irritating remark, to encourage
the combative inclination; and the old grandmother
tried, according to her custom, but for a long time
vainly, to divert the controversy to some innocent side-
issue—about as one, in case of necessity, reins a runaway horse into the drifts at the side of the road.

"Be so good as to tell me one thing," finally
exclaimed grandmother, elevating her voice. "Did
Charles XII really fall by the hand of an assassin, as
would seem from some expressions in the previous
story?"

All present were ready to answer the question with
yes. The Surgeon alone added the qualification that
the matter certainly was not demonstrably settled. He
had said concerning it only what many able men, and
among them several historians, had said before him.
He would not, however, deny that popular belief
always has a certain disinclination to accept the fact
that extraordinary men and heroes, who have astonished
the world, finish their career exactly like other mortals. Hercules was destroyed by a poisoned garment;
Romulus was carried away by a cloud; Charles the
Great still sits in the mountain, waiting for the last
judgment, when his beard shall grow around the stone
table; Olof Tryggvason was not drowned at Svoldern;
Charles the Bold did not fall at Nancy; Gustaf Adolf
was shot with a silver ball;—why should Charles
XII simply fall before a Norwegian bullet, from the
bastions of Frederickshall?

"Thus it is," replied the old grandmother, "the
simplest is often that which is comprehended last. It
would of course be altogether too natural that a rash
fellow like Charles XII could be hit as he stood, with
his arms on the parapet, exposed to the enemy's fire,

and fall, like any other soldier. No indeed! there must be 'a coalition of the allied powers of Europe,' or however these profound matters are expressed, in order to get the better of a pitcher* which went so often to the well after water."

" A pitcher!" repeated Captain Svanholm, blazing red. " Charles XII a pitcher!"

" Pitcher or pail, it is all the same," responded grandmother. " I beg that cousin may filter my meaning, and not my words. At all events, he fell; what was there remarkable in that? The wonder is that he did not fall long before."

" The wonder is, rather, that he fell in his right hour, before *all* fell with him," gravely rejoined the Surgeon.

" Let us not dispute any more about it," continued the old grandmother, content with having, by her little feint, diverted the strife from its most furious battle-field. "The blessed man is welcome to all the little satisfaction he can have in his grave, over the many pretty verses and other things which have been written about him. But he would certainly have done us a favor if he had refrained from conducting that Norse Christmas matin, for then we should still have had our excellent Major Bertelsköld. I cannot say that I have been especially partial to his robber-life in the forests, and his many singular adventures; but a faithful heart is as good as gold, and that can be said of Gustaf Adolf Bertelsköld. May his widow, the brave lady, live to see their little Carl Victor become a good, honest man."

" Will he be as strong as the major?" asked little Jonathan, who now made daily attempts at Bertelsköld's art of lifting a man at arm's length with each hand. This was, in Jonathan's eyes, the height of human perfection.

" Dear Jonathan, the men continually grew weaker

* *Kruka*, the Swedish word for pitcher, also means *coward*.—Translator.

in the arms, and colder in the heart," jokingly answered Anne Sophie. "In olden times they could break horse-shoes in pieces; even in grandmother's youth, they could fight as they fought at Porosalmi and at Lappo ; but now-a-days they are ready to give up the ghost when they dance the bridegroom down at a wedding."*

"How much influence coffee and tea, brandy and tobacco, toddy and dressing-gowns, down pillows and chamber air, lessons, overshoes and warm lobbies may have had, I will not decide," remarked the Surgeon. "But I hardly believe that the present generation is, on an average, much weaker than were the Carolins. The difference is that strength and manly courage were both valued and needed more then than now, and for that reason people were disciplined in them from childhood. Ninety were destroyed by the ordeal, but ten became strong by it, and then they forgot the ninety to praise the ten. Keep on wrestling, Jonathan, and you too will be able to lift your man and fold a silver plate !"

"Charles Victor Bertelsköld was fortunately born at a period when people were learning to place a higher value upon virtue and knowledge than upon rude physical strength," replied the schoolmaster, with a defiant glance at his military antagonist.

"If he was born a coward he may remain a coward, as far as I am concerned," retorted the postmaster, nettled ; "but if he was born a man, and took after his father and mother, it will be seen that Charles Victor Bertelsköld some day does justice to his name. I hope he will have better teachers than his crafty, herring-like uncle, whom I cannot tolerate on my

* " Dancing the bridegroom down " is a part of the amusement at every Scandinavian peasant's wedding. In a dance, especially a wedding dance, the serious Northman lays aside that dignity for which he is pre-eminent, and enters into the frolic with a zest inimitable by his warmer-blooded brothers of the South. In one dance, the Flalling, all the young men try to kick the ceiling ; the most successful one becomes the hero of the evening, and he who fails becomes the laughing stock of all.—Tr.

premises. Shades of heroes! Brother Svenonius has a drill-master there according to his fancy."

" Is anything further known about those Carolins who survived the king?" asked Anne Sophie.

" It is known," replied the Surgeon, " that the few who, highly esteemed, survived the king by forty or fifty years, never neglected to uncover their heads at the mention of Charles XII's name, and always spoke with a reverence and an admiration without equal, of the hero king and his great achievements, his simple manners, his sincere piety, and his inflexible iron will. I think no one will easily forget that veteran soldier, 'the very last on earth who had seen King Charles.' The last Carolin survivor of high rank was General Cronstadt, who died in 1750. The last known officer was Captain Guttofsky, who died in 1784, at ninety-nine years of age. The last known soldier was named Nils Örberg, and died in 1816, at one hundred and eight years of age, in Dalsland, Sweden."

" But then he was not more than ten years old at the time of the king's death," remarked grandmother, with her practical head for calculations.

" That is true," said the Surgeon, " but young as he was, he probably served, as did many another also at that time, as piper or scullion. Örberg I did not know ; but I knew another old Carolin who was certainly one of the last on earth. His name was Abraham Lindgrist. He was born in 1696, served as dragoon under King Charles, and after receiving his discharge, settled down to a little country trade in Tammerfors, from whence he afterwards removed to New Carleby, and died in 1801, at one hundred and five years of age. He was one of the few mortals who could say they had lived in three centuries. Moreover, he had, in his youth, lifted both horse and load over the fence when he was pursued by the Cossacks ; but in his last years the tall man had shrunken to a little bowed figure, snow-white with age, who was looked upon almost with surprise, as a ghost from antiquity."

The company relapsed into silence. The belligerent powers seemed inclined to conclude peace on the graves of the Carolins. Finally the old grandmother asked what, after all the dreadful tumult of war, was to be expected in the next story. The Surgeon, who had been looking out at the wild snow-storm and the snowy window-panes, now turned to his blooming auditor, Anne Sophie, grasped her hand, and with a kind look, said:

" Spring in the Wilderness."

CHAPTER I.

THE PEACE OF NYSTAD

L ONG, sorrowful years had fallen like hail and winter snow on the over-bled heart of Finland, and many already believed that it had forever ceased to beat, when, toward the autumn of 1721, a message of hope flew from mouth to mouth, over the kingdom of the North. It was the news that after three years of negotiations, often broken off, and hitherto fruitless— after stratagems, delays, intrigues, faithlessness, threats, bribes, flatteries, stubborn objections, and renewed war dangers of all kinds– the longed-for peace had at last, August 30 (O. S.), b :n concluded at Nystad, thus ending the great northern war, which had lasted, without intermission, for full twenty-one years from the beginning of the century. War's death angel, born in the secret cabinets of monarchs, and openly nourished by the blood and tears of the people, had just arrived at maturity, when, for lack of sustenance, he was obliged

B   1*

to release his prey. But he did not leave it before he
had, like the vampire, sucked out all its blood, and
palsied its vital power so that the giant race of the
North, after this terrible crisis, shrunk to a dwarf.

What had it not cost—that peace which forever inscribed the name of little Nystad in the history
of the North! The fruit of the victories and conquests of two centuries : the rich Livonia with its active
commerce ; fertile Estonia, Finland's sister-land, and
with it all the coast of the Southern Finnish waters ;
Ösel and Dagö, with other islands inhabited to this
day by Swedish colonists ; Ingermanland's bloodily
contested morasses, and Neva's mighty arteries, emi-
nently fitted by nature for the center of a great empire ;
broad, glorious Ladoga, a sea and kingdom in itself ;
old Wiborg, the uttermost bulwark of the Swedish
dominion, whose ramparts had so often hurled back
the surge of the Orient, and with Wiborg, its territory,
the south-eastern corner of Finland, where brother was
torn from brother, on opposite sides of an unnatural
boundary—all together more than a kingdom, more
than a maritime state ; the control of the Baltic Sea,
the bridge to the Occident, the sea breeze under the
wings of the eagle, and the ascendency in the North.
There was promised, it is true, on both sides, "an
everlasting, eternal, sincere and inviolable peace on land
and sea, with true unity and an indissoluble and eternal bond of friendship" between the two governments,
so that the former animosities "shall never more be
thought of," and in like manner, the royal majesty of
Sweden, "in the most effectual manner possible, for
all time renounces for himself, his successors and de-
scendants, and the whole kingdom of Sweden, all right,
pretension and charge, as his royal majesty and the
kingdom of Sweden, to and of all the above-named
provinces, islands, countries and regions, possessed and
capable of being possessed, etc.," and in return it was
promised that his majesty the czar, his heirs and suc-

cessors to all eternity, should not possess or claim to possess any right or title under whatsoever pretext or name
it might be, to the now restored grand-duchy of Finland, together with the remaining part of the province
of Kexholm. History has recorded that " eternal
peace " among very many other similar ones, prov-
ing the uncertainty of written words, and the inability
of any period to judge what shall take place in other
times and generations.

And yet, with all these enormous sacrifices, with all
the threatening future calamities which peace induced
rather than averted, seldom has a message been received
with greater delight in the North than was this same
peace of Nystad. Posterity can haggle over the conditions, and censure the ambassadors for their unwarrant-
able negligence ; but at that time the weariness was so
great, the need of rest and quiet so imperative, that
peace, peace at whatever cost, was the innermost thought
in all hearts, the sonorous cry upon the lips of all. The
kingdom of Sweden resembled a failing champion who
day and night had watched at his post with superhuman
exertions, until his arms had become numb, his knees
had given way, his eyes had closed, and his heart des-
paired. In such circumstances one does not select the
softest couch, but sinks down upon the first little hillock in his path, indifferent to what his rest may cost,
if only he can wrap himself in the tattered flag, and
preserve his honor for better days to come.

But in the bitter chalice of that renunciation,
there was a great drop of sweetness. Nine-tenths of
the lost and sorely regretted Finland had been regained.
The mother had still saved out of the ruins of the
burning house where her wealth was buried, her most
beloved child—weak, unconscious, exhausted, with
scarcely a sign of life, but saved, still saved, for hope
and for the future. She might, perhaps, have offered
up that one also, and still have lived ; such indeed
became her fate at a later time   But the child could

not have lived if it had been separated from her in 1721. No part of all which, after a century's development, befell Finland for her good could then have befallen her. And thus, powerless, broken, crushed even to death as was the country at the time of the peace of Nystad and under the prevailing spirit of the age, Finland might have become irrecoverably buried, like a disappearing fragment in the billows of the ocean, and at this hour its name might only have been known as that of a Russian dependency, scarcely able to vie, in standing and importance, with Estonia.

In comparison with this gain, the rest of our advantages in the conditions of the treaty—King Frederick's secured place on a tottering throne, the free export of grain from Livonia, and the two millions of rix-dollars which Russia granted as an alms to bankrupt Sweden—were to be regarded as matters of little moment, hardly able to counterbalance the humiliation of not having been able to effect an amnesty for the Cossacks of Mazeppa.

The now active little Nystad, founded in 1617 by Gustaf II Adolf, had during the same century arrived at a certain prosperity, chiefly by means of its wooden-ware and lumber, which were industriously exported in small sloops to Stockholm. In 1685, on the 14th of September, a conflagration had destroyed the town, which had not fully recovered from this calamity, when famine, war and pestilence also came to ravage its peaceful neighborhoods. At this time, 1721, the new stone church, the building of which was begun in 1706, was not yet finished. The houses were small, red-painted, one-story wooden cottages, and the streets narrow, so that the town offered very few conveniences for the distinguished negotiators of peace, of whom the Swedish envoy, councilor Count Liljenstedt, and prefect Baron Strömfelt, together with the great Russian master of the ordnance, Count Bruce, had arrived the previous spring ; but privy-councilor Osterman, the powerful favorite of the czar, had let them wait for him, and purposely protracted the time in order to drive the Swedes to extremity and extort one more tribute from impoverished Finland. On Kivikarta island, just outside the city, a large house had been erected, solely for the ambassadors and their numerous retinue. Here the Swedes certainly objected somewhat, but it was not to this transaction that the well-known saying referred :

"Much they did not object, but half at first was objected."

Finally came the controversy about Ösel and Wiborg. Ösel was quickly lost, when the cry of distress at Nystad was heard from the Swedish coast, where the Russian fleet, for the third summer, was now committing depredations by land and sea. After this, and when Osterman bade the Swedish envoy read more carefully a certain point in their secret instructions, Wiborg also went. A two-months' truce, beginning July 20th, preceded the conclusion of peace.

Scarcely had the truce become known, before a great number of boats and small vessels from the nearest coasts hastened to Nystad, as the surest place for ascertaining the direction in which the winds of the times were blowing and the flags turning. Even from Roslagen, on the opposite shore, boats arrived with Finnish refugees, trembling with impatience to learn Finland's fate, and with it often their own ; for many among them, in the prevailing poverty and insecurity of Sweden, suffered scarcely less distress there than at home in their own ravaged land. A tolerably animated barter arose ; Russian and Hollandish merchants, who accompanied the ambassadors and their suite, would not accept the worthless Swedish coin, but sold salt, meal and hemp, in exchange for butter, tallow, furs, iron, and sheet copper, which the Finns were here and there able to scrape together.

Around that house wherein the boundaries of kingdoms and the position of the North were at this time decided, there stood for many summer days, from early morn till late at eve, a restless, waiting crowd, endeavoring to read in the countenances of those great gen- tlemen and their companions, peace or war. Every liveried *valet* who, with plumed hat and wide-sleeved embroidered coat, showed himself, with mysterious mien, on the stairs or in the door, was stared at by the crowd, as an oracle, and assumed an importance as great as though the fate of the North rested upon his shoulders. If in these portentous faces the beholders fancied they read bad news, many half-suppressed sighs and inconsolable tears were visible amongst the crowd ; but if the barometer of masters and servants indicated fine weather, the sinking courage of the mul- titude was again revived, and every one spoke only of his plans for the immediate future. So far had this gone, that every embroidered fool in Nystad was able, by simply knitting his brows, to terrify this otherwise undaunted people, who for long years had braved the severest misfortunes and the most overwhelming enemies.

Notwithstanding the truce, disquieting rumors some- times gained circulation. Now it was that war had again burst into blaze, and that the czar, in his own person, was pressing forward with a large fleet toward Stockholm ; now that the distinguished gentlemen within had fallen into a violent dispute, and had threat- ened to leave Nystad immediately ; and again that all Finland had been given over to be plundered at the conclusion of peace. The frequent couriers and the daily conferences at last led to the surmise that the decisive hour drew near. Every day the disquiet in- creased, and the Cossacks, stationed outside the con- ference house, often had trouble to keep off, with their threatening pikes, the too importunate crowd of the inquisitive.

One day—it was the 31st of August, early in the

morning—it became known that the diplomats had been
assembled all the preceding day, and that late in the
evening a new courier had departed for St. Petersburg,
while another courier, in a swift-sailing cutter, was dis-
patched to Stockholm. The meaning of these messengers did not long remain a secret. Nystad, unconscious
of the veil of sorrow with which this day was to envel-
ope its name in the history of Sweden, awoke to a day
of rejoicing. From breathless expectation, from the
various pangs of uncertainty, the emotions of the populace passed to an unrestrainable delight. The stolid
Finnish temperament had for a moment laid aside its
phlegm. They wept, they laughed, they cried out, they
embraced each other, acquaintances and strangers,
friends and enemies; even the savage but jovial
Cossacks, who had so long been the terror of
the land, rollicked arm-in-arm with sailors and peasant women at the harbor, with flask in hand and
cheers upon their lips. All was forgotten—all that
had been suffered, all that had been renounced, years
of misery, rivers of blood, a hundred thousand
graves, poverty, hunger, exile, death, despair, all—all
was this hour forgotten in the unspeakably blessed feeling of once more possessing a country, a home and a
future. They felt themselves suddenly lifted up out of
the abyss of utter distress where they had lain in such
deep humiliation that they had almost forgotten to hope
for better days. What now signified all that they had
suffered and lost? They felt that they once more possessed the right to live ; and with this feeling, they
were suddenly rich, fortunate, happy and free.

The ratifications of the monarchs, on the conclusion of peace, both dated the 9th of September, were
not slow to arrive. But already, before the bray-
ing trumpets announced the glad event to the people,
the news had flown around the land and the kingdom,
and bleeding Sweden and exhausted Finland once
more breathed free.

Had the posterity that cast gloomy glances back
upon the peace of Nystad, only for a single day lived
through those sorrows without equal, and those emotions without name, it might perhaps with gentler
hand have lifted aside the veil of sorrow from the
memory of Nystad, and inscribed her name among
those dispensations of Providence which bear upon
their forehead the impress of the inevitable.

CHAPTER II.

IN NYSTAD HARBOR.

NYSTAD was not that sort of place which could
offer every day diversions to the aristocratic
young gentlemen who, as suite and aids, accompanied
the ambassadors. They therefore made use of a
couple of hours' leisure in the afternoon of this same
31st of August to walk down to the harbor and look
at the motley multitudes, who, so unaccustomed to a
glad hour, now conducted themselves the more uproar-
ously.

The scene was a very animated one. All the vessels
and boats with flags had hoisted them, and those which
had none tried to make up for the lack by using green
birches, which were hoisted in such numbers that the
harbor resembled a young forest. The September
sun (for according to the new style it would already be
the 11th of September) shone brightly on the calm
surface of the water, which had just made its peace
with the storms of ocean. Temporary trading-booths
were erected on the shore, in which there was no lack of
ale and whisky; and the Russian soldiers, the only
portion of the throng who had money, were liberal

customers. Freely and gaily they treated their new friends, especially when young girls were in the company. Many of the soldiers during their long abode here had married Finns, to whom there was comparatively free access, as among the surviving inhabitants there were at least three women to one man. Some had formed engagements in the place, and others were hastening to do so, for they knew that within four weeks the country would be evacuated. Very few ceremonies were necessary in these transactions, for usages had, alas! become so deteriorated during the long wretchedness that almost any woman allowed herself to be sold to the most detestable foreigner who offered a few shining silver rubles or a milch cow, regarding herself as fortunate in not being taken for nothing, as often happened when women and children were carried away as colonists to Russia. Also discipline, which had been rigidly maintained by the lamented Prince Galitzin, as far as his arm extended, had of late years, under the new governor-general, Douglas, the robber of the people, been allowed to grow lax, so that the army was accustomed to all kinds of excesses in the conquered country.

The Finns, debilitated by hunger and all kinds of privation, were not able to bear many drops of whisky in their blood, and the day-old "eternal" peace was already, on a small scale, very near seeing the end of its short eternity. There was jealousy and humiliation on the part of the Finns, perhaps envy also, at the happy lot of the Russian soldiers, with everything in abundance and money in their pockets. Here and there at the booths quarreling arose, and from quarreling they came to fighting, which usually ended to the disadvantage of the Finns, very few of whom were young and strong, but almost all were gray old men or half-grown boys. Fortunately, through all this, the delight at the close of peace was so preponderant, and the women, the cause of the conflict, came forward so zealously as peace-makers, that the disputes were closed as hastily as they begun, and the greater part of the crowd did not allow themselves to be disturbed by them.

Two young and fine-looking gentlemen, Baron Sparrfelt and Von Weidern—the former private secretary to Count Liljenstedt, and the latter acting in the same capacity for privy-councilor Osterman—were walking arm in arm, like an illustration of the treaty of peace, and amusing themselves with the noise, when their attention was attracted by a new commotion near the shore. A tall Russian grenadier, laughing and swearing, was pursuing a young Finnish peasant girl, who, in order to escape him, sprung into a boat, and shot out from land. The grenadier sprung after her in the shallow water, and seized the stern of the boat. The girl threatened him with the oar, and, as he did not let go of the boat, gave him a quite justifiable sound rap across the shoulder. Irritated at this, the grenadier pressed the stem of the boat under the water so that the girl lost her balance and slipped into the water also, where a new struggle arose between her and her pursuer.

Curious to watch this scene, the young gentlemen drew near. The girl once more escaped, but instead of fleeing to the shore, she resolutely stopped and menaced the grenadier anew with the oar.

" *Morbleu!* " exclaimed Sparrfelt, with a genteel oath, "it seems to me as though I had seen that brave lass before. I declare! if it is not little Marie, from Stockholm, she who bewitched my own brother, the captain of horse! How the devil has she become a peasant girl, and got to Nystad ? "

The grenadier, without heeding a new blow, seized the girl by the waist and wrenched the oar from her hand.

" Upon my honor, I have a mind to beat my brother at that game ! " exclaimed Sparrfelt, as he sprung to the shore, to aid the weaker party. But he arrived a second too late. A young man in a peasant jacket reached the place before him, sprung into the water, and in his turn seized the grenadier about the waist. The latter let go of the girl and turned furiously upon his new antagonist. A violent scuffle ensued between the two, and meanwhile the girl hastened to the shore, and paused there, with glowing cheeks, awaiting the issue of the combat.

The grenadier, a head taller than his adversary, threw himself upon him with all his weight, to bear him down into the water. Contrary to the expectation of all, however, he had found his master in the short but broad-shouldered youth in the peasant jacket. It was not long before the peasant, with a powerful jerk, lifted up the grenadier and threw him at full length into the muddy water, which at that place was not more than about two feet deep.

The crowd on the shore sent up a shout of applause. Sparrfelt meanwhile made use of the opportunity to pay his respects to the still waiting girl, whose uncommon beauty, heightened by her excitement, drew from Von Weidern an exclamation of surprise.

"I am indeed happy, lovely Marie, in being able to offer you my protection against these rough soldiers and peasants," said the young knight, in French, and in a tone of gallantry strongly mingled with an aristocratic patronage. "Come; I will conduct you to the ambassador's house, and there, in quiet, you can relate to me by what strange chance I meet you here, and in this unexpected costume."

The young girl was so absorbed in the combat, a little distance away, that she did not at first observe her new protector. But scarcely had she heard her name mentioned before a sudden paleness succeeded the flush on her cheeks, and she hastened to draw the woolen cloth farther down over her forehead.

"The gracious gentleman is mistaken," said she, in

Swedish, with a little trembling of the voice and a rather Ålandish accent.

"*Mille tonnerres!*" responded Sparrfelt, in amazement; "can it be possible? . . . . But no, beautiful Marie; do not try to deceive me. Who, having once seen you, would not at the first glance recognize Marie Larsson, Countess Horn's lovely *protégée*, who has been fostered so many years in her house in Stockholm . . ."

"I know neither horns nor hoofs," replied the girl again, with a loud laugh, and a still stronger accent. "I am from Åland, and have been seven years with my aunt in Roslagen. 'See, that is the confectionery,' as the old woman said of the herring; but I happened to lose aunt in the crowd, and then that vile fellow came."

"The devil, you say!" again responded Sparrfelt, with an aristocratic toss of the peruke-ornamented neck, but evidently quite nonplussed. "If you are not the same Marie with whom I had the honor of dancing a Spanish quadrille last winter, at Count Bertelsköld's, then some Finnish witch must have copied your portrait, and mingled a love potion in the Rhenish wine in which I had the honor to drink your health at Count Liljenstedt's dinner. By all the freaks of Cupid, beautiful Marie, your ladyship may be any one whomsoever, so I claim the privilege of being your declared knight to-day."

"Attend to Cupid, if your honor has a horse by that name, but let me alone! I am no witch," snappishly replied the girl. "But here comes Elias," and with these words she abruptly left him to meet the young man in the peasant jacket, who, after his victory over the tall grenadier in the water, was now approaching her.

The circumstances were these: The Russian commander, who had that day received strict orders to prevent disagreements with the Finnish populace, had

SPRING IN THE WILDERNESS.

sent out a patrol, who arrived in due time, to seize the grenadier, and take him to the guard-house at head-quarters, as a disturber of the peace. By this means, a continuance of the angry encounter was averted, and the man in the jacket arrived on dry land without further adventure.

"Come, Elias," said the girl, grasping the young man's arm, "let us find aunt!"

Baron Sparrfelt objected, but in his uncertainty as to who the young girl really was, he allowed her to escape, and in a short time she had disappeared with her companion in the crowd.

Weidern shrugged his shoulders. "With us," said he, "such ceremony is not observed toward a serf, though she be as beautiful as St. Ann, or as the empress Catherine herself."

"With us there are no serfs," replied Sparrfelt, answering the shrug of the shoulders. "*Morbleu!* I may have been mistaken in that brown hair and those roguish blue eyes; but I will still wager Count Liljen-stedt against a common scribe that she is the real Marie Larsson, who has been bewitching all the gen-tlemen in Stockholm for the last two years. Explain this enigma to me, my dear Baron! Is it she, that charming being, who has suddenly been transformed into a rough Ålandish fisher-girl, or is it we who have drunk, in honor of the peace, somewhat too deeply in the noble count's excellent Rüdesheimer?"

CHAPTER III.

THREE FUGITIVES.

THE peace of Nystad was to have been kept secret until the ratification of the monarchs had arrived from Stockholm and Petersburg. But, as in the darkness of night, light forces its way out through every crevice of the bolted cottage, so in the very beginning the great news trickled out over leaky lips, and quickly, if not officially, became known. Alderman Jacob Fahlander, of Old Carleby, to whom posterity is indebted for the best contemporaneous description which Finland possesses of the great war, heard the news from the peace commissioner's own mouth in Nystad, and, under a half-promise of secrecy, obtained the message to the Russian commander in Wasa that the commissioners had not been together in vain, and the commander, "overcome with delight," could not keep silence concerning it. So the message of peace flew northward along the coast, received with great joy also by the Russian troops, who by this time were wearied with their wretched quarters in the desolated land.

The morning after the event described in the previous chapter, Count Liljenstedt summoned his secretary, Baron Sparrfelt, and gave him a reprimand for his conduct of the day before. "The baron had been seen engaged in conversation with highly suspicious persons," he said.

Sparrfelt described the little adventure. "The young girl," said he, "if indeed it was she, is the daughter of a Finnish peasant from Wasa, and, with many other Finnish refugees in Stockholm, had been favored by the protection of Count Horn. Countess Horn had paid especial attention to the little peasant girl, and had her educated in a manner far above her rank, for which reason she was sometimes allowed to take part in the aristocratic evening gatherings. It was natural that the unexpected sight of such a person, disguised, and in such a critical situation . . . . "

"——Should appeal to a young gentleman for his knightly protection—I understand. But does the baron know that her companion, a young man in a peasant jacket, has been recognized as one of the notorous Löfving's boldest partisans—in a word, a *kivekäs?* "

Sparrfelt protested his ignorance of the fact.

"It is nevertheless true," continued the count. " Scarcely three weeks ago—after the truce was agreed upon—the same young man was recognized as the leader of an armed horde of freebooters, who attacked, plundered and burned one of the enemy's galleys anchored among the islands of Pargas. His appearance here has attracted attention. Count Bruce speaks of it with indignation, and it is feared that the scarcely concluded peace may be endangered by new enterprises of the same extremely suspicious tendency."

"But the promised amnesty?"

"That does not extend to robbers. There is no other way now of designating those perverse *kivekät*, who exasperate our enemies at the very moment when everything depends on pacific measures. The Swedish authorities must show themselves equally as zealous as the Russian to suppress such brigandage; and my wish is therefore that you immediately join a Russian command which has received orders to search out and seize the person in question, with all his adherents and companions."

Sparrfelt bowed, secretly not displeased at having an opportunity to appear once more as the mysterious girl's protector, and now armed with legal authority. Neither did he probably feel particularly disposed to be lenient with the young man in the peasant jacket, in whom, not without reason, he suspected a favored rival. He therefore executed the command of his superior with despatch ; and a half hour later found him in pursuit, together with his *valet* and a Russian command consisting of one officer and twenty Cossacks.

It was not long before they had searched through little Nystad, and convinced themselves that those they sought were not to be found in the town. They asked the peasants, who had thronged to the town with the butter which each taxable person had been commanded to pay to the peace congress. No one knew, or would admit that he knew, anything of the fugitives. The majority of the peasants were in secret understanding with the freebooters ; and those who were not, feared their vengeance.

At the command of Count Bruce, it was now announced with the beating of drums on the streets of Nystad, that a prize of one hundred roubles (an enormous sum at that time) was offered to any person or persons who might seize and deliver to the Russian authorities the coast-ranger, Elias Pehrson, accused of having attacked and burned the galley "Golupka" belonging to his majesty the czar, and also of having broken the truce. For the same purpose, Count Liljenstedt offered one hundred dollars in silver coin, and twenty in addition for each of Pehrson's adherents.

An old woman finally allowed herself to be bribed to the acknowledgment that early in the morning a young man and a young girl had traveled northward out of town in a cart drawn by an ox. But at the same time it was reported from the harbor that two similar persons, accompanied by an old woman, had, as early as the previous evening, sailed away to the northward in a boat. Sparrfelt, who missed the boat into which the girl had sprung the day before, regarded the latter account as the right one, and hastily manned a swift sailing yacht, taking with him a few Russian soldiers, together with an under-officer. But the Cossacks rode northward, to seize the fugitives in case they betook themselves to land.

A brisk south-wester was blowing, and the yacht, running before the side-wind, headed toward Lökö lighthouse and Pyhämaa. Every little sail which steered northward was pursued, overtaken and searched. Now it was a fisher setting his nets at Kukkaistenmaa ; now a Eura peasant, returning from Dystad with a peck of salt. Meantime the wind freshened and compelled the pursuers to keep at a proper distance from the coast.

Just at this point a little sail was seen gliding close along the shore. Sparrfelt made every effort to cross its path before it reached the sound at Kursila ; but in vain. The boat glided into the sound, but the yacht gained upon it, the distance was diminished, and now a man and two women could be plainly distinguished in the boat.

Sparrfelt set all sails and followed them into the sound. The yacht was now only a couple of musket-shots from the boat, and called out to it to lie by. For a moment it seemed inclined to obey the order ; the sail was hauled up and the yacht approached. Sparrfelt was now positive that he recognized the same young man who on the day before had thrown the grenadier into the water. So assured was he, that he had ropes mâde ready to bind the freebooter.

But the maneuver of the boat soon proved to be only a bad joke. The yacht had proceeded but a few fathoms when it found itself in the lee of the dense forest of Kamela ; the sail hung limp, and began to shiver before one of those currents of air common in the sound. But the boat thrust out two pairs of oars, and with even but brisk strokes made off to the open sea, where its sail was once more seen to swell before the keen south-wester.

Sparrfelt was furious. It became necessary to use the oars of the yacht also ; but this craft moved slowly,

C

and when at last there was wind in her sails, the fugitive boat seemed but a small white speck among the
foaming waves in the north.

"The devil take the fellow!" exclaimed the police
officer who accompanied the yacht. "Soon he will be
creeping behind Pitkäluoto, and in an hour it will be
dark. We shall scarcely get the better of the bandit
to-day."

"The clouds are thickening and the storm is increasing; would it not be well to make land before dark?"
inquired the under-officer, a Saxon land-lubber, who
began to feel a certain uneasiness at the increasing
commotion of the sea.

"Luff more to the windward and sheer the course
of the sail there!" was Sparrfelt's reply. He had served
in the navy, and wished to show that he was not afraid
of a sprinkle of salt water. The command was obeyed
and the yacht shot forward like an arrow through the
darkening billows.

We will now leave for the present the elegant baron
with his police and soldiers, arduously battling against
the billows of the Bothnian Sea, and cast a glance at
the suspected boat, which was the object of their zeal
and the hoped-for game in this hunt.

It was an ordinary small-sized sail-boat, with the
kind of hull which is at once sharp and well-propor-
tioned (indicating a good sailor), and carrying only a
mainsail and jib. At the helm sat the same youth who
had had the scuffle with the grenadier, and who, in the
announcement concerning his capture, was called Elias
Pehrson. He could not have been much over twenty
years of age, had light hair, an open and somewhat
sunburnt countenance, honest gray eyes, and an expression of shrewdness, vigor and cheerful kindness in all
his bearing. If those hands were stained with blood
and pillage, it could not have happened from cruelty
or rapacity. This robber appeared capable of giving his
own jacket to one destitute in the storm, rather than

of robbing him for gain, in the darkness and calm water. His boat he managed with secure hand, and with a boldness which seemed almost to border upon rashness.

In the middle of the boat sat an old woman of about seventy years, clad in an old sheepskin cloak, and somewhat hard of hearing. Every time the boat careened before the breeze, she leaned anxiously to windward, and muttered a prayer between her teeth.

The third person, in the prow of the boat, was the same young girl whom Baron Sparrfelt had called Marie Larsson, and who had so bravely defended herself against the tall grenadier. She was short, rather than tall, and elastic and vigorous in all her motions. She had long brown hair, arranged in two braids, thoughtful blue eyes, delicate and handsome features— too handsome for a peasant girl, too sprightly for a city lady,—and in her whole manner an expression of natural agreeableness ennobled by careful culture. She had been rowing in the sound, and was still warm from the vigorous exercise; but the blisters upon her hands betrayed her want of practice at this kind of work. She had evidently been more frightened than she would admit, when the boat came so near being overtaken; but the young man's assured manner had restored her courage, and only when a sprinkling wave whirled in over the gunwale and deluged her wadded jacket of black camlet, did she shrink before the swelling of the sea.

So perceptible was this young girl's superior bearing, beside that of her companions, that, regarded with a hasty glance, the three fugitives might easily have been taken for a young lady escorted by her duenna and accompanied by her faithful servant. But upon a closer look it became evident that her assurance was only a reflex of the confident manner of the youth, hiding behind the mask of seeming indifference a young heart's

variable emotions of fear, hesitation, hope, anxiety, and
—who knows?—perhaps also some of those memories
before which the heart melts in mournful thoughts.

CHAPTER IV.

THE AUTUMN STORMS OF 1721.

" IS it far to Raumo?" asked the young girl, who had
for some time been uneasily studying a black
wall of cloud rising from the horizon in the southeast.
Elias sat in the stern, facing the north, so that he had
clear sky before him.

"It is still a dozen good miles to Raumo, and we
are not likely to be very welcome there," replied the
youth. "That is, Marie can go there well enough, but
not I," he added.

"And why not you?" inquired the girl.

"Why, ever since noon have we had that blood-
hound at our heels?" answered the youth, smiling,
as he cast a glance back at the yacht, which, about a
mile to the southward, had set all sails, and was darting
at full speed through the surging water.

"You have not yet told me that, Elias. We first
met, you know, in Nystad,—after the Ålander, who
conducted me from Stockholm, deserted us. I recognized you immediately, in the peasant clothes, although
you did not know me, and you were very kind to take
it upon yourself to conduct me as far as Wasa."

" I could not leave you defenseless in such company,
that is plain. First, we are cousins by birth, as my
mother was your father's sister. And besides, a good
boy must help a good girl. But you see, Marie, that
white rag of sail wishes to get too near us for our safety,

and will have support in Raumo, for soldiers are quartered there. But it will miss its game this time. In half an hour, thank God, we shall have darkness, and a bit of storm and snowfall for our benefit. See this little string! My grandfather got it of an Åbo witch named Black Jane, but he would never use it. There used to be thirteen knots in it; but now there are only two. I untied one to-day, there by the sound, and have a mind to untie the second now."

"Fie, Elias! Can it be that you use such witchcraft at sea! What do you do with it?"

"It is a fine thing to have. It has helped me more than once, when the hounds have been near nabbing me. If I untie one knot, I have wind from whatever quarter I wish; if I untie two, I have such a storm that it whistles in the cordage; and, if I untie three, no ship can weather the sea, and the snow comes like a white coverlet over us, in the middle of summer, and the storm sweeps away forests and houses, and it thunders and crashes like the day of judgment. You see I have still two knots left."

"But how wicked it is! If you were not so good, Elias, I should really be frightened for you. We shall get storm enough to-night, without the aid of that. Tell me, why are they pursuing us?"

"It is a little story. That night when Majniemi castle was blown up, my father had my mother and us children taken to a holm in the archipelago, intending to come and get us; but father chanced to be wounded. We suffered three weeks, till we got away in a Pargas boat to Sweden. There we lived some years, and there I met you at Count Horn's. One day my father returned bringing the gallant Löfving with him; and when Löfving once more betook himself to adventure, I begged to go too. It was hard, you may believe, both for father and mother; but I was as persistent as sin, and had my way at last. So I accompanied Löfving for four years, amid a thousand dangers, and learned his manner of carrying on war.   It was the only way that could accomplish anything now, you see.   It would take too long to tell you of all the times I have worn the garb of old women and beggars, all the times I have been near the Cossack pike, the muzzle of the musket, and the end of a rope.   Löfving had wearied of making incursions by land, and we made them by sea instead.   The Russian galleys came loaded with plunder from the Swedish coasts ; we took a small share of the booty back ; what harm could there be in that? There was no truce for us.   One fine moonlight night, it chanced that we came to the archipelago of Pargas. A galley lay there, moored by the~strand; 'Golupka' was its name.   The crew had gone ashore for a carouse, and the watch was asleep.   There were twenty of us ; we had three boats.   It was a quick maneuver.   We boarded the galley, took what we could and burned the rest.   The galley sunk like a burdened conscience. There were church-bells on board, which will ring matins in the bottom of the sea until the day of judgment."

"It would be dreadful if they knew that you did that, Elias ! "

"As if they did not know it ! Every one knows me, and one after another in Nystad gave me the wink to get myself off.   Douglas is not friendly to me, and Bruce has set a price on my head.   As soon as I caught sight of that Estonian sail I instantly thought, 'there we have our tatterdemalians ! '   Never mind, Marie ! If need be I will patch them with these knots, so that not a rag shall remain dry on them."

·   Twilight set in.   They had reached Wärknäs point, which, a mile and a half south-west of Raumo, juts out into the sea, and were about to double the point, with fair wind, when the boat suddenly struck so violently against a submerged rock, that both the girl and old woman were thrown down from the thwarts.   The next moment the boat was lifted by an on-rushing wave, and found itself again afloat. But the danger was not yet past. The lower eyelet which held the rudder fast had been broken off, and only with the utmost exertion was it possible to steer the boat. To increase the misfortune, the water streamed in through a considerable leak close by the keel.

The young man's first thought was to calm his two female passengers. "Sit very still!" he cried. "I know that treacherous rock; it has deceived more than one honest fellow. Never mind! In less than a quarter of an hour we will be ashore."

The old woman would not allow herself to be comforted. She shrieked aloud that the boat was sinking, and at every careening threw herself toward the opposite side. But Marie seized the scoops, and worked briskly to keep the boat dry.

Elias was compelled to clew the sail and grasp the oars. While this was going on the yacht was seen approaching with a favorable wind. Notwithstanding the twilight, it probably had the boat still in sight.

"What are you doing?" inquired the girl, when Elias ceased rowing for a moment.

"Nothing," replied he. "I am only untying the second knot."

And as though the elements had only been waiting for this signal, the storm quickly increased with terrible force, so that the bay, far around the point, was covered with foam, and the hidden reefs began to roar like wild beasts in the darkness. The short distance they had still to make at every moment threatened the boat with destruction in the breakers. But at last they reached the shore in safety, with the boat half full of water.

"Off with that white handkerchief!" hastily exclaimed the youth. Marie obeyed. The cloth which she had tied around her head might betray the fugitives.

Their caution came perhaps too late. From the

shore they could still see the yacht scudding past the headland, then beat south-east before a half-wind, and soon come under the lee, so that she was able to cast anchor a little distance from shore.   Scarcely was this done, before a well-manned yawl put out from the vessel's side and directed its course toward Annila, with the evident intention of cutting off the retreat of the fugitives from the promontory to the mainland and the highway to Raumo.

When Elias observed this from his lookout on the rock, he smiled.   "The last knot!" he muttered, as he untied the string and threw it far from him into the forest.   Suddenly he grew light of heart.   It seemed to him as though he had freed himself from the last remnant of superstitious sorcery of his ancestors, about which he had heard so many wonderful traditions in his childhood at Majniemi.

Whether the spirit of Black Jane now hovered over the water to give potency to the last inheritance of her magic art, or the bad weather, in a wholly natural way, had long been gathering in the black snow-cloud, there indeed set in such terrific tempest as within the memory of man had not been heard of in these stormy regions. The wind veered suddenly to the south-east, and increased to a hurricane, which raged across the coast on snowy wings.   Everything was enveloped in impenetrable darkness in an instant. Snow, mingled with hail, fell so furiously that in a few minutes all roads and paths were impassable.   In that freezing cold, that terrible darkness, nothing around was heard but the roar of the sea, the screaming of the sea gulls, the howling of the wolves, the din of the storm, and the crashing of century-old pines, which, one after another, sometimes in long stretches, fell, trunk over trunk, in the path of the hurricane, as though one of the judgment angels of the Apocalypse had swept over the region with the vial of wrath, and had laid waste everything in his course. It was as though nature had need of one violent crisis before it could regain its equipoise, after such a series of unusual and destructive phenomena as distinguished the close of the seventeenth and the beginning of the eighteenth century. The authors of that period all speak of the autumn storms of the year 1721 as the most violent ever known; and those storms covered the coasts of unhappy Finland with splinters of ships and with shipwrecked refugees who, upon the first rumor of peace, were hastening home to their beloved country, only to be stretched dead upon her shores.

In a natural grotto, formed by an overhanging ledge of rock, sat the three fugitives, only half protected from the horrors of the tempest. They did not dare to kindle a fire, for fear of betraying their place of concealment; and even if they had dared, the attempt would probably have proved fruitless. The chief effort of the young man was directed toward protecting the two defenceless beings whom chance, or Providence, had entrusted to his care. He gathered moss from beneath the snow, and pine branches from the forest, to prepare them a passable resting-place. Notwithstanding their remonstrances, he took off his short jacket to protect them from the cold. He encouraged them by the assurance that by the dawn of day they should be out of all danger. And when he was rewarded with a kind look from the girl's loving eyes, he felt so happy that he forgot his wild perilous life of adventure, and, under that snowy ledge of rock, in the midst of the storm, darkness, cold, and the uproar of the elements, he felt more blessed than for many years before—even since the happy days of his childhood at home in Majniemi.

" Marie," said he, with a tenderness in his voice, unusual with him, " I will not ask you why you left Stockholm, where you were living in quiet and comfort, with the noble count and his kind countess, to exchange your happy life for the many dangers and privations that meet you here in our own rent and ravaged land. But you certainly must have had a good reason for it."

"You know I have come to search for my old father," replied the girl, evasively. "For six years we have not heard the least news of him. But I am sure nothing could have induced him to move across to Sweden, when he sent my mother and my brothers and sisters out of the country, when the enemy came. There were eleven of us, eight brothers and three sisters. Six of the brothers fell at one time under Major Bertelsköld, shortly before the battle of Storkyro. Two brothers remained at home with father; one of them was carried away to Russia, the other went to the field, and afterwards froze to death in the mountains of Norway. My mother is now dead, and my sisters have married in Sweden. Of all the eleven, I am the youngest, and the only one left to take care of our old father, in case he still lives, perhaps in distress and poverty. Would you, Elias, have stayed in Sweden and lived in luxury, if you had been in my place?"

"But why this costume, if you only wished to search for your father? Why not, rather, travel in a larger vessel, and under better protection, which surely Count Horn could furnish you? Why not come to your father rich and well provided for, rather than poor, and yourself in need of support? The countess loved you as her own child; she would gladly have enabled you to rescue old Thomas Larsson from need."

Marie was silent, and had it not been so dark her clear blue eyes might have been seen to moisten and fall toward the snowy moss.

"Do not ask me about that now," said she at last, entreatingly. "The day will perhaps come when I can tell you all."

The young man questioned her no more. A momentary gloom perhaps filled his soul. The girl suspected it, and grasped his hand. "I cannot tell you now," said she, humbly; "but believe nothing bad about me, Elias. I tell you that you shall sometime see all as clear and light as now it is dark around us."

But little more was said that night under the ledge of rock on Wärknäs Point. Only once in awhile the noise of the storm was interrupted by a cry of distress from the sea, where vessels were foundering, or from the forest, where lost wanderers were freezing to death. But the three fugitives did not venture to leave their asylum ; and what, indeed, in this night of horror, would they have been able to accomplish, against the fury of the elements?

CHAPTER V.

AN EXPEDITION TO RAUMO.

THE morning following the terrible storm was clear and calm as a mirror. A thick white coverlet of snow spread over all the streets and roofs in old Raumo, which at this time presented a more striking aspect of decay than Nystad. One midsummer night in 1682, the greater part of the city had burned down; and only the venerable church of the Franciscans survived the devastation. The horrors of war had now passed over the place. Raumo had at this time six burghers. The lately flourishing school, also an inheritance from the middle ages, was abandoned, and teachers and pupils were scattered or dead. For seven years no axe had sounded, no brush painted, no glazier cut a pane for the preservation of the houses. The city resembled a deserted and desolate village, in which here and there peered forth from the dilapidated windows a pale emaciated face. There had, alas ! no delicate female hand needed the noted Raumo laces, which to this day are an inheritance, removed thither from the industrious nuns in the ancient cloister cells of Nådendal. But even in that dark and wretched time, a few old crones continued, from force of habit, to lace and interlace their Penelope's web, in the hope of better days when a bit of finery might again be needed in Finland—an innocent, delicate, and pleasing luxury, which well deserved some encouragement for its antique origin and subtle dexterity of art. Happy will be our Finland, if it shall never allow itself to be mis-led by a more ruinous luxury than the pretty Raumo laces!

On the morning of which we speak, the poor lace-makers laid aside their work, and hurried to the windows. The company of grenadiers, quartered in the city, marched out, and the Cossacks occupied the otherwise depopulated streets. The good women crossed themselves—it is asserted that they still secretly used this Roman Catholic custom, which had, moreover, been revived by the example of the Russians. They could not believe otherwise than that war had again burst into full blaze. Nothing less was expected than a hostile debarkation on Cape Wärknäs, and those who did not comprehend for what purpose this could be, were convinced that at least a horde of bold freebooters had landed on the cape during the night, to surprise and put to the sword the Russian post.

The truth was that the Cossacks had arrived from Nystad in pursuit of the fugitives; and at the same time, Baron Sparrfelt, on the same errand, had arrived from the beach, with a remnant of his shipwrecked company. The yacht had gone down in the storm, with all on board; the yawl had capsized in the breakers at the point, and half the crew had perished. Instead of caging the fugitives on the point, Count Liljenstedt's ardent deputy, half dead from cold, and with a dislocated foot, was obliged to seek shelter in Raumo, where he did not neglect to report to the military command how the bold freebooter, with his party, was in the immediate neighborhood.

Freebooters were feared to such a degree, even in western Finland, that the Russian commander, who supposed he would have to deal with a considerable horde of these desperate guerrillas, considered that he ought to take extraordinary measures. A couple of field cannon, which were found in the city, were drawn out, and as all the horses were needed for the cavalry, the burgomaster, Hans Reinman, was commanded to procure draught-horses for the baggage. But in this hurry, notwithstanding all his zeal, not more than four horses could be got together in the city of Raumo.

The cavalry, infantry, and artillery, about one hundred and fifty men in all, thus marched in the morning to Wärknäs. As all the roads were blocked up with snow-drifts, the men of the town and the nearest villages were summoned to clear away the snow; but for this purpose the burgomaster was not able to get together more than thirty or forty workmen, the most of them old men and boys, so that also their wives and daughters were obliged to join in the work. An advance guard was sent out to reconnoitre the enemy's position and designs, after which, the whole force, in battle array, and prepared for instant attack, marched into the rugged woodlands which form the point projecting into the sea.

Among the lesser parties sent out, was a sergeant with four men, who were ordered to reconnoitre the southern part of the cape, nearest the mainland. The sergeant was a man about forty years old, rather stout and clumsy, with a pair of ferocious whiskers, and a couple of jovial gray eyes, peering from under the shaggiest eyebrows that ever shaded a brave warrior's martial glance.* Notwithstanding his threatening

---

* With this description, the [schoolmaster darted a shrewd glance at his friend, Captain Svanholm, who, excited and attentive in expectation of the approaching combat, was twirling his red mustaches.

aspect, he seemed to be so little entertained by his laborious march, that when scarcely out of sight of the main force, he sat down on a stone to rest, and in a comical gibberish, compounded of Russian, Swedish, and Finnish, with a strong admixture of his German mother-tongue, commanded his soldiers for the devil's sake to go where they pleased; there was peace now, and he did not intend any longer to run " *mitunterein-ander wie ein Eselsjunge* for these cursed *kivekät, und Teufels nasibratten. Marsch !*" *

The soldiers, uncertain what they ought to think of this order, betook themselves to a dilapidated barn near by, in the hope of being able to close their campaign there at their ease in the soft hay. But scarcely had the first one set foot within the broken door, before he . rushed back shrieking, holding both hands to his head, which was bleeding from a rather rough blow across the shako.

Amazed at this reception, the three other soldiers discharged their muskets at random toward the barn, and then, with their wounded comrade between them, ran away, as fast as they could, to the main force, without questioning further about their nearest superior, the sergeant.

This man had taken a short tobacco pipe out of his side-pocket,. and was just engaged in the agreeable business of drawing the first puffs, when he heard the shriek at the barn, and, immediately afterward, the shots. Quite unpleasantly disturbed in his plans, he thought best, after some reflection, to rise and approach the barn, cutlass drawn and the pipe between his teeth. He had no gun, the good man.

" *Was der Henker ! perkele, stuj, durak !*" ejaculated the sergeant, shouting after his men. But they were already a long distance out of sight, and the valiant leader was a general without an army.

In such a position, generals are accustomed to look upon retreat as belonging to the common course of events; but the brave sergeant resolved to try the chances of war, and clambered rapidly forward.

At this juncture there emerged from the barn a young man clad in a gray jacket, and armed with a drawn sword—one of those long swords which at that time constituted the favorite weapons of the Carolins— in a word, the young Elias Pehrson himself.

"Surrender, or you are a dead man!" exclaimed the youth, as he fell upon his antagonist.

"*Wech mit palaschen, und* on your knees mit that *koiran! oder den Teufel take dich!*" exclaimed the sergeant on his part, and was immediately ready to parry the blow, without, however, letting go of the tobacco pipe.

It was soon evident that both the champions were practiced fencers. Whatever advantage the younger possessed in strength and dexterity, the sergeant compensated for by his imperturbable calmness. He gave and parried blows with the greatest coolness, and at the least breathing-space did not neglect to blow a cloud of smoke from his pipe, which hung six inches in front of his long mustache.

This enraged the youth. His blows fell more rapidly, but at the same time less cautiously. Almost simultaneously the point of his sword cut off the stem of the pipe, and the sergeant's blade had torn his jacket at the left shoulder.

"I will *mans* teach the devilish *perkele* to cut my good *stambulka*!" yelled the sergeant, furious in his turn, and pressed more hotly upon his enemy, but now with less success, for at that instant the blade flew out of his hand through a skillful *croisade* of his antagonist, and the sergeant stood disarmed.

"Surrender!" once more exclaimed the youth, as he threateningly raised his powerful long-sword.

"*Schtill, nur ganz sachte,* comrade, I will *mans* give the sword, and mend the *stambulka*," replied the vanquished. "*Aber a gut Rath* will I *mans* give *dazu.*

Pack yourself off, *padi suda*. *Den kokojoukko ist ganz in der Nähe.*"

"You are right, comrade," replied Elias, thrusting his sword into the sheath, with a feeling of friendship for his disarmed antagonist. Run away now—that is, if you are made for running," he added, with a merry glance at the corpulent form of the sergeant.

"*Noch ein aberdass,*" responded the sergeant. "*Oletko kivekäs?* Which way are you going?"

"I am a *kivekäs*, I am frank to admit; but further I do not mean to confess to you. Bundle yourself off now, and that quickly," replied the youth.

"*Wain minäkin kivekäs!* * I will, *verdamme mich*, go with you, *waikka polyan perään*. You can take *mich mit*. I will give the service *tausend Schweinefleisch*, we *hawe den* peace."

Elias laughed. The man appeared to be in sober earnest. But the moments were precious. He made a motion as though, with the flat of his blade, he would drive the tedious fellow off.

"Don't strike the honest Eric Burchard, burgomaster of Wasa. *Ein* burgomaster *give* on the back, not take on the back," continued the sergeant, with an air of insulted dignity.

"What!" exclaimed the youth. "Are you Eric Burchard, the noted Saxon dragoon, whom Schmidtfelt made burgomaster of Wasa, and who cannot write his own name?"

"I am that burgomaster, that *ganz kunniotettawa und* celebrated person. I write my name *mit* the falchion, *und mit* the *nagajka*. Not *tjinnownik* now—soldier, *durchaus!* Not soldier now—*kivekäs, durchaus! Nur immer mit dem Strom! Zwanzig mal besoffen im Arreste gesessen; njeto dobra! Marschiren nach Wasa, freies Leben*, peace *und den* amnesty!"

Elias found himself in a singular difficulty. The sergeant looked to be anything but trustworthy, and

---

* I too am a *kivekäs*.

yet he spoke with a candor which could hardly have been assumed for treacherous purposes. For a jolly fellow, who had wearied of military service, the temptation to desert must now be great in the same measure as the danger of after-reckoning was diminished by peace and the departure of the troops from the country. Being unable to get rid of the man, Elias resolved to make the best of his company, as it could not be avoided, but did not forget to keep a watchful eye upon him. He called Marie Larsson and the old woman, who had been concealed in the barn; and then all four quickly set out toward the mainland and the great highway.

"*Den Teufel marschiren in lunta poron!*" ejaculated the clumsy sergeant, who with difficulty kept up with the rest. "*Alter junge weta guten Rath.* Comrade, *nehme den duschinka*, I save *den matuschka. Marsch!*"

And with this Burchard drew the old woman, half dead with terror, to the highway, where the baggage had halted, and some sledges were found, ready for traveling. Elias understood his meaning; the fugitives took two of the sledges on credit, and the baggage driver, who knew the valiant sergeant very well by his formidable whiskers and his still more formidable gibberish, dared not make the least objection.

The snow which had fallen on the grass melted immediately; but the sledging was now excellent, and they bore away on a gallop toward the town. In order to proceed farther northward, it was necessary to pass close by the custom-house; and here was the house where · Baron Sparrfelt was still lodging, and busy bathing his dislocated foot. The zealous Baron was sitting at the window, perhaps secretly satisfied that he did not himself have occasion to renew his acquaintance with the wildernesses of Wärknäs, when he saw the sledges coming, a considerable distance off, and recognized the fugitives who had been so eagerly pursued, and were now probably captured. He therefore opened the window to enjoy his triumph, and once more offer the young girl his protection. But who can depict his anger and amazement when the sledges hurried quickly past, and the youth in the peasant-jacket saluted him with a mocking inquiry as to how my lord baron had enjoyed the chase of yesterday.

Sparrfelt was furious and did what he could to set the whole city in motion; but this was more easily thought than done. The six burghers of the town had something else to do; the militia was out on a campaign; and all that Sparrfelt could effect was that a few yards less than usual of lace were made that day in the city of Raumo.

It need not be added that the expedition to Wärknäs Point returned without loss of men or any other loss, except a few run-down boots—if we omit the remarkable fact that Hans Reiuman, the burgomaster, was caught fast by the wig in a pine tree; however, the worthy official escaped the fate of Absalom by the very reasonable resolve to let his wig hang rather than be hung himself. And thus was ended, in these regions, the last campaign of the great war, not less troublesome, indeed, but much more harmless than many a previous adventure.

CHAPTER VI.

A DECEMBER DAY IN WASA.

THE autumn of 1721, with its storms and shipwreck, had prepared the way for an early and keen winter, which still wore the warlike mood of the winters immediately preceding. The memory of the great war has left behind it, even to this day, such deep

traces in the remembrance of the people, that in East
Bothnia one still hears allusions, half jest and half
earnest, to the time when it was "so cold that the fire
froze in the chimney." Another tradition speaks of a
time when it was "so dark that one could not see a
torch burning in the wall." Imagination could not
find illustrations forcible enough to express the terrible
distress of those times, and posterity therefore fancied
that during the great war an extreme darkness and an
unprecedented cold prevailed. Possibly also the rigor
of the climate was felt the more keenly as the means
decreased by which the wasted country protected itself
against it. All the stories of that time harmonize in
this: that the winter during the years of the war were
unusually cold.

One day, in the beginning of December, a large
company had gathered outside the church in Wasa. It
was Sunday, at noon, and a storm from the east was
whirling masses of snow over the city. The people
had just come from church. The venerable stone
temple had been humbly put in order, and service had
been held there, with few interruptions, during the
whole of the Russian rule. Stackelberg, the last prefect, had had the windows repaired, so that no longer,
as in Schmidtfeldt's time, the rain and snow beat in on
the congregation. But the church was stripped of all
its decorations, which the inhabitants, upon the invasion
of the enemy, had concealed or carried over to Sweden.
Gone was the altar-picture, and even the frame was
destroyed ; gone were the old organ, the ornaments of
the pulpit, and the chandeliers in the roof; even the
simple sockets of sheet-iron in the backs of the pews
had been taken either by the enemy or by some zealous
watcher who would rescue to the very least the property of the church. Everything was in decay; the
seats were mouldy, the plaster here and there had fallen off, some of the graves under the church floor had
been broken open and robbed, and some of the grave-

stones, with their inscriptions from the seventeenth century, mutilated. .But the town itself was less dilapidated than most of the other towns, as it had to some extent been kept as a place of residence by the authorities. But this appearance of preservation was on the surface only. Outside of the barracks, and of the residences of Korsholm and those civil officers appointed by the enemy, everything was deserted. Of ten large vessels which Wasa owned in 1714, not one remained.

Patiently and expectantly stood the people in the driving snow, outside the church. In the midst of winter and desolation, a new hope had arisen for these regions. Peace, peace was upon all lips; and the next thought was how the great derangements of war could be repaired. So long as the organized government of the enemy was still active, the political machinery moved on, often indeed awry, but still it moved. Stackelberg, the last commander, had been a well-meaning governor. But now the clock-work had stopped. The Russian officers had gone away, and the Finnish had not yet taken their places. All was in a state of dissolution; the whole commonwealth as good as without a government. And yet the same wonderful order was seen, as existed twenty-five years before, during the great famine. Law reposed, but no one made a motion to trample its mandates under foot. The executive power was without arms, but it did not occur to any man that he could now do what he pleased. Crime had no accuser, no judge; these impoverished peasants and burghers had the power to play the master, and take all that remained to be taken, but no one did it. Since the wise government of Charles XI, so strong was the law-abiding habit of the community that after such terrible joltings it still stood the test, and never had the laws of Finland more brilliantly demonstrated their strength than during this very transition period, when everything was in chaos, and any other country might have succumbed under the unbridled passions of the liberated, hungry and desperate masses.

Thus was the whole deportment of this people, during that hard trial, a model for all ages. When the clergy in the year 1715 excused themselves from the compulsory office of bailiff, the Russian government in East Bothnia selected peasants and sons of peasants who could write. These bailiffs chose as sergeants in every parish a peasant like themselves. The instruction for all of them—bailiffs as well as sergeants—consisted, according to the custom of the time, in the knout or gallows if they did not promptly levy and deliver the taxes. There was no mention of a salary; the peasants were merely bidden to support their bailiffs, so their maintenance commonly consisted of a few cakes of stamp-bread,* a small quantity of fish and fowl, and very rarely butter or milk, for the cattle had been slaughtered and almost exterminated. The present bailiffs and sergeants can fancy themselves in their places. 'With this instruction, and this pay, it was nevertheless the opinion, in 1721, that "they were quite agreed among themselves, so that, upon any distress arising, they always consulted together, bearing in mind their responsibility, not only during this administration, but also in a future changed government. They thus selected, in each parish, the most judicious and prominent peasants for advisers and overseers, who should always be at hand, to fill orders received, to attend to reparations, taxes, supplies, and the collection of arrears and accounts; so that at the investigation in the winter assize of 1722, in the presence of the prefect, nothing was to be said against them, but on the contrary they received commendation for their management."

Honor to those obscure and upright men, who for a hundred years have lain in their unknown graves ! A

---

* A coarse kind of bread, adulterated with ground chaff or the bark of pine trees.—Tʀ.

people that has stood a test like that, shall surely stand in any trial.

Public notice had been given in the church, that the long expected new prefect, Baron Reinhold Wilhelm Von Essen, was finally to come to Wasa, and that the people could present their difficulties and complaints to him. The grievance was great; all needed help, and all saw in their new prefect a rescuing angel. But there was also a violent fermentation of the passions. Several tools of the miserable tyrant, Schmidtfeldt, had by their extortion incurred the bitter enmity of the peasantry. Stackelberg had made a rigid investigation concerning the worst of them. Two peasant-plagues—Sergeant Martin Essevius of Lappajärvi, and John Ahlgren, his colleague, whose names have come down to posterity—had during the previous summer been condemned to suffer loss of life, of honor and of estate. A third sergeant, Anders Widbäck of Laihela, had been dismissed from the service, and sentenced to restore all that he had plundered. But a rumor had now spread that these petty tyrants were to become participants in the amnesty of peace; and there were other weeds besides to be cleared away. The peasants had therefore made up their minds to urge the prefect to severe chastisement; and on the church square many a word of exasperation was now heard against Schmidtfeldt's assistants.

"Anders is hiding here in the city! Anders must be found! We must have Anders for the rack and wheel!" shouted some of the most vociferous.

Schmidtfeldt had had two infamous servants, Israel and Anders, whom he sent around the province as collectors, and wherever these brutal bloodsuckers appeared they had, partly for their master and partly for themselves, extorted the last farthing. Israel had certainly got himself out of the way when the government of Schmidtfeldt was ended; but Anders had been seen in the vicinity. It was thought that he had buried his stolen possessions, and was sneaking around to find a chance to make off with them.

Scarcely had the cries been heard before a clamorous crowd, the greater part consisting of street boys, came marching up Köpman street, leading between them a ragged wretch whose matted hair and wild aspect were calculated to inspire pity rather than fear.

"We have him! We have him!" triumphantly shouted the boys. "Beckman's Joseph saw him creeping under the floor of Hidén's drying house, and we dragged him out by the feet."

The offender was the same Anders for whom the people had just been shouting.

"Kill the dog! Whip out of him every single dollar he has stolen from the widow and the fatherless!" cried the enraged crowd.

"Let *mans* the *hohe Obrigkeit* beat the devilish *perkele koiran* black and blue! That back *ist von härkän nahka;* I know that back; but the *Obrigkeit muss* be respected!" declared a stout personage in a sheepskin coat and with a dogskin cap drawn down to his eyes.

"Burk! Burk is here! Burk too has an account unsettled!" muttered the mob as they crowded around the last speaker, who, now that he had betrayed himself, sought vainly to make his escape. The smallest boy in Wasa knew the famous ex-burgomaster Burchard by his odd gibberish, and in the city he was known by the nick-name Burk (meaning a pot) as much for his corpulence as for the sake of the name.

"*Es lebe Carolus!*" shouted the deposed magistrate, careful, in this unexpected pinch, to show his loyal principles.

"Stop Burk's mouth!" exclaimed some. "Why is he shouting for Carolus? Is he not in the Russian service?"

"He grew too fat at the common council," replied

others, "so he needed a low diet, and at the next deal became a Russian sergeant."

"I was not sergeant!" bawled the burgomaster. "I was the honest deserter, the *karkuri*, the *kivekäs durchaus! Zwanzig mal in Arrest gesessen! Sto djelat? Pratschaj!* I desert *nach* Wasa! I like Wasa, I live in Wasa. I *schwöre den grossmächtigen Fridericus! Durchaus!*"

"I am sure we have had worse burgomasters than Burk!" pleaded an old burgher. "He drank at home and snored in the council, but if he had a drop left in the mug he offered to share it with the rest."

"He had twenty lashes given to me because I shouted 'Hurra for the king's return!'" muttered a bearded fisherman, threateningly.

"*Immer den Obrigkeit respektiren!*" replied the burgomaster. "Yesterday the czar, to-day the king, *nur immer den rechten potentate, durchaus!*"

"Away to Korsholm with Anders and Burk!" again shouted those standing farther away.

"Silence!" exclaimed a courageous man, who now advanced amid the clamorous crowd. "Do you not know that the prefect is hourly expected in the city? He must judge them, not we. And as to Burchard, every old granny knows that he is a fool, and that is the worst that can be said of him. For the present he can go home with me."

"Larsson is right! The prefect shall judge them!" was echoed from all points, and after they had assured themselves that the two suspected persons were in safe custody, the noise subsided.

CHAPTER VII.

THE LARSSON FAMILY.

THE authoritative man who so opportunely put in his plea for the deposed burgomaster, was at that time the wealthiest merchant in Wasa, and a son of that Larsson whom Count Bernhard Bertelsköld visited during the great famine. Since the appearance of the family in these stories, during the first half of the seventeenth century, it had separated into two main branches. One branch had remained as peasants in Storkyro, at the Bertila family-seat, and there worked their way up to considerable wealth. But this branch of the family had become almost extinct during the war. All its fortune was wasted ; the father, Thomas Larsson, had disappeared; the mother was dead ; eight blooming sons had fallen; two daughters had fled to Sweden, and only the youngest, Marie, poor and defenceless, returned to her native country, amidst difficulties and dangers, to search for her lost father.

The other branch had again become merchants in Wasa. It originated with one Lars Larsson, who had worked his way up from servant-boy to bookkeeper, from bookkeeper to partner, and from partner to son-in-law of the rich tradesman Hagelin, who every year sent five ships to Stockholm; and thus dated the beginning of the wealth of the Wasa Larssons. The present head of this house was also named Lars Larsson. When the thunders of war began to roll near, the cautious man, as early as the autumn of 1713, sent his wife and children, together with his most valuable possessions, over to Stockholm; and when, after the battle of Storkyro, the country was given over to plunder, he himself suc-

ceeded in escaping by the north road across Torneå.
To the enemy he left his family residence, storehouses,
pitch-works, and dockyard; but he would still have
been a rich man, if the real pillage had not begun after
the king's return, and with the government of Gortz.
Larsson had then established a grain trade in Stockholm; but now came one arbitrary tax and import duty
after another, and the city of Stockholm was finally, in
1718, commanded to order one hundred thousand barrels of grain from abroad.   Larsson's last bright carolins deserted him in this affair; but hardly had the grain
arrived before Gortz fixed its price so low that the
merchants lost from six to eight dollars on every barrel.
It was now all over with Larsson's trade, as with that
of most of the others; and upon his final return to
Wasa, immediately after the peace, he could regard
himself fortunate in still possessing, of all his immense
wealth, a few old hidden silver goblets, one hundred
copper plåts,* and a few thousand worthless coins.
Little as this was, nevertheless it was more than any
one else at that time owned in Wasa, and Larsson appeared in his native city with the reputation of being a
prudent man who had saved his neat splinter out of
the general shipwreck.   This reputation he knew how
to use in obtaining foreign credit, and he was therefore one of the few who could immediately recommence
his trade with great profit, as he was able to purchase
tar at a low price, and ordered salt.   Those who then
had cash did a prosperous business.   So high was the
value of money, and so great was the lack of this commodity, that one old man traveled from Uleåborg to
Brahestad—fully eight miles—on foot, to get a six-öre
copper coin,† which he had hidden behind the oven in
a bake-house.
      Larsson had lately got his plundered house into
some degree of order.   The walls were whitewashed,

* A plåt equals about four English pence.—TR.
† Equal to about one dime.—TR.

and once more there was glass in all the windows; but
double windows were at that time, even in the keenest
winter, an unknown luxury. From the enclosed outer
steps, and through a small passage, one entered a tolerably spacious but low room, whose accessories consisted of a huge open fireplace, a large dining table,
unpainted benches, an arm-chair of veined wood for
the master, a capacious cupboard, and on the wall a
portrait of Charles XII, every Sunday garlanded with
fresh pine boughs by the young people of the family.
All that rancor which Larsson and the other merchants
of that time had harbored against the late king who
had cost them so dearly, had long ago been transferred
to the odious Gortz. He alone was forced to bear the
bitter blame of the burghers, for the ruin which the
king's thirst for war had brought upon trade and the
civil professions. And although Larsson had had too
much to do with the debit side of Charles XII's ledger
to be quite able to cherish admiration for the hero, he
nevertheless allowed his sons and daughters, in this
respect, to have their own opinions.

To the right of the main room there were two
smaller ones, one for the host and hostess, the other
for the daughters. To the left were also two rooms,
of which the outer one constituted the store, and the
inner one at once the office and lodging-room for the
sons. Besides these, there was a loft for the laborers
on the second floor, and above that a so-called night-
room for more distinguished guests. If we add that
the furnishing of all these rooms was still simpler than
that of the larger one, one can form an approximate
idea of the house of the richest merchant at that time
in the city of Wasa.

Some hours after the scene at the church, we again
find Larsson and his family at the supper table. It is
seven o'clock in the evening. To the left of the merchant sat his wife, mother Larsson, a somewhat serious
matron of five-and-forty years; and next to her the

daughters—Kajsa, twenty years of age, of a more resolute than quite agreeable appearance, and little Veronica, a bright-eyed but pale and delicately built girl of
about twelve years.   Next to the father sat three vigorous sons.   Of these the eldest, Lars, twenty-six years of
age, had already paid his tribute to the war, having
served under the king in Norway, where he lost his left
eye; but he was now his father's head bookkeeper and
right-hand man.   The second, Matthias, twenty-two
years old, had been chosen to take charge of the
country estate, succeeding his father's cousin, the vanished Thomas Larsson; and the youngest, Bertel, who
was only fifteen years of age, had attended school in
Stockholm, and was meditating upon a scholarly career
as soon as there was once more an academy in Åbo.
Farther down the table sat a Swedish bookkeeper by
the name of Grenman, together with two old male
domestics and three girls; and among them the ex-
burgomaster, Eric Burchard, had taken his modest
place.

The rigid etiquette prevailing at that time allowed
no one to speak at the table unless directly interrogated
by the master.   But this one, who ordinarily treated
adventurers whom chance had led to his house with
all the *nonchalance* of a solid business man, now con-
descended to ask a few questions, the interest in which
was evidently shared by those who sat silently around
the table.

"You have been in Nystad, have you, Burchard?"
asked Larsson.

"I *war den* Nystad *mit und* make the place," replied the ex-burgomaster, as he let a good-sized roasted
turnip follow a large strömming* through the long
whiskers.   "I was the *kivikarta*, the island, the *saari ;
woden grossen house war aufgebaut und wo der grossmächtige graf Bruce die Schwedenhunden zog an der
Nase.*"

* A very small kind of herring.—T꜡.

"What do you say?" inquired Larsson, with a frown.

"I say, *wo der grossmächtige graf Liljenstedt die Russenhunden zog an der Nase*," continued the burgomaster, without allowing himself to be in the least troubled. "*I kenne den grossen potentaten, alle zusammen, kaikkityyni, durchaus! Den Liljenstedt, den Ostermann, den Bruce, den Strömfelt, den Sparrfelt; guten Tag, mein lieber Burchard kapuschewaite?* I present *das gewär. Gott befehle your Gnaden, so und so, grosser Durst, aber the bottle soganz pikku little! Da hast you ein Ducat, Burchard,* we make *zusammen* the peace. *Schön Dank,* your *Gnaden, es lebe der grosse Czar!*"

"Indeed!" murmured Larson, smiling.

"*Wollte sagen: der grossmächtige Fridericus soll leben!*" quickly corrected the burgomaster. "*Nur immer den rechten* monarch *durchaus!*"

"Well, and did you meet a young girl there, who was inquiring in the village after Thomas Larsson?"

"*Den Nystad I get prodoroschna nach* Raumo. *Den Raumo I marschire gegen the kivekät. Ebenaus dem Arreste wech, schlecht geschlafen, miserabel getrunken pfin! I sage zu mir: bin ein gut* Finlander, *bin wirkamies, tjinownik, burgermeister* in Wasa *gwesen, marschiren nach* Wasa, *den alten, prächtigen Larsson zu sehen, und den trefflichen Bier—mit Erlaubniss;* I drink your health,—*und so bang! drei* scoundrels in the *alten* barn! I bind *alle zusammen—nein,* I bind the old woman *nicht,—nimmer grausam gewesen.* I say to them: *Hinder, lasst uns gute Freunde, und kumpanit werden. Hagel! das junge* girl *fiel mir um* the neck, so *verdammt froh war sie.*"

"There were three of them, you say, Burchard? And where did you become separated from them?"

"I conducted them, *alle drei, bis nach den Malaks, kirkonkylässä Alleweil spatsiren, la la, zuweilen* ride the horse, *kataj! Den junge kivekäs war verdammt ver-*

*gnügen mich zu haben. So ein verfluchter Bummler!
Den Preis* on his *Kopf hundert Thaler, und hundert
Roubles verdienen — ete sto rublej!* I *nichts verdiene,* so
ein Kerl ist der alte Burchard. I protect them ; *die alte
Mume jammerte nur immer fort :* ' The good Burchard,
*den Herzens ystävä.' Wei sie verliebt war, Donner
Wetter ; ganz verpicht war sie wegen des alten Burger-
meisters. Nun so,*" and at this point the burgomaster
interleaved his story with a quantity of porridge,
sufficient for half the company, "*in the Malaks,* I came
across *ein miserables* liquor, *nawodki! Nahm ein
tscharka, den ich hatte grossen Durst, und war so ein
wenig besoffen — halloh! Die junge Duschinka ward
terrified, der Teuffel's Kerl schliess den owen küne, und
das ganze Gesellschaft war putzwech.*"

Larsson's countenance darkened, but he was silent.
All at the table had finished their repast ; the burgomaster alone was still earnestly engaged in making
amends for what he had neglected while telling the
story of his heroic adventures, when the door opened,
and a young girl entered the room. Notwithstanding
the snowy jacket, and the woolen cloth drawn down
over her forehead, all present recognized at the first
glance the beautiful blue eyes and slender graceful
form of Marie Larsson.

The younger members of the family rose to give
her a kind welcome. Even the burgomaster laid aside
the wooden spoon which had made such an enormous
breach in the oat-meal porridge. But the commanding
look of the master kept all in their places.

"Grace!" said he, in his usual tone, and without
even deigning to give the new-comer a greeting.

Veronica, whose turn it was to say grace, falteringly
performed her duty. The glances of all moved stealth-
ily to the girl, who, shy and silent, remained standing
by the door.

When grace was ended, Larsson went to Marie, and
without saying a word, led her to her room, after which

he bolted the door, and looked at her with the severity of a judge.

"Before I bid you welcome in my house," said he, "I must know whether you are worthy to enter it and be one of us. I stand in the place of a father to you, and I must know why, in the darkness of night, you ran away from Stockholm, and so deeply offended against your noble benefactors, the Count and Countess Horn."

"I wrote to the countess, from Waxholm, and begged her to forgive me," answered Marie, struggling with her tears.

"A letter which no one understood, and in which you confessed nothing. I want to know *why* you fled."

"Forgive me, oh, forgive me, uncle! I cannot tell it now. It might perhaps plunge us all into ruin. Believe me, I am innocent; I could not be otherwise! I must—I was obliged to flee."

"Marie, you can never imagine that I mean to be satisfied with empty evasions. Tell me all, and I will try to make your fault right."

"I am not to blame, uncle, and still I cannot tell you now how it is. Be merciful to me. Have you the heart to drive me away from your house?"

"No. But I will not allow you to speak with any-one here, or reach your hand to your cousins and your aunt, before you have justified yourself. Be reasonable, child! If you are innocent, you only need to speak the truth."

"And that truth might be your ruin. No, uncle! I cannot, I cannot now!"

"Indeed! Then hear what I promised Count Horn, when I came away from Stockholm. 'I shall send the girl back, *whenever* I find her, and *wherever* I find her;' that was my promise, and I am never in the habit of retracting. The sea is still open. At Brändö lies a Umeå vessel which to-morrow sails back to Sweden. For to-night, you may stay here; but no one, except

me, shall speak with you.   To-morrow, at dawn of day,
I shall take you out to Brändö, and take care that you
return to Stockholm.   Good night!"

With these words, the harsh uncle left the room,
and bolted the door outside.   Marie hid her face in her
hands and wept.

No one ventured with even a whisper to disobey
the feared master.   But Veronica silently slipped a bit
of her Sunday's cake on the tray where a supper was
placed for her captive cousin.

When this was done, Larsson unbolted the door
and himself went in with the tray to the captive.   An
exclamation of surprise was heard, and all followed him
into the room.   The window was open.   Poor Marie
had fled, alone and deserted, out into the dark winter
night.

CHAPTER VIII.

THE REFUGEES IN THE WILDERNESS.

THROUGH the whole autumn of 1721, and even
far into the following year, a stream of refugees
continued to pour into Finland.   Some came north by
the road across Torneå and Kemi; others came back
from Sweden by sea; and others still came from the
wilderness in the interior of the country, where they
had found an asylum, back to their former abode nearer
the coast.   Some few also returned from captivity in
Russia.   All of them had to contend with great sufferings.   There were no roads here in a passable condition, except the most necessary military roads.   On all
the rest of the roads there was not a bridge, not a ferry,
scarcely a boat by the shores; there were no inns, no
horses, no food, no dwelling houses, and no people.

When prefect Baron von Essen, on St. Andrew's day, 1721, was cast ashore by the storms, with peril of life, at Kasaböle, in the parish of Sastmola, and wished to travel thence noithward to his province, he found, even on the large coast road, no provisions made for the transmission of travelers. The Russian government, it is true, had established a postal service, and inns; but these were now discontinued. It was only with the greatest difficulty that the prefect could proceed, and to do so he was obliged in several places to use oxen. From this, one can approximately guess how it fared with other travelers.

Those who betook themselves to the parish and village roads, found in many places, not the old road, but in its place a moor, or patch of underbrush, in which might be discovered here and there the track of wheels. If they found the road, all the embankments were broken down, all the culverts destroyed, and all the fences lay prostrate around former fields and meadows. The refugees sought the church of their native parish. They found it, not without difficulty; the forest had grown up around it and hidden it from the eye of the wanderer. The enclosure around the churchyard was torn down—that is, where such had existed, for most of the dead were still buried under the floor of the church—and the cross had fallen and been trampled on. In the tower there was no bell to call the people to God's service; the winds of heaven blew in through the broken windows; the altar had no ornament, no cup, no wine, and seldom a priest, unless it were a young student who had been consecrated in hap-hazard way in Åbo. Yet in spite of all this, the refugees bent the knee with heartfelt devotion in that desolated sanctuary. They seemed to stand nearer their God, now that they could pray to him in their own church, however ruined it might be.

From the churches the refugees sought their villages and homes. They rubbed their eyes and

E   8*

looked around them with amazement, everything was so different on the old shores and the well-known hillock. The gate was gone, the well caved in, the cottage had disappeared; it was not easy to recognize the dear old farm, which was now overgrown with pines and juniper bushes. Or it sometimes happened that a new cottage had latterly arisen in place of the old one, and in it lived strange inhabitants, who had taken possession of the desolate farm. Then there arose mutual complaints and long disputes about the right of possession; and it was wonderful to see how these people disputed about that one little half-wild patch of ground, while the country for miles around lay desolate and without settlers.

Ten or twelve days before Christmas, such a crowd of refugees marched through the parish of Storkyro. There were about ten families of them, but they had only two horses to draw their little stock of household goods. The road led them over the former battle-field; once more the river lay frozen and the shores were clad with snow, as on that memorable day, almost eight years before. Here and there could be distinguished, under the covering of snow, the skeleton of a horse, or the heaps of earth which had been thrown up over the graves of the slain; but further than this, no marked traces of the great conflict remained. But the village of Napo still lay desolate and uninhabited, half torn down, half burned. A few ruined houses remained, but the people avoided them. The near battle-field was too sad a neighborhood, and was associated with bitter recollections. The fugitives marched on, and by a detour, came to the church. The broad cultivated plain was partly overgrown with young birches and willow bushes, where the wolf had made its lair and the ptarmigan its dwelling-place in the midst of Finland's largest and most fertile grain-fields. But a part of the plain still bore traces of cultivation. Some portions of the villages here were still inhabited, and the refugees found the longed-for roof above their heads. They scattered themselves among the farms, and were hospitably received by the poor people. Some of them were originally from this vicinity. It was touching to see how théy went from farm to farm, to inquire after their relatives and friends. Very few were those now remaining, but it sometimes happened that parents found their lost children again, and children found the parents they had wept. Sisters and brothers who had long believed each other dead, met once more; and the former youth found by the side of another the bride of his early years. Poor wanderers from the dear fatherland! They felt like shipwrecked voyagers, many of whom had found their graves beneath the billows, but some had been tossed upon the shore, and now, with alternate sorrow and delight, were counting their thinned ranks.

Among those who proceeded further was a company of five people, with one horse. Three of them constituted one returning family—a former soldier by the name of Heikki, his wife Brita, and her infirm father, the old Hilli. This Heikki was the son of a Storkyro peasant, and ought, as eldest son, to inherit the farm at his father's death. But when Heikki, who was thought to be dead, now returned from Sweden, he found house and farm in possession of the younger brother, who had lived there several years, and had a family around him. The farm was too small to divide, and Heikki had no desire to dislodge his brother. So he merely rested a few days in Storkyro, and then, with his wife and father-in-law, went farther northward, to Munsala chapel, with the intention of reclaiming a deserted farm which belonged to the old man. The Munsala congregation is at the present time altogether Swedish, but the peculiar name of the place (Muni-salo, egg-island), and many other names akin to it (Wäki-salo, Lohi-lahti, etc.), prove that the people were formerly Finnish. In many places the great war changed the territory of the Swedish and Finnish population by means of new immigrations.

In the neighborhood of Wasa, a young girl, accompanied by a youth in a gray jacket, had joined the company of these three. As we easily recognize in them two old acquaintances, it need only be added that Marie Larsson, after her flight from her uncle's house, found shelter with a sister of the old woman who had hitherto accompanied her, and who now remained in Wasa. Here Elias Pehrson had once more sought her, and as Marie would upon no consideration submit to her uncle's will and be sent back to Stockholm, she resolved rather, with the help of Elias, to search for her missing father alone. The two therefore accompanied the rest of the refugees to Storkyro. But here no one had seen Thomas Larsson for more than four years, since he came in conflict with the hostile command which was sent thither to levy tribute. On this occasion Bertila farm was plundered and burnt, and its old master disappeared. But there was a rumor that two years ago he had been seen in Munsala or Orawais, and this rumor induced Marie to go northward with the rest, the more willingly as she had formed a friendship for Brita, and hoped by this means to elude her uncle's attempts to find her. Elias had his reasons for not returning to southern Finland, and did not reflect long before he resolved to be the fifth in the traveling company.

The refugees required more than eight days, however, to lay behind them the six miles between Storkyro and Munsala. They were compelled more than once to rest over-night in a dilapidated barn or an abandoned farm-hut, and the poor horse was obliged to content itself with withered leaves, which were with difficulty gathered from beneath the snow. More than once, in broad daylight, the wolves were so daring that they attacked the horse, and Elias and Heikki were obliged to drive them away with poles. More than once, too, they found in the woods the remains of some lonely fugitive who had been torn to pieces and devoured by these (at that time) incredibly bold wild beasts.

Fortunately, the ice already formed natural bridges across rivers and marshes, and the wayfarers had provided themselves with food in Storkyro. They therefore finally arrived, exhausted but safe, at their place of destination, Lohi-lahti (now Lojlax), a quarter of a mile north of Munsala church, and three-quarters of a mile south of the town of New Carleby.

All that here remained of Hilli's former farm was an old grain-kiln by the highway. It was two days before Christmas. How were these houseless refugees to celebrate the Savior's happy birthday festival?

They took up their residence in the grain kiln, and it was found that, with some caution, a fire could still be kindled. After a while a fire of coarse pine wood was crackling in the furnace. Heikki and his young wife regarded each other with a feeling of content. They had never before sat together under their own roof, and this tumble-down smoky building was the first home they had ever owned. While old Hilli could not sufficiently praise the former wealth of the farm, and sigh at the thought of its present poverty, the young and newly married pair felt richer now than they had ever been before. Sad and thoughtful, Marie sat by the furnace, and involuntarily her thoughts went back to Stockholm, to the rich and noble house where, in the midst of Sweden's poverty, all was velvet and silk, mirrors and gold. The tempter, who is always at hand in such moments, whispered in her ear: "Why do you exchange that luxury for a miserable shelter among snow-drifts and wildernesses?" But the silent voice in her inmost soul answered: "Marie, you did right!" and the tempter was silent.

Elias now returned from the forest with his gun, and brought with him two woodcocks, which he had

shot, and which were immediately prepared for eating.

"I will make you a proposition, Heikki," said he,
pleasantly. "I will become your cottager, and then
we will build together. There is good timber around
us here. First, I will help you build a fine house here
on the knoll, and afterwards you shall help me build a
little cottage down by the sea. You shall take charge
of the fields and meadows, the grain-kiln and farm-
yard; but I will fish there in the beautiful bay, when
you do not need me, for my inclination is still constantly toward the sea."

"Your hand on that!" promptly replied Heikki.
"But then you too must have a brisk wife, who will
offer you a happy face, a good fire, and a warm dish
of porridge, when you come back, chilly and wet, from
the sea."

"That will bear a good deal of thinking about,
yet," answered Elias, as with some embarrassment he
pushed a pine-stub farther into the furnace. The stub
crackled, the sparks glittered, and the firelight fell
dazzlingly on Marie's face, as she sat near the furnace,
with her head resting in both her hands. Perhaps it
was owing to the firelight that she turned quickly
away, and no one knew if her twenty-year-old heart
beat fast or slow at these plans for the future.

CHAPTER IX.

DAYS OF WINTER AND OF SPRING.

THE following winter, very severe snow-storms
visited the settlers in Lojlax. They had been
celebrating Christmas matins in New Carleby, where

they were obliged to provide themselves with salt and iron, and it was three-quarters of a mile thither. The little town had experienced rather hard usage in 1714. The Russian fleet of galleys had set the troops on shore at the mouth of the river, and from this point the horrible flight and pursuit had begun in East Bothnia. After the battle of Storkyro, other hostile hordes advanced from the south by land. But the wealthiest citizens of the town gathered together all the silver and gold that the war had left them, and went with it to meet the approaching enemy on the south side of the bridge. Their neighbors in Jacobstad, who did not observe this caution, soon afterwards saw their city in flames. New Carleby still possessed one small remnant of prosperity, in its brave little open vessels, which, defying the vigilance of the enemy, repeatedly made trading trips to West Bothnia. In other particulars it was desolate here. The city had at the conclusion of peace, scarcely one hundred and fifty inhabitants; but by autumn an equal number of refugees had returned from Sweden. The wooden church, erected in 1708, then, as now, gathered both city and country to the great festival. For the first time in many years, there was once more a merrier life on the church hillock. Once again, as of yore, was heard the cheerful sound of the sleigh-bells and the neighing of the horses during the race, on the dark Christmas morning. Once again, as in former days, the church was glorious with light and devotion. To be sure, the chandeliers and sconces were only of wood, made for the occasion, and the lights were neither many nor large; but never had the church been arranged in greater splendor, or echoed with more heart-felt psalms of praise. It was as though a deep enraptured feeling of thankfulness and new-born happiness had reflected from the earnest faces of the congregation, up to the angel-forms in the roof, and through the marble slabs down to the very graves of the dead under their feet.

At the conclusion of high mass, the settlers from Lojlax returned home. It seemed to Elias as though a stout man, in a shaggy sheepskin coat, had followed them a little way, when they were going from the church to their quarters at alderman Fortell's. It must be borne in mind that Elias was an outlaw, who had his reasons for not wishing to meet acquaintances, and he therefore resolved to keep his eyes open. But when Heikki shortly afterward took a seat in the sledge, to escort Brita and Marie back to Lojlax, and Elias himself, without adventure, passed the bridge on foot, he soon forgot this transient suspicion.

Immediately after Christmas, Heikki and Elias began to build with might and main. And it was not many weeks before a roomy cottage, newly hewn and white, was standing on Lojlax hill, on the eastern side of the road that led from the hill to the sea. One of the two small rooms, commanding a view of the beautiful bay, which at that time came up to the foot of the hill, though it has now withdrawn some distance, was from the very beginning destined for Marie. Heikki and his wife occupied the next room, but Elias declined the place intended for him, in the room beyond them. Every night, he took up his lodging in the grain-kiln, close by. " I sleep first rate there, in the straw by the furnace" he used laughingly to say.

But Elias did not sleep. While the others were resting, he would go out on guard, in the frosty winter night, and listen carefully to every sound which could be distinguished from the near highway. Elias was used to living on the alert; there was peace now, but he felt something insecure in the air, and thought it unadvisable that all the inhabitants of Lojlax should sleep.

Weeks and months, however, went peacefully by, and Elias began occasionally to allow himself a little rest. It sometimes happened that a wanderer, enticed by the firelight from the comfortable cot, sought lodging here, during the darkness and foul weather. Now it was an old Carolin, who was at last on his travels back to the familiar places; now a captive finally returning from Ukraine, and asking in vain after relatives and friends whom he had left twenty years before; now a poor curate or sexton, who had started on foot back to his congregation; now a couple of half-grown children, looking for their missing home, and remembering nothing more about it than that in the yard there was a well, in the stable a horse, and by the bedside a good mother who repeated blessings over them long ago, when they were little. All these wanderers found a refuge here, just as the inhabitants of Lojlax had themselves so lately found a refuge with others. And each and all told their tales, during the long winter evenings; for the reality was at that time more wonderful than is many a legend now, and people had lived through such peculiar scenes as are seldom witnessed in our day.

One day in the beginning of March, when the first spring-sun of peace came to melt the snow on the pines of Finland, the parishioners of Munsala were gathered on the ice, near the village of Wexala, to raise the church-bell, which had been sunk there upon the invasion of the enemy. During the nine years it had sunk so deep in the loose mud that it could not be raised in the autumn, with flat-boat and crane, and they were not even perfectly certain of its location. Here, as by many another of Finland's shores, the herdsman or the old woman, as they walked to church on Sunday morning, heard the bell ringing in the sea. Indeed, people were so sure of it, that these old women and herdsmen were questioned concerning the place where the bell lay. Old people, you know, even to this day, hear such sunken bells ringing in the seas.

One wise old man, from the village of Monäs, advised the people to throw steel into the hole in the ice, where they were looking for their bell. If the bell

4

were there, the steel would be sure to clink against the consecrated metal. But the attempt was not successful, and the steel clinked only against the stones on the bottom. Some thought the fault lay in the fact that perfect silence was not observed, as when searching for buried treasures. Others thought they could accomplish nothing unless the clergyman read his prayer over the opening. Not until Elias hit upon the plan of searching for the bell with grappling irons, in fisher-fashion, was it finally found, drawn by their united strength up to daylight, and borne, amid noise and rejoicing, back to the church.

Twilight was already beginning to gather, when Elias and Heikki returned across the ice to Lojlax. The snow-water, which, under the mid-day sun, had gathered in hollows and wheel-tracks, had congealed again, in the evening frost, to a thin paper-like ice, which broke with a crackling sound under the feet of the travelers. The sky was as pure and blue as it only can be on a beautiful March evening here in the north, and a peculiar spring-like feeling pervaded all nature. Even the two travelers, who were by no means inclined to fanciful impressions, drank the pure air with pleasure, and silently watched the evening star, as it glistened above the pine forest.

They had gained the highway, not far from that enormous stone-heap which the ocean had in former days thrown up on the shore, when Elias, with the sharp glance of an experienced guerrilla, observed a pair of unusually broad tracks in the road.

"Some Russian gentleman has ridden northward to-day," said he, not without an uneasy glance toward the unguarded farm.

" It must have been a gentleman of consequence," responded Heikki, as he inspected the hoof tracks. "He was escorted by three horsemen, one on each side, and one behind the sledge."

" The door of the grain-kiln stands open," said

Elias, quickening his steps. The grain-kiln was also used as a stable for the single horse of Lojlax farm, until a separate stable could be erected.

The two came to the grain-kiln; the horse was gone, the harness had vanished. The snow in front of the grain-kiln was trampled down by horses' hoofs and human feet.

Seized by uncomfortable forebodings, the two men hastened to the cottage. But Heikki's fear was immediately calmed, when Brita advanced to meet him at the door, with her usual untroubled face. She had a few weeks before presented her husband with a bright boy, and had left the cradle only to admit the returning ones.

"Who has been in the stable and taken our horse?" asked Heikki.

"I thought you already knew about it," replied Brita. "The bailiff sent after it, and left word that he had summoned all the horses to draw the bell to the church. Yours was the tenth, he said, and there were no more horses in the whole parish."

"What can it mean?" exclaimed Heikki. "We just came from the ice, and no horses have been summoned there except three, which were quite sufficient for the whole transportation."

"Mercy! Marie must know that; she went to the grain-kiln with the men to give them the key," answered Brita, now in her turn astonished.

Elias, who had been searching for Marie around the whole house, overwhelmed Brita with questions as to which way the young girl had gone.

"But did she not follow you to the ice?" responded Brita. "I wondered that she stayed away so long, but I thought she had gone to the ice to see the bell taken out."

Elias asked no further explanation. He rushed out, went to the grain-kiln, and thence to the highway. The night was clear and calm; the moon was rising above the forest. Far around, not the least stir was heard. Of Marie, not a track was seen, not the least sound could be distinguished.

Elias stood for a few moments, silent and breathless. It seemed to him as though the world around him had suddenly become desolate and dark ; he no longer was in sympathy with that spring-like sky whose stars he had so recently contemplated with silent delight. Marie was gone; all was empty; what was he to do longer in the world ?

But this overpowering emotion gave place to a new fear. Who had taken Marie away ? and whither had she been taken? Must he not believe that this forcible treachery had some connection with that secret which had driven her from Stockholm, and which she so obstinately refused to disclose ? and if so, what fate was now awaiting her?

To find her, to save her, now became the only thought of Elias. His power of reasoning returned with his fear. He threw himself upon his hands and knees, to examine, by the faint uncertain moonlight, the track on the highway. He thought he discovered that the sledge with the broad runners had made a halt by the avenue road to the farm, and afterward resumed its course northward. Why northward, if it was Marie's uncle in Wasa who had had her taken away? More than this—he thought he perceived that the sledge, which had previously been drawn by two horses, had been drawn through the yard by three. It occurred to him that the third horse must have been Heikki's ; indeed, he thought he recognized the track of the right hind foot, where the shoe in one place was broken off. He understood now that by taking away the horse the offenders had intended to deprive him of the possibility of pursuing them.

Elias, with his now recovered presence of mind, which had been tested in many dangers, comprehended what he had to do. He hastened back to the cottage, put in his pocket the silver watch he had once taken as war booty from an officer of the enemy, and a few long-treasured silver roubles, acquired in the same manner. Then he bade Heikki and Brita a hasty farewell, with the promise not to return without Marie.

He knew that not a horse was to be bought for gold, for a whole mile in the direction of New Carleby. He was obliged first, therefore, to go southward, to the parish village of Munsala, although this road led in an opposite direction from the course of the fugitives. But Elias had no choice. He reached the village, and went to the farm where he knew the fastest horse was to be found.

"Lend me your horse, Simon," said he, "and if I should not come back, then make the loss good with this watch and money. It is more than your horse is worth."

Simon, an old horse trader, demurred more than once, before he could prevail upon himself to accept of this offer. It was truly not easy times as to horses now-a-days; they had been obliged to bring them all the way from Karelen, fifty miles away, and they were not to be bought there now for any money. They had at last, late in autumn, been obliged to bring horses over from West Bothnia. But if horses were rare, bright silver money was still rarer, and Simon could not resist the temptation. He protested that he would sooner lose his wife than the horse; but however that might be, the roubles slipped into his old leather purse, and the business was settled.

A few minutes later, Elias galloped back toward Lojlax, hitched his horse to Heikki's light church-sledge, and directed his rapid course northward, in the starry, calm, and frosty spring night.

CHAPTER X.

THE FREEBOOTER'S HUNT.

ELIAS Pehrson was not one of those who wasted time when anything of importance was to be accomplished. By eleven o'clock at night he had reached New Carleby, and stopped at the unpretentious inn in the northern part of the town.

During the winter, prefect Baron Essen had caused new inns to be erected on all the more traveled roads, and on account of the expensive times and the lack of horses, the stage fare had been raised to sixpence a mile.

The whole town was in its deepest nightly slumber. At that time, according to good old custom, people went to their hammocks at seven or eight o'clock in the evening, and were up by cock-crowing, at three o'clock in the morning. All sitting up by artificial light, where one could not content himself with firelight from the chimney or the flame of a pine knot, had, moreover, been precluded this winter, as candles were expensive and scarce. Still less was there a single light found in the streets of the towns of Finland.

Elias knocked fearlessly at the bolted street door, and when no answer followed, ventured to cry out, " In the name of the crown ! "

A suddenly awakened man-servant finally made his appearance, and opened the door with the surly question: " Who the devil is it that will not allow folks to sleep in peace ? "

" I am the prefect's courier," promptly replied Elias, " and am sent from Wasa with a message to the gentleman who traveled through here this evening, in the large Russian sledge drawn by three horses. I want to know when he left here, and if he took the ice-road northward."

The fellow, whose wits were still asleep, stared at the new-comer, and asked, with a yawn, "What gentleman?"

"The one who traveled through here this evening, between six and seven o'clock, and had a young woman and three horsemen with him."

"There has been no gentleman here, and I don't like to be bothered with foolish questions," querulously replied the servant, slamming the door in the face of the pretended crown-courier.

Elias deliberated whether he should burst open the door and wake the people of the house; but this seemed hardly advisable. Another expedient occurred to him, that suited him better.

"Be careful, Matts," said he, "or I may have you mustered in as a soldier, when I come here, in two weeks, with the prefect."

One of the greatest troubles of the winter of 1722 was the levying of new men for the army, in the then existing scarcity of people; and although it was no longer allowable, as in the time of the late king, to muster in one or another convenient man, according to pleasure, the dread of that despotic recruiting still remained in the minds of the people.

"Well," continued Elias, outside the door, "will you tell me good-naturedly which road they took from here northward?"

"They stopped at alderman Fortells', and I think they took the ice-road to Flatanabban," answered the servant, considerably more tractable. "Will the courier have a horse?"

"No; but if they left here a light sorrel horse with the shoe of the right hind foot broken, tell Fortells that the horse belongs to Heikki, in Lojlax. Goodnight."

Elias now bore off at full speed to the landing, at Åminne, and thence down on the ice, in order, by a short route, to reach Jacobstad, which is situated nearly three miles to one side of the great coast road. The March night continued to be moonlit and clear, the sleighing on the ice was fine, and the shores seemed to fly past the speeding sledge. Elias, who had once before traveled this road in the winter, dashed across the mouth of the river and the projecting points in toward the fiords among the rocks and islands of Pedersöre, and at one o'clock in the morning halted at the inn in Jacobstad.

Here the scene was desolate in the extreme. The town still lay in ruins from the conflagration of March 4th, 1714, when five ships were burned in the harbor. Jacobstad had had three years of freedom from taxes, but the inhabitants had not even cleared away the heaps of rubbish, which still formed hills and hollows under the snowy covering of winter. The able-bodied men of Pedersöre had all been wounded, and the greater number of them had died. Only here and there a small newly-hewn house had arisen since the peace. In the south of the ravaged town, gloomy and snow-covered, the venerable old stone church of Pedersöre, whose rescue tradition ascribes to a miracle, alone looked down through the moonlit spring night upon the devastation. The town church was burned November 30, 1714.

Elias repeated his story about the courier, and after long negotiation was admitted. People had not yet forgotten the evil doings of war times, and did not willingly open their doors to a stranger at night.

The first question was about the Russian sledge. The answer was that the woman was giddy from sleigh-riding and took a fancy to sit awhile in the room, but afterwards the sledge had continued the journey, at eight o'clock in the evening, by the ice-road to Old.

Carleby. Elias ground his teeth. He was obliged to rest an hour to feed his horse.

He then resumed his journey. Once more shores and icy plains disappeared under the hoofs of his fleet horse; the spring morning shone around him, and at six o'clock he was in Old Carleby.

This town was in little better condition than the one last described. It had been rebuilt after the conflagration of 1664, but was pillaged during the war, and vessels and warehouses were burned. Jac Chydenins, the annalist of Old Carleby, thus describes the appearance of the town at the peace of Nystad: "A few houses, one here, another there, stood roofless and partly torn down. Hardly any inhabitants were found here. For as many of the citizens as could get away had removed, and those who had been obliged to remain had been put to death in a violent and painful manner." Still the town carried on some trade. How little this was, can be decided from the fact that a Hollandish vessel which was bound for Wasa, but went astray, and anchored at Old Carleby, could sell only a small part of its salt, tobacco and calicos, and when the Hollander tried the customary expedient of establishing a trade of exchange, not more than thirty barrels of tar, in all that region, still rich in forests, could be raised.

Here Elias expected to find his fugitives. Vain hope! When, with palpitating heart, he asked after the Russian sledge, he was answered: "Here they took the highway northward, about two hours before. The young woman had cried, and a young man who drove the sledge had tried in vain to console her. The travelers had rested here a few hours, the horsemen had eaten like ravenous wolves, and the stoutest of them, a fellow with terribly long whiskers, at the sight of whom the children ran in-doors, had spoken a gibberish which no one understood."

This was the first information which gave Elias any

F

light in his many conjectures. The stout fellow could not be any other than the quondam burgomaster, Burchard; but who was the young consoler by Marie's side? For the first time, the honest freebooter felt a twinge of jealousy mingle a new bitterness in his anxiety for the beloved girl. What was to be done? The horse was tired out, and could not be used any longer without wasting the precious time by a half-day or a whole day of rest. But they were only two hours ahead of him. Elias traded away his good horse for a poorer one that was fresh, and continued his course northward, in the tracks of the fugitives.

He passed the high ridge in Kelwiå, and entered the plains of Lochteå. This neighborhood had suffered comparatively less. Here Elias saw thinly populated villages, and met peasants riding to town. But he had little desire now to institute comparisons over the unequal ravages of the war. At Lochteå church, he was obliged to rest his horse. Fortunately, the fugitives, who had probably no longer feared being pursued, had rested at the same place. The story about them became more and more singular. The young woman had been quite happy, the people said, and had conversed familiarly with her companion. For a moment Elias was ready to turn back. But he was too persistent for that.

With the shortest possible halt, he continued his course, passed the re-wooded Halajoki and the still wilder Pyhäjoki, those stretches of shore at the present day thickly inhabited and highly cultivated. The farther he went northward, the more terrible were the tracks the war had left behind it. From and including the northern part of Pyhäjoki, all was a wilderness. The snow-covered heaps of *débris* indicated the former sites of the villages. The grain fields were overgrown with thick forests; some few huts, which did service as lodging-places for travelers, still remained standing near the churches, but between these groups one could travel miles without seeing a human habitation, or meeting a living being, except the ever-wandering wolves. But Elias did not allow himself to be frightened back. Inflexibly, unweariedly, night and day, he continued the chase, with his thoughts constantly upon overtaking and bringing back Marie, who was now scarcely a mile or two ahead of him. In this way **he** came to Salo and Brahestad.

Externally, Brahestad was in some measure spared, but in reality impoverished. Into a part of the abandoned houses, the peasants from the surrounding ravaged neighborhood had moved, and were keeping body and soul together with fish. When the former inhabitants who had fled began to return in the autumn, obstinate conflicts arose, as the new settlers wished to hold the situation as long as possible; and burgomaster Wickman, the progenitor of a family which has ever since remained resident in the town, had great difficulty in restoring any order in the little re-barbarized community.

Scarcely had Elias passed in through one gate of the inn-yard, before a large Russian sledge, escorted by three horsemen, dashed at full gallop out through the other.

Brave and resolute, as his wild trade had taught him to be, the young man sprang out of the sledge, threw himself upon a strange horse, tied by the gate, and rode furiously after the fleeing company. They had not yet reached the city gate, when Elias rode in upon them with such violence that the near horse before the sledge was ridden down, and the whole party compelled to stop.

"I have you at last, you cursed woman-thieves!" shouted the young man, foaming with rage, and in an instant he was on the ground and beside the sledge, without troubling himself about the horsemen, who, believing themselves attacked by a madman, drew their sabres, but hesitated to use them.

"*Der teufel anamme dich, tausends perkelen koira!
Wech mit dir! Padi!*" cried burgomaster Burchard's
well-known voice, behind Elias.

But Elias did not hear him. He had drawn aside
the curtains of the sledge, and stood speechless with
amazement. An utterly unknown young woman looked
toward him, her cheeks pale with terror.

"What does this mean?" exclaimed an equally
unknown officer, who sprang from the driver's box,
and seized Elias by the collar.

"*Der Mann ist hullu ferrycht, ganz toll, durchaus!*"
again yelled the burgomaster; but instantly whispered
in Elias' ear, "Pack yourself off, *geschwind*, comrade,
sitschas! Bei Gott, I muss verrathen den kivekäs!"

"Marie! Where have they taken Marie?" whispered the freebooter, insensible to any other thought
than the rescue of the lost one.

"So, so, *die, duschinka? Gut*, comrade. *Die duschinka reise nach* Stockholm on the ice. I them *begegnet,
perjantaina, Abends bei Munsal. Der alte Larsson dabei.
Links um*, comrade; *hast mad marsch eingeschlagen!
Links um!*"

"Fool that I am! Fool that I am!" exclaimed
Elias. "They went to the south, and I sought them
in the north!" and like a maniac, he rushed back to
the inn-yard.

CHAPTER XI.

THE DIPLOMAT AND HIS CONSCIENCE.

ONE morning in the beginning of April, 1722,
president Count Torsten Bertelsköld sat in his
elegant office, listening indifferently to a number of
petitions and other business which his secretary was

recapitulating, in short synopsis, from letters just
received.   The fine count, with his extremely careful
toilet, his peruke dressed according to all the rules of
fashion, his embroidered black velvet dressing-gown,
with wide sleeves and large cuffs, short close-fitting
yellow breeches, silk stockings, and richly embroidered
slippers, sat carelessly leaned back in an easy chair,
and only occasionally let a few short oracular words
escape him, in reply to the servant's interrogatory.
But at intervals an almost imperceptible sarcastic smile
played over his intelligent but inscrutable countenance,
and disclosed all the disdain with which he thought
best to treat those who, in one or another matter of
importance, sought his patronage.

" Pastor Ringbom begs of your excellency a recommendation to the crown pastorate in Småland," reported
the secretary, as with a faithful imitation of his master's
aristocratic coldness, he laid aside one of the letters.

"If I mistake not, he voted against the monarchy,
at the last diet? " carelessly queried the count.

"Yes ! " replied the secretary, misunderstanding
the question; "he was, unfortunately, a less reliable
royalist."

"He shall have the pastorate," added Bertelsköld.

"Assessor Berling begs to come into gracious
remembrance through the office of counselor of the
superior court," resumed the secretary, somewhat bewildered.

"Was it not he who drafted the complaint of the
Wermland peasants concerning the arbitrary interfer-
ences of the factory owners, and inserted in it some
insinuations in favor of the unlimited monarchy?" responded the count.

"I am sorry to say it was he," once more replied
the secretary, taking pains to conform to the course of
the wind.

"He shall have the office," answered the count,
laconically as before.

"Prefect Baron Essen asks an extension of freedom from taxes for the East Bothnian towns that suffered by the war—Wasa, Christmestad, New Carleby."

"Who has not suffered by the war? That does not concern me. Refer him to Count Horn."

"Captain Baron Sparrfelt humbly beseeches that your excellence will hold him in remembrance in connection with the promised office of major."

"Sparrfelt? Oh, I remember; a good-for-nothing fellow, a fortune-seeker. He can wait a few years yet."

"The Finnish refugees in Sudermanland send a reminder concerning the assistance for their return home, which Count Horn caused to be promised them through your excellence."

"Count Horn? That is his matter. If he has promised them, they can apply to him."

"The French ambassador hopes that your excellence will be pleased to arrange his matter as to the sixty thousand livres he had the honor to send your excellence, as a proof of his court's high regard" . . .

Count Bertelsköld's countenance darkened. "I suppose," resumed he, "that the insolent Finns have complained of me to Count Horn. Ehrenbrand, are you in the count's pay?"

"I?" repeated the secretary, in consternation.

"*Eh bien*, I will not believe it. You are indebted to me, you know, for a coat-of-arms. You did right, and fawned upon Lord Brandt until our gracious queen, on my recommendation, thought best to introduce you among her one hundred and seventy-one new noblemen. You can rise still higher, my dear Ehrenbrand, through a *fidele conduite*."

"Your excellence, my fidelity, my zeal . . ."

"Very well. But who disturbs us to-day, so early in the morning?"

A *valet* announced Countess Liewen. The visit did not seem to be welcome, but could not be averted.

The count dismissed the secretary, and the countess entered.

Countess Ebba Liewen, formerly Bertelsköld, was still the same noble and agreeable woman with whom we became acquainted in the previous story; and although years and sorrows had somewhat paled those amiable features, her whole being still reflected the same expression of good-sense and kindness which won all hearts except the heart of her own brother, the cold diplomat. She saluted the count with some emotion, sat down beside him, and seemed to hesitate as to how she should begin the conversation.

"I wager that my amiable Ebba has again brought a subscription paper for the benefit of the Finnish refugees, and fears that from fraternal affection I shall empty my slim purse," said the count, with assumed gayety.

"No," replied the countess, with a slight tremor, which did not escape the keen eye of the diplomat. "I have come to talk with you about Eva—about Gösta's widow and her son."

"*Comment?* Then our courageous sister-in-law has it once more in her mind to undertake a new campaign against the Lapps and Cossacks, and you have concluded with her an offensive and defensive alliance."

"Nay, Torsten, your mockery shall not frighten me. I do not come to ask an alms, but justice only. It is not enough that you have caused your brother's widow to be banished from Stockholm, where she only sought an audience with the king . . ."

"I banish my valiant sister-in-law? *Ma chère*, what do you think of me? You know, of course, that our gracious queen, like all women, has her whims. She had got it into her head that Eva was intriguing for the Holstein party, and wished, *à tout prix*, to break in upon the legitimate succession."

"Do not interrupt me. You have declared war on

Eva to the death, and have begun by having her banished from Stockholm.   It was your *bon plaisir.*   I say nothing about that.   But afterwards, when she retreated, you had estate after estate taken from her, for those infamous crown arrearages which began in the arbitrary taxes of Gortz's time; and you now, for the same arrearages, allow her last possessions in Ostrogothland to go under the hammer   Your revenge, Torsten, is implacable, I know that; but it ought at least not to be ignoble."

"Continue, my countess.   One must pardon the ladies, even when they talk uncivilly."

" Gortz died on the scaffold.   You yourself were one of his most furious judges, and did not even grant him what the law grants the commonest offender.   All his work, good and evil, you have helped tear down; but when it pertains to saving your brother's widow, your brother's son, from the consequences of his extortions, then you approve of the system of Gortz, for it serves your revenge."

" My dear Ebba, for whom do you take me ? "

" Do you want me to tell you ? "

" Yes, do so, of all things.   Judging by the introduction, it does not seem to be your intention to canonize me."

"Well, Torsten, I will tell you who you are.   I will speak as though I were your own conscience."

" A sermon?   It is growing amusing."

"From our father, who during his whole life acted from principle, you received the inheritance of one conviction—the maintenance of the influence of the nobility, as an arbiter between the power of the king and the power of the people."

" *Eh bien!* what can you have against that?"

" How have you followed that principle?   I will tell you.   During the reign of the late king, you joined yourself to Count Horn, in order to climb up on his shoulders, and you still pass for his devoted adherent.

But you are ready, at any moment when your interest demands it, to ruin him."

"Really? I had not believed you to be so sharp-sighted."

"Ridicule, if you like; I will go on. You fawned upon all parties, you were regarded as indispensable by all, and you deceived them all. The princess and the duke, the aristocrats and the democrats, all believed you working in their interests. There were only one man and one woman who saw through you. The man was the king, the woman was Eva Rhenfelt, afterwards Countess Bertelsköld. For that reason, you swore them both an implacable hatred, and in that I admit you have kept your word like a man;—no, I deceive myself; a *man* is faithful to his king, and does not persecute defenseless women. You have kept your word like a Machiavelli."

"Now the sermon begins. Continue, only do not be too eloquent. I hope you will finish before noon."

"You found it for your own interest to help the princess to the throne. By that means you gained a foothold in her favor. But at the same time you found it also for your interest to conspire toward the reformation of the monarchy. By that means you gained the reputation of being a friend of liberty. Count Horn, your protector, and the greatest living statesman of Sweden, broke irremediably with the court; but you, his pupil and *protégé*, retained your royal favor; and, when the people began to find your game too double, you succeeded in displacing the crown on King Frederick's head. Once more, you were saved, you gained your point, and became omnipotent behind the backs of the apparent chiefs."

"But now you begin to flatter. That ill suits your *rôle* of court preacher."

"Patience. You continue to carry two faces, but no heart. You are at the same time royalist and patriot, as the respective parties have now begun to be called,

4*

You have admirably extricated yourself from all embarrassment on account of your faithlessness to both sides.
You have risen, and continue to rise. Within four
years you have mounted from the rank of a subordin-
ate secretary of legation, to that of president of one of
the most important assemblies of the kingdom; and
before long—that is, when you have ruined Count
Horn—you will sit among the kingdom's councilors.
That is a great deal, Torsten, for a man who has not
his genius, but chance alone, to thank for power and
advancement."

"Now, then, we come to the moral."

"Yes, chance, for that is your inmost faith. Torsten, Torsten, what advantage to us is the most subtle
brain, if we do not possess with it a heart for faith and
honor in life? You, who do not believe in either
God or conscience, you place all your trust in a miserable superstition, a folly, an amulet! You despise
yourself so deeply that you attribute all your power
and fortune to that awful magic power which pursues
our race and prepares its ruin. Your only, your most
heartfelt faith, is faith in the power of the king's ring."

CHAPTER XII.

CONSCIENCE BECOMES SILENT.

THE mocking smile vanished from the lips of Count
Bertelsköld. "Pardon me," said he, "my time
is occupied. Let us return to the subject, if you
please. How large is the demand of the crown against
the Falkby estate?"

Without answering the question, the countess continued. "If you were animated by that keen sense of

justice and generosity which actuated our father during his whole life, I would appeal only to that, and
you would hear me.   You must now know that I too
see through you, — and me you cannot hate, that is impossible.   You believe yourself inaccessible in your artful and heartless policy; but a weak point nevertheless
exists, where you can easily be wounded. Since you received back the ring, you say to yourself every day, 'This
ring shall make me irresistible ; this ring shall lift me
above the artifices of my enemies, and above even the
instability of human affairs; I shall rise, continually
rise, unconcerned as to whom I trample under my feet
in my ascent, and no one shall cast me down.' Yes,
do not look so darkly at me for saying it ; this is your
inmost thought, and it has hitherto been verified by
reality.   But how — if you again lost the ring ?"

Count Torsten forced a smile. "I shall take care
that my generous Ebba does not trade it off, another
time, for a candy kiss," said he.

"I recollect that the ring has been lost several
times before, and every time by means of a broken
oath.   You lost it once yourself, when you in jest
swore to your love for old lady Posse.   Are you very
sure that you never commit perjury ?"

"Ebba ! You abuse my patience ! "

"Your whole policy is a falsehood.   Your whole
life is a perjury.   Beware, Torsten, of the dark powers
of that destiny which you at once defy and fear !   If
nothing else will move you, then think on your fall !
Act nobly, Torsten, if not from principle, then from
fear.   You, who do not believe in God, but believe in
a copper ring,— tremble before your idol, that it may
not scorn and ensnare you ! "

The count paced excitedly to and fro across the
room.   His self-possession had forsaken him.   The
master of the faithless statecraft of that time, he who
laughed at all human feelings, had for a moment lost
his equipoise.   The countess tried quickly, but perhaps

too inconsiderately, to make use of this unwonted impression on a heart of ice.

"Well," said she, "it rests only with you to recall the claim of the crown on Falkby, and declare it void, as it is, since the conscription on which it depends was utterly illegal. You have called Baron Gortz 'the iron scraper;' you cannot sanction his measures, since you had his head cut off."

Before she had finished speaking, the opportunity had flown by, and the cold smile had resumed its accustomed place on the lips of the statesman.

"Admit, *ma chere*," said he, smiling, "that we are a couple of large children. We dispute about a phantom, and forget that reality has its claims. I will consider your *propos*. Everything shall be arranged, *à tout possible.*"

Countess Liewen saw that she had missed her mark, but she felt the courage and the pride of her race burst into flame at the injustice which menaced the friend of her childhood and the son of her beloved brother Gösta.

"I will propose an arrangement which will perhaps suit you better," said she.

"Very well. Let us leave the ethics and return to the reality."

"Europe, in two encampments, stands equipped for war. It is said that a great number of French livres have lately been distributed as subsidies to gain the coöperation of Sweden. If any of this foreign gold has accidentally fallen at your feet, then, like a man of honor, let it lie untouched. Have I understood you?"

"Subsidies? Impossible! I know nothing about the matter."

"A Bertelsköld does not sell his country. But, if I do not deceive myself, subsidies have arrived from Russia also. Happy Sweden! It is put up at auction, and falls to the highest bidder. And does not my brother know the least *soupçon* about it?"

"The gabble of the mob! *Enfin;* do you want to buy back Falkby, with this pretended foreign money?"

"Not Falkby, not my own fortune, even though I should be obliged to beg my bread on the streets. I would sooner perish from hunger. But either you will have a stop put to the auction at Falkby, or I will make all your duplicity known to the queen. She will believe me, for she would know—and God knows—what that confession cost me. Now I have told you all; you can regard me too as your enemy, if you do not rather prefer to regard me as your most faithful friend. Choose!"

And with head erect, but with flushed cheeks, Countess Liewen, agitated and trembling, withdrew. Only a word was needed, and she would have thrown herself, weeping, into her brother's arms. But that word was not spoken, and brother and sister were separated forever.

Count Torsten stood for a time astonished at this unusual outburst from so gentle and tender a being. He weighed the price of a sister's love. It would cost him only a signal, and Falkby would be saved, his sister reconciled. But would it do for him, the politic, impenetrable man, to acknowledge himself conquered, and blush before a woman? No!—the cold smile returned once more to his lips. He rang. The secretary came.

"Ehrenbrand," said the count, with a gracious smile, "I have been thinking about your promotion. To-morrow, a deputation leaves for St. Petersburg. Make yourself ready for traveling, my friend; you are to begin a diplomatic career. Be assured of my protection."

Surprised, and uncertain how to interpret this unexpected distinction, the young man paused. "Your excellency—" he stammered.

"I understand. You need money for the journey. Here it is. Let it be seen that you do me honor. Adieu!"

And, accustomed to mechanical obedience, the young diplomatic tyro, scarcely knowing how, soon found himself outside the door. But the face of the count darkened when he found himself alone.

"I must purify my surroundings," said he to himself. "In my service people ought not to know too much. How has Ebba conceived her suspicions? Can she really be dangerous to me? *Enfantillage!* A woman has her sentimental notions. But she is right; I might be suspected by the court. I need a *succès* with the king. How? Falsely represent to him that unlimited power which he is so actively trying to attain? Or . . . With *ces messieurs*, the small expedients are often better than the great. Where shall I find the thread by which to guide the babe in leading-strings? If I should? · ·"

The count rang again. The *valet* entered.

"Jacques, summon hither Captain Baron Sparrfelt!"

"He has been waiting in the ante-chamber an hour, for an audience with your excellency."

"Very well. Let him come in."

Sparrfelt came—a stately young soldier, but one who had. evidently had no actual experience with powder.

"My dear captain," said the count, complaisantly, "I am sorry that the promotion of so deserving a man has been so long neglected. If it had depended upon me, you should long ago have obtained the position of major. No one is more entitled to it than you. But Count Horn—you understand. *Apropos*—your brother, I am told, is still looking everywhere in vain for the dove flown from Count Horn's family. Do not deny, my dear baron, that you had a certain *partage* in the disappearance of the wild Finnish bird."

"Your excellency is pleased to jest. . . . . ."

"No, upon my honor. It was you who stole her away, and you are now letting your brother seek for her in the wilderness of Finland. Admit that this mischief is your invention. You **are a real Don Juan, my** dear baron. You make conquest upon conquest; and the little Marie is bewitching."

Flattered by so much condescension, the captain continued his denials, but in such a manner as could be interpreted in whatever way one chose.

At this moment a tall, elderly man, in citizen's costume, and of severe, almost rude appearance, entered unannounced. This man was no other than Lars Larsson, the merchant from Wasa.

The count's forehead, which had wrinkled at this abrupt entrance, was immediately smoothed into the brightest sunshine, when he recognized Larsson. It was as pleasant as unexpected, he said, to see once more, at this season of the year, so esteemed an acquaintance from Finland.

The merchant bowed exactly as low as ceremony required, and stated that the misery and urgent business of the country did not admit of any delay. He had come across the ice from Umeå, and thence to Stockholm, as a deputy from the citizens of the town of Wasa, humbly to supplicate for an extension of the tax exemption and an abatement in customs, concerning which he now most humbly ventured to solicit his excellency's most gracious assistance. The reasons were so and so; and, undisturbed by the presence of the captain, Larsson began diffusely to explain the motives for his embassy, among which was the necessity at the first opening of navigation, of supplying Finland with salt, iron, grain, hops, cordage, and communion wine, for the total want of the latter article had compelled many churches to use brandy as a substitute.

Count Torsten listened, apparently with much interest and sympathy, to this information, but finally interrupted the speaker with the declaration that he was perfectly convinced as to the fairness of the request of the citizens of Wasa, and should, for his part, try as far as he was able to procure assent to it. For the rest, the people now had a gentle and gracious

king, who would in every way further the best interests of his subjects.

The austere democrat from Wasa replied, somewhat
less humbly than is the worthy custom of supplicants,
that he did not ask clemency, but justice only; and as
constitutional liberty now existed, he hoped that such
a request would not be refused him.   That had also
been the opinion of Count Horn, he added.

"Without doubt," answered the count, with the
utmost complaisance, " if you, my dear Larsson, have
introduced your petition to Count Horn, and his excellency regards it as possible, I can congratulate you on
your success."

"I have not insinuated anything with the count,"
bluntly retorted Larsson.   "I only took my niece back
to the count's house, and talked privately with the
count about our affairs."

"Your niece, little Marie?"

"Yes, sir count," and Larsson's sun-browned
cheeks were colored a dusky red.

"I am glad.   Adieu, my dear Larsson—be assured
of my protection.   .   .   .   .   And you, Major Sparrfelt, you have heard:—your reputation as a conqueror
is at stake.   There is only one way of re-establishing
your attribute of invincibility."

"Can I in any manner serve your excellency?"

"Me?   What are you thinking of?   But yourself,
your reputation for invincibility.   Steal away your
beauty!"

CHAPTER XIII.

LAPLAND FOUND AGAIN.

A T Järna, in Sudermanland, there was, in April
1722, a royal hunting party. King Frederick
loved this sport with a passion almost equal to that of
his two predecessors, and was scarcely less skillful and
experienced in it. He had been a nimble gentleman,
firm in the saddle, but with increasing years had
grown more inclined to ease. The difference between
his hunts and those of the Charleses, was that Frederick's were now seldom dangerous or desperate, but all
took place with some wearying exertion on horseback
and on foot, which was followed by a keen appetite;
and King Frederick was not one who despised a good
table. Still, although he was corpulent and heavy, he
was quite a skillful horseman. In the kingdom of
Sweden there was hardly a better shot than the king,
and he not unfrequently amused himself by shooting
the ears off a hare at full bound, as he left to his
dogs and huntsmen the simpler work of killing the
game. In the meantime, the king, like the great Charles,
accepted fresh butter and golden cream at the parson-
ages, in such a way, however, that his French cook
condescendingly helped the clergyman's wife in the
preparations. Indeed, it even happened that the king
did not disdain a bowl of sour milk, served in the
peasant houses by some pretty lass; but there must be
cinnamon and sugar on it, which were never lacking in
the little silver-mounted traveling-case that the royal
steward always took along, to season the coarse taste
of the country according to his grace's finer knowledge
of gastronomic science.

G   5

Spring was far advanced and the snow mostly gone. In these more populated tracts, they had not succeeded in surrounding more than a single bear; and after this had been felled according to all the rules of the art, by the king's own ball, they attacked foxes and other game, of which the region had a plentiful supply. The hunt was now ended for the day, and the king had caused an elegant *soupé* to be arranged at the parsonage. Here, neither Spanish wines nor strong ale were lacking; and as King Frederick was a popular king, who had his reasons for desiring to stand well with the people of Sweden, a few of the most considerable peasants of the neighborhood were also invited to take part in the entertainment.

The king was usually very mild and gracious when free from the burdensome cares of government. He was graciously pleased to appear at a wedding, which, not without some slight indications of satisfaction with the honor of a royal visit and of the hope of royal munificence, took place that same evening in the large apartment used by the domestics of the farm. The hope was not disappointed. His majesty was pleased, in his own eminent person, to pinch the cheek of the bride and to lay four ducats on the bride's plate, after which he inspected, with the eye of a connoiseur, the young lassies among the wedding guests, who were extremely embarrassed by such royal favors. The inspection did not, however, appear to result exactly to his satisfaction, as he soon turned to a couple of gray-haired peasants and began to ask questions concerning the condition of the country, which highly surprised them, as they knew how unwilling his majesty usually was to trouble himself with public matters on such festive occasions.

And the peasants were not slow to portray, in candid but respectful language, the great misery of the people and the weakness of the kingdom since the long war, while at the same time they had ready a number of humble petitions which the priest had drafted for them, so as not to let the important visit pass without benefit to the place.   The king received the petitions with the most gracious attention, and promised, as he left the wedding, to do what was in his power, but did not neglect to add, with a slight shrug of the shoulders, that he was able to do so little for the welfare of the kingdom, the people should look to the council.   If, in the future, it became practicable for him, everything should certainly be done for the comfort and satisfaction of the honest peasantry.

The peasants, who did not know exactly how to explain this royal enigma, which was made still more incomprehensible by a strong German accent, were nevertheless charmed with the extraordinary condescension of the distinguished guest, and some of them took it upon themselves, at the ale-keg, to extol the present government above the one immediately preceding it.

"It is a long time since a Swedish peasant has looked open-eyed at his master and king," exclaimed one of the guests.

"And if he succeeds in doing as he desires, then we shall have prosperous times," said another.   "But the great gentlemen have put a halter on him, and do what they please with both king and peasants."

"And a halter might well be needed, too, after all that we beheld in the time of the late King Charles," responded another.

"Who presumes to speak against King Charles and his blue boys?" passionately exclaimed a scarred old Carolin, who, with his wooden leg, sat in a corner of the room.

Only the name of King Charles was needed, and the deeds of King Frederick faded in a moment.

"Old Hans is right.   Charles was a king who was good for something; and if things turned out badly, it was the fault of Gortz and the masters," clamored several voices.

"Law and freedom are our masters now," directly objected a member of the diet of 1719.

"Law me here, and free me there," responded the Carolin, stamping with his wooden leg so that it echoed in the room. " Do you want to hear a new song, boys, printed this year? It begins thus:

"When all has reached its height, we see its fall begun;
Thus has our Swedish clock now passed from twelve to one."

A loud cry of applause rewarded this generally-understood allusion to the figures of the rulers, and the acts of King Frederick appeared somewhat simple to this singular people, who would rather allow themselves to be tyrannized over by a hero than to live free under a puppet king. In vain did the first speaker plead that King Frederick was also known as a brave warrior, and that he bore on his body more scars from balls and pikes than even King Charles. The shadow of that last name, even now, while all the footprints of that sanguinary Carolinian time were still freshly bleeding, so overspread all other names, that his successor was entirely forgotten before the saga-like achievements and adventures with which the man with the wooden leg now began to entertain his comrades at the ale-mug.

In the meantime, King Frederick took his place by the table of delicacies, in the provost's apartment, and was enjoying the repast with jest and laughter, and doubtful hunting-stories, when a huntsman entered and handed a note to Broman, the king's favorite. Soon afterward, Broman, who as private secretary was then beginning his career to the future presidency, took away the king's plate, and let the note fall unnoticed on the napkin. The king continued to jest and prate, but put the note in his pocket. " *Was giebts?* " he afterward asked his secretary, in a careless manner.

"Lapland is found again," replied Broman, in a low voice.

The king immediately arose. "Gentlemen," said he

complaisantly, "I regret that I cannot longer divert myself with your entertaining company. Important matters of state call me immediately to Stockholm; but I beg you to continue, and not allow yourselves to be disturbed by this incident. Adieu, gentlemen. *Auf wiedersehen.*"

The king departed. The light, single-seated, two-horse sledge, driven by his own coachman, was hitched behind the best trotters, and immediately behind followed Broman and the *valet*, riding in a coppered sledge. Beside them galloped the usual escort of an adjutant and four life-dragoons.

King Frederick was quite as little of a "horse-pitier" as any of the Charleses had been, and, like them, rode at "king's-speed." Moreover, horses had been ordered in advance, and Södertelje was passed without stopping, in good time in the evening. After that, the rapid speed was perceptibly moderated. Broman, accompanied by two dragoons, received orders to ride forward, "to see if the ice was safe," and the royal sledge, with the remainder of the escort, followed at an easy trot, a good distance behind.

"What kind of a place is this?" asked the king, pointing to a large ruined house, at the right of the road.

"That is Gärdinge; it belongs to the Sparrfelts," replied the adjutant, who was riding by the side of the sledge.

"It appears to be uninhabited."

"It has not been occupied for many years, by any one but the steward and his people."

"Can you see, Stramberg, if it is light upstairs?"

"Not the least, sire. It is dark there."

"Young folks would do better to till their ground than to intrude themselves into embassies.——*Aber was giebts da am Ufer?* Broman, *lamentirt ja wie ein Verrückter.* Ride on, *zum Teufel!*"

The noise of a loud quarrel, in which Broman's

voice could be distinguished at some distance in the
frosty night air, was indeed heard. When the king
and his adjutant reached the spot, they found Broman's·
sledge ridden into by another sledge, which had met
it at a point where the winter road led down a meadow
slope to the ice of the Mälar. The quarrel had already
come to blows, and Broman, with his two dragoons,
were likely to be vanquished by a tall officer, with two
or three soldiers, who had all drawn their swords and
were unceremoniously slashing in among their antagonists. Peace was still a new fashion, and people
would not altogether break themselves of their old
habits.

"Drive the pack out of the road, to make room for
us!" commanded the king, and the adjutant did not
allow himself to be told twice. In a moment he was
there with his dragoons, and the fight now took another
turn. The opposite party gave up the battle as lost,
and fled to the woods. Only the strange officer still
fenced, like a maniac, by the half-overturned sledge.

"Surrender, Baron Sparrfelt!" exclaimed Stramberg, who now recognized his antagonist. "In the
king's name, I arrest you for disturbing the peace of
the highways."

"And for disturbing the peace of women!" put in
Broman, with an indignation which had a very knightly
appearance. "There is a young woman here in the
sledge who declares herself to have been forcibly
carried away from Stockholm."

The sword fell from the dumb-stricken captain's
hand.

The king alighted from his sledge. "We had not
expected," said he, with that haughty severity which he
could on such occasions so well assume, "we had not
expected to meet our officers in a situation which might
better suit robbers on the open highway. Is it thus,
gentlemen, that you observe law and decorum? Baron
Sparrfelt will betake himself this instant to Gärdinge, and

remain there until we have opportunity to investigate his behavior more closely. As to the young lady, we command you, Broman, to return her, *saine et sauve*, to her relatives in Stockholm. Every innocent person has a right to call upon our royal protection. You will account to us with your head for this lady."

The king's command was obeyed, and in a few minutes Sparrfelt was on the way to Gärdinge, while the royal retinue continued the journey to Stockholm, increased by a silent, trembling, and, in the twilight of the night, unrecognizable young woman.

CHAPTER XIV.

THE CONTINUATION OF THE FREEBOOTER'S HUNT.

WE left our brave young knight of the highway, Elias Pehrson, in a very adventurous situation in Brahestad; and it is no more than fair that we see what afterwards became of him. Frantic over the loss of his beloved Marie, without money, without acquaintances, without venturing to appeal to any of the proper authorities, as a price was still set on his head, bewildered, he saw himself far up in the north, while a dark fate drew Marie back to Stockholm, a return to which she so inexplicably feared. For a moment, Elias regarded all as lost. It seemed to him as though the ground had sunk beneath his feet.

Just then an ungentle hand shook him by the collar, and a peasant, who had run after him from the inn, demanded back his horse. A thought rushed through the freebooter's head, and grew, more rapidly than is wont in this country, into a ripe resolve.

"Convey me immediately northward until we reach

the officer who left this place just now, and take my
horse for the fare!"

The peasant stared at him. "Either the man is a
fool, or he has stolen the horse," thought he to himself.
But Elias drew him back to the inn-yard, and, however
the matter was managed, both were soon on the way to
Uleåborg. Fortunately, the large Russian sledge of the
travelers had broken down in Sükajoki, and Elias
overtook the party, this time without special difficulty.

He stepped quickly into the Gertula inn, and found
there the same persons whom a few hours before he
had so rashly attacked at the city gate of Brahestad.
Burchard, the ex-burgomaster, arose from a dish of
turnips, whose contents were fast disappearing in
his corpulent food-sack, and made a pretence of blocking the way before the in-comer. "The devilish *perkele*
freebooter will *durchaus* be hanged!" he exclaimed.

Elias thrust him aside, and advanced directly to the
officer, a middle-aged man, with noble features. "Pardon me," said he, "that I once more disturb your honor,
but it is done, God knows, with no bad intention."

"Who are you? What do you want?" asked the
officer, with a frown.

"I am one of the humblest servants of the late king,
and of Löfving, by occupation a *kivekäs*, as they call us
—the king's free-men in this country," responded
Elias. "A price of a hundred dollars is set on my head,
because I burned a Russian galley in the archipelago
of Pargas, and your honor can easily get rid of me by
informing against me before the police officer of the
place. But I speak to a Carolin. I cannot have anything to fear."

"No, in truth; if it is as you say, my boy. you need
not regret that you turned to me. I am Major Düker,
of the Uplanders, and am on my way back from Russia,
after almost thirteen years' captivity. My wife will
follow me by the northern road to Stockholm."

"To Stockholm!" replied Elias. "Sir major—

take me with you ! I will serve you as boot-black, I will drive all horses to death for you—I will fight for you—but there is no need of that now; in a word, sir major, I will die for you, only take me along ! "

"Young man," said Düker, smiling, "if you drive as you ride, I really believe you are prepared to keep your word. Why are you so eager to get to Stockholm ? "

Elias recounted, in brief, the abduction of Marie.

"That is a doubtful story," said the major. "We have peace now, my boy, and with all your resolution, I am afraid you will be the loser in the game with the girl's guardian. But to be outlawed because one has caused annoyance to the enemy, is no fault in my eyes. One of my old soldiers, who accompanied me out of captivity, stops in Uleåborg, and Burchard is speculating upon the position of sergeant there. You can occupy their place. But do not ride my horses to death—that, I reserve for myself."

"God save King Charles!" exclaimed Elias, swinging his hat.

" *Wollte sagen den grossmächtigen* Frederick," corrected Burchard. " *Nur immer den richten* monarch, *durchaus !* "

The train once more set in motion. They traveled now through terribly devastated regions.

The whole plain of Liningo was a desert, where not one stone upon another was left of the dwellings of men. Not until in the vicinity of Uleåborg did they again see here and there a hut by the roadside. The town itself had been ill-treated. Johannes Snellman, its historian (1736), tells of the entrance of the enemy into the unprotected town, on St. Andrew's day, in the year 1714, and how, during the war, everything was plundered. One hundred and forty-three of the inhabitants were taken into captivity, and many others during the flight perished in the sea. In the winter, a few of the refugees had now come back across Torneå, but the town was still half depopulated, and consisted of dilapidated cottages, which had scarcely been erected, after the fire of 1705, before the plague of 1710 and the invasion of the enemy also gave another sad blow to the prosperity of Uleåborg.

The travelers halted in Uleåborg no longer than was required for necessary rest. The progress was continued under difficulties and dangers of which one can now scarcely form an idea, constantly farther toward the north. Even to the little tumble-down village of Torneå, there extended traces of the ravages of war. After this, they were able to find at least a roof to shelter them; but on the Swedish side also, although in a less degree, the people were decimated, the poverty was great, and the country had reverted to a wilderness. Many a time were the travelers indebted to the resolution of the freebooter, and his experience in extricating himself from the most delicate situations, for their passage through all these difficulties.

At last, after eight weeks' travel through the bad sledging, they saw the spires of Stockholm glimmering in the spring sunshine. That view forced tears from the eyes of honest Düker. It was now the beginning of May. Elias bade a cordial adieu to his fellow-travelers, and started, on his own responsibility, out into the intricate maze of Sweden's capital, where Tessin's work, the almost completed but still uninhabited new palace, haughty even then as a lion's lair, looked out on the marriage of the Mälar with the billows of the Baltic.

Accustomed, like his master Löfving, to assume all characters, the shrewd freebooter immediately went to Count Horn's house, and passed himself off for the *valet* of a Finnish gentleman, who, with good words and drink-money, wished to gain promotion with Count Horn. In this *rôle* he had soon enticed from the servant-folks all that they knew about the count, the countess, and her adopted daughter. But it was, alas!

no glad news. Larsson had brought Marie back to the count's house; she had wept much, and most of the time had shut herself up. But one evening she had gone to visit her sister, who had come to Stockholm, and on her return she had suddenly disappeared. In vain had Larsson, in vain had the count himself, set half the city in motion to find the lost one. Three weeks had passed since then, and not the least trace of her had been discovered. The countess was inconsolable, and the rough Larsson sought in vain to conceal his repentance and remorse at having brought the girl to Stockholm. The wise ones among the servants suspected something. The girl had a broken heart, that was plain enough, and it would be found that she had jumped into the sea.

"What good would that do?" said the old gate-keeper, who regarded himself as wiser than all the others. "If she had jumped into the sea, she would have floated, that is plain; she has learned that much in Finland. Indeed, she ran away home to steal the art of some old witch in Lapland; but you see her uncle was ashamed of it, and brought her back, to become a Christian again—that is all there is of the Finland affair. Baron Sparrfelt's best fellow, Canute, he with the scar, swore that the countess's Marie had bewitched his master, and would some day probably rush off with him to Blåkulla."

"Is it really known that she did not do that?" asked Elias, quite calm, while he was secretly ready to chop the old gossip in pieces.

"It is not very certain," said a pert waiting-maid, who could never forgive Marie her precedence in the favor of the countess. "The same day she disappeared, I saw Sparrfelt ride past here twice, and from that day no one has seen him."

"Nonsense, my dear!" said the count's aristocratic *valet*, who always knew more than all the others. "Baron Sparrfelt has run his sword through a dragoon, and is now under arrest at his Gärdinge estate, three miles from Stockholm."

Elias had heard enough. Half an hour later, he was on the way to Gärdinge, this time in the character of a steward who was going about buying up horses for Finland. And it was not long before he had an account of the inner history of Gärdinge. Sparrfelt was there, half dead with *ennui* and grief, but compelled to remain in confinement at the house, on a charge that he and his people rode over the king on the ice, and killed four dragoons, on which occasion his majesty barely escaped with his life, for all of which the noble baron might doubtless expect the rack and wheel. The blame for all this rested upon a Finnish witch whom his grace the baron had wanted to take with him to Gärdinge, to cure the horses of the spavin; but when Adjutant Stramberg saw the witch, he had a hole chopped in the ice, and pushed her in with the butt of his musket, for it was understood that she floated.

With this information, Elias returned to Stockholm, and gave himself no rest until he obtained some information from Adjutant Stramberg. At this place, he passed himself off for an agent from Larsson, who wanted to present a petition to the king, and he managed to drop a word about Sparrfelt and the witch. "Larsson had intended to buy horses at Gärdinge, but found out that Sparrfelt was in the habit of doctoring his horses by magic."

Stramberg laughed aloud. "That would not be unlike Sparrfelt, but in this case he was outwitted by Broman, who ran off with his witch. Perhaps Broman's horses also have spavin."

With these words the adjutant turned his back to the supplicant, and Elias, grinding his teeth with rage, started off in search of Broman.

CHAPTER XV.

JUPITER AND JUNO.

IN order to make this story seem probable, or even possible, the reader must bear in mind the extraordinary change in manners and principles at the Swedish court after the death of Charles XII. In the time of Charles XI, manners were extremely severe, and the court, like the king, divided its day between work and devotional exercises. Much of the seriousness of that period evaporated under the wild youthful pleasures of Charles XII; but afterward, victories and then defeats again elevated the people to a more serious mood. The very fermenting internal discord, party hatred, intrigues, throne disputes, and the contention regarding the unlimited monarchy, steeled the senses at the outset against the depravity of mortals which for more than a generation had been extending from the frivolous French court over the greater part of Europe. Sweden continued on the whole to be a land of strict morals, and fifty years of weakness and internal dissensions were still needed, in order, with Gustaf III, to usher other principles into the higher classes of society.

But Frederick I and Charles XII had gone to different schools. Frederick had grown up in the atmosphere of the same gallant court as had August II and the Duke of Orleans, the most celebrated libertines of that period; and he strove for conquests quite different from those of his stern predecessor. Fortunately, his influence did not extend far beyond the brilliant playthings.of the court, and the parties which continued to roar around him, under him, and over him, intimidated him into an appearance of outer decency, which, however, appeared very comical to those who knew him more intimately.

In the ground-work of great events, there is always one strong thread which holds them together; but on the surface this thread loses itself in delicate cobwebs of chance and human passions, which then gain an appearance of having been the genuine leading lines of the events. At the time of this story, there was mingled with the rest of the party conflicts in Sweden, a bitter enmity between the victorious Hess party and the defeated Holstein party. Count Horn was now the man who governed the kingdom. But the independent Ulrica Eleonora could never forgive him that he, who had been tutor to her nephew and rival, the Holstein prince, had continually held his former pupil as dear as the welfare of the kingdom and the new succession could allow. Count Horn acted like a man, but his queen hated like a woman. His fall was decreed; and had he fallen in that hour, while freedom was still a perverse child, perhaps the absolute monarchy, which alone knew exactly what it wanted, might once more have uplifted its crowned brow in Sweden.

King Frederick trembled for that hour almost as much as he desired it. He did not love Count Horn, but he feared him. Unwillingly, he gave way before the queen's urgent representations that the pillar of the new order of things ought to be cast down; but finally he gave his consent.

Behind these court intrigues there stood, invisible and powerful, a man well-known in these stories— Count Torsten Bertelsköld. He had the ear of the queen. He was fixed upon by her as Count Horn's successor. No one else had grown to that position.

Everything was prepared. The day and hour were appointed. Only the king's signature was required for the dismissal and exile of the omnipotent Horn, upon which the nomination of his successor was to follow.

The king was awaiting the queen in his cabinet, and pacing uneasily to and fro. He had dismissed his favorites and confidentials, and Secretary Broman alone sat by the writing-table, occupied in composing an epistle to the council, according to the king's dictation, by which the arbitrary and hazardous measure was to be justified.

How wearisome, in the long run, did those affairs of state become! The king altered, and altered again, the wording of that dangerous letter, but never got it exactly according to his wish. Wearied, he at last threw himself on the sofa, and abruptly interrupted his dictation with the unexpected question: "*Noch nichts von* Lapland? Nothing yet about the Finnish witch?"

"Your majesty?" said Broman, with humble surprise, glancing up from the important manuscript on an altogether different subject.

"*Nun was?* You must bring her back to me. For more than half a year, she has been continually fooling me. You are an incapable blockhead, Broman; hardly fit to scrub the crowfeet crowd. Young donkey!"

"On your majesty's command, I conveyed her into safe protection in care of the wife of master Gerhard, the court tailor, who received the order to fasten windows and doors with care, and not admit any human being, before your majesty found occasion *incognito* to honor them with his first gracious visit. Unfortunately . . . ."

"*Geh zum Teufel!* The next morning she was *putzwech.*"

"Mother Gerhard showed me the window where the girl let herself down. It was in the second story, twenty-four feet from the ground. Incomprehensible!"

"Incomprehensible result of those ducats the old gossip enticed from you. Perhaps you have put them into your own ample pocket?"

" Your majesty, my humble zeal   . . ."

" Bah ! *Zuckerwasser !* What have you done to find
her again? *Geschwindt !*"

" I first applied to Count Bertelsköld, who induced
Sparrfelt to abduct the girl in order to play her into
the right hands.   He knew nothing."

" *Nichts ?*   The sharpest rascal in Stockholm yesterday knew *nichts?   Weiter fort !* "

" In Count Horn's house, where the *valet-de-chambre*
is in my pay, no news whatever had been received.
They believed there that the girl had jumped into the
sea."

" One can govern Sweden, and still know nothing.
Weiter fort !"

" Yesterday, after I had caused the whole of Stockholm to be searched through, quite as vainly as Count
Horn had just before done, a fellow came to me, under
the pretext, at first, that he wanted to present a petition.
But when he found himself alone with me, he seized
me by the collar, and forced me, with a pistol at my
breast, to tell what I knew about the disappearance of
Marie Larsson."

" And you told him all you knew, *und noch was
dazu ?* "

" I would die a thousand times rather than betray
my great king's gracious confidence," continued the
favorite, in the same tone, half servile and half insolent.   " I perceived that he knew of the occurrence with
Sparrfelt, and composed a famous story for him: the
girl was said to be concealed in the house of a court
wig-maker, in the southern suburb.   The cursed fellow
was not easy to outwit.   I was compelled to go with
him to the pretended wig-maker, where I fortunately
met police-inspector Frifält on the steps.   He understands a wink, and my good man is now sitting in the
city prison, under complaint for assault and robbery."

" *Gut*, Broman, *gut !* Let the man be hanged
geschwindt ! He might do something stupid, and be-

come dangerous. The fellow deserves credit for his modesty."

" Let your majesty be pleased to have no anxiety. It is now known that the fellow, who calls himself Elias Pehrson, is a vile freebooter, from Finland, and that last autumn a price was set upon his head, for some kind of robbery. There is cause enough to hang ten persons of his *conduite.*"

" *Geschwindt, junge, geschwindt!* He ought not to see to-morrow morning. There are certain reasons— the court has cat's ears—the queen is a prude—jealous —you understand ? "

" Your majesty shall be gratified."

" You ought to think of your own neck. You are playing tricks; *mausetodt!* You will bring Marie back within eight days, or you will have your discharge. *Verstanden? Weg!* The queen is coming."

The secretary disappeared, with the very humblest bow, disgrace in prospect and grief in his heart. "Such tools are worn out fast, and break soon," says a celebrated author.

Count Bertelsköld was announced and graciously received. Not a feature betrayed his inward emotion at that decisive moment which should conduct him to the heights of power. He was cool, calm, and calculating as ever. They exchanged only a few commonplace woras; Frederick I did not like people who saw through him.

The queen entered, but the court ladies remained outside. Who does not remember the tall stiff figure of Ulrica Eleonora, the younger, with the towering coiffure, the low-cut boddice, the disproportionately long waist (glued on, as it were, above the hoop-skirt, which stood out over her hips), and the high-heeled shoes? Her entire figure bore a strong resemblance to a bronze clock. The large eyes and thick lips of the Pfaltz race were softened in the elder sister of Charles XII by a delicate womanly agreeableness; but in

H   5*

Ulrica Eleonora they had a certain masculine expression, which, with large nose and coarse arms, would not exactly accord with those eulogies for beauty with which the flattering poets of that period gratuitously furnished her. She had also inherited all her brother's independence without his firmness, so that she often hesitated in irresolution, or flew into a passion, which, in Charles XII, was almost without example. This evening, she was not in a good humor. Immediately upon her entrance, the king perceived a thunder-cloud on her high forehead, and hastened to try if possible to turn away the lightnings.

"*Immer* beautiful as a Juno, and irresistible as the goddess of love!" exclaimed he, kissing her hand with the bombastic gallantry of that period. The conversation was carried on in German.

"The comparison is not badly drawn," replied the queen, with a certain acrimony of tone; "at least my noble consort bears a wonderful resemblance to Jove—majestic and faithful! Olympus might envy us; every day we are enacting the metamorphoses of Ovid. Your majesty has studied Ovid, of course? In practice, perhaps? There is fascinating instruction there. And behold Mercury—the messenger of the gods! I present you my congratulations, sir count! You play your *rôle, sans peur et sans reproche!*"

Calm and smiling, as though he had ears only for the queen's extraordinary wit, Count Bertelsköld bowed. The king had more difficulty in concealing his surprise. Something was wrong, he saw that clearly. His consort, to whom he was indebted for the crown, knew more than she ought to know. But which of the many adventures had now leaked out, and aroused her anger?

He made the queen take a seat in the purple velvet arm chair which had been moved thither solely for her.

"Will your majesty be pleased to honor me with your commands?" said he.

When Charles XII was angry at Demotica, the head of the Grand Vizier grew loose under his turban. When Ulrica Eleonora was enraged, Frederick I was obliged to play the *rôle* of the most dutiful subject.

The queen sat down. Higher and higher the dark flush rose on her cheeks and forehead. She was not lovely then, but there was something about her suggestive of the Kalabalik* in Bender. She still kept silence.

" I hope your majesty is well?" said the king, perhaps without observing the irony which lay in the tone. "Next summer, the mineral waters of Medevi shall recruit your majesty's precious health."

No answer. The thunder-cloud was not yet sufficiently charged for the lightning.

"But to come to the affairs of the kingdom," continued the king, visibly troubled, and with the evident view of exorcising the storm at any cost. " I perfectly share your majesty's opinion that Count Horn cannot any longer be retained. We must purify our government from suspicious tendencies."

" Radamanthys ought to be deposed from the Areiopagos of the gods, in order to be replaced by Mercury—the god of thieves ! Wise Jove, is not that your meaning?" burst out the offended consort.

* Kalabalik—the name of that fight in Bender, where the Turks, February 1, 1713, attacked Charles XII, in his quarters, in obedience to the Sultan's command to capture the king living or dead. King Charles and his handful of Swedes defended themselves a long time, and drove back the assailants, until the latter set fire to the wooden roof, so that he was obliged to hasten out and try to make his way to the Chancery House, a stone building, fifty paces away ; but he tripped up on his spurs, and fell. A multitude of Turkish soldiers then rushed upon him, took him prisoner with his companions, and conducted him to the Pascha, who treated him with respect, but did not give him his sword. King Charles was afterward taken to the Castle of Demotica, at Adrianople.—Tr.

CHAPTER XVI.

JUNO'S REVENGE.

THE king exchanged an embarrassed glance with Bertelsköld, who remained as cool and calm as though he had come to listen to one of the tedious pastorals of that period. But without waiting for reply, and more and more unable to restrain her boiling rage, the queen continued.

"Yes, God knows I hate that Finnish unicorn, that arrogant oligarch who now plays master over the crowned head, and the day will come when I shall trample him under my feet. But to sacrifice him, a man of capacity, a man of honor, for a miserable intriguer, a hypocrite, an ignoble faultfinder !—your majesty, our inherited crown has not yet sunk so low ! Remain, sir count ! Your queen commands it. You are smiling still. You are charmed at being witness to a scene in our royal house ; but you will never be the successor of Count Horn ! Look ! read, and judge how deeply the queen of Sweden must despise you !"

With these words, the queen handed him a note, without address or signature, in the well-known hand of Count Bertelsköld, and containing only these words :

"To-day, between 6 and 7 o'clock, P. M., Lapland was abducted by Sparrfelt, and taken to Gärdinge. *Avis au lecteur !*"

Bertelsköld read the note without changing a feature, and with a cool bow returned it to the queen.

"May your majesty be graciously pleased to pardon me," said he ; "this note was really written by me. I accidentally found out that a young girl in Count Horn's house was the object of a fool's persecution, and thought I ought to warn her guardian—a merchant of Wasa, by the name of Larsson."

" Bah ! Let us return to the affairs of the realm ! " interposed the king, who, after the last explanation, began to hope a better issue of the Kalabalik than he had at first feared.

Ulrica Eleonora tore the note to pieces, and scattered the fragments on the floor.

" That may answer for the messenger of the gods !" she exclaimed. " *Attendez!* I will do your majesty and sir count the honor to somewhat refresh a bad memory. In Count Horn's house there has been for the past year a Finnish girl, of peasant origin. I have forgotten her name, but with certain high personages, who have honored her with their attention, she was known under the name of Lapland. *Voilà*, a pet-name of bad taste, Messieurs ! This girl was beautiful, it was said—that is indifferent to me—and had received a kind of education. Unfortunately she was no Danaë. Jove found no favor in her eyes, and I wish that a person of higher rank than she had possessed an equally good taste. It was even said that she was perfectly innocent, and her honor without stain. That is possible ; at least she fled from Count Horn's house, to escape the persecutions of her mighty adorer. Nevertheless, she kept silence about those persecutions, as inviolably, as sacredly, as one keeps silence about the errors of a father. She subjected herself to all kinds of shameful interpretations of her step, rather than betray the frailties of a prince, which, if they were disclosed to this people, which does not know how to jest with its honor, would degrade the reputation of the crown and the prestige which the crown once wore. What does your majesty think ? That girl—did she not deserve a better fate ? "

The king tried to laugh. " Esop," said he, " would envy your majesty the talent for telling moral fables in the most ingenious and entertaining manner ! "

" Patience, sire ! We will directly come to the pith of the matter. The girl braved all dangers, to find once more her home and her lost father. Unfortunately, she had an uncle who fancied .that the faith and honor of olden times still had some value in Stockholm. Angry at her flight from her benefactress, the Countess Horn, and ignorant of her motives, of which she kept an inviolable silence, he compelled the girl to return with him to Stockholm, and beg pardon of the countess. The girl did so ; and she did it, sire, without even then betraying a secret which might have compromised persons of such high positions that not the least reproach from the lower orders of society ought to fall on them."

The king answered merely with a shrug. How could a distinguished lady of thirty-four years, a queen, too, concern herself with such small matters? Frederick I forgot that what a woman of thirty-four years least pardons is a younger rival.

The queen continued—her anger rising, as, with her large, clear blue eyes, she transfixed Bertelsköld: "The girl was finally forced to speak. A person at the court had the infamy to arrange an abduction, in order to change her—the simple daughter of a burgher —to the rank of a Diana de Poictiers or a Duchess de la Vallière,—I do not know which. It is enough to know that this person gave the sign to a certain Leporello of the service, and the girl was for the second time abducted from Gil Blas to fall to Don Juan. Fortunately her despair gave her courage to save herself, as when she tied the curtains together and let herself down from a window in the second story. Once more she escaped from her pursuers. In the middle of the night, and shivering with cold, she sought refuge with the Countess Liewen, one of my court ladies. To her, for the first time, to her, sire, in order to justify herself, she disclosed that series of scandal and intrigues of which she had so long been a victim ;

and you, Count Bertelsköld, can oppose your sister, if you have the courage to do so. But you have not. You have deceived me, count, infamously deceived me ! I looked upon you as a nobleman, a statesman ; I was about to confide to you the highest interests of our crown, and you have forced your own sister to unmask you. Miserable charlatan that you are ! think you that Ulrica Eleonora will allow herself to be treated like a Duchess of Orleans? Do you not fear, you double-tongued adventurer, that my anger will some day crush you ? Oh, Monseigneur of Hesse ! and you, Count of nowhere—where your countship yourself may be in time !—because *he* before whom you and the world tremble is no more, you think you can trample under foot the most sacred rights of a woman and a wife ; but you have forgotten, Messieurs, that that woman is still the queen of Sweden ! ”

For a moment, Ulrica Eleonora covered her face with her fine lace handkerchief, as she pushed away the king's hand, which laid hold of hers to press it to his lips. With somewhat more self-control, she then continued :

“ This girl, this ‘ Lapland,’ as you called her, had a lover, a plain but honest person like herself. He followed her hither, to rescue her out of your claws, Messieurs, and your assistants had him thrown into prison to get rid of him. Was it not so ? ”

“ Your majesty, who is omniscient,” sarcastically answered the king, “ probably knows also that this fellow is a Finnish robber, who committed an assault in Stockholm, and that a price is set upon his head.”

“ I know, sire, that at that time when your great talents as general were not able to keep the enemy from burning and plundering the coasts of Sweden, this young man was one of the Finnish guerrillas who, within his own territory, opposed the enemy. His crime, sire, consists in his having, during the truce, burned up a Russian galley, and having in Stockholm sought to protect a defenceless girl. I have just had him released."

The king lost patience. "As your majesty pleases," said he; "but allow me to suggest that a *scene de famille* might have been more suitably saved for a *tête-à-tête.*"

"In order that you, sire, might afterwards, in your libidinous hunting *societé*, make a woman who had the weakness to procure you a crown, an object of derision! And in order that your servile cabinet-nobility might go on unpunished tampering with the honor of their queen! Count Bertelsköld may understand, better than your majesty, why he has had the honor of witnessing this controversy. For the rest," continued the queen, with an air of haughty disdain, "it is perfectly indifferent to us what my lord count pleases to think about our royal personage."

"My humble admiration," ironically replied the count, "shall always be submissive to the great talents of your majesty, even when I have the misfortune to have my zeal called in question."

"We do not wish for your opinion, my lord count. You have an estate, I believe, have you not? Somewhere, to some extent? Your tendencies have always been toward the hights. We hope the country air will agree with you. No, stop a moment! you have still one scene to witness."

"Has your majesty any further commands?" interrupted the king, as he wiped the perspiration from his forehead.

"Will you permit me, sire, to speak a few words in your name, as you have for the last two years spoken in mine?"

"If I am not mistaken, your majesty has spoken all the time. Can I more than keep silence?"

"Yes, sire, you can—consent. Very well!"

And the queen rang. The doors were opened, and Marie Larsson entered, trembling, and accompanied by Elias Pehrson, who with some embarrassment saw himself in this distinguished company. The queen's waiting-women and gentlemen remained outside, and the doors were once more shut.

Ulrica Eleonora for some moments fastened her eyes sharply on the young girl. Perhaps, as a woman, she felt a strong desire to crush and humble the innocent rival also; but the certainty of her triumph conquered that feeling of hatred which jealousy was upon the point of kindling anew in her soul. She now tried to embody in her words the greatness of a gracious queen.

"My good child," said she to Marie, "his majesty, who has with displeasure found that you have been an object of persecution by unworthy men, and who wishes nothing higher than that all his loyal subjects may enjoy perfect justice, has been pleased to desire me to take you under my especial and gracious protection. And in order that upon your approaching journey home you may not lack a defender who can shield you from all affronts, it is his majesty's gracious will—provided you yourself have nothing against it— that next Sunday, in our court-chapel, you be joined in wedlock with this young man, who loves you, and who has been as unjustly persecuted as you yourself. I believe that is your majesty's high command, if I mistake not!"

"Perfectly! Her majesty has in the most gracious manner been pleased to anticipate my wishes," replied the king, biting his lips.

"For the rest, I will look to obtaining your guardian's consent, and attend to your dower. You have the privilege, upon your return, of selecting the best town residence, or the best farm, whichever you wish, in the province of Wasa, and drawing a bill on my pocket-money for the purchase-price. In order further to make good all that reproach which you, my child, have so innocently suffered, his majesty and I, together

6

with our court, will honor your wedding with our royal presence. Is it not so, your majesty? And you, Count Bertelsköld, who have taken so generous a part in this girl's fate, will certainly not be absent on this happy occasion?"

The king nodded, Bertelsköld bowed; both of them mute, exasperated, and humiliated.

"I thank you, sire; I thank you, sir count," continued the queen, with a prick in every word. "What happiness, my children, when a high-minded king and a loyal nobleman unite to protect innocence and justice, even among their humblest subjects! Farewell, my friends; we shall meet again. Farewell, sire; do not expose yourself too much at the next hunting party. Farewell, sir count; greet Count Horn, when you meet him, and assure him of our gracious favor!"

CHAPTER XVII.

THE SPRING OF 1742.

IF burned dwellings, devastated corn-fields, ruined splendor, and human beings slain or tortured or led away into captivity and thralldom—if even political misfortunes, such as loss of lands, exhausted revenues and general imbecility—were the only consequences of a long and wasting war, then the prospect would be far from the most dismal which meets a human eye in the fraternal feuds of this world. These dwellings could be rebuilt, these fields once more be sown, these populations once more spring up, by the wise law of nature, which, after great havoc, redoubles her fecundity. Even the kingdom might by degrees be once more uplifted out of its impotence, and lost lands, by cultiva-

tion within proper limits, be reclaimed. But the severest of all misfortunes, and that which fills the beholder
with the deepest sorrow, is the sight of a great moral
debasement, which usually accompanies the ravages of
war, and which in Finland was the concomitant of the
great contest. You who in this story may have shrunk
from a glimpse here and there into the moral corruption
of this period, be assured you have suspected only a
small part of it. Some fragment has been necessary
to the truth of the picture ; but you have been spared
the grossest and most shocking debasement in the
lower classes of society, where no surface of culture
veils the unrestrained and odious selfishness whose
seeds are implanted in every human heart. He who
would paint the great war in all its terrible reality,
must depict that woman who, alone on the ice in the
winter night, devoured her dead child ; or—perhaps
the more significant—her who, the day after a bloody
defeat, for a miserable Judas-coin kissed the murderer
of her husband and the enemy of her land.

Happy may we esteem ourselves, that during this
deep debasement the Finnish people, crushed to the
last extremity, as a whole sunk down with honor and
manliness, to arise again at the dawn of a better
morrow. Beside the gloomiest pictures which history
presents, there comes mitigatingly and atoningly the
memory of noble sacrifices, faithfulness and renuncia-
tions in the bitterest trials of want, at which the heart
leaps with admiration and delight ; just as the darkest
shadows frequently serve but to heighten the lights of
virtue and goodness. Pity it is, that the night of
almost a century and a half has buried the most of
those noble faces in oblivion ; but those who remain
are still sufficient to justify the memory of the fathers
before posterity.

And now, kind reader, we lead you from adventure,
peril, sorrow, and want, peacefully away to a beautiful
spring evening on the northern shore of Finland, in

the beginning of June, 1722. The spring had been late, but afterward came on so rapidly that trees were leaved out within a few days. Never had any spring in Finland been greeted with such wonderful emotions. It seemed to the wandering refugees as if they were returning to a new life. Everything around them seemed wonderfully strange. At first, when the snow melted, they regarded with some painful emotions the rubbish-heaps that were once their home, the corn-fields that had lapsed into a wilderness, the forest that had thickly overgrown the former site of the villages, the caved-in wells, the decayed fences, and even the dismantled churches. But when the grass began to brighten and the trees to put forth leaves, and the well-known murmur of the sea's blue billows was again heard purling around them, it seemed to them that this land, in all its wildness, was so indescribably beautiful that they had nowhere beheld its like. And it was their own dear land, their childhood's beloved home ; and they needed no more, like the ancient Jews of Babylon, to hang their harps on the willows of that unknown shore, and moisten the uncertain bread of strangers with their tears. What did it signify that great want and many cares were yet to come, before they could get their new dwelling-place in order, and while awaiting harvests which not yet were sown? They now worked with delight and ardor, for they were working for a new home and a better time; they once more had a country and a future, and once more thought it worth while to live.

One evening, as we have said, in June, when the birches, with their newly-budded mossy tassels, were reflected in the clear bay at Lojlax, a gray-haired man, once tall but now bent by sorrow and years, was seen to wander slowly along the highway leading from New Carleby southward to Wasa. When he came to the new gate of the yard, in the equally new white fence, he sat down on a stone to rest. At the left of the road was the new-built gard, where two cows were eagerly grazing the still tender pasture-grass, and a man and woman were busily turning the soil of the nearest little field. On the right of the road extended the bay, and on the shore a man was at work, framing the timbers for a small ship; while a young woman, not far from him, was occupied in clipping the thick fleeces from some fine sheep. The evening was clear, calm, and mild. All nature seemed to smile with peace, as though the new hopes of humanity were reflected with double beauty from her tender maternal face. The old man seemed to hesitate whether he should go further, or seek here a shelter for the night; for walking had evidently reduced his strength.

Before he had yet decided upon his course, the man and woman by the beach had finished their work, and returned across the road to the yard. When they approached and found the old man resting on the stone, they kindly invited him to rest over-night at the farm. With a stiff nod, and without thanking them for so friendly a hospitality, he thereupon accompanied them home to the dwelling-house near by.

By the time they entered, our old acquaintances Heikki and Brita had also returned from the field; and the supper, of the simplest kind, stood ready on the table. Elias Pehrson and his young wife Marie—for they were the ones who had been at work by the shore —ordinarily took a place of honor at the table, next to Heikki's father-in-law; Heikki and his wife had constrained them to do so, since Elias had now bought the whole farm. But for this time, the most honorable place was given up to the gray-haired man from the highway, who took it without ceremony. To give such an honor to old age, as a matter of course, belonged to the beautiful customs of those days.

When the old man, at grace, took off his winter fur cap, thus uncovering a bald head and a ghostly white-bearded face, Marie suddenly grew very pale, but soon

recovered her composure, and listened with rapt attention to the conversation of the men.

" We have done a good bit of work to-day," said
Elias to Heikki. " You and Brita have got the pea-
field ready, and I have set up the frame of my little
cutter, which before autumn is to bring us what we
need from Stockholm. The boat shall be named
Maya—all Mayas carry luck with them," he added,
with a glance of admiration at his handsome wife.

" And all Britas, too," replied Heikki, good-naturedly. " Yes, dear father, you may believe there is a
good deal to do here before autumn. The corn-field I
have already sown, and the pea-field we will sow in
the morning; but the rye-field will give us work all
summer, and afterwards make us wait a year for the
harvest. Most of the time the past winter we ate
nothing but stamp-bread; but since Elias and Marie
have come home from Stockholm, with the royal money
of our gracious queen, pure bread is to be had here,
as you see. He is master now, you see, and I am only
laborer; but as he has his old habits of going to sea
and struggling out to the open waves, I am attending
to the tillage till I can get me another farm. Marie,
you see, is not too proud, either, to sit at the table
with us, though she has served an apprenticeship with
countesses, and was married in the gracious presence
of the king and queen. We have a dreadfully gracious
king now-a-days, and the queen is said to look as radi-
ant as a bright brass fiddle at a midsummer-night's
wake."

" There seems to be a good time coming, if Heaven
is so kind as to give increase on land and wind on the
sea," said Elias, interrupting his friend's praises of
royalty. " It would certainly not come natural for such
an adventurer as I am to settle down in a steady dwelling-place, like any other human being; but when I find
the shore too confining, I will take my blessed little
Maya and go to Stockh . . ! No, Maya will not go to

sea with me, she would rather knit and weave here at home. It is she who rules, you see; otherwise I would have thought of trying to become a burgher in New Carleby, as navigation and agriculture do not go very well together; but Maya has no fancy for town life, and her pleasure is mine. Now you can taste of the home-brewed ale, father; we have malt, you know, this year. God bless the peace, old man! Without it, we would all be on half rations. You can believe me when I say it—I, who have hitherto lived by war."

"Peace?" murmured the old wanderer, as he gloomily shook his gray head. "What good does peace do the dead?"

"That sounds as though you had lost a good deal by the war, old father," said Elias, with frank sympathy. "Do not let your sorrow always master you; God will surely govern all things for the best."

"Eleven children! Eleven children!" continued the old man, absorbed in a single thought. "Eight sons, tall, straight, strong boys, all of them six feet and three inches, by measurement, except the youngest! My poor Benjamin—the delight of my old age—was three inches shorter. The seven have fallen; Bertelsköld took six; ... you have perhaps heard about it? In Ilmola—in the winter—on skates—all six on one morning; it is an old story. The seventh the king took with him to Norway; you have heard that too; it was on Christmas night; the very mountain shivered with cold; a poor boy could not be more enduring than stone. And afterward, Benjamin;—you ought to have seen Benjamin, he was so gentle of eye, like that young woman there; yes, she may well weep her eyes red. One day we were harvesting the trampled rye; then the Cossacks came, and lifted my little Benjamin upon their horse's back. Never since that day have I believed in God!"

"But," said Elias, suddenly attentive, when he saw Marie hide her face in her hands, "who are you, old man, who have lost so much, and place it all to the charge of the merciful God?"

Without hearing him, the old man continued : "I ran after the horsemen as long as I could,—one day—two days—weeks, months ; at last I no longer knew where I was. I was far in Russia, where no one understood me. They saw that I was perishing, and they gave me bread. I said to them, 'Give me back my last, my only son! Jacob had eleven sons left, when they brought him Joseph's bloody coat, and still he rent his clothes and strewed ashes on his head. I have not one! not one!' But they did not understand me. After that, I could not find my way back; I begged my way on—alone, poor—and yet I once had four large farms and eleven children. But there is no God! If there was a God he would long since have had pity upon me!"

"And are you very sure he is not doing so now, although you, in your blindness and sorrow, deny his ways? You know you had three daughters too."

" Three daughters—all fair as the light of day—and the youngest of them was, next to my Benjamin, the fairest and the dearest of them all. But they have all forsaken me—all, all have forgotten me ; and do I even know if one of them is still on earth?"

At these words, Marie softly glided behind the old man's bench, and embraced him with hot tears.

"Do you not know me, my father?" she whispered sobbingly, on his breast. "I am indeed your own little Marie, who was still a child when you sent us over to Sweden, and that is why I did not instantly know you. How I have searched for you, my poor father! But now you shall never leave us again, you shall now live with us—you shall now believe once more there is a God!"

Steadily and unmoved, the old man looked at her. He had lived through such bitter scenes that he had almost forgotten what joy was. But now his heart melted. He closed his eyes, and opened them again to look upon that beautiful and blooming daughter, as though to convince himself it was not all a dream of former days. Perhaps when, lonely and poor, he wandered around in that strange land, he had often before seen this vision in his dreams, and it had vanished, to leave him doubly lonely in his poverty and sorrow. But now it did not vanish; he was now suddenly rich again, and, trembling, he arose from the bench, but only to kneel, happy and humbled, and praise that God whom he had just denied.

"May the God of Jacob bless thee, my child, and him whom thou holdest dear!" he whispered. "As I am now, so is our whole Finnish land this spring, having lost ten children out of eleven, but when it has found the eleventh, behold, it once more feels happy and rich, as though it had never lost its joy. Come, children, it is too close here in the house. Let us behold the sun of God's grace go down in light and rise in mercy!"

And with reverent emotions they went out into the spring night—that spring when so many tearful eyes in Finland vainly sought a trace of their dear ones, but also when so many separated hearts once more beat against each other. The sun sank behind the pines upon the promontory, and gilded the calm water-mirror of the bay; there was a flutter and rustle in the first corn-field; the smoke of peaceful valleys and clearing fires rose against the horizon; again in the distance was heard the song of the shepherdess, and the tinklé of the bells away in the pastures;—all was peace, light, trust, and hope; and thus again struggled in the first green spring over the waste of Finland.

PART II.—THE BURGHER KING.

"WHERE did we leave off last?" asked the old grandmother, when the usual circle was again gathered one evening between Christmas and New Year's day. The holidays had brought with them so many cares that a busy housewife could easily be pardoned for having forgotten the past for the present.

"Where the freebooter burned the Russian galley," promptly answered little Jonathan, only half aloud, for discipline was rigid, and children rarely presumed to open their mouths in the presence of older people, unless directly questioned.

"I think it was at the peace of Nystad, when human reason was taken captive," responded the schoolmaster, as with the dignity peculiar to him he drew forth his blue-checkered snuff handkerchief.

"Begging pardon—it was at the campaign on Wärknäs point, and the affray at Gärdinge," suggested Captain Svanholm, the postmaster, whose memory was inclined to dwell upon every glimpse of war.

But Anne Sophie had fixed her thoughts on milder events. "Do you not remember the spring in the wilderness, grandmother?" exclaimed she: "The king and queen, you know, were at the wedding of Elias Pehrson and Marie Larsson, and we afterwards saw them, one evening in June, at Lojlax farm, when old Thomas came back from his wanderings in Russia."

"I remember it now," replied grandmother. "It is well there was a regular wedding for once; for, in truth,

not everything had been ended as it should have been.
It is a pity that such a rare occurrence was so briefly
related. I had expected a full description of the
wedding; how it all happened, how the bride was
dressed, what the guests wore, and what they had to
eat It would then have been something one could
comprehend. But if this or that high gentleman, president or king, played this or that trick to deceive honest
people, it concerns us very little, according to my
opinion, especially as it comes down to us in half-sung
ballads. I must insist that I could never get along with
Torsten Bertelsköld. He was crafty, even when a boy;
and he grew worse. But after he became president he
was perfectly intolerable. Fie on such a conscienceless
fellow!"

"When everything is weighed by his standard, he
was perhaps neither better nor worse than the politicians of that period," responded the Surgeon. "Why
did the world stare at Charles XII? Certainly not for
his heroic exploits alone, but just as much for his
honest zeal, which impelled him to dash his head
blindly against the wall. For otherwise the principle
would always have held good, between states, that the
most artful deceiver was the greatest master; and there
was no deceit which at that time did not receive the
name of political wisdom, when it referred to robbing
a neighbor. I admit there may be two opinions as to
whether the diplomacy of our time is not tacitly of the
same kind; indeed, it really looks so; for two hundred
years we have had a law of nations on paper, yet
nevertheless the different nations live in a state of
nature still, so that he who can get the richest booty,
by cunning if possible, by force if not, is the best fellow. But the difference is that there is now a public
opinion, a consciousness of justice, which condemns
fraud, and not infrequently sweeps away the cobweb
with a breath. And for this reason deceit does not now
venture out without a heavy gilding: it no longer pre-

sumes to be principle; it no longer dares preach that
doctrine which Charles Gustaf Tessin wished to im-
plant in Gustaf III when he was yet a child, that
'virtue is a compound of good and evil,' according to
circumstances. Mark well that, after Arvid Horn,
Tessin was in his time the greatest diplomat of Sweden,
and regarded as a brilliant genius—which indeed he
was, and in other respects no bad fellow either."

"Yellow glitter—base gilding—a belt without a
sword!" triumphantly muttered Captain Svanholm, in
his inveterate hatred of diplomacy.

"Everyone to his trade," interposed the schoolmaster, not without heat. "Without judicious men in
the council-chamber, we should all stand with bare
backs under the open skies. I recollect that the statesmen of the eighteenth century also used to appeal to
public opinion."

◀ "Oh, yes!" replied the Surgeon. "When Peter I,
August II, and Frederick IV formed an alliance against
Charles XII, they took the precaution to justify themselves in circulars to all the important European
courts. Charles XII—or, more correctly, Piper—took
the precaution to confute them with the pen no less
resolutely than with the sword. This became both
custom and necessity as the balance-of-power system
developed, and war began with alliances. The celebrated Sinclair murder, in 1739, which gave rise to an
animated literary dispute throughout all Europe, was
one example among many. But the battle was fought
out, then, between courts, cabinets, and authors in
their pay. The difference is that in our days the
people also will have their opinion, and discuss such
questions with the fluent tongues of the press; and
while in the eighteenth century it depended upon success whether a matter was in the end stamped as violence or justice, it now happens that public opinion
offers a protest even against such matters as had long
been common custom. And at the same time the mask

sits all the more loosely on the forehead of deceit, whether it be called statesmanship or individual fortune-seeking. In our day, Torsten Bertelsköld would be— I will not say impossible, but more easily seen through."

"In case he was not a Talleyrand," suggested Captain Svanholm, somewhat mockingly.

"Brother is a brave warrior, and, above all, an enthusiastic postmaster," resumed the Surgeon, with that satiric seriousness which so well became him; "but I do not believe that a man who dethroned- Napoleon and reconstructed the map of Europe can be weighed as lead. . . . . To return to Bertelsköld: characters like his belong peculiarly to periods of transition, when one principle has fallen, and another has not arrived at full development. In the year 1721, freedom in Sweden was scarcely more than a repudiation of despotism; upon this point all parties were agreed, and thus had common ground. But when it came to building something positive on the new foundation, there was a chasm immediately between 'Hats' and 'Caps,' and then no one could longer stand well with all parties, to deceive them all. We should try to view that time in its true light."

"If I might speak my mind," said the old grandmother, in her usual decided tone, "it would be better if we could escape all diet contentions. Be so good as to put plumes in the hats and ribbons in the caps, aud afterwards place them on heads with perukes, or brushed-up hair with a little powder on it, and then it will be something which people can comprehend. And how does the king's ring get along? I will never suppose that the ill-boding thing is at last to ruin also little Charles Victor Bertelsköld, son of Gösta Bertelsköld, and his wife, whose maiden name was Falkenberg? I cannot deny that I have a kind feeling for the boy; his parents were honest and intelligent people; I hope the boy did not inherit their taste for rambling around the world. I wonder if he will become a soldier?"

"That is a matter of course, if he has the least back-bone in him," interposed the captain. "He will hardly become a schoolmaster, I fancy."

"If he is not fit for that, he can be a postmaster," retorted the offended target of Captain Svanholm's sarcasms.

"Let him become something really great and agreeable, godfather; let him become a king, or at least a general, who wins brilliant victories, and transforms countries and times!" exclaimed Anne Sophie, beaming with her happy inspiration to rewrite the history of the eighteenth century in favor of little Charles Victor Bertelsköld.

The Surgeon nodded with an indulgent smile. "It is a pity," said he, "that Anne Sophie was not one of the Norns, who spin the threads of fate and unroll periods; we should then have genuine heroes and beautiful epics. That blood which drips in the footsteps of heroes, she would change to raspberry-juice; and all those tears that shower around them would be transformed by her to the gentlest summer-rain. No; with Charles XII romanticism had finished its *rôle;* and Frederick II, that hero who succeeded him, was a genius without heart, a cold egotist without a breath of enthusiasm. The middle of the eighteenth century was just such a cold, egotistic, and hollow period, which brought forth great things by its wise cogitations, but very small ones by any power of real emotion. It was the era of Voltaire, Frederick II, and Pompadour. . . ."

"And of Klopstock, Haydn, Swedenborg, and Linnæus," pleaded Anne Sophie.

"It may be. Tell me the time when the heart of humanity ceased to beat! But do not expect in that period any epic princes. I cannot help it if we seek in vain in Sweden and Finland at that time those famous

warriors who so lately had gone forth to astonish the
world. We find, instead, industrious hands ditching
the wastes, building towns and villages, covering the
land with harvests, the sea with fleets, and extending
culture and prosperity in the ravaged regions. Such a
time of utility, when everything was to be built anew,
and the prime necessity was daily bread, does not glitter
with points of light which dazzle us against the background of dark shadows. But if one has any regard
for that honest work, if the good offices of peace, the
progress of education, and the treasures of human
happiness, have any value, this period shall show a
picture which, after so many jolting trials, will give a
soothing impression. Anne Sophie, I fear, will be difficult to satisfy. What are we to do? The dramatic
tension of the heroic period is irremediably past ; we
must search out new springs, and it will be seen how
we shall succeed."

"Then it is an idyl we may expect now?—Atis and
Camilla, with shepherds, shepherdesses, and—sheep?
But in rosy ribbons, or how?"

"I will not promise. Do you think the embers of
passion burn less ardently within a citizen's jacket than
within the velvet cloak of a nobleman?"

"So it is romance in homespun? Do I guess rightly?"

The Surgeon knocked out his pipe against the
chimney-jamb, and raised a couple of fresh long logs
upon the fire. "Now we will dig our treasures," said
he.

CHAPTER I.

THE ELECTION OF THE DIET.

IN the forenoon of the first day of May, 1738, the councilmen and citizens of the town of Wasa were called into the presence of the magistrate to elect their delegate to the impending session of the imperial diet in Stockholm. Already early in the morning there was an unusual stir in the little town. Groups of mechanics, and other lesser citizens, had left their work, to discuss the important questions of the day on street-corners, or in the inn, which was also the ale-house. The more distinguished of the citizens had decided to meet with the burgomaster, to consult upon some important measures, and the fiscal of the town was seen going from house to house upon some secret commission among those who had the most to say. Divers influences were evidently at work, and the scene presented a perfect imitation in miniature of the pulley, with the many little alternating wheels which together made up the complicated machinery of the imperial diet.

And a member of the diet was no inconsiderable personage in these times, when the states of the realm governed the kingdom of Sweden, with the assistance of a king and a council who were scarcely more than executive tools. These states, with royal power, were indeed a hydra-headed personality, divided, moreover, in four parts, so that each member of the diet seemed to represent but a very small fraction of the power. But besides the fact that the sovereign rights of the people gave even the little fraction the weight of an integer, there was the question which of the many fractions could obtain the best hearing in the diet, and swing themselves up to a whole number, with a crowd of ciphers after them ; and what soldier cannot carry in his knapsack the staff of a general?   The citizens of Wasa were therefore fully convinced that the destiny of the diet, and with it that of Sweden and Finland, lay in their hands ; and for this reason the wigs had been brushed with the greatest industry ; brass buttons and shoe-buckles shone with an unusual luster ; and the best black festival stockings were drawn up to the knees, without fear of the bad sledging of spring in the narrow and unpaved streets.

In order to get a glimpse behind the curtain in this miniature representation of the storms of the diet, the reader might kindly accompany us on a visit to the then acting prefect of East Bothnia, Count Charles Frölich, at his official residence in Korsholm. The old stone house had disappeared during the throes of the time, and in its place a large·but low wooden house, with two wings, rose within the ramparts. Korsholm was now a curious cross between a fortress and a dwelling-house.   The magnificent ramparts had lately been repaired, the gate had been more strongly built, and the high stockade which constituted the inner for- tification had once more been put in perfect order for defense.   Above the gate was the arms of the king- dom, carved in wood, and in this escutcheon the arms of the city, the royal sheaf ; but below it flaunted the arms of the noble house of Frölich.   All this clearly made known that the lord of this modernized knightly castle was first a warrior, secondly an aristocrat. Neither did the personality of the old Carolin, Count Frölich, contradict this view, as he sat in his office, highly distinguished, and yet with all the simplicity of a soldier. He was at that time fifty-eight years of age, but appeared ten years older. It was not age, nor the long hardships of field life, but rather two severe wounds received thirty-seven years ago at the passage over the Duna, which had somewhat bowed his tall

6*

figure and whitened his hair.   As one leg had become
stiff, he walked with difficulty ; but the air of command
and the eagle-eye beneath his bushy eye-brows gave
all, both high and low, to understand that the old lion
still had claws and teeth for whomsoever ventured to
approach a step too near him.

It was eight o'clock in the morning, and the old
gentleman was engaged in an interview that tried all
his mettle.   Before him, as he sat in the high-backed
walnut arm-chair, stood an old man as tall as he, and
scarcely less dignified in his bearing.   And it was no
insignificant man in Wasa—it was the richest merchant
of the town, our old acquaintance Lars Larsson, at
that time about seventy years of age, although contrasted with the count he did not appear to be more
than sixty.   His hair had as yet hardly begun to turn
gray ; his sinewy arms seemed able to throw a giant to
the ground ; and in his steady glance shone wisdom
and shrewdness, coupled with power and assurance.
Had he not remained standing while the count sat, a
strange eye might have been uncertain which of them
was the official ; for such they both seemed.

" So," said the prefect, evidently displeased, " do
you persist in your resolution not to conform to my
wishes ? "

" My humble opinion is that an upright man does
what he thinks best for the interest of the kingdom,"
replied the burgher.

" You intend to adhere to the Russian alliance ? "

" Your grace regards the treaty as indispensable to
the trade and welfare of the kingdom.   I see nothing
bad in it."

" Indeed ?   You stuff your mouth full of Russian
meal, and your purse full of silver dollars ; that is your
politics.   You do not understand that it humiliates us
at a point where we ought to have the most pride.   You
support Count Horn ? "

"I venture to believe that the custody of the kingdom is in good hands."

"Well, how much has Horn paid you for your valuable adherence?"

"Your grace, I sell my corn but not my convictions. They are not for sale, by fair means or foul—neither to one count nor another."

"*Au diable*, fellow; keep your convictions. I ask what privileges you intend to procure for the town of Wasa. You will not be satisfied with less than freedom from customs, I suppose?"

"My opinion is that our Finnish towns will never make any progress until their commerce is free."

"Nonsense! That is the ridiculous fallacy of them all. As though they did not get rich enough by commerce with Stockholm! My lords the shopkeepers want to traffic in the Mediterranean sea, in order to return Spanish grandees!"

"The people of Stockholm offer us what they like, so long as our market is closed to others. In 1729 they offered us sixpence for a barrel of rye. A gracious God has not created Finland, with its extensive shores and beautiful harbors, to be a kitchen-maid to Stockholm."

Count Frölich, the Carolin, who, neither in the character of warrior nor nobleman, entertained especial respect for the long-repulsed and often cringing body of burghers, regarded with astonishment and anger the brave merchant, who, erect and undaunted, ventured to contradict him in his own house. The old soldier-mood bubbled over. "I have not had you called hither to dispute with you about your commerce, but to ask which system you will support, in case you are to-day elected member of the diet," burst out the count, with vehemence.

"I have told your grace that I believe the weal of the kingdom is in good hands," replied Larsson, with-

out changing a feature or avoiding the angry look of
the prefect.

"Indeed! Then it is my will that the town shall
elect Aulin."

"I do not know whom the town will elect, but I
know this : that the constitution of the kingdom of
Sweden, of the year 1720, insures to the citizens the
right of choosing their own delegate, without troubling
their superiors with the matter."

"The devil take you, fellow, if you presume to
conspire against the government. *Sacre nom!* Then
does my will in Wasa signify less than nothing?"

"It signifies much, your grace ; but it signifies less
than the law of Sweden."

"Out with you!—out, cursed corn-jew! you venture
to thwart my plans! I will teach you, grocer, to act
puff-paste here, so long as I conduct the government!
Out, I say!"

Lars Larsson bowed his proud head a little, a very
little, and without further waste of words on his incensed
superiðr, slowly withdrew.

Count Frölich was no despot at heart. But freedom
was still new, the monarchy still held its place in the
instincts of the old stock, and the more remote a prefect
was from the center of the kingdom, the greater was
the temptation to play the Satrap.

On the stairway, Larsson met Spolin, the fiscal, who
had come to report, and who a few minutes afterward
was seen on the jump to execute orders. Larsson
smiled coldly ; he was acquainted with his East Both-
nians, and knew of old what a despotic command
signified.

Immediately after nine o'clock the election began,
and continued until twelve o'clock. It appeared from
the beginning to be a hot contest, with uncertain issue;
for the lesser of the burghers had, as usual, a grudge
against the money-aristocracy of the town, and had
made up their minds to vote for Aulin, the huckster,

who promised to insist upon rigid laws against botch-workmen and country trade. If all these had held together, the multitude would have been able to counterbalance the votes of the wealthier class, and imperil Larsson's victory. But as it became known that the fiscal was running on the prefect's errands in the interest of Aulin, one after another deserted to Larsson's party; and when all had voted, Larsson was found to be chosen as member of the diet for the town of Wasa, by such a preponderance that his opponent had received scarcely a fifth of the votes.

Count Frölich foamed with anger. "I must find some means to dethrone the burgher king," exclaimed he.

The threat became known, and, from that day Lars Larsson was known by the name of " the burgher king."

CHAPTER II.

THE MAY RIDE.

THE site afterwards covered by the ornament of Wasa, the magnificent court-house erected by Gustaf III in 1784, opposite the hill of Korsholm, and finally transformed into a church, was at the time of our story almost entirely unoccupied. In the place of the present beautiful old avenue, where the memory of King Gustaf withers each autumn before the frost of time, and every spring starts forth anew into fresh verdure, was seen, in the days of Lars Larsson, a series of small vegetable gardens, planted with turnip-cabbages, parsley, and dill, here and there garnished with raspberry and currant-bushes. But on the north of Korsholm, and westward as far as "the sound," extended a pasture field, where the young folks used to play in summer, and where schoolboys engaged in warlike attacks upon the innocent ramparts.

In the afternoon of the same first of May on which the diet election had taken place, a large number of children and youth had gone out to the pasture. The ground, which had only recently become bare, was still yellow and damp with the spring moisture, the trees were still leafless, and only on the sunny side of the ramparts the eye was delighted by fresh green grass. But this little glimpse of spring was all that was desired ; and what more was needed, when the heavens were high and blue, and the sunbeams were glittering on the clear surface of the sound ? The young folks were having a good time; they played ball and nine-pins, and rolled hoop ; they played cat and rat, tag and widow, and danced "Simon wants to go courting."

The little schoolboys, who had a half-holiday in the afternoon, did not omit to play " Swedes and Russians," with which praiseworthy design the smallest came marching out by classes, with drums and muskets, ready to conquer the world and Korsholm first of all. It is not recorded whether Swedes or Russians won the day in this noteworthy engagement, but the two bellig- erent powers probably concluded an alliance with each other at last, as later in the evening they turned their united forces against a new enemy, the apprentice boys of the town who had collected at the ramparts to watch the games. The little fellows already displayed the tendency of their race ; for, when the East Bothnian does not have war on a large scale, he is much inclined to get it for himself on a small one. He is the most peaceful fellow in the world, if he can only raise a dust occasionally to his heart's content. Moreover, there were old defeats here to revenge and new victories to win, and before they were aware there was a new Kal- abalik between the Christians and Turks ; and as victory must rightly and properly fall at last to the

Christians, it happened that the apprentice boys, with torn jackets and swollen cheeks, were, after a brave resistance, driven from the field.

While this was taking place on the side of the town towards Korsholm—and literally under the eyes of the rector as he stood on the rampart, and with an old school champion's delight secretly laughed at the heroic exploits of the boys, contenting himself with sending a school officer to admonish them not to use dangerous violence—at the same time two horsemen were seen to approach from the south along the road from Christinestad, and wheel past the curve of the ramparts, where they halted to watch the fight. One of them, who rode in advance, was a slender and handsome youth, in the well known Carolinian uniform, half covered by a light traveling cloak. He rode a young dapple-gray horse, which seemed to dance under his bridle, and was with difficulty followed by the fagged-out sorrel of the other rider. This latter was an older, shorter, broad-shouldered fellow, half soldier and half servant-man, if one might judge by the knapsack on the back of the gray jacket, and the military fashion in which a couple of bundles and a pair of boots were tied to the pommel of the saddle.

When both had arrived at the castle gate, the elder horseman halted, as though to await his master, who had ridden past. The young officer did not, however, observe this, but continued riding. At the same moment he had an opportunity to show that he was no novice in the saddle. The Turks had just been utterly routed, and were rushing in full flight past the rampart, pursued with noise and shouts by the victorious Christians. The dapple-gray horse shied, and dashed off at full speed, like a tempest. Christians and Turks had to look out for themselves; but the horseman sat as though moulded to his steed, and after a rather long half circle, more perilous for others than for himself, succeeded in turning back, at a moderated pace, to the ramparts.

"Well, well !" he exclaimed, patting the mettlesome and proud animal's neck. "Isn't Bogatir ashamed to show his bad manners in Wasa? Be still, I say. Does he think he has the steppes before him?"

At these words the horse stopped, but continued to twitch his ears and listen to every suspicious sound. Horse and rider meanwhile arrived at the west side of the ramparts, and not far from the sound, when all at once a new sight caused the cavalier to forget his recent exercise. On this side, the more peaceful youths were playing: children, young girls, and a part of the older boys, who did not trouble themselves about anything so common as the battle on the north side. But the sight of the strange rider, on his wild horse, was something unusual in Wasa, and did not fail to excite a great curiosity. Running and playing ceased, and they began to ask each other who the strange gentleman could be.

But two of those engaged in the sports had either not observed the stranger, or in their excitement had not allowed his arrival to break off the game. These were a young, slender, brown-eyed girl, in a short white dress, almost a child as yet, and her pursuer in " hawk and dove," a long-legged schoolmaster, whose seven-league steps she easily eluded. She ran like a roebuck, in a hundred curves, and always, when she was just upon the point of being captured, slipped away at one side. But when the chase had continued for some little time, she began to be driven nearer the water, and there it could be foreseen that she would be obliged to give herself captive. This seemed to vex her; and she paused a second near the storehouses on the shore, as though intending to seek a refuge there. She probably thought this a doubtful course, however; sheered once more aside, and thus came to an old alder, which stood close by the shore, half leaning forward over the water. Here she was a prisoner, for retreat was quite cut off. But the moment her pursuer approached, she seized hold of a branch of the tree, and climbed up like a kitten. The tall school-master, sure of his prey, was not slow to follow her example. And thus the two sat, like birds in the tree. But soon a crash was heard; for the branch that had borne the flying dove broke under the heavier hawk, and the schoolmaster dropped plump, full-length, into the water below.

The strange horseman, amused by the flight and the chase, had gradually ridden nearer and nearer, and was thus a witness to the dangerous close of the fool-hardy sport. He did not reflect long, but with a leap was out of the saddle and hastening to the shore, to rescue the drowning man. This was, fortunately, not so dangerous as it appeared. The waters of the sound, which a hundred years before had floated large ships, were in 1738 made considerably shallower by the land elevation, the great natural phenomenon of East Both-nia; and therefore the hopeful twig of Wasa common-school fell, very softly and harmlessly, into two or three feet of water, with a little sediment of gray mire below. Before the stranger had time to extend to him the broken branch, he had scrambled ashore, dripping with water and mud.

So decisive a defeat could not be accepted without an effort at revenge. The dejected and highly exas-perated hawk once more caught sight of the dove, who, in the first surprise, had slipped down from the tree to run for help, but who now, when she saw her pur-suer out of danger and in so doleful a condition, took the unwise course of laughing heartily and kindly, as only a dove can laugh.

"Just wait!" shrieked the schoolmaster, wild with anger. "I'll teach you to laugh!" and with this he again started at a seven-league pace, with evident dan-ger of the pursued one's white clothes acquiring an

K   7

extremely dubious portion of the water and mud of the sound. She therefore betook herself once more to flight, but with lessened prospect of escape. The more she surveyed the distance back to the rampart, the more plainly did she perceive that to reach it was impossible. What should she do? She took the only course that remained, but which, nevertheless, not many a little girl would have taken in her place: she sprang to the waiting Bogatir, very cautiously put her left foot in the stirrup, and mounted, no one knew how, into the saddle. This was evidently not the first time she had been on horseback. But as to what it meant to ride Bogatir, she had no idea; and this game bade fair to terminate worse than that of hawk and dove. Scarcely did the spirited horse feel his light burden in the saddle, unaccompanied by the restraining rein of his master, before he careered out across the pasture toward the town at such frighful speed that hearing and sight forsook the astonished rider. She was seen to let go the bridle, lean forward, and instinctively grasp the saddle bow. Horse and girl were soon out of sight. The schoolmaster had achieved a brilliant revenge, and, pale with dismay, it was now his turn to look after the rapidly fleeing girl.

The strange officer tried all the caressing words and threats to which his Bogatir had formerly been wont to listen. In vain; and he apprehended that the so lately frightened horse had fallen again into his wild mood. The girl seemed lost, and nothing remained but to hasten on foot in the track of Bogatir, with the probability of finding her somewhere, thrown, with crushed head, to the ground.

Then, from the neighborhood of the ramparts of Korsholm, a whistle was heard, so sharp and shrill that it was plainly distinguished far away, above the din of all that multitude who were shrieking at the sight of the running horse. The stranger seemed to recognize that sound; he stopped; he listened; his pale cheeks were colored with a flush, as though he was ashamed that he could not himself produce the same sound.

"That is Istvan, that is my faithful Stephen," said he to the schoolmaster, who was with him. "No one can imitate that whistle. Bogatir knows it; he was born in Hungary, and that is the signal with which the Hungarians call their horses from the steppes. Hark! he is whistling again!"

The shrill penetrating sound was repeated, and then again; and behold, at the third whistle, Bogatir, apparently perfectly quiet, was seen to follow the sound and at a gentle trot approached the ramparts, where the other horseman easily stopped him.

The stranger and his companion hastened thither. The white-clad girl still convulsively held fast to the saddle. But she was unconscious.

"Esther! My Esther! O God! she is dead!" exclaimed a pale and handsome young woman, pressing forward among the crowd.

"Do you not see, Veronica, that the girl is still holding fast?" said one of the school-teachers who was lifting her off the horse. It was really only with difficulty that her hands could be pulled from the saddle.

"Who is that young girl?" inquired the strange officer, with lively interest.

"It is Esther Larsson, the youngest and most beloved child of the rich Larsson," replied the school-teacher.

"Well, well! Larsson will find out now what it means to fly higher than the wings carry," muttered a butcher, who at the election that morning had gone with the adherents of Aulin. "He will be seen to ride in grand pomp to the diet; but how he will ride home again, and who will whistle to him then, cannot be so well known."

"Yes, indeed!" said the nearest old woman in the crowd; "upon my word, this is a warning for Larsson. Vanity, vanity! What says the proverb?"

CHAPTER III.

THE COUNT AND THE BURGHER GIRL.

THE strange young officer seemed anxious to make amends for the mishap in which his wild horse had had so great a part. He hastened to bring water from the nearest well, moistened the fainting girl's forehead with it, and caused her to inhale a delicate essence, which he took out of an *étui* in the holster of the saddle. He now had opportunity to look more closely at her features, and his interest was not diminished by the fact that they were uncommonly beautiful. Esther Larsson could not have been at most more than fourteen or fifteen years of age; a child she still was, as her rashness had sufficiently proved, but a child on the verge of maidenhood. She was slender and delicate, with hair of shining brown, and a complexion not without traces of the influence of the spring sun. Her hands were too delicate for a village girl of plebeian origin. A small but costly ring on the left hand, and little frills of that subtle Raumo lace which, as it was unable to compete in price with the Belgian machine-work, has now little by little gone out of use, did not contradict the stranger's first supposition that the young girl was the spoiled and darling child of a rich man.

Perhaps the reader may still remember the little Veronica, who, on the night when Marie Larsson was so sternly received by her harsh uncle, sent her a piece of her Sunday cake for consolation. Veronica Larsson had grown and flowered in love. She was no longer young; she had seen her twenty-nine summers; but she still spread a fragrance of love around her. She had rejected many suitors, in order to attend to her father's house, and devote her whole heart to her youngest sister Esther, who so greatly needed her care since their mother's death, as their father seldom had an hour of leisure now for the training of his children, and as he did what he could to spoil the little pet whom heaven had granted for the delight of his old age. Veronica alone ventured to oppose Esther's caprices; she alone ventured to deny her anything; and when the headstrong girl succeeded in having her own way, as now in these May-games, it was always Veronica who watched over her, and made amends for all faults which she could not prevent. The neck-break ride she had not been able to hinder; and it was now, as always, her lot, with a mother's solicitude, to nurse her little imprudent child.

"Do not be afraid now, Esther; the danger is over, and you are with me!" she tenderly whispered to the pale sister, who in her embrace began to recover from her terror and open her eyes. In her words there was no hint of upbraiding for all that cruel anxiety which she herself—the good Veronica—had so lately suffered.

Esther looked confusedly around her, and caught sight of her pursuer in the game, the long legged schoolmaster, who, still breathless with amazement, was gazing at her over her sister's shoulder.

"See, Ringblom," said she, with a still weak but triumphant defiance on the pale-red lips. "You know I told you that you should never get hold of me."

At that moment she met the sympathizing looks of the strange officer on the other side, and instantly her white cheeks were overspread with the purest blush. Shy as a bashful child, she immediately hid her face in her sister's lap.

This amused the stranger. He laid his hand on the girl's brown hair, and said with a smile: "Do not be afraid. Bogatir is an audacious scamp who needs strong reins, and I have seen old horsemen thrown out of the same saddle where you held your seat. Next time it will go better. Do you want to learn to ride?"

Esther looked up; it may have irritated her to be treated like a child. "Will you sell your horse?" she asked.

"I hardly think so," replied the stranger. "I fancy you have already had enough of him."

"My father will give you as much money as you want."

"Bogatir is an Hungarian—he will not allow himself to be sold," merrily responded the young officer. "But if I should sell him to you, what would you then undertake to do? Would you try your luck again?"

"Yes, that I would!" replied the girl, casting a defiant look at the impatiently stamping horse.

"And if he was not pleased to obey your rein? If he threw you out of the saddle, my brave little maid?"

"Then I would have him shot," answered Esther, very decidedly, and without the least hesitation.

The stranger laughed. But Veronica did not like this jesting. "Come, let us go home;" said she; "you can lean upon me. Come, Esther, before father has a chance to hear from others that you have been in danger."

Esther quickly changed countenance, and sought in vain to conceal her anxiety. "No, Veronica, no," said she, "you must not speak about it before father. He would be angry at the strange gentleman. And father is not kind when he is angry," she *naïvely* added, with a glance at the stranger.

"What is the discussion about?" said a commanding voice behind them, and there stood the prefect, Count Frölich, who was returning from a walk to the harbor, and with some surprise became aware of the crowd of people by the gate of Korsholm. At the same moment he observed the young officer, who respectfully lifted his hand to the three-cornered hat.

" What do I see ? " exclaimed the prefect, in French. " Count Bertelsköld here ! Be heartily welcome to our extreme north ! My young cousin rains down from the moon ! "

. The lieutenant of the engineer corps, Count Charles Bertelsköld, related by the mother's side to Count Frölich, forgot at these words the supposed little . burgher girl, who cast a long and furtive look of surprise at him. Wasa had never possessed any great supply of counts, and the only one who had been there before was regarded as such an extraordinarily grand gentleman that his equals could hardly be found in Stockholm. Who would have thought that Wasa would now, in such a twinkling, be supplied with another count ? Esther at once felt so perfectly restored that she could by no means be prevailed upon to go home. She only left the place to the distinguished gentlemen, and, with childlike curiosity, continued to look at the young stranger, with whom she had just now spoken so freely and familiarly. But in Esther's opinion this was not very serious; there was hardly any one in all Wasa, except the prefect himself, whom she did not accost in the same confidential manner. All that was remarkable in her eyes was that the young gentleman was so stately and tall, so noble in his whole manner; that he had such bright blue eyes, although his carefully arranged hair was so black that it almost had a bluish luster; that he did not wear a wig ; that the little hat became him so well; that he wore a sword and belt under the short traveling cloak; that he appeared so kind, although strange fate had created him a count; that it chanced to be his horse which almost frightened her to death, and that he laid his hand on her forehead, and promised to teach her to ride. All these thoughts swarmed in the brown curly head of the rash

little girl, and made her deaf to the tender admonitions
of sister Veronica.

Count Charles Victor, for thus we will call him, in
contradistinction to his uncle, the diplomate, Count
Torsten Bertelsköld, in a few words spoken in French
now described the object of his journey to Finland.
He had the previous autumn returned to Sweden from
Vienna and Hungary, where he had taken part in a
campaign against the Turks, and for five years studied
the art of war in the excellent school of the great Prince
Eugene. His mother had now put it into his heart to
become acquainted with the land of his forefathers,
this Finland which his father had defended to the last
man, and .loved even in death. His uncle, Count
Torsten, had then procured him a commission from
the council to inspect the fortresses in Finland, and
propose plans for the defence of the Finnish coast in a
possibly impending war, and as a vessel was going to
Christinestad with equipments for the regiment of East
Bothnia, the occasion had been used to make a first
journey to Wasa. He was now here, and, with the permission of his gracious uncle, Frölich, would stop for
a week or two at Korsholm.

"Though not on bread and water," responded
Count Frölich, laughing. "Are you aware of the fact,
mon cher ami, that crawfish and noblemen do not pros-
per in East Bothnia?"

"My family knows it of old," replied the young
count, in the same tone. "Almost all the Bertelskölds
have been at variance with the democrats of East
Bothnia. I myself had scarely set foot in this territory before my horse was seized and run off with by a
little hector—little Larsson."

"A Larsson? I congratulate you; I too have had
the privilege of profiting by acquaintance with a Larsson. But come; let us see whether the fountains of
Korsholm yield anything but well-water."

CHAPTER IV.

FISCAL SPOLIN.

A WEEK or more had passed since the arrival of Count Charles Victor at Wasa; and during this time he had come to the full conviction that Korsholm was not made for a fortress, according to the more modern requirements of military art. But he had contrived a plan to fortify the entrance to Wasa against a hostile surprise; and with these plans in his head, he had now accompanied the prefect, Count Frölich, on his customary evening ride out to the harbor. The ice still lay in the inner fiords, but farther out toward the archipelago of Replots a strong southwester had broken up the band of ice, and the two horsemen halted awhile to enjoy the animating view of the sea. They saw the blue rim in the west widen and grow clear; far away, they saw the fresh waves rise and fall in beautiful curves; they saw them break against rocks or icebergs in the distance, and, falling again, sprinkle their molten silver high in the transparent vernal air. The seal-hunters returned from their perilous trip on the ice-floe, dragging their sledges filled with slaughtered seals; while others, who had been shooting sea-fowl by means of decoys along the margins of the ice, carried their game in bags on their backs.

Eight vessels were lying in the harbor, all making ready to sail as soon as the ice and winds should permit. The five largest belonged to the rich capitalist and merchant, Lars Larsson. One of the chief sources of his wealth was his sale in Stockholm every year of three or four new vessels, built solely for speculation. But the fifth vessel, which bore the name "Esther" on

the stern-post, he had fixed upon to make journeys, on
his own account, but in the name of a Stockholm capitalist, to Rostock and Wismar.

With dark looks, the prefect regarded these preparations ; and then turned to his companion with the
sudden question if he expected war.

Bertelsköld replied that in Stockholm warlike plans ·
were cherished for regaining from Russia the great
sacrifices made in the peace of Nystad.   But there
were two triggers to the present peace—the council of
the realm, with Count Horn at the head, and the peace
majority in the last diet.   The war party hoped to be
able soon to spring both triggers ; and then a soldier
would once more signify something in Sweden.

"*Justement!*   It is high time, before newly-baked
gentlemen of the yardstick grow above the heads of
old cavaliers !" responded the prefect, not without
heat.   " Do you know, Charles, that one of these days
a member of the diet, who carries peace in his pocket,
is to embark on this vessel ?   The mole thrives in his
hole, and a merchant's views extend from the counter
to the shop-door.   These peace heroes are ready to
sell Riga for a barrel of apples, the trophies of Narva
for a measure of salt, and all St. Petersburg for a scrap
of sole-leather.   But can I hinder it ? · No, *pal malheur*,
we have the misfortune to be free fellow-citizens ; a prefect in Wasa now-a-days signifies less than a burgomaster in Jacobstad.   Oh, we might achieve a splendid
success !   We might win a victory which would restore
our possessions away across the Neva.   We might
take revenge for all our defeats.   And then they tell
us that we ought to wait !   As though we had time to
wait—we old soldiers of King Charles's school !"   And
the prefect lifted his hat, as the surviving Carolins
never neglected to do when they mentioned the name
of the king.   "*Parbleu*, Charles," he continued, "those
who succeed us can be patient, *à bon plaisir;* they can
revise the map in the next century.   But we, who have

only a few days left, must rehabilitate our honor, and not allow the memory of King Charles to be overgrown with moss!"

"My uncle means to say *mössor,*"* responded Bertelsköld, smiling, but warm with the re-awakening memories of the old warrior.

"How does that apply?"

"My uncle has not heard, then, that the utterance of King Frederick, '*Sie sind alle Nachtmützen,*'† has become historic?"

"King Frederick sometimes has his flashes of wit; it would become a king of Sweden not to draw the night-cap so far down over the ears. *Enfin,* this Larsson is a desperate fellow, and, with his resolution, his shrewdness, and his influence in the house of burghers, is able to ruin our whole glorious enterprise. If I had had the power, and decreed the choice, he would never have been elected. That is the result of Horn's system; the rabble wrests the power from the nobility, and tramples the honor of the kingdom in the dirt. But the fellow is now a member of the diet, and the devil cannot help it. He is getting ready to embark for Stockholm. I would donate a year's revenue of my whole province, to the one that could place some obstacle in the way of the journey."

"Pardon me, uncle, that I remember the fable about the tempest and the sunshine. Would not a flattering condescension on your part—an invitation to dinner, for example—be sufficient to bend that obstinate man, and win him to your party?"

"Wasted powder! I know these East Bothnian democrats; from time out of mind they have not known any other aristocracy than that of the church and of money. A principle incarnate is always redoubtable, and such is Larsson. For him there exists only

---

* The Swedish word *mössor* means cap.—TR.

† *Sie sind alle Nachtmützen :—*"You are all nightcaps," *i. e.,* dull fellows.—TR.

a king and a people, with nothing between. With King Frederick he is personally intimate, favored by the queen, and is on confidential terms with Plomgren, Kjerrman, and other influential persons among the citizens of Sweden, not to mention Finland, where he has an incontestable preponderance. There is only one means of crushing him."

"And that is . . . . ?"

"Envy among his own peers. If his departure can be delayed a few weeks, so that he is not present at the beginning of the diet, he will be disarmed. But I am not skilled in wire-pulling. I have a fiscal . . . . Hallo! If there the fellow is not coming now, as though he had been sent after! Spolin!"

The person accosted was a little, pale, thin, light-complexioned man, clad in a worn but well-brushed brown coat with large brass buttons, riding alone, in a shabby peasant-cart. At the call of the prefect, he stopped, jumped nimbly out, and approached with a bow as humble as though he had wished to pick up stones from the highway.

"Well," continued the prefect, "how do matters stand?"

"Good or ill, according as your grace commands," cautiously replied the fiscal, with a questioning side glance at the young count.

"What is that to imply, Mr. Shrewdness? Speak freely; this gentleman is a relative of mine. In a couple of days we shall have practical navigation, and our merchant intends to try his luck at sea. Well, my dear Spolin?"

"The custom-house cannot be prevailed upon to lay obstacles in the way. The papers are clear."

"Indeed? Why do we have a tariff system? You understand, of course, fellow, that I cannot refuse a passport to a member of the diet?"

"Your grace—I beg to inquire humbly if my back is sure not to suffer?"

" H—m ! That savors of the rod. I will not suppose that you have any rascality in view ? "

" My highest desire is only to obey the commands
of your grace."

" Very well. Do as you like. And remember, my
unhanged friend, that you exposed me at the election,
the first of May. You have a great mistake to make
good, my dear Spolin. I have nothing against your
trying to make reparation. I shall bear in mind your
advancement."

" Your grace, the person in question shall not go
to Stockholm—at least not in May."

" The deuce he shall not ? Well, well, Spolin, do
as you like ; that is your affair. Come, Charles ! "
and, evidently troubled to continue the conversation,
the prefect put spurs to his horse, to return to town.
But Fiscal Spolin, whose back had curved considerably again, gradually straightened himself up the farther
his high superior withdrew, and at last stood at his
full height of five feet and two inches ; upon which he
climbed quickly up into the cart again, and continued
his course to the harbor, muttering to himself :
" Before Michaelmas I shall have the stewardship of
Korsholm ! "

" Was that a specimen of the Finnish democracy?"
said Bertelsköld, as they continued the ride. "I do
not know why my riding-whip had such a surprising
attraction toward that fellow's back."

" Mine, too," laughed the prefect. " Bless me !
Is it my fault that the walking-stick needs a ferrule to
stir in the mud ? What would you have me do ?
Liberty may be good enough for proletaires and peasants, but, *enfin*, it annoys a prefect. Indeed, I prefer the
absolute monarchy under the late King Charles.
' March, fellow ! ' and the fellow walked. ' Halt,
scoundrel ! ' and the scoundrel stood still. But now
. . . *Apropos*, who broke your Bogatir?"

" My groom, Istvan."

" The fellow is either the maddest hot-head, or the most accomplished horseman who ever put a bit between the teeth of a fine colt. Just see how the little scamp is listening to the least sparrow-twitter in a circle of half a mile ! Quite different was your father's Bogatir ; I remember him as though it was yesterday, when we crossed the Düna : of Finnish stock, which indulged in no undue haste ; a stout leg, a long neck, broad breast, and good lungs ;—held out, when the Russian and Polish horses perished like calves. Tell me where you got that high-headed kitten, with his splinter legs, and his slender ears, which are continually on the *qui vive !* "

" It is quite a story, uncle."

" Good. Then we can reserve it until we again bivouac beneath the batteries of my old Rüdesheim. *Par miracle*, I am curious to see which of the two gets worsted, Larsson or Spolin. The rhinoceros has encountered a crocodile."

CHAPTER V.

THE MONEY PRINCE.

AT the time of this story, the house of the wealthy Lars Larsson still stood in the same condition it had occupied sixteen years before, when it was put in order after the great war. The same low hall, the same four rooms, and the same dormitory and guest-room, with their belongings ; only the house was more elegantly covered with boards, and a part of the furniture had received the great luxury of white paint. In the square at the right of the old garden was a newly-built residence, inhabited by the eldest son,

Lars, with his numerous family; and at the left, an older garden, occupied by the daughter, Kajsa, who had married the distinguished and powerful Councilor Blom. All three—Larsson, his son, and his son-in-law —pursued their separate trades at their respective places of business, and, in East Bothnian fashion, competed with each other in the tar, butter and salt trade, but carried on their business as shipowners in partnership, and thus controlled the navigation of the place. It might be said that there was peace and union between them in business abroad, but constant feuds and rivalry concerning the market at home. If two of them were on the way to some of the great markets in the interior of the country, they were sure to drive past each other in the night, in order to arrive an hour in advance and secure the best of the customers; and if a previously unknown peasant from Tavastland or Savolaks came down to Wasa, as they then used to do, he was sure to be allured, by the one first on the spot, with the promise of a heaped-up measure of salt, and this or that number of clay pipes in the bargain;—all of which did not prevent the son and son-in-law from outwardly showing the old burgher king and his estimable stocks exceedingly great deference, so that they never spoke of him out-of-doors otherwise than hat in hand, and never answered him in-doors otherwise than standing. Moreover, all that large family gathered on Sunday, after divine service, to dinner in the elder Larsson's house, and then the old man sat like the patriarch Abraham, stately and absolute, surrounded by children, children's children, and servants, as many as could find place at the long table in the family room.

It was not Sunday now, but a busy and bustling week-day; nevertheless, at eleven o'clock in the forenoon, the residents of the two neighboring farms, with children and flowers, and in holiday attire, as they always were on such occasions, were seen to set out for the old mansion. To make their way among horses and people which filled the yard was no easy matter. Peasants and sailors, mingled with one and another townsman of higher social rank, had crowded on the stairs and in the vestibule waiting for admission. In the smaller room a table was spread for customers from a distance. From the bake-room, where Veronica, with Esther as assistant, commanded three or four peony-red servant girls, exhaled a pleasant odor of newly-baked bread. The guest-room was occupied by recently arrived travelers. The meaning of all this was that the archipelago had lately become clear of ice, and Larsson, with all five of his vessels, was about to sail to Stockholm. A thousand necessary matters were to be put in order for the journey, and all affairs which demanded the personal examination of the chief were now to be arranged. But the family were also to eat a farewell meal together, before their father and head set out to sea.

Just at this juncture, and amidst this crowd, the young Count Charles Victor Bertelsköld appeared upon the premises, to present to Larsson a letter of credit from Stockholm. Elegant and noble as he was, with a toilet which in Wasa could not fail to awaken the admiration of all maidens, he seemed somewhat annoyed by the close contact with so many unbrushed rustics, and evidently expected that the crowd on the stairs would voluntarily make room for him. But in this he was mistaken ; no one moved, and a couple of tarry sailors seemed rather to take delight in blocking the way before him. The lord count had to wait and wait, perhaps too long for his young patience.

" Be kind enough to make room," said he at last to the sailors, in a tone which did not anticipate any opposition.

" Lay by so that the gentleman will not run into you," said one of the sailors, as he inspected him with a mischievous look.

"Make room ! I have no time to wait !" repeated Bertelsköld.

"God bless you, there is no haste !" calmly responded the other sailor, with his hands in his trowser's pockets.

At this moment, a slender girl, perfectly white with meal, ran straight across the yard, bounded up the stairs, and glided nimbly as a kitten through the crowd—not, however, without leaving evident traces of the bake-room on the fine blue cloth of the count's coat.

" Esther !" called Bertelsköld after her, " tell your father that I wish to see him ! "

The girl paused a moment, looked at him with a pair of lively brown eyes, and then disappeared in the passage.

" Halt, cruiser ! Don't tack into the current, you'll go adrift ! " muttered the first of the sailors, as he very familiarly laid his pitchy hand on the count's shoulder.

It was probably not so badly intended, but Bertelsköld was not in a mood to tolerate a parley with sailors. Instantly he seized the fellow, who was unprepared for the maneuver, by the collar, and threw him headlong down the stairs.

This was more than a Wasa sailor could reasonably bear. The fallen hero was no sooner on his feet again than he rushed wrathfully back to the stairs and seized the other son of Neptune, Bertelsköld, by the collar.

" Port the helm, Dick ! " shouted the sailor.

The situation was critical, and would have become still more so if the little meal-covered girl had not once more pressed forward between the combatants, and succeeded in making the sailor let go.

" Father is coming immediately ! " she whispered, and darted like a rocket back to the bake-room, where she hid behind the door to witness the result of the fray.

Bertelsköld improved his opportunity, sprang down

L   7*

into the yard, placed himself with his back against a wall, and drew his sword. "The first who comes must look out for his ears!" exclaimed he.

"All hands aloft!" replied the sailors, as each one seized his cudgel and prepared for battle. Noise and confusion prevailed in the yard. Several sailors joined their comrades. A couple of soldiers, who happened to be present in the crowd, promptly placed themselves on the side of the assailant, and the peasants, highly entertained by this rare spectacle, did not neglect to pour oil on the fire.

"Pitch in!" they exclaimed. "Wood against steel! Knock the spots off from them! Roast herring on them! Thrash them till the chaff flies!"

It seemed likely to become one of those frays which were formerly, and in some places are still, an almost every-day delight in the East Bothnian towns, when the sight of old Larsson's tall form on the stairs suddenly put an end to the confusion. "Who presumes to raise a brawl in my yard!" cried he, in a voice of authority. "Away with the clubs! So surely as I am master here, God defend the one who ventures to mutter a word! And you, young gentleman, who forget that you are not standing among Turks and heathen, if you value your life, put your sword in its sheath, and come in with me! I promise you no one shall hurt a hair of your head."

The noise in the yard immediately died away, and the uplifted weapons sank of their own accord.

Bertelsköld would have been a poor pupil of the great Prince Eugène, if he had not borne an honorable retreat from a critical position where even victory might easily have become a defeat; so he accepted the invitation, quite carelessly, quite indifferently, and, through the dividing multitude, entered Larsson's living-room. This was half filled with waiting people, while one at a time was admitted into the office at the left. The count was obliged to remain standing like the humblest day-laborer, until his turn came. Was it by design, or was it rule? He did not know; but his young and noble blood boiled again at what he regarded as a new humiliation before the boundless arrogance of the money-prince.

It was finally his turn; and he entered the unpretending room which constituted the only office of the wealthy and respected house. A press of walnut, a table of unpainted oak, a desk of the same material, an iron chest, a plain single bed, and three or four clumsy chairs, made up the meager furniture of the room. At the desk the old accountant, Grenman, was sweating under a thousand cares, with a pen behind each ear; at the table sat the mighty Lars Larsson himself, before a heap of letters and ledgers. That was the extent of the *personnel* in this office.

Bertelsköld produced a letter of credit for one thousand rix dollars, but added, more haughtily perhaps than Larsson was wont to put up with, that he hoped it was the last time he should have occasion to trouble a man who had so little time for such small matters.

"My lord must be a stranger in this country," coldly replied Larsson, as he took some bags of bright rix dollars out of the money chest. "If you knew our condition you would perceive that a ruined land like ours is not lifted out of its weakness by compliments and bows to imaginary honor, but by honest industry and the greatest exertions. You, who have never seen other times, may think that we plain burghers ought to esteem it a great honor to meet you on the stairs with the humblest request that you would accept our money. But, my young gentleman, I have seen the time when this country, for fifty miles around, did not possess enough to buy ten barrels of salt, and when Gortz was obliged to draw blood to scrape together this sum which you now call a small matter. God grant you may never have to see it, sir; you would then learn a greater respect for labor and the fruits of labor. Here is the money. Farewell! I wish **you a** happy journey."

CHAPTER VI.

A FINNISH JOURNEY IN 1738.

"YOU ride out through the north gate of the city. When you have arrived at Weikars, a by-road branches off to the left, toward the coast; but you follow the large road along Kyro river, to the bridge by Lillkyro church. From that point the shore-road runs northward to Wörå and Ny Carleby; but you continue the upland road, to the right, which goes to Storkyro. That is, in case you do not prefer to lodge over night at the Lillkyro parsonage, which would be the safer plan, as the roads in that vicinity are troubled by vagabonds."

"I thank you, uncle, and hope to be back the day after to-morrow."

"I would prefer to have you delay your departure until I am in a situation to procure you an escort. For the present, I cannot spare a single man; the rabble is in motion; you have yourself seen its humor. *Par honneur*, Charles, I have had enough of liberty. To be governor of the province, and at every step to feel a snare about my feet, which is called constitution, privileges, court of justice,—it is insupportable! Confound it! Give me a little liberty, too, for private use —liberty to slash in among the villains, when they become too daring—a good *choque*, as we used to do with King Charles in Poland — and we should see that the country and the kingdom would be the better for it. *Apropos*, you have not told me yet what procures the peasant clowns of Kyro the honor of your visit."

"Amusement—a desire to see something more of this country than the old ramparts of Korsholm. And besides, uncle, I wish to find my father's old war-comrade, Lauri, or the Laurikain, who is said to be somewhere in Kyro, and whom my mother charged me to hunt up in the event that he was in need of assistance."

"Be careful! Those old *kivekät* do not always enjoy the best reputation for loyal *conduite*. A part of them have settled peacefully down on their old domains, and now attack the forests and fens just as obstinately as they once assaulted the Russian transports ; but others, who could not exactly accustom themselves to peace, have taken up a residence on deserted farms, deep in the forests, and there carry on all kinds of by-trades, which do not exactly please the officers of the crown—for example, depredations on the crown forests, the distilling of brandy, smuggling, and now and then, for variation, a little robbery on the highways. We have to construct a new society, Charles ; and such a work is not completed in one generation. Much is still undone; much, which we can only by degrees set right by constitution and statutes, must still be tolerated. Those old freebooters are a great perplexity. The people fear them as the very devil, but it is impossible to obtain evidence against them ; the police do not venture to their dens without a heavy force. Once more, my dear Charles, be careful! Do not venture into the forests !"

"You can be at ease, uncle; I am armed, and Istvan accompanies me."

"As you please. I have cautioned you, but do not intend to persuade the son of my old friend to any cowardice. So *au revoir !* In the mean time, I will see what can be done with that usurer, that Larsson, who may get into a troublesome lawsuit through that affair. By-the-way, you have not yet told me your opinion about the quarrel in his yard. If it might be the means of putting off his journey—shall we not arrest the sailors?"

"No, uncle, no. I beg you, for my sake, let the matter drop. Do you want to mix me up in a lawsuit?"

"You may be right. I would perhaps better find some other expedient. Farewell! and—one word more! If you are attacked in the forest, let the scoundrels know your name. There is not a *mauvais sujet*, from the Lochteå forests to the bridge of Lappfjärd, who is not ready to be hung for the son of Gösta Bertelsköld. God bless the villains! At any rate, the dogs have hearts in their bosoms, under their ragged jackets!"

A quarter of an hour after this conversation between the prefect Count Frölich and his guest, the young Count Bertelsköld, the latter, accompanied by his faithful servant Istvan, rode out on his dapple-gray horse, Bogatir, through the newly-built yellow-painted north toll-gate of Wasa. The young nobleman had donned a plain riding costume, and put into the holster of the saddle a pair of large cavalry pistols, inherited from his father; but the enormous broadsword had, under the influence of peace and fashion, been exchanged for a small pointed sword of choice Hungarian workmanship. But Istvan wore a Turkish sabre with a Damascus blade, and carried across his shoulder, with his knapsack, a short musket.

It was three o'clock in the afternoon. The day was beautiful and clear, though somewhat cool. The two horsemen rode at an easy trot toward the northeast, and had soon left the low wooden houses and the venerable old stone church of Wasa far behind. The first mile was then, as now, pretty much without forest, level and uniform, only here and there broken by green fields of rye, which grew luxuriantly in the fertile clay soil. Villages and farms were rather scattering too, considering that they were so near the metropolis, and the most substantial town at that time in southerly East Bothnia. Broad tracts still lay deserted ; but those residences which were to be seen were almost all large and built of newly-hewn timber. Various transports were met on the road, crowding the riders to the border of the ditch. It was easy to see that the Swedish population of these neighborhoods, with their more restless disposition, a large proportion of them following tar manufacturing, navigation, country-trade and ship-building, had not yet had time or inclination to repair the ravages the great war made upon agriculture ; especially as the East Bothian peasant had a right to ship-passage in Sweden. The celebrated Wasa rye grew only to an insignificant extent in the immediate vicinity of the town, as the real granaries of that particular kind of grain are to be found in the surrounding Finnish parishes of Lillkyro, Storkyro, Laihela, and Ilmola.

As soon as the horsemen entered upon the territory of the Finnish population, which, a slender wedge of land between Swedish settlements, shoots forward as far as the shore in the parish of Lillkyro, the landscape assumes another color. The road here followed for the most part the bank of the usually calm Kyro, which, lately freed from its icy fetters, now foamed in youthful wantonness between its low clay banks, which were overhung with alders and willows. The open plains were now broken by good-sized forests, which had found opportunity, during war times, to grow up again, and had not as yet been laid low by the axe, for the benefit of the tar-makers. Between the forests extended closer and better tended grain-fields, not, as yet, covering the whole of the former acreage, but well fenced and ditched, and with an appearance which plainly indicated that in these neighborhoods agriculture was the chief industry. The residences were closer together, but at the same time smaller, and the

most of them retired, except in the vicinity of the
church—for here, too, the Finn retained his predispo-
sition to solitude, independence, and free scope about
him.   It is only the Tavastlanders who were sometimes
crowded together in large, closely built villages, as
though to band together against the oppression of the
nobility.   The appearance of the people grew more
silent, serious, and reserved.   The sight of the horsemen enticed children to the fence and women to the
window, but seldom was a cap lifted in greeting, and
the travelers had usually to open the gates themselves,
which had not been the case in the territory of the
more active Swedish population, nearer town.

Something that surprised Bertelsköld was the
numerous crowd of children which everywhere seemed
to people the smallest cot.   At a few places he dis-
mounted, and went in to ask for a drink of water.
Everywhere he met the same sight : A half-score or a
score of bare-footed, white-headed children, clad in
nothing but their linen ; a youngish man, assisted by
several women at out-door work ; a few gray-haired
old women, rarely an old man, and occasionally a man
of forty or fifty years.   The reason was plain :   At the
conclusion of peace, seventeen years before, 'there was
hardly one grown man to four or five women, for
nearly four-fifths of the male population had been
swallowed up by the terrible war.   But since that time,
here and in all Finland a singular power of nature had
been evinced, which, everywhere in life, endeavors,
after great disturbances, to restore the lost equilibrium.
All or nearly all marriages were at that time blessed
with a fruitfulness never before or since known, so that
ten, fifteen or twenty children in each household were
a very common sight.   The population rose so rapidly,
partly by the return of refugees, but mostly by this
extraordinary procreative power, that twenty-seven
years after the peace, according to the best information, the number of inhabitants had doubled, and

increased from twenty-nine to sixty persons to the
square mile. But it was a nation of children. The
greater part of the sons and daughters of Finland were
now looking, with the clear blue eyes of a child, out
toward a happier future. Those were strange times,
and they never recurred. What might not then have
been done to make all things new, and to bring a new
race, free from the old defects, in the fear of the Lord
and the light of truth, up to knowledge and virtue !

It was already evening when the travelers; following the direction of the prefect, reached Lillkyro parsonage, on the hill overlooking the river. The venerable pastor, Gumse, a shivering old man in sheepskin
overcoat, large boots, and leather skull-cap, sat upon
the projecting porch, and seemed to be engaged in the
praiseworthy business of reprimanding an inoffensive
miller, who, cap in hand, and greatly troubled, was
repeatedly pulling his floury forelock.

"I tell you, Anders," expostulated the provost, in a
fatherly, benignant tone, which contrasted strangely
with the tenor of his speech, "yes, I tell you, old
gate-post, there is not a more worthless house-dog
than you to be found between Lillkyro bridge and the
boundary-line of Wörå parish ! To let the Philistines
steal the horse out from under your very nose, you
dried-up sponge !—and not even lift a foot so that the
sergeant found it out before they reached the woods,
you old groat-mill ! Do you suppose that they will sit
down in church next Sunday and wait to be complained of, you jackass ? Little do you know Lauri, if
you think he will bring the jade back ! "

At these words, the miller repeated the foretop ges-
ture, and responded, with embarrassment, that the horse
had disappeared from the pasture, but he could not say
who had taken it. He only knew that his son Jaako,
who was picking cranberries in the woods, had seen
Lauri, with a fiddle on his neck, coming from a wedding in the village, and so he thought . . . .

8

"Your head is as full of meal as your hair, my dear Anders," continued the angry church-shepherd, in the same good-natured tone ; but he was interrupted in his exhortation by Bertelsköld, who now approached, curious to know if the man for whom he was searching was the same one who seemed to be suspected of nothing less than having stolen the miller's horse.

CHAPTER VII.

THE TRAP AT LILLKYRO PARSONAGE.

"I AM a traveler, and wish to find an old soldier by the name of Lauri, or Laurikain; and in case the right reverend provost knows of his abode, I should be much obliged to learn it," said Bertelsköld, with a polite salutation.

Provost Gumse took out a pair of brass-bowed spectacles, wiped the glasses with much deliberation, equipped his worthy nose, and looked at the stranger with evident surprise.

"Abode ? " repeated he. "Lauri's abode ? Your pardon ; but where does my lord live ? "

"I come from Wasa, and have an errand to the person mentioned, who is supposed to have settled in this region."

"Settled ?" repeated the clergyman. "If my lord, as I suppose, is the fiscal—hm, hm, though the gentleman may need to grow in the official gown, then— pardon me—do you fancy, sir, that Lauri has any abode ? "

"I only know that he was one of the last of those who defended their country during the war, and had a desire to know more about his present situation," replied Bertelsköld, who did not care to enlighten the provost as to his mistake.

"Situation?" again responded the obstinate old man. "Young man, you might as well ask about the situation of the north-wind, when it is whistling over there in the birches, and where that is' settled. The war was a great calamity, which the Lord inflicted upon us for our sins; and God preserve any one who experienced it. You are so young that you have as yet seen nothing but the scars; but ask that ground on which you stand: the hoofs of the horses of Ammon's children have tramped upon it. Only mention the great contest, and you will hear the stones speak out."

"Pardon me; but can it be the same Lauri who is suspected of stealing the miller's horse "

"What, pray? I have no proof, sir, no proof. Did I say that he had stolen the horse?" and a certain uneasy blinking behind the spectacles indicated that the venerable pastor had some apprehensions about engaging further in a conversation on that subject.

"If that is the case, I most humbly beg to receive some direction as to where I ought to look for the man. If he has been visible here as lately as this morning, I might perhaps overtake him to-night."

"Overtake him? Hm, hm; if you will accept a bit of good advice from an old man, remain here over night, and put up with what the house affords. Brita, go and inspect the guest-room. I think you might as well have the place as any one else."

A strong-limbed, ruddy, full-faced girl now showed herself in the yard, and after some moments returned with the information that as yet no one had taken up quarters in the guest-room except the judge's tall clerk.

It was one of the beautiful and hospitable customs of that day that a large and warm room, with beds prepared, stood continually open to all travelers, who made use of it without ceremony or introduction, and

were provided with what they needed, often without the
host and hostess even knowing who the guests were. In
the mornings some of the domestics were sent to see
who had been lodging there and what they might
want ; and this was called *inspecting the guest-room*,
just as fishermen in the morning inspected their
wicker scoops and salmon nets to gather the night's
catch.

These hospitable places of entertainment, at a time
when so few other conveniences were at the command
of travelers, had their mutual advantages. Neither
host nor guests troubled themselves more than they
chose. There was not a single public journal in the
country, but every traveler answered somewhat the
purpose of a newspaper in our days, and paid for his
entertainment with fresh news from near and far.
For this reason, many an honest country parson
thought himself defrauded of the newest chronicles of
the day, if the guest-room was inspected and found
empty.

There was, perhaps, something in the appearance
of the supposed fiscal which led Provost Gumse to
expect a richer harvest than usual ; for he renewed his
friendly invitation, with the injunction to Brita to
prepare the bed for the traveling gentleman, and let
the clerk lie on the folding-bench. The attendant
could find a bench in the servants' room. The horses
ought to be watered and put into the stable, for the
grazing in the pasture was still too light, and there was
no certainty that the animals might not get out. They
should bear in mind what had happened to Anders'
horse.

Bertelsköld would consent only to take supper at
the parsonage while the horses were being fed. He
was ushered into the long hall, which, with two bed-
rooms and a kitchen, accommodated the clergyman of
a wealthy pastorate, and his whole family, except the
curate, who lived in the attic, and had a salary of

thirty plåts.　At the spread table, he found the
pastor's wife, a domestic-looking woman in a short
gray woolen jacket, home spun, and woven from the
product of her own sheep.　She was surrounded by a
crowd of hearty children and grandchildren, who were
silently making headway in the deep porridge-dish.
There was no ceremony.　Every day, guests sat here
by the same table; and that the supposed fiscal received
a place at the upper end of the table, beside the venerable host, was probably an extraordinary distinction,
explicable by something unusual in his appearance,
which unconsciously indicated a person of a different
rank from that of the daily customers of the parsonage.

Provost Gumse had many questions to ask :—what
was said in Wasa about the diet ; what was thought
of the election ; what was paid for rye ; what was the
prospect of war ; what butter was selling for ; what
was the condition of Polish affairs ; if much brandy
was being smuggled over to the Swedish side ;
if the Roman emperor was very sick ; who was going
to be bailiff of the district of Korsholm, and if it was
true that the Pope was going to abdicate.　After
Bertelsköld had told all he knew, and perhaps a little
more, he once more tried to lead the conversation to
Lauri.　But scarcely had he for the second time spoken
this name, before an embarrassed silence ensued ; one
looked at another, and one of the smallest of the boys
was heard to ask his mother, in a whisper, " if the
strange gentleman wanted to put Lauri in prison."

It was plain that such a reserve must have its
reason ; and as the wandering young horseman had no
desire to reveal his incognito, he expressed his thanks
for his pleasant entertainment, and declined all invita-
tions to remain over night, with the courteous explanation that his time did not admit of any delay : he must
immediately continue the journey, and would be much

obliged if he could get some one who, for a liberal recompense, would show him the way to Lauri's dwelling.

The venerable provost coughed a little, looked alternately at the large wall clock and at the point of his wife's neckerchief, as though in search of some happy inspiration, and finally stated that the miller's Jaako was acquainted with all the paths in the forest, and was the one who could best show him the way "in case he must needs prefer to make the acquaintance of bandits, morasses and night-fogs rather than that of a warm bed with honest people."

As Jaako had accompanied his father to the parsonage, and was just then occupied in the praiseworthy business of devouring a dish of porridge in the servant's room, the proposal met with no particular hindrance ; and soon the two horsemen, guided by a slender bare-footed lad of thirteen or fourteen years, and with an appearance of shrewdness, left the parsonage, not without the perceptible astonishment of all its inmates.

Lieutenant Bertelsköld had been reared far from the land of his father, and had already become better acquainted with many another country than with this ; but he was not altogether ignorant of the Finnish language. He had spent a part of his childhood in intimate companionship with old Tobias, who, years before, had accompanied his mother on that adventurous journey to Kajana castle, and from him had learned the language of his fathers. Much had since escaped his memory, but enough remained to allow him to make himself somewhat intelligible to the boy, who, with the agility of a beagle, bounded rather than walked alongside the ditch, before the two horsemen. In this way he discovered that about a mile from the parsonage there was a small house in the forest, where Lauri was sometimes in the habit of staying ; and if he was not there, they might perhaps, by reward or persuasion, find out where they ought further to seek him. With this slender information, the ride was continued in the light spring evening.

It was between ten and eleven o'clock at night, when the horsemen, under the guidance of Jaako, left the great highway and turned off on a smaller by-road to the left. This road also narrowed by degrees, after they had passed a few farms, where the barking of dogs attracted one curious face after another to the little windows, some of which were single panes, barred or protected by shutters. Bertelsköld observed that the front doors of these houses were fastened ; a precaution elsewhere seldom used in this peaceful and sparsely inhabited country.

The road at last became as narrow as a footpath ; wheel-tracks disappeared on the clayey ground, and, owing to the stones, shrubs, and juniper bushes, the horsemen could no longer without inconvenience ride abreast. They had left the last farm far behind ; the barking of dogs ceased ; the cow-bells no longer tinkled from the forest-hillocks in the distance ; the peculiar odor of smoke from the piles of chips lighted on fallow fields to protect the grain from insects, was no longer distinguished. The vigilant May sun had gone to rest behind birches and pines ; the night-fog arose from the fen, and spread out like a veil over moist and low places.

The forest became denser, the air cooler ; the silence was broken only by the hum of insects, the measured hoof-beat of the horses, the rustling of some broken twig, or the voice of a thrush, singing his melodious song in the tree-tops.

CHAPTER VIII.

PERILS IN PEACE-TIME.

THE deeper the horsemen penetrated into the forest, the narrower became the footpath, so that at last there was hardly anything to indicate a road except the track of a lost cow, where the ground was soft. The horses were continually stumbling over windfalls, and the pine branches struck the riders in the face. No signs of wood-cutting, or other traces of humanity, could be discovered in this uninhabited wilderness of forest, stones, hair-moss, and moor.

"What now, you rascal ! Why, the road has come to an end here !" impatiently exclaimed Bertelsköld, when the density of the forest finally compelled him to dismount and lead his horse by the bridle. The last tracks had ceased ; but Jaako, with the nimbleness of a squirrel, still continued, half creeping, to work himself forward through the thicket.

"Has the road come to an end ?" repeated the boy, with an expression so stupid that under other circumstances it would not have failed to call forth the laughter of his companions.

"If we do not soon come to the cottage I will lay you across the saddle and let you taste a bit of birch," continued the exasperated count.

"The cottage ?" repeated the boy. "Can that be the cottage that we see between the trees ?"

There really seemed to be a dark object in the dim shadow of the pines. At that moment the boy darted off between the tree trunks like an arrow. Istvan, who had been watching him with distrustful glances, let go his bridle and pursued the boy. Both were very soon out of sight.

Bertelsköld, left alone, and uncertain what to think of the boy's disappearance, had no other choice than to tether the horses and start off on foot in the direction in which the dark object was faintly discernible through the night-fog. He had not gone many steps before he discovered his mistake. What had been taken for a human habitation was nothing but a large wolf-trap, built of tree-trunks and provided with a pit-fall within. The trunks were broken down in several places, and the dilapidated condition of the entire structure indicated that for several years it probably had not been looked after or kept for its original purpose. This trap was in all respects less inviting than the hospitable "trap" at Lillkyro parsonage.

Bertelsköld paused to listen. Round about him all was as silent as the bottom of the sea : not a bird, not a breeze ; only in the distance a soft hum was heard, like the wings of myriad insects. The ground here was high, but close by was a morass above which hovered an impenetrable fog. It seemed to spread out more and more ; it flowed, like a light sea of down, over the roots and trunks of the trees ; only the tops. were now seen in the peculiar splendor of the spring night. Little by little the fog stole higher up on the circle of vision, and it was not many minutes before our wandering knight found himself so completely enclosed in mist that he could not distinguish an object ten paces distant.

He shouted : no echo ! He whistled : no answer ! He thought he heard the sound of a broken twig, and groped his way in that direction : he was mistaken ; it was a woodcock, flapping against some dried branch. He could no longer doubt ; the treacherous guide had purposely led him astray in the wilderness,—and he thought he guessed the reason. He had been taken

M

for a traveling fiscal; and the more he recalled the
reserve that had been observed concerning Lauri, the
more clearly he understood that Jaako must be in
some complicity with that adventurer, and desired to
lead his supposed pursuer astray in order to inform
the freebooter of the danger.

Impatient and irritated, Bertelsköld continued to
grope his way forward in the wilderness, not knowing
where he went. It did not trouble him that the grass
was wet and the night air cool; now here, now there,
he thought he heard some sound from his companions.
But when he had continued this difficult wandering for
nearly a mile as he thought, he found himself once
more at the wolf-trap which he had left long before.
He had traveled in an almost complete circle around
the spot.

After a while a step was plainly heard in the forest.
Something was moving through the fog, and in another
moment a slender figure darted close by him. It was
a girl; she wore a white head-cloth over her head, and
probably did not see him, for upon his calling out,
"Wait a little!" she started, looked around in surprise,
but immediately fled again with the rapidity of a bird,
and vanished in the mist.

Quickly as she flashed by, Bertelsköld had nevertheless, to his great astonishment, thought he recognized her features. If she was not a form of air, a
fairy, or a phantom, she bore at least a surprising
resemblance to a well-known person whom he had met
twelve hours before in Wasa—the rider of the first of
May—his deliverer in the tumult of the forenoon—the
rash and roguish little burgher-girl, Esther Larsson.

"Esther! dear little Esther! Have you the heart
to leave me alone in this wilderness?" exclaimed the
young lieutenant, in the first surprise at this unexpected
meeting.

No one answered. It seemed to Bertelsköld as
though the capricious girl had hidden herself a few

steps away behind a large pine. He hastened thither, but what he had taken for her white head-cloth was only the white trunk of a birch, which in brotherly concord had grown beside the pine. He could not resist a laugh at the mocking illusion of his lively fancy. How could he imagine for a moment that the rich merchant's daughter, her father's pearl and the apple of his eye, would be alone, in the middle of the night, in this pathless wilderness so far from Wasa?

Dissatisfied, he turned once more to the wolf-trap, in the hope that Istvan would yet search him out by that beacon in the forest; but he had scarcely reached the spot before a new form pressed forward between the tree trunks.

It was a man, about fifty or sixty years of age, unusually short, but broad-shouldered, clad in the ordinary peasant costume of the neighborhood, and carrying an axe on his shoulder. The man came from the same direction as the girl—and Bertelsköld now saw that there was a small, scarcely perceptible footpath— then stopped as though surprised, and asked: "What is the gentleman doing here in the woods?"

"And what are you yourself doing, my friend?" responded the count, in his turn, glad to have found at last some one who could conduct him out of a situation of which he was already very tired.

"I am cutting masts," drily replied the man.

"And I am trying to find a cursed boy, who was to show me the road, and has deserted and run off. Have you seen him? Or have you met my servant, who went in the same direction awhile afterward?"

"I *do* remember meeting a boy," said the man.

"Where did you meet him? And when?"

"At noon, on the highway."

"See here, fellow, you would better tell me honestly where I ought to look for my people, for I do not relish fooling."

"And the gentleman would do better about this

time to be sleeping in his bed, instead of hunting black-cock in the underbrush."

" I do not ask advice," retorted Bertelsköld, some-what haughtily, " but I wish you would show me the way out of this infamous forest. You can earn a good day's wages."

" Possibly enough, sir; but I do not care anything about that," replied the man, indifferently. " I cannot show you the way; I have my contract, and must have my pines at the highway before night. But I can give you some good counsel, and if you are not too proud to take a mast-hewer's word, then listen to that sound over there. Do you not hear something ? "

" I think I hear a humming no louder than that of a horsefly buzzing against the window-pane."

"That is a big horsefly, sir, and, if you were a few miles nearer, you would perhaps better understand its morning psalm. Have you never heard the dogs of the Bothnian Sea yelp against the rocks ? "

" Do you believe that is the murmur of the sea ? "

 " Yes, you can depend upon it. Now help your-self. Should you not see the sun for the fog, then listen to the barking of the dogs; there you have the west, and then you can steer after your own compass. In about two hours the southwest wind will begin to blow; you will then lose the fog, but also the compass, for from that time the sun will creep in a fleece, and we may hear the footsteps of Thor. Farewell, sir ! If you wish well to your father's son, do not be sparing of your shoe-soles. I wish you a lucky walk ! "

" Do you not want to earn ten plåts ? "

" My mast is worth fifty. God be with you."

And with these words the man disappeared at the same point where the girl had just before vanished.

Bertelsköld felt a strong inclination to pursue the impudent fellow and compel him to earn the proffered reward; but he had too lately seen a proof of the suc-cess of such pursuits. His situation appeared to him

more laughable than dangerous, and at the thought of
all the long and perilous nights he had spent by the
bivouac of the advance guard in the Hungarian forests,
he resolved to sit patiently down and wait till the fog
was dissipated.

Fate seemed, however, to have decreed that Charles
Victor Bertelsköld, lieutenant of his royal majesty's
engineer corps, should this night enjoy not even a
quarter of an hour's rest; for it was not long before, at
some distance, a shrill, penetrating whistle sounded
through the solitude. This time it was surely Istvan;
and if any one had still been able to doubt it, the animated neighing of Bogatir showed that he too was
listening to the well-known signal. Bertelsköld answered with the common battle-cry of the Hungarians,
and it was not long before his faithful servant appeared
from a quarter entirely different from that in which he
had disappeared.

Istvan now made his report. He had chased his
deserter nearly an hour, but the shrewd lad had used
his knowledge of the locality so well that some obstacle
constantly interrupted the chase; now it was a morass;
now a thicket; now one of those bowlder-heaps, large
as a house, which strew the whole East Bothnian coast.
Behind such a great cairn Jaako had disappeared, and
when Istvan had persistently continued to seek for
him, he had "seen people inside the rock."

He said this with an air so serious as to bring a
smile to the lips of his incredulous master.

"Then did you go right in where they were, and
ask them to show you the way?" queried Bertelsköld.

"I go into the rock?" repeated Istvan with undisguised astonishment. "I will go where your grace
commands, where steel can bite the skin, and where
balls do not turn back from their mark; but I am a
human being, your grace, and do not want to have
anything to do with what I saw there. I became satisfied that everything is not just right here in the forest,

and got away as quickly as I could, to find your grace; but I am sure that that vile fog is sent out solely for our sake, and so I have been running around in a circle like a hare with the dogs at his heels."

"You are a fool. I have heard that there are yet many hiding-places here in the forests since the time of the great war, when people concealed themselves in dens and mountain caves to escape the enemy. Who knows but in that very cave we may find the fellow we are seeking!"

Istvan had meanwhile got something else in his head. He laid down with his ear against the ground, remained thus a minute in silence, holding his breath, and then suddenly asked: "Has your grace let the horses loose?"

" I tethered them not far from here, and they cannot have broken loose, for I heard Bogatir neigh at the place where I left him."

Istvan continued to listen. "They are loose,—they are a good distance east of here,—they are going the other way,—now they stop,—now they are going again,—they walk slowly,—they are trampling on sticks and dry twigs,—their pace is heavier and evener than that of horses that are running loose. . . . . Your grace! our horses have been stolen. A nag travels in that way only when he carries a rider on his back!"

"Come," said Bertelsköld, who well knew that Istvan had grown up from childhood among dangers and deserts, where the senses are sharpened far beyond the common human standard; "we shall soon see if you guessed rightly, and then we will have a chase beside which our former one has been child's play."

CHAPTER IX.

THE QUEEN OF THE MIST'S GARTER.

THE two wanderers of Lillkyro parish were not
slow in forcing their way through the thicket to
the place where their horses had been tethered ; and
the first glance convinced them that Istvan's delicate
sense of hearing had not deceived him. The place
was deserted ; the soft moss appeared to have been
trampled by fresh foot-prints, and the horses were
gone. It was not possible that they had drawn their
heads out of the halter or broken away. Not even the
bark of the trees where they had been tied showed the
least trace of a forcible jerking loose.

Istvan was beside himself. He threw himself on
the ground, he crept on all fours, he scented the tracks
like a hound ; he snorted with anger. "See here !"
he shrieked, "Bogatir has reared. They did not get
upon his back very easily ; and not easily do I think
they would have kept the saddle if the cursed forest
had not been so dense."

"Hold ! They have lost something !" exclaimed
Bertelsköld, as he stooped down and picked up a shining object from the nearest juniper bush. It was a
small, dainty, silken garter, with a silver clasp that
glittered like a gem among the drops of mist on the
juniper.

Istvan regarded it with what he thought a very just
horror. "Did I not say so?" said he triumphantly.
"I recognize that — I know what it means. I
found it just so once on the mountain in Bukovina, between Zablatov and Kolomea. It was at night, in
clear moonlight, but somewhat misty by the river bank.

We heard the horses of the infidels neighing in the
valley. I had it in my power to be as great as a
pascha, but I did not understand my good-fortune. I
threw the charm into the Pruth! At dawn of day we
had the enemy upon us, and got a beating instead of
a victory. Why was I so stupid!"

"A little scrap of ribbon is surely not very dangerous," responded Bertelsköld, smiling "I think it resembles a girl's garter remarkably."

"Resembles? Yes, sir, it resembles everything,
sometimes this, sometimes that. The one that lost it
can also resemble one thing or another: sometimes a
shrub, sometimes a stone, sometimes an old hag, and
sometimes a girl. It all depends upon what time of
day it is, and what is the humor of the creature that is
skurrying about in the mist."

"Why should I throw away anything that may perhaps be a means of discovering the thieves?"

"I tell your grace that when I threw the thing
away I was stupid as a Bosnian. I did not understand
it until afterwards. I ought to have put it away inside
of my jacket; then I would have been invulnerable;
and the one that lost it would have been compelled to
come to me and ask to have the thing back. I could
then have fixed my own terms, your grace, even if they
had been a crown. And there, in the mist, it would
have given me what I demanded. Put it away, master,
but put birch-bark around it, or, still better, lay it between two flat stones in your pocket; it might burn
through the birch-bark."

"Fool! if there is anything singular in all this it is
meeting a girl here like .... But while I am listening to your silly superstition, we are letting the thieves
escape us."

"Yes, by Sandeç's mountain! it is as your grace
says. Follow me if you can, and if we get on level
ground again I will show the rascals who is Bogatir's
master!"

At these words, Istvan again laid down, breathless, with his ear to the ground, and after he had
assured himself of the direction they ought to take in
order to overtake the horse-thieves, he began, more
creeping than running, to make his way among thick-
ets and tree trunks with such rapidity that his master,
although considerably younger, had the greatest difficulty to keep up with him.   It was wonderful to see
with what sagacity the Hungarian, in his ardor, observed every mark which indicated a trace of the horses ·
in the wilderness.   Now it was a trampled tuft, now a
broken twig, now a hoof-mark on a fallen and crumb-
ling tree-trunk ; now the trail seemed to lose itself in
a rocky tract, and then a place with newly-scraped
moss, or a little stone which had been turned out of its
position and lay with its moist side upward, served to
guide him.   Bertelsköld thought he observed that their
present course was toward the east, and at almost a right-
angle to that on which they had entered the forest; but at
another time it seemed to him as though he had seen
this or that crooked pine, and this or that moss-grown
boulder, the evening before.   From this he concluded,
and perhaps not incorrectly, that their treacherous
guide from Lillkyro parsonage had intentionally led
them on a crooked detour into the forest, in order to
render more difficult the task of their finding the way
back unaided.   In this supposition he was strengthened
still more when the two wanderers, after an extremely
difficult tramp, and sooner than they had hoped, saw
the forest grow thin around them, and once more approached cultivated tracts.   Judging by a brightening
in the east, it might now be about two o'clock in the
morning ; but the fog, which lay thick over the moist
meadows, shut off all view at a distance greater than
fifty paces.   They now came to a fence, on the other
side of which was a newly-ploughed fire-clearing.   Here
Istvan could not use his art of laying his ear to the
ground, for in that soft, muddy, clay soil every echo of

8*

sound in the distance was lost. Being compelled to
run along the grassy borders of the dikes, he came to
a little road, the first he had seen since the evening before. When he and his master had followed the road
some minutes, a little farm was seen in the fog.

"Halt!" cried Bertelsköld, worn out with weariness
and impatience. "Knock, you dog, and let us rest an
hour; I cannot stand it any longer. I have marched
more than one night on the Hungarian steppes, and
have had just as good sole-leather under my feet as
you have; but the deuce take me if you cannot out-
walk me! March, fellow! What are you gaping at?"

"I think there is a large rock under this hill," replied the servant, without seeming to hear his master's
commands. He undertook, instead, to scrape away
with his fingers the soil at the foot of the hill, by the
fence, and immediately afterward he stooped once more
to listen.

"I have them!" he cried. "They are not a quarter of a mile away. We shall now see if Bogatir understands the language of his fathers."

No sooner was this said than Istvan began to
bound up the little ascent as though he had not tramped
a weary step that night. Reaching the summit, he
scrambled up into an aspen tree that was growing
there, and gave one of those shrill whistles with which
he could pierce the air as with an awl. Notwithstand-
mg the morning fog, the whistle must have been heard
very far away, as the sound was carried by the gentle
breeze which was beginning to be perceptible on the
height, and was blowing toward the northeast, the point
which Istvan faced.

For a minute or two it was perfectly still around
them. Nothing was heard but the purling of a little
spring-brook which was filtering out from among the
stones at the foot of the hill. Istvan repeated his
whistling a second time, and a third time. No sound
replied. But after the third signal, he descended from

the tree, resumed his listening posture, and declared,
with animated gestures, that he heard Bogatir's hoofs
approaching. Soon Bertelsköld could no longer doubt
it. Before the fog admitted of distinguishing anything with the eye, he heard the well-known hoof-beats
of his trusty pony, approaching on that fleet gallop
which had thrown the rider at Korsholm into so great
a terror. And in a few minutes Bogatir really came,
in obedience to the signal, galloping with the wonderful instinct of the animal straight through the fog
toward the narrow by-road.

But he did not come alone. To the satisfaction
and surprise of the wanderers, a figure both pathetic
and laughable was seen on his back, who, kicking with
all his might, was leaning forward and holding fast by
the horse's mane, while a pair of bare feet, which were
too short to reach the stirrups, thumped like drum-
sticks on each side of the saddle. And who was the
doleful rider but Jaako, the boy-changeling, the guide,
who was now, by a singular disposition of fate, brought,
against his will, to account to those who by his evil
trick had been forced to stray around all night in the
forest! His punishment was complete when Bogatir,
well-broken in military maneuvers, having reached his
master, stopped almost instantly, and, as a natural consequence, his unhappy rider was immediately thrown
heels over head over the horse's neck to the ground.
On the whole, this was a very fortunate circumstance for
Jaako, as it was of exactly the right nature to save the
hopeful youth from an otherwise inevitable lathering
with twigs from the nearest birch. His judges had
now, instead, the trouble of helping him on his feet
again, and examining whether he had received any injury by the fall. He had fortunately tumbled very
softly into a clay puddle by the roadside, and arose,
certainly not in the neatest condition, but nevertheless
as sound as ever a clodhopper arose, with two lively
arms and legs, after such a neck-breaking summersault.

Still, poor Jaako's afflictions were not altogether ended. While Istvan contemptuously shoved him aside, and went to caress the horse with those little confidences which on such occasions are bestowed upon a long-lost and newly-found friend, his master began at once the inquiry which the circumstances demanded. The little villain was not so easy to unravel. As soon as he had somewhat recovered breath and realized his dilemma, he began to howl in a fashion which a young wolf might have envied him. It was impossible to get an intelligible word from him.

"Istvan," said Bertelsköld, with assumed sternness, "go and braid a stout rod from the birch yonder!"

The howling was now redoubled; but as that did not avail, the rogue thought best to resort to the prayer-book. The gentleman should forgive him; it was not he who had taken the horses, it was Lauri who had loosened them from the tree, and compelled him to help him. The girl had been afraid to sit on the dapple-gray, and so got leave to ride the other horse, while Lauri led him by the bridle. Then Lauri had taken the gray in order not to be overtaken by the gentleman; and then Jaako had thought it would be nice to ride a little; and then—"*Boo-hoo!*" (here the sobbing began anew at the thought of the pleasure Jaako had so shamefully missed)—and then they had come out on the highway, when the gray horse all at once caught the witch-distemper and took a notion to run away, out in the fog, and afterwards—"*Boo-hoo!*" And the music began anew, until a little stroke of the switch produced a proper effect.

"Was that Lauri who a little while ago went past the wolf-trap?" inquired the count.

The boy said it was.

"Who was the girl that was with him?"

"The girl?" repeated the rogue, with his silly air. "It must have been his own girl."

"Do not try to deceive me!" responded his inexorable chastiser. "What do you know about the girl?"

"*Boo-hoo!* people say that he is her godfather," sobbed the boy.

"Master," whispered Istvan, "it is not well to talk about such beings while the mist still lies thick upon the meadow."

"You remind me of something else," rejoined Bertelsköld. "I will not have fatigued myself in these infamous morasses altogether in vain. March, scoundrel!" continued he to Jaako. "Show us the way to the stone-heap in the forest where the people are hidden. We will take care this time that you do not fool us."

The objections of Istvan were as unavailing as the music of Jaako, and the company was soon in motion toward the interior of the forest,—Bertelsköld on horseback, and before him the refractory boy, bridled like a skittish colt by means of a willow rope, with which Istvan thought best to secure his valuable person.

CHAPTER X.

THE BARROW IN THE FOREST.

THE morning sun had not yet penetrated the fog which, inaccessible to the wind, veiled the inner portions of Lillkyro forest, when the adventurous procession, with its intractable guide, approached a large grave-hill, situated scarcely a quarter of a mile to the west side of the great highway. The ground in this region was extremely sterile, cut up by marshes and broken by enormous blocks of

stone, so that both caution and patience were necessary. But so enticing were these difficulties after the
monotonous quiet of Korsholm, so briskly stirred the
inherited spirit of adventure in the breast of the young
nobleman, that an undertaking which, in view of its
needlessness, would for any other reason have seemed
childish and foolish, made him forget hunger and
weariness in the prospect of getting on the track of
that mystery which had so lately frightened his brave
but superstitious companion. It was to him a peculiar
pleasure to rove through these solitudes, where his
father had once carried on his wild partisan warfare
against an overmatching foe ; and if the son could not,
like him, defend his country, he might possibly receive
some benefit by becoming acquainted with it in its
poverty and wildness, which still at every step bore
traces of the great devastation.

Jaako evidently knew the way better than he was
inclined to admit, for, after some little abortive attempts
at escape, he led the wanderers into a little highway,
broken by fresh cart-tracks and leading past fens and
rocks to the cairn indicated, which Istvan confessed
was the same that had inspired him with such just
apprehensions. It was one of those mighty bulwarks
of nature which are sometimes met with on the East
Bothnian coast, and resemble monstrous giant-hows
heaped over fallen Titans before the deluge. This
mound was at least a thousand paces in circumference ;
the base, or foundation, was made of large moss-grown
blocks of stone, worn at the edges, thrown upon each
other in wild confusion by some tremendous power,
but piled in a definite direction, as though washed
thither by an irresistible wave. On the top of these
rocks lay stones of an inferior size but similar shape,
all of them rounded at the edges ; and above these
were still smaller stones, some of the uppermost ones,
forming the crust or summit of the mound, being

hardly larger than a hen's egg. The whole formed a
ridge rather than a pyramid, and was finished, with
all its chaotic disorder, in an almost regular curve,
about like a large overturned trough.

With delight and curiosity Bertelsköld contemplated this magnificent freak of nature, which seemed
to him to be a most fitting mausoleum for the great
Charles XII, when Istvan, who had with great reluct-
ance consented to make the circuit of the mound,
significantly pointed to a singular stone, the shape of
which assumed in the fog the figure of a colossal
horse's head.

" Was it here ? " inquired his master, with softened
voice.

" I think so," sullenly replied the servant. " The
one who lives here left the horse's head behind him
when he rode in."

Bertelskold now left the horse and boy in the keeping of Istvan, and set out alone to make his way to the
stone indicated, which lay in about the middle of
the mound, half way to the top. It was a short but
difficult walk : now his foot slipped on the treacherous
moss, which covered these remnants of the revolutions
of antiquity ; now he displaced a stone, and caused it
to roll down with a rumbling, hollow sound, as though
on the roof of a cellar. The mound had upon nearer
view lost its appearance of regularity, and seemed wild
and chaotic ; the gray blocks of granite appeared as
if thrown helter-skelter and piled fantastically upon
each other. And that which at a distance resembled a
horse's head, was nothing but a shapeless mass of stones,
almost hanging by the extremity, so that it seemed
every moment ready to tumble down.

Under this stone there was a hole large enough to
admit a man, and the aperture, which was now exposed,
seemed to have been covered by a flat slab of stone
lying beside it. The mound had here formed a natural

grotto,* which in times of distress and danger must have offered the inhabitants of the neighborhood an excellent asylum, one that in case of need could be defended against a superior force. But hardly for amusement would human beings have sought a refuge in this open grave, which in silence and darkness yawned under the hoary rocks of the mound. It seemed to Bertelsköld as though there was something here which had reason to shun the light of day. As he stooped down, a faint scent of smoke floated toward him ; he thought he discovered a faint glow of fire in the depth, and just then caught sight of the uppermost round of a ladder, which was leaned up toward the mouth inside and plainly showed that the hole was not inhabited by spirits, who would have had little need of such means of ascending and descending.

After having examined the priming of a couple of pocket pistols, which ever since the Hungarian campaign he had carried in his belt, our young adventurer resolved to descend the ladder and examine the grotto. As a precaution, he dropped a small stone into the orifice, and satisfied himself by its fall against the bottom that the depth was not too great for the length of the ladder.

He stepped upon the ladder with good courage, but still not without examining occasionally the strength of the rounds, and casting a long look behind him, as the descent had to be made backwards. He advanced a few steps from the clear morning light down into a twilight which from the aperture was faintly illuminated by the day. A few steps more, and even this twilight disappeared, and the passage above showed like a round spot of light in the roof of the grotto.

* The Surgeon fancied he observed that his auditors regarded the story of the grotto as an off-hand romance, and took occasion to remind them of the famous Troll-mountain in Wöra. Tradition attributes such grottoes to the giants, or looks upon them as the abodes of evil spirits, and the hiding places of long buried mysterious treasures. It is more than probable that in former times they were places of refuge for fugitives, bandits, and counterfeiters.

After the count had descended twenty steps or
more, he reached the bottom, which consisted of gravel
and small stones, slippery with moisture. The first
sight which met him here was a fire, half turned to
coals, which was burning in a corner of this subterranean dwelling, and spread a faint glow over the
dusky stones, which constituted the walls of the grotto.
Bertelsköld found himself in an irregular cellar-like
cavern, no larger, but somewhat higher, than a common
peasant cottage.

Among the rocks in its wall purled a little spring-
vein, an invaluable treasure for such a hiding-place in
times of danger. With the exception of a couple of
frogs, which were slipping and sprawling on the wet
stones, there seemed to be no living being in the grotto,
but everything indicated that it must have been quite
recently occupied. It could not have been more than
an hour since the fire had been cared for; on one flat
stone by the wall there appeared to be remnants of a
meal, while two others had served as a bedstead, and
were still covered with sheepskin coverlets.

Besides these objects, there were various implements in the grotto, such as melting ladles, an anvil,
hammers, tongs, crucibles, casting-moulds, and traces
of several kinds of metal which seemed to have been
worked up in this underground shop. Bertelsköld had
seen too much of the world to surrender himself to the
general superstition, still prevailing in his time, and
was therefore inclined to attribute all these implements
to a very natural although uncertain purpose. But he
was nevertheless too young to be able to free himself
entirely from the mystical impression of that deep
silence and that sepulchral twilight which spoke so
powerfully to the imagination, and which was increased
by the feeling of finding himself alone, thirty feet under
ground, shut away from light and life, in a situation
where no human power could come to his assistance,
though the rocks fell over his head. The sensation

N   9

was so overwhelming that Bertelsköld for a moment
fancied that by the light of the dying fire he saw the
dwarfs creep forth out of the clefts in the rocky wall,
and with their small black hands seize the hammer, to
continue their work, which had been interrupted by the
entrance of the unbidden guest into their subterranean
dwelling.

Vexed at this caprice of fancy, and deceived in his
expectation of finding those he sought, the young soldier resolved to desist from further investigations, and
return to daylight in the upper world. So he searched
for the ladder, and, found it with some difficulty, for
it had become darker in that part of the grotto, perhaps
because the fire was almost out.

He began, however, his return by his Ariadne's
thread, step by step; but the darkness continued,
though he ought by this time to have seen the round
aperture to day-light above his head. It was not
visible. He clambered impatiently on, and the height
seemed to him doubled, when suddenly his head struck
against a hard object. He groped with his hands in
the darkness, and found that he had reached the upper
end of the ladder, but the opening had disappeared,
and in its place a heavy slab of stone, which must have
been the same that upon his descent lay beside the
orifice, was lying across the entrance. With or without
design, some one had barred his exit, and he was a
captive in the dismal, dark, and deserted mountain
cavern.

CHAPTER XI.

IN WASA HARBOR.

WITH the same unmercifulness with which capricious fate sometimes leaves mortals to be racked by the pangs of uncertainty, we are obliged now to leave for awhile the young lieutenant in his unexpected captivity, and move some miles away, to Wasa, where the imperturbable member of the diet, Lars Larsson, was at last upon the point of setting out on his proposed journey to Stockholm and the diet.

It was a Saturday morning, and, it may be well to note, the very same morning when Count Bertelsköld and his groom had some hours earlier trotted through the fog of Lillkyro forest. Various obstacles had caused delays in Larsson's journey. Some formality had been lacking in the application for a passport from the prefect, and the certificate of election as deputy of the diet had not obtained all necessary signatures. The custom-house had not furnished the vessel's papers, and Fiscal Spolin had only the day before caused two of the sailors to be put in jail for a disturbance in the street. In short, something had given way in the tackle, as the mariners say,—and perhaps also something had given way in Larsson's own resolution, for the day of departure first decided on was a Friday, and that was regarded by many as of itself a sufficient cause for delay. Who, except in an extreme case of necessity, could or would begin his journey on a Friday? According to the common belief of the time, it would have been a blind exposure of one's self to the influence of all malign stars.

What value Larsson himself was disposed to set

upon the ideas of his friends and kinsmen, concerning the unlucky signification of Friday, we have not been able to ascertain ; but certain it is, that, like a prudent business man, he did not neglect to make use of the delay in the best manner to his own advantage. They continued throughout the night to increase the cargo of the vessel with the common articles of export from that place to Stockholm : first grain, then butter, meat, and salt fish ; but also tar and pitch, which in the bustle they had not been able to stow away. The old bookkeeper, who was himself on the spot to oversee the loading, spent a sleepless night, while his employer took a few hours of rest ; but as this faithful assistant had sat up the preceding night also in making arrangements for the journey, his eyelids by degrees grew heavy, and finally the curtains fell quite down before his Argus eyes, as he sat on the wharf by the harbor, noting in his memorandum book the transportation of the various commodities.

During that involuntary pause in his ardent service, it happened that a load of small kegs, resembling eighth-barrels of pitch, which was sometimes used as ballast, reached the wharf, and waited to be entered. But as the bookkeeper was asleep, no further ceremonies were observed, but the goods were taken on board, and accepted, with all the rest, without question.

Meantime the sun rose higher and higher, and shone straight in the face of bookkeeper Grenman, so that he awoke just the right time to receive his employer, who, accompanied by his family, arrived at the harbor between nine and ten o'clock in the forenoon. Passports and documents were at last correct, the sailors freed from arrest, the wind was favorable, and the anchor about to be weighed. The family came on board, to say the last good-bye ; and as some of the citizens showed their member of the diet the attention of accompanying him to the harbor to wish him a happy journey, an extra supply of French wine was dealt out to the more distinguished guests, and whisky to the crew.

The son-in-law, Councilor Blom, made a speech to his father-in-law, in which he called him the ornament of his country, and likened him to a fully ripened ear, (upon which Widlund, the tanner, whispered to his neighbor that Blom was only waiting for a chance to thrash), and presumed that with the grace of his royal majesty and the favor of the lords of the realm, he would not only guard the privileges of the community, but also manage that the city of Wasa should acquire staple-right, and hold it alone in East Bothnia . . . .

Larsson here impatiently interrupted his enthusiastic son-in-law with the declaration that he held his royal majesty in all due honor, but, concerning the lords of the realm, he was a free man, in a free kingdom, and knew no other lords than the king and the law. And, as the wind was beginning to rise, he would now thank his friends for the honor they had shown him, and bid them a kind farewell.

It was not easy to avoid this hint, and however much the good friends may have wished to view the "Bothnia" at half-anchor, they concealed their disappointment by a loud cheer in which the whole crew joined.

"Honor and thanks!" replied the shipmaster. "And now, boys, stand by to heave anchor!"

"Hurra for the patron!" again sounded on the fresh morning air.

"It is pleasant to see the gentlemen all so gay!" at this moment said a well-known voice in a somewhat nasal tone, and through the gate of the lumber-yard there entered a small, thin, light-haired figure, which was no other than Fiscal Spolin himself.

"Heave anchor!" continued the patron, in a commanding voice; and the captain did not neglect dutifully to repeat the order.

"Your pardon," said the fiscal, very politely, but not without a perceptible trace of ill-concealed malice in his tone. "Your pardon, sir patron; but before the vessel sails I have an order to institute a search on board."

"What does that mean?" roared Larsson, passionately. "I have clearance papers from the custom-house . . . ."

"That is quite possible," continued the fiscal, with a shrug; "but I have definite orders." And with this he produced a written order from the office of the prefect, "to institute a search of the brig Esther before permitting her to leave the harbor."

"All right, man!" replied Larsson, contemptuously, after he had glanced through the paper. "Captain Mårs, let the fiscal search where he likes, but let it be done quickly, and see that nothing is spoiled. If he bursts a single hoop, or breaks a single lid, take witnesses; it will be charged to his account in due time."

"Do not trouble yourself with witnesses—I have them myself," responded the fiscal, somewhat mockingly, as he motioned to a custom-house officer and a town sergeant to accompany him on this unexpected intrusion upon the sacred domains of the customs. And after he had hastily peeped behind some presses and cast a fleeting glance into the cabin, for appearance sake, as it seemed, he boldly directed his steps to the freight room, where his peering eye immediately discovered one of those little kegs which had been smuggled into the vessel while bookkeeper Grenman was sleeping the sleep of innocence on the wharf by the harbor.

"Break open that keg!" he authoritatively commanded his amazed assistants.

"Why, it is nothing but pitch!" said the custom-house officer, somewhat nettled by a sense of his injured dignity.

"Break open the keg!" was the concise command.

The fiscal was obeyed, and scarcely had the cover been broken with the axe before a quantity of bright new silver rix-dollars rolled out of the keg.

The customs officer and the town sergeant opened their eyes. The captain and a couple of the crew, who had been curiously watching the operation, were no less surprised. Like wildfire the rumor spread around the vessel that Larsson was exporting silver to Stockholm, and had introduced his precious kegs as ballast among tar and pitch.

Not less astonished than the rest was the wealthy merchant himself at this unexpected discovery. His first piercing glance fell upon his son-in-law, Councilor Blom, who more than once had been detected in attempts to beguile his venerable father-in-law into various mysterious speculations. But the right honorable councilor's whole appearance disclosed such artless amazement that he might rather be thought to suspect his father-in-law of an iniquitous attempt to outwit him of his coming inheritance. There was a very expressive pause of mutual surprise down there in the hold.

"This money does not belong to me, and I have not the least knowledge concerning it!" Larsson finally ejaculated, with a wrath he did not trouble himself to conceal.

"It is quite possible that is the case," replied the fiscal, quite meekly, "but the patron will pardon me that under such circumstances I must provisionally stop the vessel."

Larsson's patience gave way. "And by what right," he exclaimed, "do you venture to hinder a member of the diet from appearing in his place? Where is a case recorded that vessels were stopped for carrying silver from one part of the kingdom to another?"

"Silver?" responded Spolin, as he held one of the new coins toward the light from the large hatchway.

" Oh, patron Larsson may carry silver where he pleases within the kingdom, but I do not think the same can be done with stamped pieces of tin. This money is all spurious! "

CHAPTER XII.

ESTHER'S DISCOVERIES.

HAD the brig Esther fallen to pieces and suddenly commenced to sink, it would scarcely have aroused greater astonishment than those two little words, " spurious coin."   While the heavy copper plåts of Charles XII and the coin of Gortz were still pretty generally in use, silver coin was rare, and was regarded with no little respect.   Rough attempts to imitate this highly esteemed coin had, indeed, sometimes been made, and German pewterers had succeeded in now and then smuggling in a parcel of this false commodity. But though the fraud was thus not altogether unfamiliar, it was nevertheless extremely surprising now to find the spurious coin not only in an unusual quantity but also in an imitation so unusually good that it required the keen scent of an old hound to discover its real quality at first sight.   Meanwhile the suspicious murmur which met the first assertion of the fiscal subsided when the eager officer let the coin carelessly fall against the lumber ballast in the hold, and its faint muffled sound made all further doubt impossible.

To a business man like Larsson, there was hardly an object on the face of the whole earth more detestable than spurious money.   After he had recovered from his first consternation he declared emphatically that underneath this there was some base conspiracy, and that, as an unmolestable member of the diet, he did not intend to pay any attention to it, but continue the journey; upon which Fiscal Spolin, with all politeness, observed that he was perfectly free to do so, and that it was only his good brig Esther which for the present was obliged to put off the journey.

Larsson insisted on a rigid examination, and the ardent fiscal declared that it should certainly take place, but in due order, before a court of justice and of record. The angry owner then took it upon himself to institute a strict inquiry. But that was unavailing; his Argus had slept, and it was only found out that some strange men had brought the kegs to the wharf, and they had been put aboard with the rest of the goods.

The remaining kegs were examined, and found to contain the usual contents—not coin, but pitch. Nobody knew what to think of the matter.

Meanwhile, among the relatives and friends who had accompanied the member of the diet was a slender person, who, silently and unobserved, had hitherto been watching the progress of affairs with a pair of shrewd eyes; and this was Esther Larsson, the merchant's youngest daughter. She now glided to her father, and, with a glance at the fiscal, whispered : " Ask him how it came about that he immediately pounced upon the only keg that contained coin."

The observation was a wise one; and the father, who rarely took advice from any mortal, for once thought best to follow his daughter's direction.

" Why?" responded Fiscal Spolin, with visible embarrassment. " Because the keg of coin happened to be uppermost."

Esther now, as though accidentally, pushed with her little foot the empty keg which lay on the deck, and remarked carelessly that it had a notch in the edge, which was not found on the other kegs.

The fiscal declared it was an accident which did not concern him. But he had now to deal with a troublesome person, who did not allow him to escape so easily.

"Where was Fiscal Spolin last night, between one and two o'clock?" shrewdly inquired Esther, as her brown eyes flashed with so wonderful a luster that the perplexed officer stood for a moment confused and nonplussed. With difficulty he made out to stammer that he stood here as complainant, not as defendant, and that he was not obliged to answer stupid questions. He had slept all night quietly in his bed.

"The fiscal answers for all that," put in Esther, with the same sharp look. "But if the fiscal slept, then perhaps the bed was not very well made up. Shall I tell where the fiscal slept?"

"Take away that impertinent changeling,* and give room for me, on behalf of the great crown, to seal the hold till due search is made," resumed the official, anxious at any price to get rid of his tormenting spirit.

But Esther leaned close to his ear, and whispered very softly, "Do not deny that at one o'clock last night the fiscal was at the grave-cairn in Lillkyro forest."

If a thunderbolt had fallen among the records and warrants in his very office, the effect could not have been greater on the dumbstricken man. He seemed to seek, in the astonished faces of the bystanders, the confirmation of some extremely unwelcome discovery, and his defence reduced itself to a feeble attempt to murmur the word " proof ! "

But Esther did not release him. "Will the fiscal allow the brig to sail immediately, and explain everything as a misunderstanding?" she whispered again, with emphasis on the words.

---

* It is impossible to express the meaning of the original word *flickby-tingen* in English. There is a superstition, still prevalent in the less frequented parts of Scandinavia, that the evil mountain spirits are on the alert to steal human children, whom they carry off to the mountains and bring up to their horrid practices, leaving one of their own uncanny brood in the cradle instead. This young troll is a changeling, "*flick*" or "*goss*" " bytingen."—Tr.

The unhappy man was like a fly, which, in the midst of its gay flight, had blundered into a cobweb. "This is the result when parents do not discipline their children!" exclaimed he, at the same time drawing nearer the port in the gangway, in order to have a retreat open.

"What is that you are saying, Esther?" inquired Larsson.

"I say that the fiscal can meet old acquaintances, if he really wants to do so," replied Esther, and turning on her heel, she pointed to an elderly man, who was sitting in one of the boats at the ship's side, wrapped in a loose gray jacket, and appearing to be one of the boatmen. Fiscal Spolin could not refrain from giving a side glance from the gunwale at the person in question, and the result was so remarkable that he immediately, with his foot on the stairs, declared the whole of his great discovery to be a misunderstanding. It was evident, he thought, that patron Larsson had no knowledge of the illicit affair, and he would on no account be the one to hinder so estimable a person from taking his proper place at the assembling of the diet. He, Spolin, would at some future time see that this disagreeable affair had all possible explanation, and of course had nothing at all against the brig's immediately setting sail; so he would not trouble them further with his presence, but wished one and all a happy journey.

With these words he descended into his boat—not, however, without several times looking backward as though he feared a tar-bucket upon his head; and with rapid strokes of the oars he quickly withdrew from the side of the brig.

It was perhaps a fortunate circumstance for the officer, that the task of resuming arrangements for the journey did not leave any time to inquire into the reasons for this singular change in his official ardor. Activity again reigned, the guests trooped off from the deck down into the boats, and the brig was cleared for sailing. Only Larsson himself had time enough left to press his daughter to his breast, as he whispered something which implied that he would bring her elegant dolls and sugar-plums from Stockholm, in reward for her sagacity.

Esther probably felt nettled by promises of things which she thought she had long ago outgrown, for she blushed deeply, and turned away. Her father looked at her ; it seemed to him as though she had grown a head taller since yesterday. His under lip protruded, as was its wont when any important resolution was on foot, and after a little reflection he asked abruptly if Esther would like to go with him to Stockholm.

The bold little girl started, regarded him with dilated eyes, and immediately declared that it was of all things what she most earnestly desired, but had not ventured to ask. "And can I see the king? And the palace? And the handsome officers, with the plumes in their hats? And will I have a chance to look on when there is war ? "

The stern father frowned ; but the cloud went quickly past. " I promise that you shall see the king," he replied, "but with that you must be content. A sensible girl does not care about glittering follies. Remember, child, that you go not only to amuse yourself, but to learn something useful which you cannot learn here at home. I will put you in the best school ; you shall have a chance to learn more than many young ladies, and you shall do honor to your old father."

"I shall see the king! I shall see the king! " exclaimed Esther, who forgot, at this remarkable news, the trivial addition about the school. And in her rapture she immediately completed her idea : " I shall see Charles the twelfth ! I shall see war ! "

" *That*, I hope, by the power of God and the states, you will not see," said the father, smiling. " But it is time for you to get ready, child. Veronica, see to getting the child ready right away ; we have already had too much unnecessary delay."

" But, father ! " objected the sister, who now for the first time heard, to her great amazement, this unexpected news. " Esther cannot go just as she is. We must at least send home for her linen and stockings, and her black holiday-dress, and her new buskins, and her traveling-hood and riding-cap, and her gold chain ; and she cannot possibly go without her gray woolen gown, and she will need her sack on the sea, and the new veil she got last summer, and her lace ruffles, and her little work-box, and her New Testament, and her psalm-book, and her muff, and her pearl beads, and. . ."

"No— stop ! What a terrible jargon ! Why didn't you think about it before? But of course the child ought not to take cold. So hurry to town, and get what is most needed, but the finery may as well stay at home.... Well, that is to say, you can bring the gold chain along, and the pearl necklace, and the rings ; she must not look like a beggar-child, and it costs money to buy all these things new. And see here, Grenman, you go with Veronica, and send the child a few raisins and almonds from the shop, to eat on the journey. Look well to the servants, man, and do not sleep without a light. Give the servants only a moderate amount of whisky, so they will not become unruly ; and be sparing of the tobacco, Grenman,—it is enough if folks get a couple of leaves at a time, on a bargain when the tar is thick and the barrels good measure. But," and this was whispered, "keep an eye on Blom, that he does not overbid us, and if you observe any signs in that direction, then do not mind a measure of salt or a couple of clay pipes, to keep the peasants in good humor. And do not measure any more camlet and calico to the girls than to the old women, you fool; and see that the boys do not get into the licorice drawer. Wait—we need at least fourteen hundred dozen planks for harvest-time ; it makes no difference

if Blom has to wait.   Look after the hop-yard, and be
sparing of the spices : more than one ounce of ginger
ought not be used at the table in a week.   And one
thing more : If the prefect or his people ask for credit
at the store, answer politely, but plainly, that it is not to
be thought of.   I know those grand gentlemen from
the reign of the late king ; they have helped themselves
in war so long that they have forgotten to pay in
peace.   But if the young man Bertelsköld does not
happen to be in funds, for the time being, and has a
fancy to try our Flemish cloth or our Spanish wine, do
not be strict with him ; he has good paper and can
pay twenty per cent. for credit, and — well, God be
with you, my dear Grenman ! It is time you take yourself off."

At the close of this confidential counsel, expressed
half-aloud, Esther suddenly became attentive and
thoughtful.   She sprang down into the only remaining
boat, which was to convey her sister to town, where she
conversed earnestly, and in a low tone, with the same
man whose countenance had had such a singular effect
upon Fiscal Spolin.   The old boatman shook his head
several times in a dissatisfied manner, but finally seemed
to yield to some importunate demand, and was heard
to mutter something about willful children having their
own way.   The conversation was soon interrupted,
however, by Veronica and Grenman, who descended
into the boat, which, after Esther had climbed on
board, quickly withdrew from the brig.

CHAPTER XIII.

RESULT OF THE ADVENTURE IN LILLKYRO FOREST.

IT is now time to return to a captive whose fate has perhaps inspired some unnecessary apprehensions, and we will therefore seek again the burial-cairn in Lillkyro forest, where Count Charles Victor Bertelsköld so unexpectedly found himself shut up within the mountain cavern.

For a hot-headed young man, whose patience rarely extended farther than from the hand to the sword-hilt, this involuntary captivity was a good lesson in the art of waiting. Not, however, without considerable resistance did he accept his loss of freedom. After convincing himself that the cave had only this one entrance, which he could reach only by the ladder, he undertook to try, by means of an iron bar found down below, to break the slab of stone which covered the opening. This seemed to him not impossible : he had inherited some share of his father's uncommon physical strength, and although his position was extremely uncomfortable, the slab yielded by degrees, so that a beam of daylight flickered through the aperture. A few more efforts, and he could thrust his arm out through the orifice. His impatience increased ; he pushed against the stone with all his power. But this was one tug too much for his frail foothold ; the 'ladder broke under his feet, and he was precipitated with its fragments down into the cavern.

Luckily for him, his perilous plunge resulted better that might have been expected. Glad to find arms and legs still left him, the young warrior arose and began to reconnoitre. All hope of reaching the opening

by his own efforts was now lost; and the gleam of
daylight at the top seemed only to mock his fruitless
anger. He was thus obliged to submit to his fate. He
went to the fire, now almost out, and succeeded in re-
lighting it. By its glow he found a coarse cake, a box
of butter and another of salt fish. To one who had
been roaming all night in the forest, such a discovery
is not without its advantages, even if one has never
been in the field ; and Bertelsköld was not scrupulous
about making the best of the meal. It was excellent ;
and the vein of spring water in the cleft of the rocks
served as a relish. Nothing but good company, and
the prospect of soon being free again, was lacking to
make this situation fully as supportable as many he
had known in the bivouac. With hunger appeased, his
careless and youthful disposition reasserted itself, and
without troubling himself particularly about his future
fate, Bertelsköld threw himself down on one of the
furs, after which, wearied with the toils of the night, he
soon sank into a calm and refreshing sleep.

He had probably slept a long time, for he felt perfectly rested, when he was awakened by some one
tramping over his feet. He sat up, and saw beside
him five or six men, directing upon him the light of a
crackling torch.

His first impulse was to seize his weapons ; but
they were not to be found. The sword had been withdrawn from the sheath, and the pistols which he had
laid beside him were no longer there. He did not
reflect long, but sprang up, seized the iron bar which he
had used in his unsuccessful attempt to break through
the stone slab, and placed himself with his back against
the rocky wall.

All this took place so quickly that the new-comers
did not even attempt to hinder him. They alternately
looked at him and at each other, and seemed at a loss
to decide what to do.

Finally one of them stepped forward, and began

questioning the stranger as to who he was, whence
he came, and what was his business in the mountain
cave. Bertelsköld replied, without hesitation, that it
was no matter who he was ; he came from Wasa, and
was looking for a person named Lauri, or Laurikain,
whom he supposed was to be found in this cave. When
he had desired to leave the place he had found the
exit barred ; and now if they would help him find the
person he was seeking they might expect a generous
reward.

This reply led to a consultation, which was carried
on in low tones ; and Bertelsköld now observed that
one of the strangers wore his pistols, another his
sword, and that the rest were armed with axes, to say
nothing of the common knives which all, according to
the custom of the place, wore in leather belts at their
sides.

The man who had first spoken now took up the
conversation again, and plainly declared that they well
knew with whom they had to deal—that it was with
the Swedish provincial fiscal who had made inquiries
the evening before at the parsonage. He, the provincial fiscal, had now stolen in here to spy out their business and capture Lauri ; but it was more easily said
than done ; he would better say his prayers, for they
were not such fools as to think of letting him out to
inform against them, and he would scarcely get out of
there quite as sound as he came in.

Bertelsköld coolly answered that he was not the
one they took him for, but a lieutenant in the service
of the crown, and they would have to pay dearly for
it if they harmed a hair of his head. He did not intend to inform against them ; but he cautioned them
against making too intimate acquaintance with the
iron bar, for it might disagree with them very seriously.

Secretly, the young warrior was not quite as much
at ease as he assumed to be. He could not hide from

O   9*

himself that he had to deal with one of those remnants of the lawless times of the great war, against whom prefect Count Frölich, who knew his people, had warned him before he set out on his adventurous jaunt,—old-time freebooters, lapsed into savagery, who had no desire to submit to the civil order of things, but continued to roam the forests and apply themselves to forbidden trades ; in a word, the after-effects of the irregularities of a long and terrible war, which required generations in which to become once more calmed and brought to order,—just as the swelling of the sea, even long after the storm has ceased, continues to break in foam against the shores.

His threat had probably not failed to produce a certain impression, for a new consultation began among the attacking party. But the result was not very tranquillizing ; for the torch was thrown to the ground, leaving a twilight in which the clicking of the locks of the two confiscated pistols plainly indicated that the strife was soon to take a more dangerous turn. No time was to be lost. Bertelsköld seized his iron bar with both hands, resolved to throw himself upon the bandits, and rather venture a battle alone with them all than unresistingly to allow himself to be shot down with his own weapon.

But before he had time to take this desperate step, the result of which was more than doubtful, against ruffians so familiar with all kinds of skirmishes, the faint sound of a little whistle, or so-called grouse-pipe, which hunters often take with them into the forest, was heard near the entrance. The men seemed surprised, but after some hesitation they answered the signal in the same manner. The aperture was then immediately darkened, and a man in a gray jacket climbed down a rope which was hanging from the entrance to the bottom of the cavern.

" What have you done with the strange young nobleman? " inquired the new comer, in a stern and commanding voice, as, coming from the bright day-light, he could not immediately distinguish objects below.

"Hallo, comrade! If you are a good and honest man, then help me chastise these miscreants who have stolen my weapons!" exclaimed Bertelsköld, as he struck the iron bar against the rock, so that the sparks flew.

"Are you there?" responded the man. "I hardly thought that any one who did not belong to the trade would have remained alive ten minutes in the grave-cairn. Antti, give the sword back to the gentleman;—Mört, give him the pistols! I will be responsible for him!"

The bandits seemed inclined to disobey. They angrily muttered something about the folly of letting the bloodhounds of the government thrust their noses into their hiding-place.

"What now?" roared the man in the jacket. "Have I not said that I will be responsible for him? Give the weapons back, or the devil take you! Are you not ashamed, you cowardly hedge-creepers, to steal in on a man who acted his part so ably yesterday against the pitch-jackets in Larsson's yard?"

"But the soldiers took sides with him—he belongs to the sneaks!" stubbornly and fearlessly objected one of the assailants, who had probably had something to do with the crowd in Wasa.

"It is not true," continued the man in the jacket. "I saw him throw one of the soldiers down-stairs. . . . . Get up some kind of a lie for them, and for God's sake don't breathe a word about your rela-tionship to the prefect!" he whispered at the same time, in Swedish, to Bertelsköld, in a tone which evinced that he apprehended mutiny.

But this caution had the opposite effect from that intended, by exciting the pride of the young nobleman. "I have told you scoundrels," he exclaimed, "that I

shall not inform against you ; but know that I live
with the prefect, and am his kinsman ! "

Now the tumult rose. " There ! do you hear that !
And it is you, Lauri, that he is going to arrest ! " At
the same instant one of the pistols was discharged so
near that it singed Bertelsköld's dark hair. The other
was aimed scarcely three paces from his head, but the
arm which lifted it was met by a blow from the iron
bar, and dropped the pistol to the ground, where it
exploded.

The strife would undoubtedly have been bloody, if
the person called Lauri had not, with great danger of
being hit by the axes and knives which were being
brandished in the dim light, thrown himself between the
combatants. " Madmen ! " cried he to the furious
assailants, "have you never heard of the Strong
Major ? "

That name had a wonderful effect. The blow that
was aimed did not fall ; yells and oaths abruptly
ceased ; the bandits seemed to hesitate.

Lauri did not neglect his advantage. " Cowards ! "
he exclaimed, " in the Major's time, we stood one against
six ·fully equipped men ; and here you stand six
against one, after you have taken his weapons ! If
you had the least honor in you, you would bear the
son of Major Bertelsköld on your shoulders ! "

"Is he the Strong Major's son ? " muttered the men,
with evident embarrassment.

The " Strong Major " was the name by which
Gösta Bertelsköld was known in these regions, and
the name under which his exploits continued to live in
memory at the time of this story.

" I tell you that it is his son," continued Lauri ;
" and if you knew why he came hither, you would
thank me for preventing you from committing the
greatest blunder of your whole life. He has come
hither, boys, to get us something to do. He will give
us war."

No sooner was this said than all was changed. The murderous weapons fell from the hands of the bandits; these desperate outlawed men now crowded around the young warrior, to press his hands, to beg his forgiveness; and the one whose right arm hung maimed by the blow of the bar, sobbingly extended his left hand, that he too might receive pardon from the one whom they had so nearly sacrificed to their revenge and fear.

"Young gentleman," said Lauri, with a peculiar expression of simple dignity, addressing the one who, touched and astonished, was the object of these unexpected demonstrations of affection, " you will, perhaps, sometime leave behind you a son. See that he inherits from you a name that will make the weapons fall from the hands of his foes, and will be capable of warming the hearts of posterity ! . . . . But come," he whispered, "it is time we leave this place ; you are sought for everywhere, and I do not care to have the hounds seek you here in the grave-cairn."

At these words, all betook themselves to the entrance of the cave, where the dependent rope served them for a ladder.

CHAPTER XIV.

ISTVAN'S ADVENTURE.

WHEN Count Bertelsköld ascended out of the cave in the burial-cairn, the sun had already passed its meridian. What delightful emotions to a young mind to arise from the damp and chilly darkness of the interior of the earth, as though from a grave, to the bright sunshine, to spring, to freedom, to life, to the fresh air and the songs of birds in all the boughs! The impression was so powerful that the young warrior offered up a silent thanksgiving to the Lord of all things for freedom and life; for no stormy scenes, no temptations of the already beginning infidelity of the period, had been able to efface from his heart the prayers taught him in his tender childhood by his mother—she who in the crucible of adversity had learned to fear God. A child's prayer is thus the vein of a fountain in the earth. Winters snow over it, and the rocks lie heavy on the sand; but that hidden vein courses its way, and the grass above it grows green in the dew and sunshine.

Bertelsköld's first inquiry was for Istvan. The faithful servant had disappeared. Neither Bogatir nor the guide were to be seen. . . . . But instead of imparting the information which Lauri succeeded in getting from the men, concerning the fate of the missing ones, we will go back in our story to the time when the servant saw his master descend into the cave while he remained standing at his post at the foot of the grave-cairn.

He had not remained long on his double guard, one hand on the horse's bridle, the other on the boy's neck, when he observed a horse and cart, escorted by eight men, toilsomely making their way through the rugged forest. The men seemed surprised to see a stranger by the grave-cairn, and four of them separated from the rest, worked their way straight toward Istvan, and offered him a flask of whisky. But they had to deal with a man who had stood at his post a hundred times against perils and foes. Istvan calmly drew one of the pistols out of the saddle holster, and thus awaited the arrival of the strangers.

The four evidently did not like this sight. They stopped to deliberate; then separated and approached him cautiously from four different points in a manner which no longer left a doubt of their hostile designs.

Istvan used his disadvantageous position as wisely

as he was able, placed himself with his back against the horse's side, and cocked his pistol. Unfortunately this maneuver compelled him to let go his hold on the boy's neck, and no sooner was this done than the crafty changeling crept under the horse's legs, and found himself at liberty. The attacking party gradually drew nearer, and the following short conversation took place:

"Comrade, will you take a dram in the chill of the morning?"

"Many thanks, comrade; will you take lead in pay?"

"See here! what is your horse worth?"

"The skull of a thief, if you really want to know."

"A pretty creature; how old may he be?"

"A little older, I think, than the rope with which you are going to be hung."

"Just let me see his teeth."

"Take care;—he bites!"

But the brave servant had no opportunity to continue the squabble longer. He felt something seize him by the legs and drag him down. Unprepared for this foe, which was no other than the same little gallows-bird that had perpetrated so much mischief during the night, Istvan tried to free himself from the entangling hold, when at that instant the men were upon him, and one of them threw a horse-blanket over his head. In the desperate struggle which ensued, the pistol went off, and notwithstanding the bravest resistance, Istvan was overcome and bound by these freebooters, who were evidently quite as experienced as himself in this kind of adventures. It was probably one of these, who, after having won the victory, was prudent enough to replace the stone over the entrance to the cavern.

In his impotent wrath, and unable to see or shout under the horse-blanket, Istvan felt the villains lift him up on Bogatir's back, after which one of them climbed up behind him and sped away with his booty at a speed scarcely to be expected in this rugged region.

After a time the captive's experienced ear detected, by the evener and softer hoof-beat, that they had entered on a trodden path, and the ride now continued with increased speed, without interruption, as Istvan thought, for about two hours. By degrees he perceived that Bogatir's strength, exerted during more than twelve hours' incessant toil, was nearly exhausted; and the idea that this noble animal, which was dearer to him than a human being, was at last to drop dead under this inhuman treatment, afflicted him much more than his own strange and inconvenient situation.

Meantime Bogatir's trot, which had been brisk in the beginning, was moderated, and he was finally allowed to stop, either because he could hold out no longer or the captive and his conductor had reached the end of their destination. Istvan was lifted off the horse, carried into a room, and thrown carelessly on the floor. In this position he remained lying about an hour, vainly attempting to get free. The only thing he succeeded in doing was to get loose from the blanket; and he now observed that he was in a bath-house, whose only daylight came from a loophole above, sufficiently large to permit the passage of a cat, but too small to leave his broad-shouldered body the slightest prospect of escape.

There was nevertheless something in this otherwise ordinary place which attracted the especial attention of the captive, and that was a cross, cut in the stones above the rudely-built fireplace, probably a remnant of Catholic superstition, the design being to increase the healing power of the bathroom (a very important matter to all Finns), and defend it against the mischievous influence of witchcraft. Istvan could not turn his eyes from that cross. It seemed to him as though he had seen it long before, and had bathed in this very place, red and warm with steam from the furnace.

with a tuft of young birch leaves in his hand, and surrounded by men and women in the same situation. While he was seeking to disentangle these dim remembrances, the same man to whom he was indebted for this involuntary journey entered, loosed his cords, and handed him bread, cheese and sour milk. Istvan's first inquiry was for Bogatir, and his mind was relieved when he learned that the faithful animal was indeed very tired, but otherwise in good condition, beside a crib of oats in the stable. The next question was what they particularly wanted of him ; and the answer he received was very short—that he was to close his mouth for the present ; it would be seen just what kind of a fellow he was when " Gray Jacket " came home.

Istvan kept his keen eyes on the door, but before any plan could be carried out, his adversary had left the bath-room and barricaded the exit. Nothing remained but to make the best of his meal, which was spiced with fasting, night-watching and toil. This being done, Istvan climbed up on the bench to see how this part of the world looked through the loophole.

He saw before him a long stretch of luxuriant grain fields, green with rye blades, and transversed by a broad river. On the bank of this river was a village, which he thought he recognized ; and close by the bath-house was a well, where he was sure he had some time helped in drawing water for the horses. Near this well stood an old crooked pine, whose low, shaggy branches formed an inviting seat ; and this not very unusual sight filled Istvan with wonderful emotions. His brown, inflexible and weather-beaten features were by degrees distorted to a grimace, half laughing, half crying ; and as he looked and looked again, and wiped his eyes, which were dimmed by unwonted tears, this impression became so strong that he finally threw himself down on the straw, and—not wept, that would be stating it too feebly ; he howled like an old

10

bear that has chanced into a trap and vainly struggles
to escape.

Poor Istvan! He now understood plainly that
some time he must have sat in that same crooked pine,
and thrown pine-cones at these same boys who now
came riding barebacked to the well ; but how and when
it was impossible for him to comprehend, he only knew
that it must have been very long ago.

His master, who arrived at the place some hours
afterward, accompanied by the singular man who was
called Gray Jacket, found Istvan immersed in so deep
a sleep that it required some strength of arm to recall
him to consciousness. "Come," said the confused
servant, staring before him, and mingling old memories
with new; "come, let us ride to the well and water the
horses! Father said I must not ride the colt, for it
kicks ; but I will ride Musti and take my little sister
Maja in my arms, and then we will fight with the
boys there by the pine-tree—and all seven brothers
shall see how strong I am—and there comes father
from the field and drives them all to the grain-kiln,
and—up comrades! St. Stephen! St. Stephen! the
infidels are upon us!"

"Wretches!" cried Bertelsköld, intensely angry.
"What have you done to my faithful Istvan? The
poor fellow has lost his reason!"

But Istvan had meantime collected his wits, and
sprung up from the couch. "Where am I?" he asked,
with undisguised astonishment.

"On Bertila farm, in Storkyro," replied the man
who was called Gray Jacket.

CHAPTER XV.

BERTILA FARM.

FOR fear the kind reader may regard this story as romantic and improbable, it can do no harm to listen to the following conversation between the young Count Bertelsköld and the person who was sometimes called Gray Jacket, sometimes Lauri, or Lauri-kain (Lauri the Lance), and who now took his companion into a little cottage, not far from the bath-house where Istvan had quite recently been assailed by such wonderful fancies. It should be remarked that the open-hearted and resolute bearing of the young nobleman during the two miles they had traveled together in the search of Istvan had considerably diminished the distance between him and Gray Jacket, while the name and memory of "the Strong Major" in connection with the friendly service in the grotto had knit a bond of confidence between the old freebooter and the son of his former beloved chief.

"Is this Bertila Farm?" inquired the young count, as he cast a curious glance around the unpretentious sitting-room, whose chief ornament was a rude portrait of Charles XII in a home-made wooden frame, while a couple of heavy rifles with a long sword and an old canteen hung in brotherly concord on the smoky wall, with an axe, a saw, an augur, and other implements of a more peaceful character.

Gray Jacket drew his bearded visage into a kind of smile. "Heighho, your grace!" said he; "this turnip-shell, which answers for an old freebooter, and which is always a trifle warmer than the hair-moss in the forest, is perhaps the smallest cottage on the Bertila place. My lord can look out through the window westward ; that is a neat bit of ground—four taxable farms, according to the old ground-rent book—and your grace might look all over Finland to find its equal for full-weight rye. This is all comprised in Bertila Farm ; it has been acquired, farm after farm, during the time of the Larssons ; and although the property has not yet recovered from the effects of the great war, it is still, all told, worth perhaps sixty or seventy thousand dollars to the brothers. Your grace may well look at the patch. of ground, as it is from here that your forefathers sprung and acquired their name. And people say that your grace's—let me see—yes, your great-grandfather's grandfather—that was it— became angry once at the mother of your grace's great-grandfather, and willed the whole farm to the Larssons ; every old woman in the village knows that ; but how it took place, according to Swedish law, is nothing to me. People say that ever since that time the Counts Bertelsköld, generation after generation, have been here once to look upon that which ought to be theirs, but only once in their lifetime, and it has always boded some great calamity to the country. The Strong Major was here last, and got the six Larssons to enlist under him. They all fell in a skirmish, and a few days afterward the battle of Storkyro took place. . . . . But what is the use of talking about last year's snow ? "

"On so large an estate there ought to be a residence of considerable size, and I see only small cottages," said Bertelsköld.

"Large estate ! " wrathfully rejoined the freebooter, with the common repugnance of the East Bothnian for estate owners in the country. "No such estates exist here ; the people here are peasants, who own the ground themselves, and the Larssons are too sensible to plough their fields in velvet jackets. There was a splendid farm here before the war, but it was ruined and much else with it ; and Mathias Larsson, the son of the burgher king, occupies the little red cottage which your grace can see a few musket shots from here, by the river. The rough garb of a peasant can find admittance through that door too."

"How did the burgher king come to undertake agriculture on so large a scale ? "

"Your grace must ask his nephew, old Thomas Larsson, who is lying in his grave. The old man was out of his wits at last, after his wanderings in Russia, to search for his boy whom the Cossacks dragged off one fine day, and who was never heard of afterwards. Lars Larsson, of Wasa, saw that there was business to be done here, and why should not a grain-jew export grain from his own granary, as well as from those of others ? It would of course be but loading with one's own powder. Now Thomas Larsson had three daughters living, and all the boys were gone ; two girls were married in Sweden, and ready to kiss the fur gloves of the burgher king for the eight thousand dollars which fell to their inheritance. The youngest daughter, Marie, is married to Löfving's darling, Elias Pehrson, of Munsala, and for such perch other hooks were used. Besides money, Elias received a small fleet-sailing schooner, just sharp enough in the stem to sail in less than a week to Dantzic, and that on Larsson's account; confound me, but that man does something for nothing. When this was well done, Mathias moved hither and began to cultivate all the wasted fields, until he once more got a hundred barrels of seed-grain, of the two hundred which were sown here in old times. As for me, I got the cottage to hold till the day of my death, for a trifling service which I did the old man in war-times ;—but that is nothing to the point."

"See here, Lauri, something is wrong about your comrades—the fellows there in the cairn."

"Ho ! what are you getting at ? Those are the boys who stole the turnips while we were beating the

Cossacks.   But they have not degenerated, and one must get a living some way."

" All those melting ladles and dies and other things down there in their creep-hole,—admit, man, that it is a handicraft which might possibly concern the police."

" Well ! bless my heart, why did your grace allow the scoundrels to believe that they had the provincial fiscal before them ?   Rumor has long legs, and before my lord was outside the gate the message had already gone to the boys in the forest to keep a good lookout, although that hole was the means of their letting them- selves be fooled by Fiscal Spolin."

" What connection could the fiscal have with those lawless freebooters ? "

Gray Jacket winked. " I will tell your grace some- thing," he replied. " When the king is out of money, he makes it of silver ; and he can afford to.   When Gortz was out of money, he made silver dollars of copper ; that, he could afford.   When brave boys in the forest get out of money they coin silver dollars of tin ; and they can afford to do that.   But when Fiscal Spolin gets out of money he coins his vile soul, which is not worth a bit of tin ; and he can afford to do that.   He repre- sented to the boys that he would help them smuggle their home-made dollars over to Sweden, and share the gain, you understand ; and as it was not the first time, the blockheads allowed themselves to be outwitted by the evil-minded brute.   Fictitious cargo, your grace ! First, Spolin had proof in the money ; and besides, he had an excellent opportunity to torment Larsson.   But he grew very long-faced when Esther got the advan- tage of him, for the little creature had chanced to see him that morning in the forest."

" So it was Esther Larsson who ran past me in the fog, and helped you steal my horses ? "

" Steal ?   I must beg your grace to speak with more respect of my god-daughter.   To tell the truth, she had gone on an errand for her father, in the evening, as in the hurry and excitement no other trustworthy person was found to send, and it was not the first time; she has her father's courage and judgment—the young witch. But the boys in the forest happened to make the mistake of snapping away her horse and attendant, precisely as they afterward did with your Istvan, or whatever his name may be ; and that was lawful, military strategy, your grace, as they every moment expected the provincial fiscal. The little girl had no desire to lose her horse so cheaply, and hunted up her godfather. I then took it upon myself to pilot her to town again, where the horses arrived in due time. But she is a Sunday's child, she sees more than others, and stood in awe of the dapple-gray. It has a delicate nose, your grace, for while we were riding the cursed creature pricked up its ears, turned squarely around, and shot off like a rocket, with the boy booby on its back. Oh, well ! People have their peculiarities, and animals have theirs. But we rode to town and arrived in time to help Spolin with the keg of silver. Chop me to pieces if I would put myself to the inconvenience of going out again and helping your grace out of the pinch, if the little girl had not begged me so persistently. But she will always have her way, though all Wasa, and her father in the bargain, should oppose her."

Bertelsköld remained for a moment silently by the fireplace. His thoughts wandered to the past. He bade Gray Jacket come with him, to the grave of the mother of his race, in Storkyro churchyard.

" That is well," replied the freebooter, "but so far as I know it is not much to see, for all people of quality are buried under the floor of the church, and the sexton hardly knows any longer where your grace's ancestors lie."

" My grandfather's grandmother and her father are buried in the northwest corner of the churchyard," responded Bertelsköld. " Look at this; I would not come to Finland without this drawing, which is pre-

served in our family, and which was made by my grandfather, when he visited Storkyro to buy grain, during
the famine of 1697."*

"Good! We will travel by the chart, then,"
replied Lauri; "but it is now forty-one years since it
was made, and human memory is like an exploded
cartridge, it smokes a little while, and then dies in the
morning dew, is trampled upon and forgotten."

Gray Jacket was right. When they arrived at the
churchyard, they sought in vain for the three gravestones which Bernhard Bertelsköld had sketched for
the remembrance of posterity. They had probably
sunk in the soil, or fallen down and been carried away
by heedless peasants. Gone was the monument of
the peasant-king; gone, too, was that of Larsson, his
old comrade-in-arms. Only one of the gravestones
still remained, so overspread with moss and dirt that
only its corner projected above the surface of the
ground. The descendant in the fifth generation raised
this neglected stone, and after scraping away the moss
he read on its face the letter E. It was the grave of
Emerentia, the mother of his race. Gone was all
memory of riches, of heroic deeds and worldly renown;
and only love, only the goodness of the heart, had survived. The purest and noblest of the three had lived
longest in memory. The gentle spirit of Emerentia
had for a century after her death guarded even the
insensible stone from forgetfulness and decay.

* " The Surgeon's Stories," Second Cycle, page 357.

CHAPTER XVI.

IN THE STATESMAN'S CABINET.

FROM the forests of East Bothnia we now transport ourselves, some months later than the
events last described, to the metropolis of Sweden. It
is late in autumn of the year 1738. A cold northeaster
is driving showers of snow and sleet over the streets
of Stockholm—the fitting accompaniment of the unrest
of the period. The impatient, unsettled, Viking mood of
the Swedes had now reposed for seventeen years, and
seemed to have slept enough, and accumulated new
powers, after the great exhaustion under the twelfth
Charles. A new race had grown up during the period
of peace—a race which remembered victories, but forgot what they cost; and this race was eager to make a
bustle again in the world. Young Sweden brooded on
thoughts of the future; it looked so infinitely changed
after these seventeen years, after the center of gravity
of the North had been shifted from the Mälar to the
Neva, and the giant of the East had awakened to life
and tasted the salty waters of two seas; it could not
bear to see itself transformed from a grandee to a
peasant; hero-dreams began anew to haunt its brain,
and it swore to overturn the new order of things.

But in order to do this, it was first necessary to
establish family government in its own house. This
authority had, ever since the change of government
and the peace of Nystad, remained in the prudent
hands of Horn and his friends. They must now retire;
and efforts had been earnestly directed to this end ever
since 1731. But the matter was not so easily accomplished. Those in power had on their side two who,

P

from old custom, added weight to the scale; and they were the king and the queen, who did not love them, who, on the contrary, had called them " night-caps," but who nevertheless had their reasons for depending still less upon the party struggling for power. And in the eyes of the people, Horn could point with just pride back to these seventeen peaceful years, during which the kingdom, with unexpected rapidity, had regained a part of its internal prosperity—that happy period which, even far into the storms and dissensions of the eighteenth century, was lauded by the old as good and golden times, when peace, freedom, unanimity, and piety, ruled the land.

The threads of the political skein of this period ran out over all the country of Sweden, and had been twisted as early as the diet election. They had by degrees been knit into a great net, in which it was desired to catch at one haul the king, the council, and the states. The fishes were surrounded, the fastenings made, and the draught accomplished. Those who pulled the rope were not seen. People saw only various swells in the billows of the time, and the gayly-colored trimmings of the great net, which flaunted the fine name—patriotism.

One morning, President Count Torsten Bertelsköld, the head of the state family, was sitting in his private office, on Drottning street, overwhelmed, as usual, with work and visitors. This man had the rare ability of attending to everything and everybody at the appointed time. He always had a few minutes of leisure for every visitor, high and low, each of whom fancied he appointed his own time; he was seldom seen to work, and yet he despatched everything, and had time enough left for evening parties at the court, and the witty French comedies at Count Tessin's. The secret of his efficiency was that he slept only three hours in the twenty-four, was extremely temperate in all his habits of life, and knew how in one minute instantly to regain what he had lost in another. The queen hated him, the king ridiculed him; Horn distrusted him. He had enemies in all parties, for he failed them all ; but all feared him and all needed him. Cold and selfish, he sat with a haughty satiric smile on his lips, like a spider in the center of his web. His features, always thin, had become more austere and sharp during the sixteen or seventeen years since we last witnessed his conspiracies; but the carefully-kept peruke concealed from all except his *valet* the fact that his hair had become snow-white, although he was nut more than fifty-six years old ; the black-velvet coat, with its gold embroidery and disproportionately wide cuffs, according to the fashion of the time, did not show the least grain of dust from the protocols, and the black-silk stockings which reached to the knee, beneath the yellow close-fitting pantaloons, displayed a pair of calves so well rounded that one might almost suspect the presence of a good quantity of wadding there. Indeed, if one closely observed his still youthful complexion, and the measured curve of his gray eye brows, one felt a suggestion of a skillfully applied cosmetic; but few were those who approached so near him. And this artificial youthfulness was not at all unusual in the court of Charles XII's successor, for Frederick I was himself an exquisite gentleman, and French customs poured in with the worldly breezes through the open windows of the new royal palace in Stockholm.

Before this distinguished gentleman, who sat in a plain but elegant writing-chair of mahogany inlaid with mother-of-pearl, stood a tall, stiff, straight old man, in a coat of blue cloth without ornament. His bearing had nothing of an entreating supplicant's, but was rather that of a man who demands a natural right; but the answer of the count indicated that he viewed the matter from a different standpoint.

"Be at rest, my dear Larsson," said the count to

him. "I have had the grace to present your humble
petition concerning free trade for the town of Wasa,
and his majesty has been pleased to take it into favorable consideration. But, as you know, the matter
depends upon the consent of the estates; and now, my
dear friend, it turns upon the merits you have there to
cite. I will tell you frankly that the conduct and
tendencies of the house of burghers are suspicious. It
is said that its members place their own interests
before the honor and welfare of the kingdom. The
house of burghers goes so far as to approve of the
treaty with Russia."

"The house of burghers desires peace, and thinks
it accords best with the true good of the kingdom,"
unhesitatingly replied the stern member of the diet
from Wasa.

"Very well, my friend, very well! I perfectly
share your opinion; but let us understand each other.
You know that the council, when it renewed that
treaty, overstepped its power. Law and justice, my
dear Larsson, go before everything. You have great
influence; you have a controlling power in your body
which you must use for the good of the kingdom. I
am sure that you do not approve of the proceedings
of the council; you will prevail upon your colleagues
to vote as they ought."

"Yes, your excellency. As they ought."

"And then, my friend, when you have voted for
the good cause against the despotism of the council,
it will be in order to give a merited regard to your
propositions—the staple-right, among others. Next
summer I am certain your ships will sail into the Mediterranean direct."

"But if I think the council has acted as it ought,
and vote accordingly?" coldly responded the member
of the diet.

"Well, what can I do? You will then have

forfeited the fortune of your town, and your ships will sail into Stockholm, as before."

"Farewell then, your excellency. I know now what Wasa has to hope in this just cause."

"Everything, my friend, everything; your cause is progressing admirably."

"I believe that also. When one acts according to his duty and his conviction, everything results well. Permit me only to tell you, sir count, that we merchants of East Bothnia export grain and tar, but we do not export our consciences, even though it might be to the Mediterranean."

With these words the burgher withdrew, with a stiff bow, which would hardly have been deemed sufficiently low in the presence of the burgomaster of a small town. The count frowned.

"Always obstinate!" he muttered. "Frölich is right; these shop-keeping princes begin to overtop us. It is high time that we check their presumption. The man must become ours; he carries two-thirds of the house."

He rang the bell. "Call in Plomgren," said he to the *valet.*

Plomgren entered. He was one of the most important merchants of Stockholm—wealthy, scheming, and not very scrupulous. He and his colleague, Kjerrman, both members of the diet, were the ones who most industriously manipulated the house of burghers in the interest of the Hat party.

"Well, my dear Plomgren," carelessly queried the Count, "how are matters progressing? I hope your wife and your coffee-sacks are doing well? People are beginning to drink a great deal of coffee in Stockholm. I suppose you have got the contract to furnish it for the court?"

"Your excellency has been so kind, and given his gracious assistance," replied that representative of his rank, with a bow which ought to have met the approval of majesty itself. "That is a trifling transaction—thirty-four sacks; but with economy one can get along, your grace, in case Kjerrman does not get the furnishing of clothes next year for the army."

"One must 'live and let live,' my dear Plomgren. Kjerrman, like yourself, is a man who is watchful of the weal of the kingdom; still, I do not quite see why he should get the clothing contract in preference to you. . . . . *Apropos*, how are matters in the house of burghers now-a-days? I have not had time to think on the subject for a long while."

"Bad, cursed bad, your excellence; pardon my boldness. There is one man in particular who plays false, and that is Larsson of East Bothnia. Your grace knows him: an obstinate royalist, a grain-jew, who is ready to break the neck of freedom if he only gets well paid for his seed-rye."

"You are right in that. He was here just now, and what do you suppose was his errand? He demands staple-right for all the northern towns. What says my good Plomgren to that?"

Plomgren turned pale. "Staple-right for the northern towns!" repeated he, with undisguised amazement. "Winds of heaven! Staple-right for those miserable northern boroughs! Is there no more justice, then, on earth? Staple-right for the commerce of Finland! Why, it would be the ruin of Stockholm."

"Undoubtedly; decided ruin. But what can I do? His majesty is said to be not averse to thinking of the matter; and who knows what the states may get into their head? There is a slim prospect for business, dear Plomgren, if the Finns begin to export their tar and lumber themselves, and perhaps begin to supply Stockholm with salt into the bargain."

"Impossible!" ejaculated the frightened merchant. "It would turn the world upside down! It would be all over with liberty; it would be the sure downfall of the kingdom ! "

" I think so, too; and although the matter does not concern me, I will see what I can do, if you continue to be zealous and do all you can to move the house of burghers. You can also find me some person from Finland—some one who knows the circumstances of that Larsson. It would perhaps do no harm to counterbalance his designs, or—what is your opinion ?"

" The robber ! The deceiver of the realm ! Yes— let me see: I know a man who came from Wasa a couple of weeks ago—Fiscal Spolin."

" Good. Send him to me at the first opportunity. I will think of your cloths, my honest Plomgren. Present my regards to your wife, and beg her to accept this little perfumery-case from Paris. It is the same perfume which the queen herself uses.''

CHAPTER XVII.

THE SPIDER AND THE GRASSHOPPER.

DURING the quarter of an hour following representative Plomgren's departure from the private office of the president, Count Bertelsköld, this gentleman had found opportunity to despatch four items of business—one of them being the appointment of two members of the diet, who were clergymen, to lucrative pastorates, and the other two being promotions for anti-government men in the house of burghers, one of whom was nominated as counselor of commerce, and the other as burgomaster. Private secretary Feldman was then sent out with secret instructions to secretary

Troilius of the body of peasants.   On the majority in the house of lords, his excellency could rely ; but one not altogether unimportant political power still remained to be won over to his designs — and this power was majesty itself.

There now entered, as if in response to a call, the king's favorite, at that time chamberlain, and member of the board of trade, afterward president, Broman, or *de Broman*, as this favorite did not neglect to write on his rose-colored perfumed French visiting-card. Since we last saw the *valet* and caterer to the private pleasures of Frederick I, his outer appearance as well as his rank had undergone a considerable change. He was now extremely fashionable and elegant, with a deportment in which the *parvenu* incessantly protruded from beneath the courtier's borrowed feathers, and gave him a kind of comic grandee dignity, which admirably accorded with his substantial and jovial figure. Broman, although no longer young, was what would in our days be called a *toujours* boy ; ingenious, good-hearted, prodigal, and ruined, but still never at a loss for money, for as Tessin said of him, " he could sell a hen for more than I could get for a Spanish horse," he borrowed money at twelve per cent., and, when necessary, on security of double the amount, which did not hinder him from loaning it to his friends at six per cent., with such success that the debts he left behind him amounted to nearly four hundred thousand rix dollars.   In a word, this man " only needed to own a Peru, in order to be the solidest, most magnificent and serviceable fellow in the world," and all these peculiarities made him the one favorite who succeeded, in the long run, in maintaining himself in favor with the fickle king.

President Bertelsköld received him with that air of familiar equality which so highly flatters all upstarts. This time it was not " my dear Broman," but " my courteous chamberlain," who was obliged to sit down, and converse awhile—in French, of course, although the chamberlain had never advanced far in that path— about the last ball at the court, and the new French dancers who were expected, about the proper cut for a masquerade costume, or about the latest novel of Mlle. Scudery. He was having such a good time, the agreeable count, that for the time being he had "nothing which could equal the delight of conversing awhile with this knight of the court, *sans peur,*" if not exactly *sans reproche;* and, besides, he wished to ask some good advice about the new landau which the president intended to order next spring from Paris. In reference to that, Bertelsköld was well informed. The chamberlain owned a carriage possessing the very peculiarities which the count desired ; it had cost him six hundred rix dollars, and he said he would give it up now with delight, if he could by that means do his excellence the most insignificant service. His excellence, on his side, consulted a price list from Paris, and found that the carriage he had intended to order would cost at least a thousand rix dollars ; so he would regard it a real act of friendship, if the chamberlain would give up his carriage for the same price. The negotiation was not long, for it was accepted on both sides freely. The bargain was concluded, and both had reason to be satisfied ; one had bought a useful vehicle, and the other had received money to pay his hungry lackeys.

Then, as though by chance, the count asked, "between friends," about their majesties' present opinion concerning the council. The chamberlain, with equal familiarity, replied that if the Caps were not in particular favor, the Hats were in still less, and that their majesties did not intend to involve themselves in all the entanglement about the possession of a power which . . . ."

"Which their majesties would rather retain on their own account," interruped the count, with a wink which

10*

one diplomat regards as sufficient to be understood by another.

But Broman was annoyed, and descended from his diplomatic *rôle*. "The devil take those who disturb his majesty's appetite with this cursed diet-wrangle!" he ejaculated, inspecting his shoe-buckle, while, with legs crossed, he lounged in the velvet *fauteuil*, as though it had been one of his own lackeys. He probably thought that his dignity required him not to incommode himself.

"And to that pious wish I answer amen!" resumed Bertelsköld. "But confess, Monsieur de Broman, that the council has treated her majesty lightly, not to say parsimoniously! Four hundred thousand dollars for the journey to Cassel—how ridiculous! I ask, can majesty be represented with such trifling sums? Can a king, with such an appropriation, worthily reward his faithful assistants?. No, monsieur; the government of the kingdom must be placed on another footing; you, with your talent for finance, perceive that, better than I. Ought we to tolerate Jews in the council-chamber? —Horn for instance, who never has money for the dignity of the crown, but always an abundance, when he himself wants to shine! Bjelke, who for four years has not given a ball! Peasants, who refuse to invite such distinguished persons as yourself to their stiff evening parties—you, the most agreeable man at the court, and who have thé good fortune to belong to his majesty's most intimate company! I will not speak, monsieur, of Count Hård, who allowed his son to make that epigram, you know, about your gallant adventure! You will find that such a government cannot long exist."

Chamberlain Broman was not one who blushed for trifles, but his blooming cheeks did not fail just now to take a higher color.

"Bah!" said he, with a *nonchalance* which became him admirably; "your excellence is pleased to flatter me. It is always an honor to me to be esteemed worthy a lampoon ; my gracious master and king amuses himself frequently with such things. That of Lieutenant-Colonel Coyet, for example ; what does your excellence think of that ! "

"Coyet ? " repeated the count, who had now come to the very point he wanted ; " what is it about Coyet ? Has he had too little or too much luck with the ladies? Sometimes both happen at once."

" I did not know your excellence was ignorant of a certain scandal, or rather a song, on the streets of Stockholm," responded the favorite, with vexation. " The virtuous Coyet recites his witty production before everybody who has patience to listen to it. There is said to be a memorial to the states . . . . "

"Yes, I remember now that I have heard some· thing about it. He urges that the servant-girl, Hagar, with her sons, may be driven out of Abraham's house. Poor Coyet ! I believe, *par honneur*, that he has killed himself in being witty ; it must have cost him a tremendous effort. In truth, he has not done his majesty a great honor in comparing him with the patriarch Abraham ; but whether Miss Taube finds herself equally flattered by the comparison, I will not de· cide."

" To mix himself in his majesty's domestic concerns—what the devil is all that to Coyet ? "

"That depends. *Our* virtue, Monsieur de Broman, can feel perfectly satisfied with his majesty's having allowed himself a marriage, *sub rosâ*, with Miss Taube; why not ? I know sovereigns who do not trouble themselves with so many formalities. But permit me to call your attention to the fact that Charles XII was a bachelor, and since that time there has been a multitude of people here in Sweden who have regarded one wife as too much, and two wives as a luxury. Her majesty is without doubt as sensible a lady as one can wish, of her years ; but nevertheless there are matters which even a queen does not willingly forgive her husband, especially if they obtain a certain *éclat*. And since Coyet conceived the unfortunate idea of likening her majesty to Sarah, who was no longer a beauty. I fear our gracious queen—you know she is thought to bear a family resemblance to her late royal brother."

"I can testify to that, for I have been threatened with more than one embarrassment by the gossip of the court. *Parbleu*, I make no secret of it, and besides, it has stopped with mere threats."

"You are right; what does not one suffer for his king? Nevertheless, it is you, Monsieur de Broman, who is to be the first victim."

"I? It is impossible. I am as innocent as a mummy in that whole love affair.

"Who would doubt it for a single moment? And yet—do you remember the fable about the lions that quarreled and made up again? It is you, my amiable and virtuous chamberlain, who will be the price at which our gracious king re-purchases his domestic peace."

The favorite blushed no more. The color left his face. "Your excellence may be right," said he. "What are your suggestions?"

"Well," continued Bertelsköld, as he resumed that tone of superiority, mingled with disdain, which, toward the close of this conversation, he hardly took the trouble to conceal, "I will save your precious existence to the fatherland. You will go immediately to the king, and tell him,—as though of your own accord you understand,—that Coyet's memorial is in the mouth of everybody, and that it will without doubt be presented to the states and cause an immense scandal, to say nothing of the fact that the king would be obliged to send Miss Taube out of the country, if his majesty does not give his unconditional assent and consent to the measures against the council. To the queen you will say—what you please. Am I understood?"

"Yes, your excellence," replied the humiliated favorite, with a much lower bow than before.

"Farewell, Monsieur de Broman! When opportunity offers, you can send me your carriage."

CHAPTER XVIII.

A MEETING ON SKATES.

AT the time of this story, the ancient island of Wallmar, or Waldemar, which afterward became so widely celebrated as the zoölogical garden of Stockholm, was for the greater part a hunting ground, consisting of rocky ledges, swampy lowlands, and beautiful foliferous forests, where the deer, destined for the balls of the king and court, grazed for the most part undisturbed by the proximity of the metropolis. As early as the year 1658, Charles Gustaf had given orders for the transformation of the island into a "pleasure garden;" and the Frenchman, De la Vallée, soon afterward designed one, from the well-known sketch by Hedvig Eleonora, after the Versailles model, with "fountains, avenues and parks," and other appurtenances. But the sun which was to unfold the verdure of the zoölogical garden had not yet risen. At the bishop's promontory the work had stopped; the period of Gustaf III slumbered far behind the gray cloud in the distance; no Blue Gate, no Valley of Roses, proffered anticipations of pleasure to eye or palate; and the material regulations of the time of Horn and Frederick I went on undisturbed on the shores of this island of the future.

After the removal of the fleet to Carlskrona, the admiralty leased its former possessions in these neigh-

borhoods.   Lodsach, an important merchant, then built
a dock on the southwestern point of the island, after
the best foreign models ; and this dock was at the time
of which we now speak the object of the admiration
and curiosity of all Stockholm.   It was therefore not
unusual, and was regarded as a fitting proof of favor,
that his majesty, with a part of the court, sometimes
honored the useful industry of the dock by a gracious
visit.

One night in the latter part of November, 1738, a
sharp frost—a presage of the approaching unusually
severe ·winter—had covered with ice both the salt sea
and the Mälar, near Stockholm, with the exception of
the river-course nearest the sluices.   This was followed by a calm sunny day, with continuous frost and
without snow ; an occasion that it was not thought
desirable to let pass without entertaining with a northern
winter-scene the French ambassador, Count St. Severin
d' Arragon, who was every way flattered, after the
so-called defensive alliance that had recently . been
formed with France, which brought into Sweden annu-
ally 300,000 marks, Hamburg currency, in subsidies,
for that war which was already in sight, although at a
far distance.

His majesty and the court, together with the
ambassadors, rode out in the forenoon in carriages, to
the zoölogical garden ; but the queen, irritated and in
bad spirits on account of Coyet's memorial regarding
her rival Miss Taube, and all the scandal which might be
apprehended from it, declared herself ill, and kept her
room.   The day's programme included an excursion
around the zoölogical garden in carriages, a visit to
the dock, skating on the salt sea, a hunt in the zoölogical garden, dinner on the dock at one o'clock, return
to the city at five o'clock, a ball at the court at seven
o'clock, and supper at eleven o'clock.

Everything passed off admirably.   The excursion
was magnificent ; the views, with a little hoar-frost in

the trees, were charming; the dock proved very interesting; the hunt cost the lives of four or five stags
"with noble wounds," and the dinner was found to be
gotten up with all that gastronomic talent which King
Frederick so highly appreciated. Times were different
now from the year 1725, when the good old chamberlain Düben ventured to entertain his king with the
household fare of the Carolinian time, and so much ado
was made over old sweetmeats and undrinkable wines.
King Frederick had since then given the most rigorous
instructions regarding his wine-cellars; and no count
on the banks of the Rhine could place on his table a
nobler article than he. And for that matter, there was
certainly no other luxury lacking, in that good old
period of hooped petticoats. How little Sweden
needed to wait for her Gustaf III, to get a share of
foreign finery, is already proved by Count Tessin's
complaint that he had seen parsons' wives strutting in
the streets with long silken trains (*à la robe trainante,*)
and assessors riding in magnificent equipages, with two
liveried lackeys on the back of the carriage.

After dinner, there came the race on skates. The
ice was smooth as a mirror, and sufficiently strong, if
one did not go out too near the current; and as a safe-
guard against all danger, the company was attended by
the lackeys of the court, who pushed long light sledges
before them. The cavaliers of the court showed their
skill to the best of their ability; and, for those of the
ladies who ventured out on the ice, there were small
velvet-covered chairs on runners, behind which a gallant
knight was always found ready to propel the young
beauty, and during the rapid journey to whisper the
most agreeable courtesies in her small, red, cold ears.

Among these gentlemen was Lieutenant Count
Charles Victor Bertelsköld, who in the autumn had
returned from his journey to Finland. His lady was a
young Countess de Lynar, French, and related to Count
d'Arragon. This vivacious child of the South was

beside herself with rapture at the ease, speed, and pleasure, with which she thus, for the first time in her life, glided forward over the polished icy way. She clapped her little hands, both from delight and cold ; she wanted continually to go farther and farther out on the resplendent plain, and history does not allege that her knight objected. It is possible that the mysterious conversation at the red, cold ear, had for them both an interest which made them forget how far they were wandering out on the ice ; and yet it was so far that they were already nearer the opposite shore of Danvik than the dock of the zoölogical garden from which they had set out.

At length, however, the young count halted, and proposed that they should turn about ; for he remembered that the stream from the Mälar side went nearer the southern shore. But Mlle. de Lyner objected to this. "See !" she exclaimed, " over by the other shore a woman is skating ! It would be a great pleasure to me to make her acquaintance and steal her art. See how skillfully she turns in a circle around that old duenna, who stands there so astonished, and is hardly able to keep on her feet ! "

From the crowd of spectators on the opposite shore who were watching the diversions of the court, a young girl in a close-fitting capote of pressed black flannel— a cloth which then constituted one of the first rudiments of Swedish industry—had really skated out on the ice, and there, moving in the most beautiful circles. showed a skill that won the admiration of her companions not less than of the French Mademoiselle. In her hand she held an iron-shod balancing-pole, probably from caution, to use in case the ice was too weak; but the little implement became rather a means of coquetry. Now she held the pole before her like a spear, now she swung it over her head, now she thrust it in the ice and pushed herself along with it like a racer, and now she ventured a bold attempt to jump over it, alighting on her feet with a dexterity which might have honored a rope-dancer. All her motions were at once so capricious and so graceful, that Mlle. de Lyner turned to her cavalier and asked him, somewhat sarcastically, if they had the ballet in Stockholm. " This little fairy is destined for a *danseuse.*"

" I venture to dispute that," replied the count; " first, because no one would presume to vie with the French in grace, and next because no *danseuse* would risk her feet in skate straps."

"*Mais si*," said the young lady, vexed by the contradiction; " be kind enough to skate a little nearer. We can easily settle the matter."

" I do not know as I ought to venture," responded her cavalier; " the ice may be weaker over there."

" What, my lord ! " exclaimed Mlle. de Lyner ; " I did not know before that the Swedes were capable of everything—even of being a little timid sometimes ! "

" Thank you for the compliment," replied the young count, nettled in his turn, " and if it will amuse you, I will have the honor of accompanying you in death."

With these words, he skated briskly forward, possibly not without the secret wish that the little piece of French rashness might receive a suitable lesson.

And indeed, they had scarcely gone a hundred feet farther when the weak ice suddenly broke under their feet, and lady and cavalier sank in the cold treacherous water of the sea.

"*Au secours!* I am dying ! " exclaimed Mlle. de Lynar, utterly terrified when she felt herself sinking. But her situation was not so dangerous, for the chair sledge was sufficient to support her slender figure. Count Bertelsköld was in much greater peril, while trying to keep the chair from capsizing. Every time he attempted to support himself on the edges of the ice, it broke under his arm. The spectators on the Danvik shore sent up a loud shout. The skaters and lackeys of the court became aware of the danger, and hastened in that direction. But they had a good distance of glare ice to traverse, and there are predicaments in life where one has not time to wait long.

The young stranger who had been the innocent cause of this mischance, had meanwhile approached the place, and with a sagacity equal to her courage, had resolved on a means of rescue. She laid herself down on the ice, approached the hole with great manifest danger to herself, and extended the balancing pole to the sinking pair. Fortunately, the ice supported her. The count grasped the pole, and with its help succeeded in keeping himself up, while with the other hand he clung to Mlle. de Lynar, who, wild with terror, was struggling to get free. Before any of the court had arrived to their relief, Bertelsköld, with the assistance of the proffered support, had succeeded in getting upon solid ice, and at the same time in rescuing his drenched companion in misfortune.

Mlle. de Lynar no sooner felt a firm foundation under her feet, than she began laughing, with the happiest humor in the world. At her feet she saw a pier-glass of the purest crystal—the polished ice—which reflected the forms of herself and her escort, in a condition too doleful not to produce a comic effect.

" Good heavens ! " she exclaimed, " you and I ought to be put on exhibition ! In Paris people would pay two sous for an opportunity to admire us as we are now."

But the count did not hear her; he had eyes only for the unknown, who with a spring had risen up on her skates, and was hastening away. He must have seen her before; and the maid-of-the-mist in Lillkyro forest suddenly rose before his memory. " Esther ! " he shouted after her; " Esther Larsson ! stop and let us thank you ! "

But Esther, if it was really she, did not allow herself to be stopped, but quickly vanished amid the crowd of spectators on the shore, where an elderly woman, with gestures of fear and reproof, was seen to receive her.

"Was I not right?" again exclaimed Mlle de Lynar, with gayety. "She *is* a *danseuse*, and the proof of it is that she has bewitched you, my dear count, with her *pas de glace.*"

Bertelsköld really felt something within him which resembled witchery. "She is a Finn, and all. Finns can bewitch," replied he, in the same tone. Secretly, he thought: "Is it possible that the merry child from Wasa has in these six months become one of the graces?"

CHAPTER XIX.

LESSONS ON THE HARP.

IF all the currents in the ocean flowed constantly toward the same point, navigation would be a simple study; and if all the desires in this world were directed according to the same compass, it would be no art to learn the lessons of life. But no course is so straight that a side-wind does not here and there drive the sails awry; and no character is quite so steel-like that not a spring presses unevenly in the mechanism. Life is full of variations of the compass; and this remarkable story bears witness to the fact.

Ever since the young Lieutenant Count Charles Victor Bertelsköld, in November, 1738, had again met Esther Larsson, the youngest daughter of the burgher king, on the ice between the dock of the zoölogical garden and Danvik, near Stockholm, on the occasion when both he and Mlle. de Lynar were indebted to her presence of mind for their lives, it was no longer in his

power to drive that rare and captivating image from
his thoughts.   Curiosity to become acquainted with a
girl whom capricious chance had for the fourth time
thrown in his path, seemed to him to be a sufficient
motive for trying to seek her out.   But, unconsciously
to him, his enthusiastic temperament, which was perhaps an inheritance from his grandfather Bernhard
Bertelsköld, had colored the image of Esther Larsson
with that mysterious luster which so powerfully charms
the youthful heart.   The pleasures of the court, the
allurements of noble ladies, and even the charming
French coquetry of Mlle. de Lynar, had all become
matters of indifference to him; and the time not
unavoidably taken up by conventionalities and the
duties of his office he now passed partly on the streets
of Stockholm and partly on the ice-covered shores of
the sea, in the hope of regaining some trace of the
little, self-willed, Finnish burgher girl.

This was not so easily accomplished; for he soon
found out that Representative Larsson lived alone in
an unpretentious apartment, up two flights of stairs, on
Köpman street, and that nobody knew a word about
his daughter.   Bnt the young count did not allow himself to be discouraged.   Stockholm at that time was
not so large that people could disappear in it and
leave no trace behind ; and so it was one day discovered that Larsson was in the habit, in the evening, after his work was done, of visiting a house on
Vesterlång street, where the wealthy Madam Sager had
her linen-draper's store.

Lieutenant Bertelsköld now suddenly discovered
that his linen wardrobe needed a considerable addition,
and at no place was there to be found such superfine
Hollandish handkerchiefs, such white linen from Norr-
land and Åbo, and such excellent German and Swedish and Finnish damasks, as at this very Madam
Sager's.   And as an agreeable young man, who never
disputes the price, but always pays cash down, and

always has a pleasant word about the excellent quality of the goods, the fair price, the elegant display, and perhaps even about the well-ironed cap which becomes the lady of the house so well—as such a young man is a welcome customer in all stores, it was not long before Lieutenant Bertelsköld had the good fortune to win the favor of Madam Sager, as she herself, according to the good old custom, stood behind the counter, selling goods, assisted by a one-eyed old maid, and a surly apprentice lad, who resembled the polished clerks of Stockholm about as a shaggy wolf-dog resembles a sleek-combed washed and perfumed poodle.

That Madam Sager was the widow of a member of the diet which had reformed the monarchy, laid the foundation of liberty, and helped King Frederick to the throne ; that she herself was an important personage, who hated tyranny and gave her powerful support to the free constitution; that (probably on this account) she had the good fortune to stand particularly well with the customers of quality, and daily、had visits, in her store, from counts, barons, and wives of the councilors of the kingdom ; that the Countess Tessin bought her bed-linen of her, and that the afterward bloodstained shirts of Count Horn, and other comrades of Charles XII, came from her stock ;—all this, and more besides, she had already found time to relate, at first acquaintance, while she was measuring off a piece of first-class linen, which was " fit for the king." Bertelsköld next found out that the mighty woman was of Finnish birth, and a distant relation of Larsson, "whom they call the burgher king, over there ; " although God knew, she added, that she had more trouble than honor from the relationship, since he had taken it into his head to quarter a spoiled child at her house, who drove her to her wits' end every day . . . . Here the garrulous madam suddenly stopped, and cast a glance toward the gate as though she feared some improper auditor. In

vain did the lieutenant make known that he had lately
come from Finland, and had messages of friendship to
Esther from her own neighborhood.   Madam Sager
tossed her head, as much as to say that such greetings
were useless trouble; and for that day, all further
investigations were fruitless.

But as early as the following day—for the new linen
must be constantly tried—Bertelsköld (after the old
woman had talked herself warm on politics, and, like a
righteous Cap, wished all the Hats in the debtor's
prison, if not in the " Rosechamber" seven days in the
week) found out that she had her hands full with the
many tutors with whom Larsson worried her on his
daughter's account.   Now came one who was to teach
the girl how far it was to Rome ; now another who
scribbled slates full of figures ; now a third who had
his mouth full of the histories of the old world ; now a
fourth who knew the art of embroidering trifles with
glass beads ; now a fifth who was to teach Esther
German ; now a sixth who taught her to ride worse
than a Turk, on the wild dapple-gray which she had
obtained of her father ;— in short, all possible useless and vain wisdom, except God's word and French,
for the Bible she read with her father, and anything
pertaining to French, Larsson could not endure ; that
was an invention of the Hats.   To be sure, all these
tutors and governesses were old people, with gray
hair,—though, God help us, not greatly better for that;
but now came the worst, for the father had got it into
his head that the girl ought to learn to play on the harp,
as that, he thought, was a righteous and godly art, to
which even King David, the man of God, applied himself betimes with so much fame.   And behold, in the
whole city of Stockholm there was no skilled instructor
in that—at least none of sufficient years of discretion . . ."

"If my small talent in harp-playing could be of
service to any one . . . " interrupted the young lieu-

tenant, himself somewhat embarrassed at this timid
proposition to a simple linen-draper.

Madam Sager measured him with an astonished
glance, and asked if he knew the burgher king.

"A little," replied Bertelsköld.

" If your grace knows Larsson," responded the honest woman, "your grace knows that King David himself
would not be a good teacher for the girl, if he bore the
title of count before his name. This is what I told
Larsson ; he ought to be sociable, like me, with high
and low, and measure the council of the kingdom with
the same measure which he applies to shoemaker-boys ;
that, I call trade, liberty in all honor, you understand.
But it is like fire and water this time—he can not tolerate the nobility, and yet wants to make a lady of his
daughter. . . . Did not your grace order napkins of the
same kind as Count Horn's ?"

Bertelsköld departed, but returned the next day.
He ascertained that Madam Sager had a son who
played the flute.

" Well, as to Calle," said the woman, when the tender chord had been skillfully touched, " he has all he
can do in his royal majesty's service, on the revenue
board. Calle could have become as good a linen-
draper as any one in Stockholm, and perhaps a little
more than that ; but he has a head, your grace, yes, a
head like four common people ; he knows Greek and
Latin, and French, when it comes to that ; and so I
thought there was a chance of his becoming something
in the world and the revenue board ; for I was enough
to attend to the store, and, thank God, he will have a
spare penny when many other distinguished gentlemen
are pawning their shoe-buckles. I always stand on the
side of liberty ; but, God bless the king, my son may
become assessor if he lives, and then—what if he plays
the flute ?"

" On the contrary," interrupted the count, " it will
always give him a certain advantage. With Count

Tessin, for example." (Count Tessin could not bear music.)

"Does your grace think so?" inquired the mother, with a sunshiny smile. "Perhaps your grace might be so kind as to put in a good word for Calle."

"Not only that, my dear Madam Sager, but I might perhaps, through my uncle, manage to have her majesty get a sample of those fine damasks . . ."

"Oh! what does your grace say? Would her majesty's high person be pleased to eat on my table-linen? And perhaps stop in front of my place with her royal carriage, when she goes out to Ulrich's dale?"

"Nothing is easier than that, if her majesty only gets a suitable signal. And as Calle plays the flute, you know upon occasion we might try the flute and harp together . . ."

"Your grace is pleased to jest . . ."

"Certainly not; one does not find a good flute every day. Perhaps Esther has more inclination to learn the flute than the harp."

"Such a person at guessing! If your grace has not hit the nail on the head, then I don't know the difference between kersey and damask. To tell the truth, the children have had a good eye for each other some time, and although Esther is badly enough trained, I do not doubt that with proper effort she may become a capable wife. And she would not come entirely barefoot to the house, either; so that—yes, if it pleases your grace, my humble house is heartily at the service of so courteous a gentleman, and your grace is perfectly welcome to bring the harp along. It may be as well as to hire a tippling old organist, for a quarter of rice an hour."

The young nobleman from the court of Frederick I smiled at the comparison, and accepted the invitation. Even the sharp antithesis possessed something enticing and piquant. On one side, his uncle, the president, the haughtiest aristocrat who ever looked with disdain upon the rabble beneath him; on the other side, Larsson, the most inveterate democrat who ever cried woe upon the power of the nobility; between them a shop-keeping woman, who vociferated about liberty, and was ready to kiss the hem of the nobility's garments; further, a child of nature, who was to be trained according to the newest fashions of Stockholm; finally, he himself, the heir to a brilliant name, coming direct from the court, that he might, in the midst of packages of linen, accompany Calle Sager's flute, for the pleasure of seeing a little burgher girl whom his uncle would hardly have thought worthy a place as waiting-maid, and all this under the risk that, if he was discovered, if he was suspected, he would be disinherited by the one and thrown out of the window by the other; in short, this situation seemed so delightful to the young lieutenant that he left Madam Sager's store with the heartiest smile that had flitted across his lips since the adventure in Lillkyro forest.

CHAPTER XX.

THE THREADS OF POLITICAL INTRIGUE.

ONCE more the course of this story takes us to the private office of the president, Count Torsten Bertelsköld, that secret center of so many intricate threads, which ensnared the diet and aimed at nothing less than changing the *personnel* of the government and the political system of the realm.

All was unchanged. There was the same marked order, the same choice elegance; not a grain of dust was on the statesman's fine velvet coat, not a disturbed

lock on his peruke, curled according to all the rules of
the art; not a trace of hurry in the heaps of carefully
filed papers, in the *étagères* of mahogany and ivory;
everything had an appearance of almost philosophic
calm, but a calm which coquetted and was intended
for appearance.   The large pier-glass, placed just
opposite the door, allowed every visitor, upon his first
entrance, to admire his own person.   The soft Flemish
rug seemed laid so that not the least creaking of a
silken shoe might interrupt the devotional silence of
the room.   A bust of Charles XI looked grimly at his
neighbors, the Louises of France, XIV and XV, who
in their turn looked down on a bust of the then all-
powerful minister, Cardinal Fleury; but on the taste-
fully ornamented pedestals the high-borne head of
Charles XII was sought in vain.   Count Torsten was
too proud to deny his antipathies, and one and all knew
that he belonged to the sworn enemies of the hero-
king.   One more pedestal was finally found, on which
one would have expected to find a statue of Frederick
I; but no—he had ceded his place to a French *danseuse*,
Mademoiselle Zoë.

It was eight o'clock in the morning, and the count,
who seldom retired before two o'clock, had been at
work since five.   Visitor after visitor was announced.
At one time, two tall and stately gentlemen entered.
The one, a military officer, affected to retain in his
costume some portion of the old Carolinian uniform,
which during the time of Frederick I had been displaced by the Prussian model, which, with its stiff
cockade, its powdered peruke, its long vests and knee-
breeches, was only an extremely emphasized copy of
the French uniform.   This gentleman wore riding
boots and gauntlets, and the long Carolinian sword, as
though setting out on a campaign.   His bearing was
bold and commanding, not repellant, but rather open,
generous, even knightly, although somewhat blunt.
When he spoke, it was with vehemence, as though no

contradiction were possible; but a skillful counter-argument confused him, and an artful turn quickly led his ideas astray. One could almost guess that the times had made this man a head taller than he really was; other times might come which would make him a head shorter again. His reputation was at its hight; he was the hero of the approaching woful war, General Count Charles Emil Lewenhaupt, sometimes called by his boldest adherents "Charles XIII."

The other gentleman was a middle-aged civilian, clad plainly, but with a taste and elegance which threw even the fastidious diplomat into the shade. Every inch of lace in his neckcloth was of the choicest quality; a pair of delicate frills shaded two of the whitest hands, which incessantly accompanied his discourse with animated gestures. And he talked like a master, this gentleman of grace and wit; only, when the conversation was carried on in Swedish, he constantly intermingled a refined French, which seemed to be really his mother-tongue. His manner showed the accomplished man of the world; his whole noble personality possessed something in a high degree captivating to the fancy of the multitude, and insinuating, for he knew how to yield with the greatest flexibility before opposite opinions, in such a manner, however, as to keep his own chiefly to himself. He seemed to appreciate his own importance as a reconciling link between the extremes of a stormy period—a function in which he perhaps overestimated his ability, for, outside the *salons* of the court, he betrayed a lack of firmness of purpose; and the Sweden of the year 1738, which had outgrown Lewenhaupt, at last prevailed over the high aristocratic republican, Count Charles Gustaf Tessin, speaker of the palace of nobles, also.

These three potent gentlemen—the cold, crafty, refined diplomat; the impetuous, knightly, but narrow soldier; and the intelligent, witty, but superficial courtier—were now, by the force of circumstances,

united under the same banner, to sway their fatherland. The conversation was carried on mostly in
French.

"I am charmed to see your excellencies at so
decisive a moment, when our native land needs more
than ever the support of valor and genius," said Count
Bertelsköld, well knowing that Lewenhaupt would
immediately advance from the common phrases to the
direct subject of consideration.

Tessin, however, came forward with a compliment
of a similarly pointed character. "Your excellency,"
said he, pointing to the busts, "is surrounded by
virtues so illustrious that we can hardly flatter ourselves
with being able to add to the collection. Cardinal
Fleury and Mademoiselle Zoë! That is drawing
inspiration from both this world and the next."

"You remind me, my dear count, that we have
neglected to consult the oracle about the next ballot.
Perhaps your excellency, who has the fortune to be
intimate with Assessor Swedenborg, will take it upon
himself to . . . ."

"Let us come to the point, gentlemen," put in
Lewenhaupt, impatiently. "We have only a few minutes at our disposal before the session. His majesty
is hesitating. The assent of England to the prince of
Hesse's succession to the throne pleases his majesty
better than the French alliance."

"Fortunately," resumed Count Tessin, "France
possesses something which is to King Frederick's
taste. His majesty is said to have given the cardinal
to understand that a few hogsheads of French wines,
prémière qualité, to the value of one hundred thousand
ecus, might have the greatest influence on the disposition of the same toward the kingdom of France. It
would be un-Christian of the cardinal to haggle over
such a bagatelle, when the welfare of Europe is at
stake."

"Possibly. But who guarantees us his majesty's consent to the removal of the councilors?"

"I," calmly replied Bertelsköld.

"May I venture to ask what makes your excellency so sure of a more than doubtful *consentement?*"

"Nothing is simpler. Coyet's memorial to the states, about Miss Taube, has produced the desired effect. His majesty wishes at any price to avoid scandal; and the anger of a queen still signifies something in Sweden.

"Accept my compliments, sir count," said Tessin, somewhat sarcastically. "You play chess like a master. That move has checkmated the king."

Bertelsköld answered with an easy bow. "Allow me," said he, "to count myself as an unworthy member of that diplomatic school in which your excellency, under the regent Orleans, won the doctor's degree."

"But, gentleman," resumed Lewenhaupt, annoyed at this war of words, "do you realize that there is a desire to buy us with Russian money? Bestuscheff has lately received six thousand ducats, which he has deposited in the bank. With that gold, he will buy half of our adherents."

"Oh, *fi donc!* Six thousand ducats! What a trifling sum for Swedish liberty!" exclaimed Bertelsköld angrily, while the cold scornful smile on his lips gave the words an intentional ambiguity.

"Have we then gone so far," exclaimed Tessin, "that the honor and conscience of Swedish men are bought with foreign gold? Gentlemen, I appeal to the ancient honor of knighthood. As speaker of the palace of nobles, I cannot permit the least taint of so gross a suspicion to fasten itself upon the reputation of the house."

"Allow me to make a little suggestion," resumed Bertelsköld. "Bestuscheff has rendered us a service which cannot be highly enough appreciated. As soon as he draws that six thousand from the bank, we will take care that the fact becomes known, and those who have the slightest fear of appearing to be bought will thus be compelled to vote with us."

"Which will not prevent people from saying we are bought with *louis d'ors*," objected Tessin, with a shrug. "Gentlemen, the house ought to be purified, and foreign gold once for all stamped with infamy."

"And what are subsidies but a purchase?" said Bertelsköld. "Is not Sweden sold, every day, to the highest bidder? To-day it is France, to-morrow England, the day after to-morrow perhaps Russia. How will a trade be prohibited individually, when it is carried on by wholesale through the entire country?"

"I think with his excellency, the speaker," said Lewenhaupt, "that a purification is unavoidable. The evil-minded must be silenced or expelled from the palace of nobles, the incompetent sent away, the militia called out, and pernicious books and writings forbidden. Otherwise we will never be sure of the vote, and traitors will have free play."

Tessin and Bertelsköld exchanged ironical glances at this strong interpretation of constitutional liberty. The speaker of the palace of nobles observed, very moderately, that an expedient might perhaps be invented which would not interfere with the right of opinion in a free commonwealth. According to the information he had obtained, the victory would not be uncertain in the palace of nobles, and the clergy always voted according to the opinion of the king. As to the peasants . . . .

"The peasants think like their secretary, and Troilius is a scheming fellow," responded Bertelsköld.

Tessin smiled. "That is to say that Pierrot always has to dance after Harlequin's pipe. So everything depends on the accidental humor of our Swedish Peter Shopkeeper."

"Your excellency is right. At this time everything

depends on the house of .burghers. Plomgren and Kjerrman are playing our melodies for the shopkeepers from morning till night, but so long as that headstrong Larsson cannot be moved, we have the house against us."

" Then send him to the devil ! " ejaculated Lewen-haupt.

" What can we do, my dear general ? We live in a free commonwealth, as his excellence, Count Tessin, so truly observed. The only plan I can see is to get the shopkeeper voluntarily absent ; and I have taken measures to that end."

"We rely on sir count. . . . . *Apropos,* how fare our young wolves in the privy committee ? "

" They begin to get claws and teeth."

" Then everything really depends on the burghers."

" And ultimately on Larsson."

" Your excellency is perhaps aware that that Finnish grain-jew is known by the name of the burgher king."

" I am glad of that ; two kings in a commonwealth are always better than one. We will dethrone the one with the other, and Sweden is ours."

CHAPTER XXI.

AN ATTIC ON VESTERLÅNG STREET.

THE house owned and occupied by the wealthy Madame Sager, on Vesterlång Street, was one of the oldest in the vicinity, and stood, in old-time fashion, with its gable to the street. In proportion to its humble length and breadth, it was quite high, and consisted of three stories, besides a high attic, with a steep slate-covered roof. The ground-floor was taken up by the store in front, a back room occupied by the bookkeeper, a kitchen, a store-room, and a room for the apprentice. The next floor was the story of state, consisting of four rooms, two of which were for the son, one was for strangers, and one for old Madam Sager herself ; but of the four corresponding rooms on the floor above, two were unoccupied and used as store-rooms for goods ; the third was occupied by the shop girl, Louisa, a distant poor relation, and, under her close watch, Esther Larsson occupied the fourth room, an attic with a view toward the east.

It was to this elevated sanctuary that the worthy woman, at three o'clock one afternoon, conducted her hopeful son, of the exchequer college, accompanied by young Count Bertelsköld, with the praiseworthy intention of procuring her young *protégée* that musical instruction which her father had wished, and which, as we remember, was to consist of lessons on the harp. The good woman probably had a certain apprehension about permitting musical click-clack down on her own floor, where Esther took the rest of her lessons, as it might occasion gossip among the neighbors ; and, furthermore, Madam Sager was cautious and careful enough about her *protégée* not to allow any one to enter the attic except in the personal presence of herself or Miss Louisa.

It was now for the fifth or sixth time, and with constantly lighter step, that Count Bertelsköld ascended the steep staircase. Before him flew Esther, light as a bird, two or three steps at a time ; at his arm climbed the lady of the house, extremely flattered by that honor; but the son, of the exchequer college, had from some unknown reason stayed away, and so there was need of all that favor which the courteous young gentleman succeeded in winning from the party concerned, in order to prevent this break in the trio from putting an end to the lesson. The good woman was not without misgivings, as would appear from the conversation, or, more correctly, monologue, in which she indulged during her difficult ascent of the stairs.

"It is not that, your grace," said she, "it is not that, bless me! I have eyes, and know how to distinguish an honest young man from a titled boor, who turns the heads of simple burgher folks; but I doubt if my late husband, who had a hand in establishing liberty and King Frederick's crown, would have allowed so fine a young gentleman to visit Esther in her own room, even in my own presence,—for your grace may well suppose that we are careful of our good name, and God save the king, of course, but God save the daughters of the land, too, from royal majesty's gracious glance. ' Like master, like servant,' says the proverb; and it is not long ago that it was only by good luck that Marie Larsson got happily away. . . . Well, I will say nothing; and your grace knows that my son, of the exchequer college, is as good as engaged to Esther, and of course it can not injure his chances for promotion to play the flute, can it? Bless me! Where can he now be keeping himself, when your grace has done us this honor! But I can well understand that there is much to write. Calle has such a beautiful style—it is he who writes the title of our most gracious king in addresses. . . . Whew! that is a steep stairway, your grace; the house was built in King Gösta's time, and the Sager family have been born and have died here. But now we are up. Louisa, see to the store, while I keep his grace company, and keep an eye on Malenius, that he does not measure too much bed-linen, in case the queen's waiting-maid should come in. Annoyance and trouble one has with store-help, and there is nothing but negligence now-a-days with young folks;— they are all smitten with the people of quality; . . . . but how it is with liberty and bed-linen, I will not undertake to tell."

They had now arrived at Esther's attic. It was a long, high, antique room, which, with its single window,

R   11*

would have been extremely gloomy, if it had not commanded the most beautiful view of the entire palace hill, the wharf, and the sea. This single window possessed a remarkable peculiarity, concerning which Bertelsköld several times ventured to throw out a question, but without obtaining any answer except that it was a relic of " old times." The panes were enclosed by a strong iron lattice ; and it was probably to escape this odious sight, that Esther, capricious in everything, had placed before the window a peculiar kind of houseplant, a young pine, growing in a large wooden box. The free-born plant of the forest did not appear to suffer from this prison-like environment; the pine thrived well, and spread out its shady branches before the window and the iron lattice, with such success that the room, even in broad daylight, was half-dark.

" Esther, do take away that ugly tree ! Why, people can hardly see each other ; and when his grace is kind enough to take the trouble to come here for your sake, child, he ought at least to see your fingers on the strings," grumbled Madam Sager, in bad humor over the absence of her son.

" Your pardon," replied Esther, meekly, but very decidedly ; "that is my forest, the only one I have, and if it does not have daylight it will wither."

" Let the tree remain," interposed Bertelsköld. " It is an old rule that music lessons always go best in twilight."

" Well, if that is the case," responded Madam Sager, as she took out her knitting-work, " your grace understands such matters better than I..... Where can Calle be loitering ? But perhaps, child, you will begin with that psalm which father thinks so much of—number three hundred and fifty-four."

Esther gave a few fine touches to the large pedal-harp which stood in the room, and was just opening her lips to begin singing, when Miss Louisa, somewhat startled, put her head in at the door.

"Dear mother ought to come down right away!"
she exclaimed. (Instead of the modern title of Madam,
the good old "dear mother" was still used at home.)

"What is the matter?" inquired the mistress, as she
laid away her knitting-work.

"Dear mother ought only to come down right
away," was the reply.

"It is probably the kitchen chimney burning out
again, although we pay two plåts a year to the chimney
sweep," muttered the old woman. "It is always so;
nothing but annoyance and trouble, and times are continually getting worse and worse. Louisa, stay here
till .... beg your grace's pardon ...."

With these words she disappeared. The count and
his pupil suddenly found themselves alone in the half-
dark room, where, moreover, the November twilight
was rapidly beginning to creep in.

A pause ensued. Bertelsköld had hitherto treated
Esther like a capricious child, and a kind of fraternal
intimacy had arisen between them. But now, for the
first time alone with the wild sylphide, who had become
a half-year taller since their acquaintance in Finland,
the count was for a moment speechless.

Guided by that fine instinct which never fails the
child of nature, Esther touched the strings, and began
to sing—a whole long verse of a psalm, fresh and clear,
as though she was singing to the pines of the forest.
The count listened. There was something in that
simple and touching melody which softened his heart.
This was what Esther sung:

"If trees of the wood and grass of the plain
    Had each both a voice and a tongue;
If birds and wild beasts could vie in their strain
    With songs that the angels have sung,
Meet praise to our Lord, on their loftiest refrain,
    Not yet through the heavens had rung."

"One more verse, Esther, one more verse!" It
seemed to Bertelsköld as though he was listening to a

captive bird, singing in its cage, of the freedom of the forest.

And, as though the young girl had divined his thoughts, she immediately took up the following verse :

> " Oh, high is the flight of one wee bird to-day;
>   The tempest but bears up its wings;
> It praises its God, and is blithesome and gay,
>   As over the mountain it swings.
> And thus 'neath the valleys and groves on its way,
>   The pure joyous rivulet sings."

The song was hushed. "Tell me," said Bertel-sköld, pursuing the former tenor of his thoughts, "how did your father have the heart to shut you up in this gloomy cage? And what does that thick iron lattice mean, in front of your window . . . . you, who, more than other beings, live on liberty and light?"

Esther laid her finger on her lip, and pointed toward the outer room, as though she feared some one was listening.

Bertelsköld opened the door. "There is no one there," said he, artlessly.

"Then I will tell you," whispered Esther. "Many years ago, a crazy girl lived here, a relative of the Sagers. She loved a grand gentleman, and was deceived—that is the whole story—and it is a very common one, Louisa said. But she did not allow herself to be shut in by the iron grating, of course. She jumped out."

"Jumped out? From the third story?"

"Of course. What would she do here?"

"But it is a terrible hight—over fifty feet, and the yard below is paved with stone. She must have been crushed to death!"

"Yes—oh, yes! Indeed, that was not such a very fearful thing. You know she had been deceived."

"Do you think of jumping out of the window, too?"

"That depends. Perhaps so, if I get very melancholy."

"Who would have the heart to make you melancholy?"

"Well, then, I can jump out for fun."

"Fortunately, the grating is strong enough."

"Now I remember something. Will you promise me one thing?"

"What is it?"

"To let me see the king and queen, close by. You know I have wished it a long time. And day after to-morrow there is to be a masquerade at Count Tessin's, and the royal family will be there; one of the waiting-maids told Louisa so yesterday. Will you promise to take me to the masquerade?"

"No, my little one, I cannot promise you that."

"Why not?"

"Only the court and some of the members of the diet will attend."

"But if I wear a mask, like all the others?"

"Not even then. You are a large girl now. Your reputation would suffer, and that would make me sorry."

"Good-bye, then! Give my best respects to Madam Sager!" and with these words, before the astonished youth comprehended her intention, she had disappeared behind the pine. The iron lattice rattled, the glass clinked. Bertelsköld sprang to the window.

His first thought was that Esther had hidden behind the pine. She was not there. The lattice, fixed in a frame on hinges, was bursted open, and two panes shattered. Esther had jumped out of the window.

The young count was not easily terrified, but when he looked out at the giddy hight, and saw the stone-paved yard beneath him, but no trace of the wild girl, his heart began to beat violently.

"Esther!" he shouted.

No answer.

"Esther!" he continued; "naughty girl! Speak one word, to say that you are alive! Do you wish to kill me with anxiety?"

"Am I going to see the king, or what will you do?" sounded a fresh merry voice, quite near his ear. Bertelsköld looked around. The window was furnished on the outside with a massive iron-plated shutter, which was thrown open against the wall. Esther was holding fast to it.

"Come in instantly, or I will alarm the house!" exclaimed the count, really angry.

"Am I to see the king?" repeated the willful girl.

"No, you are not. And if you do not come back immediately, I promise you that your father shall know your foolish trick."

"Indeed! So I am not to see the king?" continued Esther, in an indifferent tone, as she removed her right hand from the shutter, placed it petulantly at her side, and, hanging over the abyss, held fast by the left hand alone.

Bertelsköld's brain reeled; but he resolved not to yield. He supported himself on his left knee, threw his left arm around the window-post, reached forward as far as he could, drew the window-shutter to him, and with the right arm seized Esther around the waist. A singularly dangerous struggle now ensued between the two. Esther in her turn became angry, and struck about her like a furious child. But she had now found her master. Bertelskold drew her in through the window, and fastened the iron grating.

Then she struck him in the face.

The cheeks of the youth colored with anger. Esther ought to be punished;—he kissed her.

She bit his cheek.

Bertelsköld was now ashamed. He, a man, had allowed himself to be transported with anger by a willful child.

With his cheek still bleeding, he **took the harp,**

swept a few rich chords from its strings, and sang the third verse of the three hundred and fifty-fourth psalm:

" Oh glorious God, three persons in one,
　With the host thy bright Heaven within,
　Defend us this day, and till life's day is done,
　From the mocking allurements of sin ;
　That Satan's envy, with time begun,
　May never the victory win."

It was almost dark in the room. When he began to sing, Esther stamped her foot on the floor. When he had ceased, she had leaned her head forward against the window, and was sobbing aloud.

CHAPTER XXII.

THE MASQUERADE.

IT was not called a masquerade—it was only a *petite cèrcle*, a *soirée* in costume, at the residence of the speaker of the palace of nobles, Count Tessin, and his lovely countess. But few were invited, hardly two hundred persons ;—King Frederick, Queen Ulrica Eleonora, the *elite* of the court, the diplomatic corps, and the high aristocracy. Still, his excellency, the speaker of the palace of nobles, certainly not without calculation, had also invited some of his most dangerous opponents in both the upper and lower houses. Indeed, the Caps* looked upon the whole arrangement as a diet maneuver, intended to flatter the refractory, dazzle them with the splendor of royalty, and possibly allow King Frederick to work personally upon their

* The " Hats " and " Caps " were the political parties of that period, representing the nobility and the common people. For half a century they continued very nearly equal in power, but the revolution of August, 1772, under Gustaf III, settled the preponderance against the aristocracy.—TR.

opinions, since they had now succeeded in drawing
him into the interest of the Hat party. The six
councilors whom it was desired to depose were also
invited, but only Counts Hård and Bonde had
accepted the invitation. Count Horn excused himself
on the ground of indisposition, and the rest on that of
pressing business.

There were whispers of a particular reason why the
guests ought to enter masked. The unpleasantness
between the queen and Miss Taube had become so
marked after Coyet's notorious memorial concerning
Sarah and the servant-girl Hagar, that Ulrica Eleonora
very unwillingly showed herself in large companies,
and least of all where she feared meeting her odious
rival. But not to invite Miss Taube would have been
to disappoint the king, and put him out of humor for
the whole evening. By entering in masks, they would
avoid compromising the one or the other ; and at the
unmasking, later in the evening, in case the queen
tarried so long, they would doubtless find some means
of averting the dangerous meeting.

At that time there was not in Sweden a nobleman
who in fine culture and brilliant qualities could
compare with Count Tessin ; not a woman of the
world who in agreeableness and amiability surpassed
Countess Tessin ; and not a house where the tone of
society was so choice, and genius and wit, art and
science, so at home, as in the house of the Tessins.
Everything belonging to the period that was witty,
enlightened and interesting, loved to gather in those
elegant *salons*, copied after the best Paris models.
During that period, when Stockholm had only an old
court, and on the throne a faded and over-wrought
etiquette whose courtesies toward the ladies were more
suspicious than flattering, daunted delights and noble
manners sought and found in the Tessin house an
asylum which in more than one respect was an
emblem of the Gustavian period, still concealed in the

obscurity of the future.   More of the courtier than the
statesman, with more of brilliant talent than of penetrating genius, Count Tessin was in his natural element
in just such affairs, where ingenuity and taste could
appear from his most amiable side.   That little entertainment, which was said to be wholly unpretentious, was nevertheless a subject of conversation
beforehand by the court, and really did all honor to
the happy inventive ability of the host and hostess.

The ponderous pomp of gods and goddesses of the
former masquerades had now surrendered the field to
more lightfooted French shepherds and shepherdesses,
dancing in a *salon* decorated with flowers and bowers.
The background of this room represented a Swiss
landscape of bewildering effect—mountain tops covered
with cockles, and glittering with crystals and with seas
set with mirror glass.   At the foot of these painted
mountains were seen the most charming Swiss cottages,
in which were served strawberries and cream, cheese
and almond milk.   In a hermitage at the right—a
hermitage of Gobelins and East Indian mats!—was an
elevated place, prepared for the royal pair ; and the
hermit of this splendid wilderness was no other than
the host himself.   One feature which produced a
brilliant effect was the large pier-glasses, skillfully
concealed amid the foliage, and placed just opposite
each other on the long sides of the *salon*, through
which they reflected dazzlingly the crowd and the
chandeliers, so that on both sides one seemed to view
an endless succession of illuminated bowers and bright
costumes.

Queen Ulrica Eleonora sat there stiff and solemn
in her monstrous hoop-skirts, like a Madonna carved
in wood, and seemed to take little part in the pleasures
of the evening.   Poor queen ! With cloudy and
suspicious glances she followed those groups of motley
disguises, as though she divined that beneath one of
the masks was concealed those features which she least

12

of all wished to behold. Sometimes, at a jest of the hermit, a transient smile flitted across her somewhat masculine features ; but she quickly relapsed into her melancholy calm. Perhaps she secretly wished to sit hidden from the world in the heart of her royal palace; but a man so mighty as Count Tessin must not be disappointed, and the queen remained.

The somewhat dull mood which, in consequence of this, prevailed among the persons nearest Ulrica Eleonora, seemed, however, not in the least to trouble her royal consort. King Frederick had that very day returned from a successful hunt, and was in a very gracious humor. His majesty, from his elevated place, was pleased to enter upon a review of the guests, particularly the young ; and gave a kind ear to the not always delicate witticisms with which the favorite, Broman, thought best to amuse his master at the expense of those present.

The king's glance quickly darkened as it rested upon a stately, stiff and erect old man, who, at the lower end of the hall, was contemplating the crowd as indifferently as a wood-cutter in the forest looks at a nut-shell.

"See, there is a timber fit to export to England," said the king. "*Wo der Teufel hab ich den Kerl schon ehemals gesehen?*"

"That is a competitor for your majesty's crown, the burgher king, Larsson," replied the favorite, without troubling himself in the least about certain less agreeable recollections which were connected in his mind with Larsson. "In Finland," he continued, "they have a custom of dipping a burgher three times in pitch, that he may acquire proper manner."

"Ah ! *das verfluchte Mädchen sein Vater!*" responded the king, as he continued the inspection, nodding kindly to the French ambassador, rather coldly at the president, Count Bertelsköld, and finally pausing with his glances on a young shepherdess, who, masked, like all the others, was standing alone at a window, looking at him through the mask.

The examination must have awakened a royal curiosity, for immediately afterward his majesty was heard to say, in French, to the host: " My dear hermit, it will perhaps soon be time for you with your wand to restore to their natural form all those phantoms that people your wilderness."

But Tessin had observed that the keen glances of the queen were following a tall masked Amaryllis at the opposite side of the hall.

" Deign to pardon me," said he, " that I abide that hour which is ordained by the stars. At this moment, the constellation shows us two planets in conjunction at the orbit of Jupiter."

"Aha !" replied the king, in the same tone, " you think that Jupiter might possibly chance to come between Juno and Venus. Great astrologer, I admire your sharpness. Do as your wisdom thinks best."

The guests changed their masks and costumes several times. Two couples, representing the seasons, now entered and performed a contra-dance. One of the four, young Spring, completely overstrewn with flowers, attracted the attention of all. Such nimble grace, such a sylph-like foot, had not before appeared in the dance. People asked each other who Spring was. A part of them guessed Miss Stenbock, and others the young Countess Bonde.

"Why, that is a veritable corymb," said Mlle. de Lyner shrewdly, to Lieutenant Count Bertelsköld, who during the whole evening had been unusually abstracted, and now, like all the others, was following attentively the dance of the seasons. " You are extremely poetic this evening, my dear count," she added. " Go and gather roses with that Spring ; I wager you will fill a whole basket."

"Our northern springs pale before those of the

south," replied Bertelsköld, almost without thinking
what he said.

"Do you think so?" returned Mlle. de Lyner.
"That reminds me of something. Admit that I
guessed rightly when I had the honor of measuring the
depth of the Baltic in your company"

"I cannot recollect. . . ."

"Then you remember nothing this evening. That
active girl on skates—she who rescued us with a *coup
de théâtre*, out of the wet,—she *was* a *danseuse*, although
you would not believe it."

"But, my lady, what occasion have you to think
anything like that?"

"What occasion? And you, who for a quarter of
an hour have not had eyes for any one but her, say
that!"

"I? Explain yourself. . . ."

"Ah, my count! you are no doubt greatly
charmed, but you cannot be so blind as not to perceive
a certain likeness . . . . *enfin*, our dancing skater
and this Spring are the very same person."

Fortunately the dance was just then concluded, and
in the admiring applause which was murmured round
about, no one but Mlle. de Lyner observed that her
escort changed color.

"What is the matter with you?" said she. "You
are as pale as your own frill. Ah, what a scar you
carry on your cheek! Have you been bitten by a
snake?"

"Yes, by a snake," replied Bertelsköld, and hurried
away to seek the unknown masker. He found her
surrounded by a crowd of admirers, among them, the
hermit, who was entreating that he might present her
to his royal guest. But Spring laid her finger on her
lip, and to all the compliments replied not a word.

"Very well, my lady," continued the always ready
host, "I respect your silence. It is your right to
speak only with the fragrance of roses."

With these words, he took the masker by the hand, and presented her to the king, as a rose from the garden of the Hesperides, " eloquent even in her silence."

Bertelsköld could hardly breathe.

King Frederick uttered some of those gallantries of which he had so good a supply ; but young Spring only courtesied and courtesied still lower. The king laughed.

" Day is dawning," said he merrily. " Away with the night from all these suns ! "

The ladies began to unmask.

Then the young Spring courtesied still lower, and glided away like an eel between the astonished groups.

" Take me away from here ! " she hastily whispered in the ear of Bertelsköld.

· " Esther ! " he whispered in return, beside himself with amazement.

" You know I said that I was going to see the king! . . . But come. . . ."

" No, lovely Spring, you shall not so easily escape us ! " exclaimed a corpulent, jovial gentleman, as he placed himself in their path. It was Monsieur de Broman.

" Make way ! " replied Bertelsköld, crowding him aside. A throng gathered. One tall figure stood in the path of escape. It was Larsson. No one moved from the spot.

" Unfortunate girl ! " whispered Bertelsköld ; " if we do not get away from here, you are lost ! "

" The mask ! the mask!" cried several voices. All had now unmasked, and Spring alone was disguised. Her hand trembled.

Then the eyes of all were suddenly turned toward the hermitage. The queen had fainted. The planets had crossed each other's orbits. . . . . Bertelsköld and his *protégée* succeeded in escaping.

For a moment the festival was interrupted. The

10*

queen withdrew, but the king remained to see Count
Tessin's new play, "*L'enfant jaune*," which was
performed before supper. In vain did the company
seek the charming Spring. She had vanished, and
they found themselves once more in the middle of
November.

CHAPTER XXIII.

THE SAME NIGHT.

SCARCELY had the masker who represented
Spring emerged from the crowded *salon* into the
ante-chamber filled with domestics, before she tore herself loose from her companion without a word of explanation, and hastened to a waiting-maid, who was in
attendance, and who threw a cloak over her shoulders
and led her away. Bertelsköld hurried after them
down the steps. Reaching the gate, he saw a carriage
roll away, and by the light of the torches he distinguished on the carriage door the arms of the Count
of Stenbock.

Surprise, perplexity, anxiety, and indignation, by
turns took possession of the young man's soul. Was
that really Esther Larsson? What childish thought-
lessness! What hardihood of a girl without birth or
knowledge of the world, to intrude, disguised, into this
rendezvous for everything eminent and brilliant that the
metropolis possessed! And how was this at all possible? Would Larsson himself, that stiff democrat,
really have allowed his paternal tenderness to mislead
him so far as that, to gratify the whim of his spoiled
darling? Would the same vanity which induced him
to give his daughter an education far above her rank,
foster in him the secret wish to allow her to exult

secretly in a personal audience before royalty and the court? Any other explanation was hardly possible. And the more certain this seemed to Bertelsköld, the more his anger turned toward a father who could so unpardonably place his child's reputation in peril. Poor child! What, then, was to become of her under such guidance, amidst the perils of that frivolous court, toward the splendor of which she flew like a moth toward the flame of a candle? And yet, in all her wild wantonness, she was an uncommon, a lovable and richly-gifted being, and must be saved at whatever price, even though it might be by protecting her from the imprudence of her own father.

Bertelsköld did not reflect long. He resolved immediately to seek Larsson, who still tarried among the guests of Count Tessin.

At that moment the doors were thrown open, and the queen, who had recovered from her swoon, was accompanied to her carriage by the host and hostess and her own ladies in waiting. But as King Frederick, who more and more neglected his consort, was pleased to continue to honor the *soirée* with his presence, the most of the guests remained, to be present at the representation of " *L'enfant jaune.*"

All were now unmasked. Several had seen Bertelsköld offer his arm to the young masker who had attracted so much attention. " Ah !" exclaimed Monsieur de Broman, "here we have Miss Stenbock's cavalier ! I assure you, my dear count, that you ought to be tried by court-martial as the person who has robbed our evening of one of its most beautiful ornaments—next to the charming Amaryllis," he added, loud enough to be heard by the king, who was not far away.

" It is impossible to deceive your sharpness," whispered Bertelsköld, glad to be able to divert suspicions; " but I beg you do not disturb my lady's little pleasure in passing *incognito*. She will no doubt soon return."

"It was not Miss Stenbock—she was taken sick last evening and cannot leave her room," interposed a gentleman of the bedchamber, who knew the chronicles of the court to a dot.

"Your pardon, sir; you are mistaken," responded another gentleman of the bed-chamber, who affected still more to be versed in the chronicles. "Miss Stenbock, a week ago, ordered those genuine Parisian flowers which Spring wore, and her carriage stopped at the gate while I was alighting."

"But her own physician has told me that she has the measles," insisted the first.

"Oh, we know the doctors! What do they not say to promote the little intrigues of their pretty patients?" returned the other.

Bertelsköld succeeded in stealing away. He had not proceeded far when a heavy hand was laid on his shoulder, and besides him stood the burgher king. "I have something to say to sir count," said Larsson, coldly.

"I am glad of it," replied Bertelsköld; "I have also something to say to the honorable member of the diet."

"Then let us speak undisturbed by these fools," said Larsson, stepping aside into one of the window niches. "Are you aware, sir count, that your groom is threatening me with the loss of half my possessions?"

"Istvan? What do you mean by that?"

"I mean that your groom, Istvan, claims to be the lost son of my elder brother, Thomas Larsson, and in that character threatens to claim an hereditary right to half my possessions in Storkyro. What do you say to that, sir count? Is it not a well-fashioned story?"

"I beg you to explain yourself more fully. Ever since our visit to Storkyro, Istvan has been an enigma to me."

"Well, I will be brief. My elder brother, Thomas

Larsson, owner of Bertila farm and adjoining farms in
Storkyro, had eight sons and three daughters. Six of
the sons fell the same day for their king and country,
and the seventh was carried off by camp fever. Then
only Benjamin, the youngest of the brothers, remained.
He had the fate of Joseph, son of Jacob, though he
was not sold, but stolen away by the Cossacks, who
carried him, at eleven years of age, with them to
Russia. Since that time—it is now twenty-three years
ago—no one has heard the least thing about the lad
Benjamin. His father Thomas, who wandered out to
seek him, returned, after the peace, infirm and feeble-
minded, to his native place. When, shortly afterward,
he died, only three daughters remained of all Thomas
Larsson's family; two of them married here in
Sweden, and the third married my skipper, Elias
Pehrson, and settled in Munsala. Fifteen years ago,
I bought their real estate, which was utterly run down
after the war; and since that, my son Mathias has by
new tillage more than quadrupled the value of the
property. Now this Istvan steps up, or rather his
lawyer, Spolin . . . ."

"Ah! I know. He is a finished knave. . . ."

" . . . and claims the hereditary right to buy my
brother Thomas's property at the prime cost, on the
assumption that he, Istvan, is the same Benjamin
Thomasson Bertila who was carried away by the
Cossacks to their native country on the Don, afterwards was taken prisoner on an expedition by the
Turks, and finally deserted from them over to Hungary, where you found him and took him into your
service. Now, I ask, what says sir count to this
story?"

"I say," replied Bertelsköld, reflecting, "that this
story is very romantic, and perhaps improbable, but not
therefore impossible. It has always seemed to me as
though Istvan had a good share of northern slowness
and Finnish toughness in him: and quite singular was

S

the ease with which he learned the Finnish language, as though it had been an awakened memory of childhood with him. When we arrived at Bertila farm, in Storkyro, the fellow was out of his senses, and raved about a well in the yard, which he seemed to have seen before, and to which he had ridden out, as a child, to water the horses. I do not know what I ought to think of it. Have they produced any proofs?"

"Documental, none at all. Confused memories, testimony of witnesses, and a scar on the left cheek, which the lost Benjamin bore after he was kicked by a horse when eight years of age."

"A scar? Yes, Istvan has such a scar."

"And that is all that sir count knows?" coldly continued Larsson. "Pardon me; I have looked upon sir count as a worthy young man, who had no reason to enter into a league with my enemies."

"Neither have I; quite the contrary. All that I can say is that in the wonderful times that we have passed through, events like the one in question are not altogether inconceivable."

"Indeed? I understand. Let us say no more about it. Was there not something which sir count wished to say to me!"

"Yes," said Bertelsköld, somewhat embarrassed. "I would beg you not to be offended if I asked you something concerning your daughter."

"My daughter?" Larsson frowned.

"I have heard it said that your youngest daughter accompanied you to Stockholm. It is a city which offers many dangers. Allow me, as a friend, to ask you if you are aware of all those dangers, and if you are sure of having protected your lovely child from them?"

Larsson drew himself up, considerably haughtier than the young aristocrat who stood before him. "Sir count," said he, "I have taken the liberty to question you concerning a matter of business; but my family relations are my own affair. I choose my friends, but permit no one to obtrude his friendship upon me. Can I be of service in any other way?"

"I obtrude my friendship upon no one," replied Bertelsköld, a head taller in his turn; "but be assured I did not ask that question without reason. Can it be possible that Esther, without your consent . . . ."

Larsson interrupted him, and laid his hand on his shoulder. "Young man," said he, "to save yourself further questions, you ought to know that between your family and mine there has been of old an inherent enmity. I ought to do us both the justice to say that we have not been at variance concerning personal interests, but rather about those which are important to the welfare of the country. You are a young man, and hence ready to yield to the first whim that occurs to you. But when you are ten years older, you will occupy the place of that man (pointing to President Count Torsten Bertelsköld, who was standing not far away) and then it will be your aim, as it was that your father's, to trample the people under your feet. But I—and, with God's help, my sons after me—adhere to the aim of my fathers: to uplift the people from their debasement, and in our turn trample their oppressors under our feet. You thus perceive, sir count, that there can be nothing in common between us—at most only matters of business. So be kind enough not to trouble yourself. The play is about to begin."

With these words, he turned his back to the young nobleman. The curtain with the Swiss landscape was raised, and "*L'enfant jaune*" was presented.

CHAPTER XXIV.

TREACHEROUS PROJECTS.

IF the kind reader has surmised that a cloud was gathering around the gray head of Larsson, the burgher king, he has perhaps not guessed so far astray. As Larsson's influence increased in the house of burghers and threatened to annihilate the subtle plans of the Hat party to draw the house into its interests, those nets were all the more industriously spun in the darkness, which were to ensnare the dangerous opponent and render him harmless. As a member of the diet, he was personally unmolestable so long as the diet lasted; but now, when matters every day more nearly approached their climax, it became more necessary every day to get him out of the way; and the instrument of this cabal was our old acquaintance in all kinds of bad artifices, the experienced Fiscal Spolin.

Without allowing himself to be daunted by his abortive attempt to detain Larsson in Wasa by means of the pretended smuggling of counterfeit silver dollars, the zealous fiscal, by means of his friends, the counterfeiters of Lillkyro forest, had obtained information of a person in the service of Count Bertelsköld, by the name of Istvan, whose adventurous experiences and credulous nature seemed to render him particularly qualified to act as the decoy in the lion hunt upon which they now intended to enter. And after Spolin had gathered in all serviceable intelligence from every conceivable source, he set out in the autumn for Stockholm; where, after receiving instructions, he did not neglect to seek Istvan.

No great art was needed to persuade the honest groom that he, and no other, was the rightful owner of that great estate which Larsson had purchased of his brother's daughters, according to rumor, for a mere song. The times immediately succeeding the great contest, moreover, were so rife with such wonderful stories of heirs who had disappeared and returned, that they belonged to the order of the day, and easily found credence with judges, parties, and the witnesses summoned.

Istvan, who had been prevailed upon to keep the matter secret from his master, had meanwhile sought Larsson, and, in his harsh laconic manner, presented himself as his nephew, and offered a peaceful adjustment. Any one who knew the burgher king,—and Spolin did,—also knew beforehand the issue of such an attempt. Larsson was not the man to bestow a whole fortune on the first one who would have the goodness to accept it. In brief, the result was that he drove his new kinsman out of doors.

Now it was in order to intimidate him with a lawsuit, which should compel him to return home and arm himself with legal documents against the threatening loss of half his property. They took care that he was reminded of several similar cases, which had been taken as far as to the king, and ended with the complete ruin of the defendant. But Larsson did not allow himself to be imposed upon. He kept his opinion to himself, and continued attending to the business of the diet, as before, in the sure hope that the victory of his party would also pave the way for the success of that plan for which he had so long and persistently worked—the plan of procuring the staple-right for the East Bothnian towns.

Spolin began to distrust the effect of his wily trick. It was of a quality to bring him revenge some day, but what was that to the mighty lords behind his back? The burgher king must be destroyed. Only upon the ruins of his throne could the Hats hope to climb to power.

Still, like a skillful fisher, Spolin had many nets spread at once   He searched around, and in an inn of Stockholm found a young fool by the name of Calle Sager, leading a gay life among a crowd of poor noblemen, who, in exchange for the pleasure of feasting at his expense, were not over scrupulous about condescending to such plebeian society.   While his honest but too short-sighted mother believed him to be immersed in important matters of state, in the exchequer college, Calle Sager found it more in accordance with his artistic talent to play the flute to the fair servant girls at the inn ; and it was after a jovial dinner with his noble friends, that he made the mistake of coming home somewhat half-seas over, that day when Miss Louisa, frightened at his hilarity, begged his dear mother to come down from Esther's attic, with the sequel that the old lady forgot to go up again.

With this excellent young man, Spolin succeeded in forming quite an intimate acquaintance, which was probably founded on certain illusions about recommending so deserving a youth to a brilliant promotion, with high patrons.   And as the same recommendations were the shortest road to Madam Sager's heart, it was not especially difficult for the artful spy to gain entrance into the same draper shop which, a short time before, had had the honor of receiving a harp-playing count.

Spolin knew perfectly well where to look for his adversary's most vulnerable point.   But he also knew that Esther was too sharp for him, for she had once before brought his plans to naught.   He was careful, therefore, not to let her know about the visit, and, instead, succeeded in winning to his side Miss Louisa, a well-meaning but simple person.   He talked so handsomely, the intelligent fiscal, about his old friendship for the poor imprisoned child, how cruelly she was

treated, and how one ought not to oppose her innocent
wishes. Miss Louisa's kind heart was touched, especially when some few courtesies gave her to understand
that the position of fiscal's wife did not belong to the
impossibilities of this world. And after it had happened
that Miss Stenbock was taken sick, the night before she
was to appear in the quadrille at Count Tessin's, and her
waiting maid was a confidential friend to Miss Louisa,
only a few necessary instructions were required, and a
suitable fee to Miss Stenbock's servants, to provide
Esther, who happened to be of quite the same figure,
with the pleasure of appearing at the masquerade in
the costume of the high-born young lady. That the
rash and inexperienced burgher girl would soon betray
herself in so brilliant a gathering, thus causing an
odious scandal, and that Larsson himself should become
a witness of this humilitation of himself and his daughter,—such was the honorable fiscal's well contrived
plan. But, alas ! even the greatest human cunning
cannot penetrate all the little crooks of events ; and
Spolin had not considered that the natural freedom of
the Wasa girl would, at the masquerade, be taken for a
well-played *rôle;* that her native grace, cultivated by
the most celebrated dancing-master of Stockholm, had
given her courage to appear in a hitherto practiced
quadrille, and that in the moment of peril she would
succeed in finding a protector who would conduct her
out of danger. Spolin's plan had again miscarried.
He must invent a new one.

To this new stroke of genius, the hopeful youth,
Calle Sager, would be a suitable lime-twig ; and to this
end a somewhat importunate creditor was set upon him.

"Do you know," said Spolin to his man, in one of
the confidential moments of friendship, in the Hôtel
d'Espagne. "It is reported in the city that you have
not much left of your inheritance."

"Nonsense ! " replied the flute-player, who took the
matter lightly. "If it was not for keeping the old

woman in good humor, I would show them what she has in the bottom of the chest."

"You cannot be so very sure about that. If I were in your place, I would capture the East Bothnian tar-barrel. It weighs something, and it would make the bears as gentle as lambs."

"Esther? Indeed, mother sings that ditty every day. But I will not have the young one, and she will not have me. She is ready to scratch my eyes out if I touch on that string."

"So you think that? Why, old fellow, you know no more than a schoolboy about the freaks of girls. Her scratching is just a proof that in secret she loves you."

"Yes, thank you. Offer to the other gentlemen."

"It is true, the haughty Larsson thinks that you are too low a match for his daughter—you, who are nevertheless one of the most gentlemanly young fellows in Stockholm! If I were in your place I would show him that the girl would take me with outstretched hands whenever I pleased to do her the honor to propose."

"Does he think that? the uncultivated corn-jew! Well, if it was only thoroughly to worry him . . . ."

"Just imagine it! I should call that revenge! To-morrow, for example, when the girl rides out on her usual excursion to Horn's gate . . . . Have you not a dinner there in the neighborhood?"

"Some of my most intimate friends—Ulfveklo, and Lejonram, and Gyllenfelt, and a nephew of his excellency Hård, and a few others of the better *societè*."

"Why, that fits together like a French comedy! For example, if her horse should run—a little—not too much, you understand—on account of a little bit of burning sponge in the ear,—you are a good horseman, if I remember rightly?"

"So the musicians of the guard maintain; but the grooms hold that I am a good flute player."

"Envy, mere envy! Have I not seen you ride like a Turk over the ditches in the field? In short, you stop the horse, which is likely to run away—you rescue your beautiful one—that is genteel, it is much used now-a-days in novels . . . ."

"I know it. I read nothing else."

"Afterward, you carry her to your friends—à little faint; that would produce effect . . . ."

"Yes, that would be pathetic."

"Then follows a tender scene . . . ."

"The devil! I may get a box on the ear."

"So much the better, as you will then have occasion to take revenge."

"Do you think so?"

"And then you declare your engagement in the presence of the whole company."

"But if I am sorry for it?"

"Be sorry afterward as much as you please. Meantime you have taken revenge on the girl, revenge on the father, revenge on your creditors. . . . . In short, it is an adventure which will make you famous all over Stockholm. They will say: 'That Sager is a very pagan for luck! He caught a barrel of gold on every finger!' And so genteelly, too! It will perhaps influence your promotion. A gentleman like you, with such enormous wealth, must inevitably be discussed at the granting of the next patents of nobility. Perhaps Baron—Baron Sager! That sounds first-rate—don't you think so?"

"Why not? We certainly hear more clownish names—Count Bonde,* for example. You are right, Spolin. My late father had a hand in establishing liberty in the land. It would indeed not be too much if his son should become a baron."

* Bonde—peasant.

CHAPTER XXV.

FATHER AND DAUGHTER.

ONE day, Representative Lars Larsson quite unexpectedly entered the residence of the Sagers, and with stiff steps climbed the steep stairway to his daughter's attic. It was near noon—a time when he was usually occupied by diet business ; but to-day there was no session of the house of burghers. The members were preparing for a large vote the second day following; everything was moving finely, and the burgher king was in excellent humor.

He had expected to find Esther occupied by some of those lessons with which he so liberally provided her; but he was disappointed. Esther had been pleased to send away her German teacher, and now sat by the open window, amusing herself by blowing soap-bubbles, which she sent flying out into the clear frosty winter air, where, to the admiration of all pedestrians, they soared like little glistening stars in the sunshine high above the roofs and streets of the great city.

The father's countenance darkened, but the girl did not give the tempest time to break loose. She instantly threw her arms around his neck, and begged him to come and see her beautiful little birds; he must see how high they flew, and how the sparrows sought in vain to catch them in their flight. The austere old man could not withstand so important a reason for a neglected lesson. He drew his lips into a rough laughter,—and it was something rare to see Larsson laugh. There was perhaps only one person in the whole wide world who could boast of having displaced that invariable seriousness, and that one was Esther Larsson, his youngest child, his daring and spoiled darling.

-"Foolish child!" growled the old man; "do you think it is becoming for a nice girl, who has been studying straight ahead since last summer, to be blowing soap-bubbles into the streets of Stockholm? Tell me, little rogue," and he pinched her ear, "when will you ever become wise and sensible?"

"I am wise already—father has often told me so, and I will by degrees become sensible, too, when I get gray hair and arrive at something like the age of a member of the diet, like father," replied Esther, as she sent a new bubble flying.

"Well, well, we must hope for improvement," muttered the father, not without a little new sunshine across the stern lips. "But then, we must also see that you have something better to think about. I will tell you something, my dear child. This is a perilous time we live in, and the bird that twitters too early in the morning is before night in the claws of the hawk. Your father is old and would like to see you provided for, my dear girl. You will soon be sixteen. What would you say if I should think of a good husband for you?"

"I?.... See! That bubble flew the highest of all! Do you think, father, it can be much lower than the tower of St. Jacob's church?"

"The bubbles burst, my child, and your father is talking about serious matters. You have been brought up in an honest and pious house, and I want you to become a righteous woman. Do you not answer my question? Has young Sager been prating nonsense to you? I understand—about that which they call a heart, love, and such stuff. I ought to have foreseen that when I brought you into this house. An old crack-brained mother and a good-for-nothing son! . . . 'That twig is not good to sit on,' said the heath-cock

of the fern. Esther, I hope you have not bound yourself by any promise to Sager?"

"I will not let myself be bound. No, father, I do
not like chains."

"That is good. You lift a stone from my heart.
A girl never ought to bind her future, which she cannot judge. Such matters are for those who better
understand. In short, I have selected you a good,
steady husband, neither too young nor too old—somewhat over thirty years of age. What do you say of
that, my child?"

"Oh, father! You ought to see my bubbles! Only
look, now! Pshaw! it burst—that one did—before it
got to the church weather-vane."

"Esther, my darling, my delight on earth, do you
think that your old father will so gladly miss your
happy roguish face, which lights up my dark hours
amid the troubles of this world? But it must happen
sometime, child, and it is better for me to choose a
husband for you than for you to choose according to
your own foolish head. Of course you have seen
young Årström—Eric Årström, partner of his father?
A worthy, good fellow ; solid wealth . . . . it
was with their house that I united in that large grain
operation, you know, in which I invested half my
fortune. That will prove a good transaction. I am at
any moment expecting a letter concerning it. There
have been bad crops in the Netherlands . . . ."

"Oh! have there been bad crops in the Netherlands?"

"Yes ; and for once we Finns will have to feed the
rich Hollanders. So, my child, young Årström will
be your husband. Many will envy you, my comfort ;
but something for something; indeed, there are those
who will envy Årström, too. It is agreed between his
father and me that your wedding shall be celebrated
at Christmas. I ought not to conceal from you that

the senior Årström has much influence in the house of burghers."

"Indeed! What do you say, father? How did he attain so great an influence?"

"Real worth, industry, and wealth—they are surer roads than all intrigues to a good name as fellow-citizen and patriot. If you knew, my dear child, what stratagems have been set in motion to ruin your father! But they shall not succeed. The old Larsson is too tough for them. And then, you know, I have you?—Is there anything you wish, little one? Perhaps those pretty bracelets, which hang in the window of the goldsmith at Storkyro hill? Or, perhaps, one of those costly Flemish lace collars, which many a young lady at the court has not means to buy? No, do not thank me beforehand—you have not got it yet, you little damsel! Do you think I am weak enough to throw away so much precious money for such a crow as you? What will you give me for those laces?"

Esther threw her arms around his neck. "Everything you wish, father, except yourself. I will not give *you* away for any Orrström, or Ormbunke, or whatever his name may be."

"Oh, well, we will talk together about that matter. But you have not let me hear how you have improved on King David's harp. Who has been your teacher, child? Some old organist, I think Mother Sager told me."

Esther was silent. She did not yet know the art of lying. Fortunately, no further information was asked on that delicate subject. The father continued:

"Some other time you will have to sing number three hundred and fifty-four for me. I have not time now. We have dinner soon, and committee-meeting immediately afterward. What do you think of doing now? Of course, you do not intend to sit here all day with your silly soap-bubbles?"

"No, father, I think now of riding out, as you know I do every forenoon."

"Indeed! You have had your own way in that matter, too. Otherwise I should not allow it—for it is not customary for girls of your rank. But I want my child to be able to compare in everything with any one whomsoever, even with the elegant young French lady at the court; at any rate, she does not ride half so well as you. But be careful, my dear child, that the dapple pony does not run away with you ; I think he twitches his ears rather too much."

"There is no danger. I have seen worse horses than he is."

"Well, well ; you have not forgotten your adventure at Korsholm. That young count is here now. He is said to be betrothed to Miss de Lynar."

Esther blanched. "It is not true ! " she exclaimed.

"What do you think ? I am going to give you a bit of good counsel, child : Never listen to the tattle of servant girls. I can well believe that Louisa regales you with stories from the court. . . . . See here! Do you still ride out with the old riding-master ?"

"No, father, I ride out now with Calle Sager, although he is a sorry horseman."

"I do not like that. If the riding-master has not time to go out, you will have to submit to staying at home."

"You do not need to trouble yourself about Sager— he is a fool. This is the last time, too, that I intend to ride out in his company."

"Well, let it be so, since it is the last time. But we have dinner now. Good-bye, my girl. Ride cautiously. And God protect you ! "

"Good-bye, father ! God protect you, too ! "

With these words, father and daughter separated. A few minutes afterward, Esther was sitting on her mettlesome horse, and, in company with her idle cousin, was riding out toward Horn's gate.

CHAPTER XXVI

A HORSEBACK EXCURSION AND ITS CONSEQUENCES.

IN the small but in its way fashionable Hôtel d'Espagne, outside Horn's gate, a select gathering of
the most dissipated young idlers of Stockholm had
thrown themselves down around a table, fully equipped
with choice Hollandish pipes and cannisters, which in
those days were in fashion. Tobacco, in all its forms,
had been known in Sweden and Finland ever since
the thirty years' war; but not until later times had it
stolen in among the higher classes, who probably
imitated high Prussian prejudices, and had afterward
taken it from Pomerania. To the elegant and accomplished French noblemen all tobacco continued to be
an abomination; but this very fact called forth opposition among the less punctilious fops of the day, and
the thicker were the clouds they puffed out of their
fine porcelain pipe-bowls, the more they regarded
themselves as standing on the side of Swedish liberty
in opposition to aristocratic prejudices. For the rest,
they stowed away quantities of Rostock's ale sufficient
to keep the pipes from becoming dry. They had no
occasion to be sparing of what the house afforded, for
the expense of the party was born by the rich Sager,
whose arrival was expected every moment, in order to
begin the real work of the day—a somewhat fashionable dinner, where the plainer viands gave place to
German and French wines, which were ready in
decanters of Bohemian glass.

Politics was the watchword of the day; and the
company, whose members had nothing to lose by a
revolution, but everything to win, naturally belonged

to the opposition.   Among these gentlemen there
were gamesters who had offered their wealth on the
altars of deceitful Fortune; lovers of ease, who had
eaten up their patrimony in expectation of the death
of uncles and aunts; and drones, who could not get
into any office under the rigorous and laborious system
of Horn.   All these were, for the moment, Hats; all
exercised their wit on the present government, which
did not understand how to appreciate their talents
properly; and they were just busy with the political
situation of Europe, when they heard the trot of a
horse in the yard, and saw Calle Sager, the expected
host, arrive.

To the surprise of all, the entry took place in a
very peculiar manner.   A slender young-girl, uncommonly supple and agreeable in all her motions, entered
the yard on foot, leading by the bridle a horse on whose
back young Sager seemed with difficulty to cling.
It was soon explained that the genteel young man had
fallen from his horse; and—as it may be as well to
relate at once the details of the matter—Esther Larsson's dapple-gray had run away, Sager's chestnut had
followed its comrade's example, and the end of the
adventure was that the horseman turned a somerset;
upon which Esther, who was a better rider, had offered
him her horse, and at his request had led him to the
inn, in the belief that he was badly hurt and needed
prompt assistance.

The injury could not have been so dangerous,
however, as Esther had imagined; for scarcely had she
helped her cavalier out of the saddle and led him into
the house, before he seemed to recover himself perceptibly, at the sight of the old friends and the spread
table.   He now declared that a bit of lobster and a
few glasses of Rhenish wine would not disagree with
him—especially if his lady would be pleased to take a
place by his side and recover her strength in the patri-

otic and very polite society he should have the honor
of presenting to her.

Esther Larsson was not the person who was in the
habit of losing courage, but having entered so unexpectedly into a company of strange men, who did not
trouble themselves to conceal their amusement, she
felt at once amazed and embarrassed. The door stood
open, and she turned to go.

But now one of the gentlemen placed himself in
her way. It was impossible, he declared, that so
charming a fairy, who had rescued their friend from
destruction, could leave them without allowing the
company to offer her its homage in a glass of genuine
Rüdesheimer.

"Oh, drink away, and without ceremony. Of
course the gentlemen all know that you are my little
sweetheart," carelessly remarked Sager, as, without
the least appearance of any dangerous hurt, he seated
himself at the loaded table.

"Your sweetheart! We congratulate you! We
congratulate you!" exclaimed the guests, as, with full
glasses, they thronged around the terrified girl, who did
not see any possibility of escaping. This was not the
first time they had heard Calle Sager boast of his
intimacy with the East Bothnia burgher king and all his
riches, the youngest daughter included. Toward such a
little simple burgher girl anything could be allowed.

"Your health, my sweet friend," cried one of the
boldest—the already somewhat tipsy Gyllenfelt.

"Drink away! this is no tar!" laughed the nearest
man, the strutting young Von Hartzdorf, who wore
the most elegant cockade in the whole company.

"I hope we will be marshals at the wedding,"
mockingly added the corpulent Baron Krauser, the
greatest cheese connoisseur in Stockholm, as he
inserted his napkin nicely between his vest and care-
fully-starched frill.

T   13

"And what mother-in-law is to bestow fine kitchen towels?" said the agreeable Lejonram, who boasted of having within six weeks lost two barrels of gold in card-playing.

"Come, my little friend, and take a dram, and some bread and butter!" impatiently resumed Gyllen-felt, as he put the climax to the shameless performance by taking Esther by the left hand, to lead her to the table.

But Esther's short patience was now at an end. She answered him as perhaps not many an insulted girl would have ventured to answer in her place. She struck him with her riding-whip straight in the face. And she did not strike amiss. On his blazing forehead and cheeks a bright red stripe immediately bore witness that the chastisement was as thorough as it was deserved.

"The cursed fool of a burgher girl!" was the elegant exclamation which, in the first surprise, escaped the tipsy gentleman, as he let go Esther's hand, and, startled, turned his attention to the smarting spot.

The anger of the gentlemen was terrible. They thronged around Esther with noise and jests. Sager left his plate, with the newly-served lobster, to express his indignation at the extremely rude behavior of the uncivil girl. Krauser alone still sat undisturbedly smiling, with his napkin at his frill, picking the bones from the titbits of a roasted flounder.

During the confusion it had not been observed that a newly-arrived guest had entered the room adjoining, and ordered a glass of wine, while through the half-open door he plainly heard every word in the hall. He now thought best to step into the midst of the company, and, crowding back the most impertinent, placed himself resolutely at Esther's side.

This new-comer was Count Charles Victor Bertel-sköld, who, as he was riding past the Hôtel d'Espagne, had recognized Esther Larsson's dapple horse in the yard, and, surprised at it, resolved to inform himself of the reason of her presence in this not over-reputable place.

"What!" he exclaimed, with the flush of anger on his noble brow. "What, gentlemen! Is this conduct befitting Swedish noblemen toward a defenceless and estimable woman? Is there any one here who ventures to throw the least stain on the fair fame of this young girl?"

The gentlemen looked at each other. "Who has given the count a right to mingle in our affairs?" muttered Gyllenfelt. "She has struck a nobleman; and a thousand devils take me but she shall kiss me, first on the hand and then on the mouth!"

Bertelsköld answered with a look of contempt.

Lejonram, the gamester, the best-hearted one of the revelers, now touched the count softly on the shoulder, and whispered: "Be reasonable—do not arouse any quarrel. Come and empty a glass with us, and we will let the girl go. Of course we all know that you were her cavalier at the masquerade at Count Tessin's."

"Who has divulged?"

"Who? Ask the first peruke-maker that dresses your hair; for it is probably now a subject of conversation in all the barber-shops of Stockholm. I heard it to-day from a little sneaking fellow named Spolberg, or Spole, or whatever his name may be."

"Yes, indeed!" again cried Gyllenfelt, who seemed to recall something similar. "You think that we are having a masquerade here, where one can without reproach bring in any girl whatever from the street?"

"Do you think we will allow ourselves to be duped so easily as certain high night-caps?"

"Let her dance her *pas de printemps!* There are partners enough here—summer, autumn, and winter, at pleasure!"

The storm was increasing. Bertelsköld took Esther by the hand, and led her into a side-room.

"Stay here a few moments," he whispered, "and if I should be unable to conduct you away,. Lieutenant Lejonram will do so. Do not fear; he is better than his reputation."

"If you die, I will die with you!" exclaimed Esther, clinging to his arm. She was beside herself; she no longer knew what she said.

"No, Esther, I still live to defend your honor. Stay here. That insult demands blood!"

"No, no! do not go! They will kill you! I will not let you go!" and she clung still closer to his arm.

"Poor child! do you not know, then, that I love you, and that your honor is mine? Will you drive me to despair?"

Esther looked at him with a pair of large, astonished eyes, and released his arm. "Go, go!" she whispered, vainly trying to conceal her tears.

Bertelsköld fastened the door of the side-room, and entered the hall. He found all prepared for a bloody reparation. They were only disputing as to who should first cross his sword with the defender of Esther Larsson.

"Gentlemen," said the young count, calmly and decidedly, "Gyllenfelt has received a blow across the face. I assert that he perfectly deserved it; and it is thus he whom I shall have the honor of encountering first. Lieutenant Lejonram will perhaps have the kindness to be my second."

"I propose that we finish our dinner, and afterward settle the business at Liljeholm," proposed Krauser, little pleased with being disturbed in his agreeable occupation.

"Impossible! Darkness is setting in! *Allons* to the matter!" cried several voices.

"That is also my mind," said Bertelsköld.

They placed themselves in position, and threw off

their coats. Gyllenfelt had suddenly become sober, and selected Von Hartzdorf as his second.

The combat began. Both the antagonists were practised fencers, but Gyllenfelt, furious at the insult, was incapable of retaining the coolness he so much needed, in order to parry the blows of his skillful combatant. It was not long before a keen thrust through the right shoulder extorted from him a cry of rage.

"Never mind! Let us go on!" he cried; but his arm soon hung powerless at his side, and Bertelsköld lowered his sword.

"It is your turn, Von Hartzdorf," said the count.

The wounded man was led away, and Hartzdorf stepped to his place. Young and effeminate, he would have been an easy prey to a less merciful enemy. Bertelsköld contented himself with scratching a mark across his right cheek, on which the seconds hastened to cross their swords between the combatants.

"Adieu! *mon plaisir* with the fair sex," observed Krauser, without compassionating his afflicted friend, whose first care was to inspect his wound by the aid of a mirror.

"It is your turn, sir baron!" said Bertelsköld, apparently as calm as ever, although from the sharp tone one might guess the rage that boiled within him.

"You might have waited till I had finished the turkey," growled the gentleman challenged, as he neatly folded his napkin, wiped his lips, and placed himself in position. "Let it go on lively—I am hungry!" he added, playing indifferently with his sword, as though he had never used it for anything more serious than to knock off apples.

Bertelsköld, however, did not allow himself to be deceived. He knew that he now had to deal with his most dangerous antagonist, the most famous duellist of Stockholm, an accomplished fencer, initiated in all the tricks of the Italian masters. He knew that this cold-blooded egotist would impale him on his sword with the same indifference with which he would cut a chicken in pieces. He resolved to be on his guard, for Krauser's plan was evidently by feigned carelessness to make his enemy feel secure, and tempt him to expose himself to the ever vigilant point of his sword.

"How many have you killed in duels, sir count?" said Krauser, quite casually, as he parried a well-aimed thrust.

"You will be the first," replied Bertelsköld, in the same tone, although his blood was beginning to boil.

"What! Not one? And I am just amusing myself. with the eighth," resumed the baron, as he directed an insidious thrust toward Bertelsköld's breast. The sword was dashed aside, but tore open the shirt sleeve, and a streak of blood stained the linen red.

"Nay, see! I think you have spilt huckleberries on your sleeve," observed Krauser.

Bertelsköld perceived his peril. Every minute he was becoming more excited, but his adversary continually cooler and more derisive. In that lay the danger. He controlled his wrath and changed from attack to defence.

"Oh! some one is afraid for his titled flesh!" sneered Krauser, at the same time purposely uncovering himself, in order to lead the count to an attack. When this plan miscarried, Krauser in his turn lost patience. "*Finissons!*" cried he.

Bertelsköld kept on the defensive. Krauser supposed this arose from loss of blood, and thought he now might venture a decisive thrust. He drew a step backward, as though to place himself *en garde*, but at the same moment he made a furious assault, in which he succeeded only in hurling himself against the outstretched sword of his antagonist, which went straight through him at the waist and felled him to the floor.

"*La pièce est finie, allons souper!*" exclaimed he, in the well-known awful words uttered at the death of Charles XII, as a stream of blood gushed from his nose and mouth. The gourmand had ended his career.

"Quick! to your horse!" whispered Lejonram.

Bertelsköld perceived that delay was dangerous. He drew Esther with him, and hastened out. Not even Sager hindered them, and the two were soon galloping across the bridge to Liljeholm.

Then the count paused. "No," said he, "I must take you back to your father."

"Sooner to death!" exclaimed Esther, in terror. "The story of the masquerade is known in all Stockholm. My father is dreadfully angry, and the best I could expect would be to be united before morning to a man whom I abhor."

"Well," said Bertelskold, "I know another refuge where you can live secure till the storm is over. I will place you under the protection of my mother."

CHAPTER XXVII.

THE MINES BEGIN TO SPRING.

THE same day on which the incident just related occurred at the Hôtel d' Espagne, President Count Torsten Bertelsköld had received some favorable advices. His largest fish—his whale, that no one before had been able to bind and capture—began to flounder in the net. Closer and closer was the entangling snare drawn around the real master and ruler of Sweden—the old man, weighed down with years, toils and honors, Count Arvid Horn; more and more was the horizon of the Hats' ambitious plans enlarged, and every day they approached more nearly their destined object—a new government and a new political system. The assurance of victory shone in the keen glances of this artful diplomat, as alone in his private office he contemplated the means of breaking down that last opposition. He was too sagacious to despise those smaller fishes which still remained to be scaled ; and, above all, did the continued obstinacy of the house of burghers annoy him. This, it is true, was only one department of governmental power, against the three in which they thought themselves secure ; but it was important to possess the key to the public cash-box, and so long as they did not have the house of burghers in their power, they feared that the key would not be obtained or would not open the complicated lock.

It was between five and six o'clock in the afternoon. Wax-lights were burning in the silver candelabra, and the count, who seemed to be expecting some one, looked repeatedly at the clock. "What if the old wolf should scent the ambuscade?" said he to himself.

But the double doors were at last thrown open, and the *valet* announced Representative Larsson. The count's brow brightened as he motioned his visitor to enter.

Larsson advanced as inflexible as a timber from the forests of his native land.

" Sir count has sent for me," said he, after a slight bow. " We were in committee in the house, so that I could not reach here at precisely five o'clock."

" It is no matter, my dear Larsson ; duty and country before everything. Be so good as to take a seat. I have been wishing to talk with you about our common business, the staple-right of the East Bothnian towns."

" I confess that I had no longer cherished any hope of sir count's favorable intercession."

"But, my dear friend, you utterly misapprehend my kind intentions. We may be of different opinions on other questions, and every one ought to follow his convictions; but who would not do your patriotic principles the justice they so well deserve? Believe me," and these words were uttered with a touching air of sincerity, "I am a real friend, and do everything that lies in my ability to serve you."

Larsson replied with a short bow, which left the declaration of friendship unchanged in value.

"You have enemies, my dear Larsson," continued the count; "enemies who are seeking to injure both you and your cause. Plomgren, for example—a selfish man! I detest such men! If you would have confidence in me, I should employ my whole influence to destroy his plans. Touching your lawsuit, do you know that the members of the supreme court maintain that you will certainly lose? And you know half your fortune is at stake."

"Will your grace permit that we return to the staple-right?"

"That is just what I wish to talk about. You understand that such a lawsuit must injure your cause at the same time as yourself. It will be said that you demand the staple-right in order to repair your ruined business. And when a man like you extends his operations abroad—in grain export, for example, which is always a difficult business, depending on conditions . . . ."

"I do not perceive what my individual affairs have to do with the determination of the king and parliament. I am associated with the house of Årström & Sons, in Stockholm, and should perhaps gain more by Stockholm's retaining its exclusive privileges of the world's trade. But it is a crying injustice to forbid industrious towns, the best places of export in the kingdom, from taking their commodities to whatever market they find most advantageous, and compel them to sell to the inhabitants of Stockholm below value, and buy of them for whatever they please to ask, that they may gain while all others lose. The trade of the kingdom will never in that way arrive at a flourishing condition ; all speculation will be crippled, and our poor towns be ruined. Finland is paying an enormous indirect tax, and Stockholm is sucking out the marrow of the land, without any permanent benefit to herself; for the more the country is impoverished, the less it consumes, and the less does Stockholm gain by her monopoly."

The austere old man grew warm as he reached the subject which he had set before himself as the aim of his life. The statesman heard him patiently, with a quiet smile ; and afterward continued, in the most friendly tone :

"To whom do you say this, my honored friend? To a man who perfectly shares your view, and, like you, looks upon this matter as the vital question of trade and commerce. But your enemies will object that you yourself are an example of the utility and adaptability of the system now under discussion. They will maintain that you yourself have under this system gained a very considerable fortune—that you own eight ships on the sea—that you are the greatest ex-porter of Finland—that your name is as good as gold in the commercial world, yes, that you have rightfully acquired the honorable title of the burgher king. . . ."

"So much the less, your grace, ought I to be charged with voting for the staple-right from selfish motives." And with these words the proud old man drew himself up, a head taller than before.

President Bertelsköld could not wholly suppress a peculiarly scornful, malignant, and ill-boding smile. "You are right," said he ; "your position is, for the present, happy and independent. Rich, respected, and powerful, celebrated, admired, and envied by all your colleagues, the happy father of a family—are you not? I believe you have kind and lovely children, and among

them a daughter who is the delight of your old age!
. . . . What more can a mortal ask of life? My dear
Larsson, allow me, a lonely old bachelor, also to envy
you your fortune!"

"Sir count, the question now is not about me
. . ."

"Exactly about you, my friend; or, what is the
same, the cause you espouse. Fancy, for example, that
all this rare and much-admired happiness, which all
envy, and which you—of course with all reason—
attribute to your own activity, prudence and industry
—fancy that this prosperity is a card house, built on
shifting sand, and ready to tumble down at the first
puff of wind, perhaps even while we are talking about
it."

Larsson looked him steadily in the face. But that
constant smile, that still cold countenance, it was impossible to penetrate.

The count proceeded: "I beg you to listen carefully to what I now have to tell you, and mark well
that I speak as a friend who only wishes your own
good. To begin with—you are going to lose your
lawsuit."

"That is possible."

"It is certain. My friend, it will seriously injure
your reputation. You will become prominent in it as
a man who wished—how shall I express myself?—to
rob his nearest relatives."

"Your excellency!"

"Hear me with patience. Why risk half your fortune, and all your reputation? Are the reasons not
sufficient for discontinuing that infamous litigation
which is ruining you? Consider who is your opponent:
an adventurer, a low fellow, a servant of my nephew.
And should a man like you allow that sort of person
to degrade him to the level of what your enemies
would call a greedy robber? It is impossible! We

must send your opponent to the morasses of Hungary,
whence he came."

"I thank your grace; but as such an accommodation
would lay me under an obligation which I cannot fulfill, I would rather face the risk, if so it must be."

"Really? Well, it is true that you still have a considerable property at your disposal, which is independent of your nephew's claim. I would remind you
that the whole of this, your business capital, and perhaps something over, is at present invested in a large
grain operation in Holland."

"I once more beg that your excellency will not
mingle yourself in my business."

"You will immediately perceive my reasons. I
have here a note which I received this morning from
the Hollandish minister. He writes me that the free
importation of grain into the Netherlands ceased on
the twenty-fifth of last October, and that, in direct
violation of the interdiction, a fleet of Swedish mer-
chantmen, laden with grain and belonging to the business house of Årström & Sons, of Stockholm, on the
twenty-sixth of October sailed into the Zuyder ⬤ee. I
am sorry for you, my friend, for you know how en-
vious the Hollanders are of your agricultural interests.
If diplomacy does not succeed in adjusting the affair,
the vessels and cargoes are subject to confiscation."

Larsson bit his lip. It was evident that the arrow
had reached his merchant-heart. But he controlled
himself. "I hope," said he, with composure, "that
the Swedish government will not permit so gross an
outrage against the property of its subjects."

"What is to be done? You remember under what
paltry pretexts Englishmen seized our vessels in the time
of Charles XI, and yet Sweden was then at the height
of her power. 'Myn heers' in Amsterdam are
unreasonably jealous, and I fear Sweden has no means
of procuring a hearing for the claims of her subjects.
You, who desire peace, *à tout prix*, of course you do

not wish to begin war on account of the grain fleet of Årström & Sons?"

"Your grace, if so infamous an outrage takes place, without a strict reclamation on the part of the Swedish administration, this miserable government does not deserve that an honest man should waste a word in its defense or a farthing in its support."

The president smiled. This was the very point he had wished to reach. "I am sincerely glad, my dear Larsson," said he, "to hear you utter a sound opinion, once, as to our political situation. You perceive the point to which we have come with this government, which humiliates us in our own eyes and the eyes of foreigners. And this government is the one you are defending in the house of burghers! No, my friend, we must have a change; and if it is longer delayed, your cause is also lost. The first care of the new government shall be to procure justice for all, and to take decided measures against the exorbitant pretensions of foreign powers."

Larsson reflected a few bitter moments; then he said : "I think I know Count Horn, and it is impossible that he can leave this matter without consideration."

Again the statesman smiled. "I doubt if Count Horn will think best to meddle with your concerns. For the present, he has enough of his own."

"He shall, he must hear me!"

"But if his dismissal only awaits the signature of the king?"

"Then I will turn to Count Bonde."

"And if his dismissal only awaits the signature of parliament?"

"Count Hård!"

"The same condition of things."

"Perhaps so But not before I have full assurance will I change my views in the house of burghers."

"Very well. You are quite free to do as you like.

I have advised you as a friend, but you prefer to be at
once dishonored and completely ruined. You can, at
all events, console yourself with your domestic happiness—your children. . . . ."

"I have told your excellency once before, that I
never sell my political convictions. Threaten or
flatter—it matters not. Is there anything else by
which I can be of service?"

"No. Heaven defend me from wishing to move
your patriotic principies. . . . . But, *apropos* of
your children—allow me, my dear Larsson, one more
question," and here the count assumed his blandest
smile. "I hope that your daughter is well? A charming being—I really admired her dancing at the masquerade at Count Tessin's."

"Sir count is mistaken. My youngest daughter is
a child, and can never have the honor of showing
herself in such high society."

"What, my friend? I was very sure that you were
an accomplice in that charming little intrigue, but I
did not suppose you any longer pretended to maintain
your daughter's *incognito*. For the rest, all Stockholm
is talking of nothing but Mademoiselle Larsson and
her lovely dance in the quadrille, in the presence of
royalty, where she played the *rôle* of Spring. I confess
that Count Tessin, and his majesty himself, heard
with some surprise that a person who had not been
invited had honored the *societé* with her presence."

"Your excellency, that is a vile slander!" The
last well-directed arrow had began to pierce the armor
of ice around the heart of the burgher king.

"But, my dear Larsson, why deny a little innocent
joke? A handsome girl can take liberties of which our
enlightened age ought not keep such accurate account.
You yourself saw what grace and confidence! Oh,
it was *charmant!* Your training would do honor to
a lady of the court!"

"When I tell your excellency that it is a lie, I ought

not to need to say it twice," responded Larsson, angry aud worried in the extreme.

"As you please. Ask the first one you meet on the street, what people have been talking about ever since yesterday. All the world knows that my nephew was the one who succeeded in getting your daughter out of the crowd. I say nothing of that. I approve of his taste."

"Base calumnies! Ah, you believe then, most honorable gentlemen, that you can, unpunished, insult the honor of a burgher!"

"Do not put yourself in a passion! Who is talking about honor. A bagatelle. Do you happen to know where your daughter is now?"

Larsson hesitated. It began to be plain to him that even his beloved child might become a victim to those machinations by which he was surrounded. His eyes flashed. "What does your excellency know about my daughter?" he asked with severity.

"Calm yourself! Your daughter is probably doing admirably. I heard, by accident, that she had ridden out to-day with a not over reputable young person by the name of Sager, for the purpose of dining with a crowd of jovial gentlemen at the Hôtel d' Espagne."

"My child! My Esther!" exclaimed the unhappy father, wringing his hands. He remembered the ride, and now believed all.

"At the hotel," continued the count, unsparingly, "some dispute is said to have arisen as to who possessed the greatest claim to your daughter's favor. Young and hot blood—you know how it goes. The consequence was two or three duels; Baron Krauser is reported to have fallen, and your daughter is said to have fled with one of the gentlemen. All this took place scarcely an hour ago. It was told me just before you came. You may be calm. So far as I know, your daughter is unharmed."

"Unharmed!" exclaimed the father, frantic with

rage, and approaching the count in a threatening manner. "Base villain! take all I possess—ah, you have already taken that—but give me back my Esther, my child, my beloved child!"

The count rung, and said to his *valet:* "Lead the member of the diet carefully down stairs,—he is suffering from a vertigo."

Larsson collected himself. "Sir count," said he, with still trembling voice, "you ought not to have forgotten the story of Marie Larsson, and the not too honorable share you had in it. There is a Providence that will revenge the wrongs of the humble on the heads of the mighty!"

"But, my dear friend . . . ."

"Insult me not with your friendship, sir count! From this hour we are mortal enemies!"

And the burgher king departed, more erect than he had come, without the least bend of his inflexible neck.

CHAPTER XXVIII.

COUNT HORN'S FALL.

WE shall now, quite contrary to the custom of the world, turn our gaze from the rising to the setting sun, from those who are climbing on the shoulders of the moment to those who are sinking beneath its weight. It must be remembered that we are speaking of past times and of a perishing greatness—noble and worthy of respect even in its fall—. not of those petty fawners whom the winds of time had undeservedly lifted to the heights, in order the next minute to blow them away again, back to their proper place in the depths.

And so far as these stories are read by Finnish eyes, it must be remembered also that Arvid Horn was a Finn, the greatest statesman whom the land east of the Bothnian Sea had thus far produced.

We now enter another cabinet, no less elegant and even more luxuriously furnished than that of President Count Torsten Bertelsköld. But this apartment, in all its magnificence, has an appearance of age. There is dust on the pictures, dust on the statues, dust on the splendid books in their cases, dust on the elegant silk and velvet covered furniture. The curtains droop in heavy festoons, and darken the room. The rugs are as soft as though the sound of the lightest footstep were intolerable to the occupant. Notwithstanding his known taste for. luxury and comfort, the possessor has not for a long time been able to prevail upon himself to have his office dusted and put in order. He places more value on not having the least article of furniture displaced or the least slip of paper removed from its place. He is conservative, even in the little habits of his daily life; and he has a right to be so, for he is seventy years old, and in his younger days helped Charles XII, after the manner of the times, to dust and put in order the kingdom of the North.

Count Arvid Horn, grown old and infirm, is now sitting by the heavily laden writing-desk. The machinery has not stopped; his secretary has but just departed, laden with letters to half the cabinets of Europe and half the offices of Sweden and Finland. Only a few minutes before, the old statesman had still been contriving new political combinations for the welfare of the kingdom, and peaceful plans for causing cultivation to conquer new realms within the much contracted boundaries of 1721. But lately, he was the soul in the political body of .his country, and the person who with steady hand held the reins of state, curbing the passions and adjusting the many hateful interests that antagonized, threatened, and sought to

U   18*

annihilate each other.   But he had now thrown from
his shoulders his worldly burdens.   He was weary.
He was seeking rest for his soul, and open before him
lay the large bible of Charles XII.   What was he
reading there?   It was the first chapter of Ecclesias-
tes: "All is vanity.   What profit hath a man of all
his labor which he taketh under the sun?   One generation passeth away and another generation cometh:
but the earth abideth forever.   The sun also ariseth,
and the sun goeth down, and hasteth to his place
where he arose.   The wind goeth toward the south,
and turneth about unto the north; it whirleth about
continually, and the wind returneth again according
to his circuits.   All the rivers run into the sea; yet
the sea is not full; unto the place from whence the
rivers come, thither they return again.   All things are
full of labor; man can not utter it; the eye is not
satisfied with seeing, nor the ear filled with hearing.
The thing that hath been, it is that which shall be;
and that which is done, is that which shall be done;
and there is no new thing under the sun.   Is there
anything whereof it may be said: See, this is new?
it hath been already of old time, which was before us.
There is no remembrance of former things; neither
shall there be any remembrance of things that are to
come with those that shall come after."

At these words the old man's venerable head sunk
to his hands.   The seventy years of his life, the thirty
years of his power, passed by him like a dream, and he
repeated the words of the preacher: "I have seen all
the works that are done under the sun; and behold,
all is vanity and vexation of spirit."

"Everything?" he asked himself.   And again
came the answer from his heart: "Emptiness, vanity,
evanescence."

Then his eyes fell upon another book, which had
lain open since the previous day.   It was the works of
Seneca.   It was opened at a passage which accorded

with the words of the Preacher, and ran thus: *" Quosdam, cum per mille indignitates in usum dignitatis subrepserint, misera subit cogitatio, ipsos laborasse in titulum sepulchri."* That is, "Some who, by a thousand unworthy means, have crept up to high dignities, are suddenly seized by the wretched thought that they themselves have been working on the inscription for their graves."

"What!" exclaimed he, "am I too one of those who were born for the dust and have artfully usurped a power which they were unworthy to wield? All my life-work—the battles of my youth for king and country—the labors of my manhood—and this free form of government, which I have founded, strengthened, and sustained in Sweden—is all this nothing but the inscription for my grave?"

He straightened himself up thoughtfully, and sunk into a gloomy meditation. Alas! what life is so spotless that an oppressive thought of one's own defects, one's own weaknesses, does not sometimes steal into the noblest heart, and displace that self-confidence which had perhaps lifted itself too high, that consciousness of great ideas and great deeds which perhaps in prouder moments was tempted to worship itself! The great and powerful man of mighty deeds was at this hour far more to be pitied than the day-laborer who counts the whole fruit of his toil by the weekly wages he receives on Saturday night. The poor workman sees a definite result before him; Count Horn saw his fatherland rent by parties, and himself gray and impotent,—and he asked himself the question: "For what, then, have I lived?"

The door opened, very softly as was the custom in this house, and the *valet* announced President Count Torsten Bertelsköld. The brow of the old statesman darkened to a veritable thunder cloud; but he said, "The count is welcome."

And with a careful step, as though in a sick room,

entered his former pupil, who had grown above the head of the master, and who now—Count Horn knew it perfectly—was the soul of that band who were working for his downfall. The two gentlemen understood each other; but however much the times had changed, there was still something left of the former relation of the master's superiority on the one side and the pupil's deference on the other. There was certainly not more than one mortal for whom Count Bertelsköld entertained a veneration, or rather a fear, which neither sneers nor artifice were ever able fully to overcome; and that was his former master, Count Arvid Horn.

And yet he had now—perhaps in the belief that no one else could succeed in it—taken upon himself the difficult task of prevailing upon the old statesman to descend voluntarily from his high place as the manager of the realm, and transfer his power into the hands of the Hats.

He began very cautiously, with some sympathetic questions concerning the health of his excellency, as though that had been the only and very natural object of his visit. All Sweden, he assured him, had heard with apprehension that the long-continued labors of his excellency for its weal had resulted in a bodily weariness, which he hoped, however, would not prevent his excellency, for many years to come, from devoting his ripe experience to the service of the country.

" Pardon me," interrupted Count Horn, in that well-known tone of frankness which the pupil very well imitated toward *his* clients, " have I the honor of receiving sir count as an individual friend, or as a deputy from the palace of nobles? "

The president assured him that he came merely from personal interest, to inform himself concerning the welfare of his excellency.

" I am glad of that. I might otherwise imagine that I had lived somewhat too long for the impatience of the lords. With the count, it is another matter.

But I am growing old for both friends and enemies. When one, like me, bears scars from two battle-fields, his vigor cannot reach eternity. My wound from Düna often reminds me of its existence; but I should perhaps forget that, if I were not now and then, on the civil battle-field, wounded by attacks both in the rear and flank. There is something which, to an old soldier, is worse than gout; and that is the imperial diet."

" Calumny will never be able to dim . . . . "

" Let us not speak of calumny. It does us the same service as those red-hot balls with which we warmed our wintry tents in Poland. Everything depends on how one takes them. *Apropos*, how do matters progress in the palace of nobles ? Are they going to get rid of me soon ? "

" Your excellency, the palace of nobles, like the other departments of government, know how to appreciate fully the eminent merits of your excellency."

" No compliments, I beg. Let us now drop our lessons in the obsequious style. How far, I ask, have they progressed with the catalogue of our sins in regard to the renewal of the treaty with Russia ? You know we have acted contrary to the precepts of the privy committee, have we not? And our fault was not diminished by the fact that its orders were sealed, and were awaiting a conjuncture which, in our opinion, had not taken place."

" Your excellency knows, better than I, that the Russian treaty is really looked upon as a gauntlet flung down to France, and that the plurality of the houses might perhaps call the council to account—just as the privy committee regards the conjuncture favorable to an alliance with Turkey, subsidies from France, and war with Russia. It is thought that something ought to be ventured for the honor and independence of the kingdom, and our lost provinces should be retaken."

" What? Favorable ? Because that adventurer, that Bonneval of Constantinople, makes you believe

all kinds of nursery tales about a Turkish alliance !
Honor and independence bought with the beggary of
French subsidies ! Lost provinces retaken by boys,
without an army, without field material, without a navy,
without money ! Are you so very sure then, gentlemen, that in such a rat-trap our Swedish lion might
not part with a bit of his ragged skin ? And where
have you the military genius that shall clear your path
to these fabulous victories ? I understand—give Lewenhaupt the compliments of one of Charles XII's old
soldiers, and tell him that countries are not conquered
by great words. Tell him that to win battles in the
field something else is needed than rostrum applause."

"I beg your excellency to be assured that the irri-
tation against the council, founded or unfounded, is
very strong; but as to your excellency a due deference
shall always . . . "

"Bah ! Who is speaking of me ?"

"And if it were not for the unfortunate note recently communicated to the Danish minister . . . "

"Explain yourself ! The Danish minister ?"

"Well—I cannot conceal it—your excellency's
haste to notify the Danish minister of the agreement
which your excellency recently concluded with France,
is thought to imply a danger to the alliance with the
last-named power, and some of the enemies of your
excellency threaten your excellency with a complaint
for that indiscretion."

"What ! We are to ask permission of France to
address questions to another power, touching our own
interests ? Is that it, gentlemen ? So it has come to
this, that a country calling itself free and independent
does not venture to utter a word without the consent
of its so-called allies !"

"Your excellency's enemies. . . ."

"What are my enemies to me ? The question is,
whether the country ought to be guided in leading-

strings by an artful cardinal in Paris or a debauched vagabond in Constantinople."

And the old man, but now so feeble, paced with the impetuosity of youth to and fro across the soft carpet. Suddenly he stopped in front of Bertelsköld, looked at him sharply, and asked : " Who is to be my successor ? You, or Gyllenborg ? "

Bertelsköld answered with composure: " May Heaven spare us that question many years ! But if the long labors of your excellency should merit a longed-for rest—if that complaint, whose absurdity your excellency is pleased to show so clearly, should really fill your excellency with just indignation—at least be assured that it is not I, who have had the honor to serve under your excellency, and am indebted to your excellency's guidance for any knowledge I may possibly possess in affairs of state, that it is not I who am aspiring to a station where *any one* must be eclipsed by his predecessor."

During these phrases Count Horn found time to calm himself. He once more sat down, and said, quite composedly : " *Enfin,* so it is you who purpose to make me superfluous."

" Your excellency, those suspicions ! " And Bertelsköld made a pretence of withdrawing, with all the indignation of insulted virtue and friendship. But Horn continued :

" Sir count, let us be candid ! I am sorry for my country, because, on account of the thirst for power of some and the desire for honor of others, it must be thrown from the peaceful career of freedom and progress into dangerous byways, where my old eyes can discover only perils and humiliations. I am tempted also to pity myself, because I have not succeeded in bringing up a school of statesmen other than talented intriguers and hot-headed politicians, whose views hardly reach to the point of their sword. Still, I have one reason to thank you, sir count, and I

do thank you. You have lifted a burden from my
heart. See here!" and he pointed to the passage in
Seneca which had just before made him so thoughtful
and despondent.

Seneca was no unknown greatness to Count
Torsten Bertelsköld, but he had long ago forgotten
that sentence. He returned the book, with the sneer-
ing remark that it was no doubt very moral.

"Oh, well," responded Horn, with that superior
greatness which for the moment swept the smile of
scorn away from his opponent's lips; "you there see
one of those symbols which the wisdom of antiquity
has launched forward through a thousand years at the
low scurfy forehead of ambition! I will now tell you,
sir count, why I thanked you. One moment I regarded
myself as having lived in vain. And before the
Almighty, small may that appear which my weak arm
has been able to accomplish. But when I measure my
work with yours, gentlemen successors, I then feel that
I have some right to say to you who are eager to be
rid of me: I have uplifted the kingdom of Sweden out
of its deepest debasement, mortal distress and desolation, to prosperity, respect and external independence.
I have plucked it out of the chains of despotism,
where it lay, impotent, bleeding, crushed, a prey to
Gortz and his compeers who were trampling it under
foot, and have restored to it its ancient liberty, the law
of 1734, and, what is more than laws, respect for itself.
I received it a hopeless ruin; I relinquish it a kingdom
of the future and of vital strength. Gentlemen, what
are you going to do with my work? What are you
going to do with that realm I deliver to you?"

Bertelsköld did not answer. This time his Latin
was at an end.

Count Horn continued: "But there was a moment when the words of the old Roman struck me
with the sharp sword of truth, as I stand at the close
of my career; and I asked myself if my expedients

had always been the worthiest—if I, too, had not been working for an empty and miserable title which was to become my epitaph. I may well confess that, in the presence of the Great Judge above, I am as impure as any other mortal, full of defects and vanity. But if I compare myself with you, gentlemen successors, I have then some right to say to you that I have not smuggled myself into power by pushing away a predecessor! I have not sustained myself by lies and fraud—I have not, with wretched artifices, deluded king and country, in order as long as possible to bask in power and elevate myself as one of the mighty ones of earth. No, gentlemen! Into the place I occupied I have been lifted by the storms of the times and by a political necessity; and I have retained it so long as I have had the consciousness of being useful to my country. And I am not cast down from it, as you shall one day be cast down; I descend of my own free will, when I see my designs misapprehended and my power broken; and I descend, myself a free man, surrounded by free fellow-citizens, from that hight to which I arose in battle against a tyranny which through me has been lifted from the shoulders of all. You there see, sir count, why I have you to thank. . . . And now you are free to act as you please. I will hand in my resignation to-day."

Count Bertelsköld wanted to say something more, but he found no words. He stood like a schoolboy before the rod of the old master; and he withdrew, mute, humiliated, full of rage, but also with the scornful smile of vengeance and victory deeply hidden within the prison of his lips.

And Count Arvid Horn, left alone, returned to the large bible of Charles XII, to lay his lost power at the feet of Him who hath the heavens for his throne and the earth for his footstool.

14

CHAPTER XXIX.

ESTHER LARSSON'S FLIGHT.

WHEN the young girl and her protector first galloped toward the highway from Horn's gate, it is probable that neither of them comprehended the whole danger of their adventurous undertaking. Esther understood only that she would not, dared not, return to Stockholm, where she had been so grossly scandalized and was now a general topic of conversation, and to her father, whose severity was as relentless in punishing a fault as his love had been excessive in spoiling a darling child. How had he not treated Marie Larsson, her cousin, who appealed to his protection, and was so received that, rather than remain in her uncle's house, she jumped from the window in the wintry night! Esther, when a child, had heard her sister Veronica tell that touching incident; it had made the liveliest impression upon her; and now she herself, more to blame than her cousin, must expect a similar, even a crueler, reception. Her only distinct thought, therefore, was that she must hasten away; but where, she knew not.

For awhile, the two young people rode silently side by side. Bertelsköld, however, older and more experienced, soon returned to a calmer deliberation, and threw out a word as to whether Esther might not repent her flight; if so, it would be better to turn about in time.

The young girl answered, impetuously, that he might turn back if he liked, but she should upon no consideration return to Stockholm.

"Well, then," said the youth, "from this hour we

are brother and sister. Your confidence shall be
sacred to me ; and as a proof of that, I will take you
to my mother."

The ride was continued. It grew dark, and gradually cooler. The two young people were glad in the
evening to reach Mariefred.

But to stop here had its dangers, for Larsson would
certainly not spare any means of regaining his lost
daughter. Bertelsköld therefore took care that their
horses were sent back to Stockholm, bought a sledge
and a warmer cloak for Esther, and continued the
journey by post through the night to Nyköping.
Thence a courier was sent down toward Norrköping,
and so on southward; and letters were sent to Malmö,
with inquiries concerning the opportunity for crossing
over to Denmark. All this was to bewilder pursuit.
The fugitives also took the road leading out of town;
but after going three miles they exchanged clothes
with some peasants, and turned off to the right, on the
road toward Örebro. They now traveled in the character of an inspector of manufactories and his sister,
who were on their way from Säter to enter service in
a manufactory in the Nora mining region; and, as
such, succeeded in forming the traveling companionship of a talkative masculine butcher-woman from
Örebro, who had been down to Stockholm to sell
hides. This honorable personage did not neglect so
good an occasion to ease her heart, in advance, from
the burden of all the important Stockholm news she
was taking with her to the country. Next to the prices
of tallow and hides, which in her chronicles occupied
the foremost place, a trifle of politics accompanied
everything, as the old woman belonged to the Hat
party—for the natural reason that if there should be
war there would be soldiers, and if there were soldiers
those soldiers would need boots and knapsacks, which
again might be a little profit to poor burghers in those
hard times. Further, the old woman's art of reckon-

ing did not extend. This again gave an opportunity to make an ado about the diet and the Caps, the burgher king Larsson included. . . . . And then he was said to have a daughter, that Larsson, a half-silly girl, who one night dressed up like a lady and went up to a dance at the court, and invited the king himself to dance; and when the queen saw it she was so angry that she fainted on the spot, as she sat on her royal throne; and then the king said that it must have been some witchcraft, as the girl had bewitched him. For you see she was Finnish, and anything whatever can be believed about the Finns. But then, when they looked after the girl, she had disappeared like smoke, whether through the window or chimney no one could exactly say; but the queen had never been able to forget it, but had said she wished the Russians had taken the whole of Finland, for only sorcery and evil-minded people came from there. For it is said to be a doubtful land; there the coffee is so thick that the spoon stands upright in the cup, and when they pour in the cream they are obliged to cut it off with sheep-shears.

To attempt to contradict the worthy old woman in her narrations would have been vain, and our travelers had to put up patiently with these stories, which were neither better nor worse than those commonly served up by rumor. In their position they were obliged to regard it as a piece of good fortune that their companion kindly offered them lodgings for the night in her house in Örebro; and the following day, after they had for the first time during their adventurous trip allowed themselves some rest, they continued the journey northward, to the old Countess Bertelsköld's Falkby estate, on the borders of East Gothland.

Of this fine estate only a small and detached portion remained to its former possessor, who now, in an unpretentious rural dwelling, was spending the evening of her once stormy life. The greater share of the property had gone under the hammer, for crown-arrears, since the time of the extortions of Gortz, and for that cruel visitation she was indebted to her powerful brother-in-law, President Torsten Bertelsköld, who, as we know, with all the thirst for. revenge of a formerly slighted lover, had sworn her an implacable enmity. Against his influence all attempts at reclamation had been in vain; and the countess now possessed, over and above her son's support, only enough to relieve her actual want. At Falkby—a life estate, which the crown, "by favor and grace," bestowed on the widow of the brave Carolin, Gösta Bertelsköld—two kinds of festivals were known, besides the usual holidays. The one took place when Countess Ebba Liewen, formerly Bertelsköld, visited her sister-in-law and the beloved friend of her youth; and the other when the only son, Charles Victor, found leisure to visit his mother. These precious visits were bright spots in the otherwise monotonous and secluded life at Falkby, and its almanac measured time from one visit to the other. Whenever the rare fortune occurred that both took place simultaneously, the countess at Falkby used to say merrily that she felt two centuries younger, as she then had on the one side the youth of the seventeenth century, and on the other, next to her heart, that of the eighteenth century. "It is a pity," added she, in the same tone, with a tear in her still-sparkling dark eye, "that the great war lies between the two."

Charles Victor Bertelsköld felt his heart beat more quickly at these memories of his mother, when in the twilight of one of the last days of November he recognized in the distance the barren frost-covered birches of Falkby. His thoughts had hitherto been almost exclusively taken up by the care of the young traveling companion whom he had so unexpectedly come to bring with him,—how for her sake he would soften all the discomforts of the journey; how he would cheer her with the hope of happier times, and with the most respectful delicacy relieve her from that depressing feeling of her loneliness and defencelessness by the side of a young man so far above her in social position. And it seemed as if a propitious star alone had reserved to Esther Larsson that bitter humiliation in order to subdue in her soul that capricious and willful defiance which by nature and training had been her greatest and most dangerous fault, and which under other conditions would doubtless have been her certain ruin. Her pride and presumption were broken; the severe trial, aggravated by the petty Stockholm gossip of their traveling companion, had penetrated to her very heart's core, and for the first two days Esther had no other answer to her protector's encouraging words than her silence and tears.   Not until the third day did she regain sufficient calmness to be able now and then to repay the attention of the count with some little reciprocal service, such as mending his torn glove and preparing for the brief dinner of both a basin of warm milk at the inn.   And one who had seen Esther Larsson so humbly and unassumingly attending to these little cares would hardly have recognized the same rash girl who but a short time before had dashed along the streets of Stockholm so that the sparks flew from under the horse's hoofs, and the crowds of people separated, supposing themselves in danger from a runaway horse.

This change touched Bertelsköld deeply.   He had avoided any allusion to those words which, in the tempestuous feelings of the moment, had escaped him in the side room of that unhappy Hôtel d' Espagne. But those words were beginning to grow in her heart. If the sculptor beholds with a feeling of love the lifeless clay which under his hand is assuming beautiful and harmonious forms, with what emotions must not a noble-minded young man, of fine sensibilities, regard a young and rich but shapeless and misdirected woman-soul, which under his hand is regaining the simple and modest grace of a noble -womanhood? "Alas," thought he, "what treasures of goodness and loveliness have lain concealed within that neglected being, and what a noble character can yet be shaped of this child of nature, if she only comes under the right motherly care—she, who has never been cared for by any mother ! "

"Courage, Esther ! " said he, comfortingly. "Courage, my little weeping sister ! Do you see the birches over there at the left, on the shore of the bay? Perhaps you can yet in the twilight discover a little red-painted house, with white window frames and a tall flag-staff at the gable? That is all that remains of my mother's estate—for my father possessed only his long sword,—and it is there you shall find a mother."

Esther did not answer. Not the twilight, but the tears, had dimmed her eyes.

"And a good and noble mother," continued the youth, warmly. "You are a wise child, Esther. I ought, therefore, to tell you that at the first meeting you may expect something cold, perhaps something haughty, on the part of my mother. Many and bitter sufferings have made her distrustful of humanity. But as soon as I have had time to tell her who you are and what you have suffered, as soon as she has my knightly word on your honor and innocence, her arms will without hesitation be open to you, and you shall not regret that you intrusted yourself to her protection and mine."

Bertelsköld had seen something of the world, but yet too little to rightly measure the strength of discretion in a sixteen-year-old heart. Esther was seized with dreadful anguish. "Stop ! " she exclaimed. " In pity rather let me go and hide myself in the poorest hut. Alas ! I shall die of shame before a single humiliating look ! "

"But I promise you, upon my honor, that you shall rest like an own child in my mother's arms."

"No, no, stop! In kindness, stop, sir count!" continued Esther, in the same tone, which still bore the trace of her former impetuous humor, as she again unconsciously addressed her companion by a title which implied the whole distance between their birth and social position.

"Well," said Bertelsköld, after a short deliberation, "I will fulfill your wish. In the little cottage by the gate lives an old woman, Flinta, my mother's faithful servant—she, too, the widow of a brave Carolin. Her heart is softer than her name; and you shall stop with her till everything is prepared and I come to fetch you."

CHAPTER XXX.

OLD ACQUAINTANCES.

WHEN the summer of life is vanished and the autumn wind sweeps through the forest, wonderful it is to see what various tracks it leaves in the tree-tops. Some of them are ravaged without compassion; the leaves wither and fall, and the branches are bare. Others wither, and in part fall, so that the side-branches throw off their verdure, while the green of summer still tarries for awhile in the tops. Others again resist the devastation, or rather they only acquire from it a new and equally perishable beauty, in those many colored motley leaves which clothe them in a touching beauty, sweeter and sadder than even the freshness of youth.

And thus it is with those perishable blossoms of womanly beauty, which, like the others, bloom and

wither, are flattered and forgotten, tremble awhile
before the whistling of the wind, and then sink away
in silent night. Unlike for them also is the period of
beauty, unlike the traces of decay ; much depends on
outer storms—the most, however, on inner calm or
inner strife. .

Two once charming women, both in their youth
objects of the admiration of Stockholm and of the
knightly homage of the proud Carolins, now sat, old
and forgotten, in the little red house at Falkby farm.
The two were of the same age, now fifty-six. Both
were noble-minded, high-spirited beings ; both had
shared the same sorrows and the same memories ;
each had loved the other sincerely and faithfully since
childhood. But as the disposition of each had changed
in unlike colors, so also the features of each bore a
dissimilar impress from the autumn of the year.
Countess Ebba Liewen, once Bertelsköld, had retained
a large share of the beauty of youth; the lovely milk-
white complexion, the sweet, kind, blue eyes, which at
the least tender emotion were filled with tears ; the
comely, full form, which had only acquired a tendency
to the dignified stoutness of the matron ; only the
blonde hair had turned somewhat thin and gray.
Countess Eva Bertelsköld, once Falkenberg, had
externally hardened, as it were, under the influence of
time. The once slender and flexible figure had become
thin and somewhat stiff. The vivacious and beautiful
features had acquired a touch of severity ; the black
hair had begun to be interspersed with a few silver-
gleaming threads ; but the dark and once flashing eyes
still retained their enchanting lustre.

Countess Bertelsköld was now celebrating one of
her longed-for festivals. The beloved friend of her
youth had been allured by the first fine sledging to
travel the seventy-five miles which separated them, and
visit her at Falkby. According to her own assertion,
she had grown a century younger, and did not suspect

V

that she was soon to gather the youth of the other century also to her throbbing mother-heart.

The two friends were seated in the twilight, by the work-table, in the sitting-room, talking confidentially of the new and the old. Countess Liewen was child-less; it was therefore natural that the love of both had encompassed that subject which stood nearest to them both, the son and the nephew, Charles Victor Bertel-sköld. They both spoke of his amiable and gentle character, which so vividly reminded them of his grandfather, Bernhard Bertelsköld, and of his inten-tions to achieve, during the storms of the times, a firm and honorable position in the community. Both were agreed that this position ought to be made sure by an advantageous alliance with some of the powerful families of the kingdom; for neither of them expected any trustworthy support from the selfish uncle, Presi-dent Bertelsköld. But both possessed feelings too fine, and knew too well all the danger of cold calculations, to decide such a match without a nobler incentive. Their mutual hope was therefore that the beloved youth might himself choose and find a bride worthy of him, at the Swedish court; and Countess Ebba jest-ingly proposed that both should, for the first time, lay aside their wonted mourning costume on the happy day when they should see Charles Victor united with a noble and engaging wife, of high lineage, and worthy of him.

During this conversation, the twilight had almost inperceptibly changed to darkness, when the door softly opened, and a man stepped into the room, where for a few moments he was a silent witness of the friendly compact. Then he stepped briskly forward, threw himself into Countess Bertelsköld's arms, and in a joyful tone exclaimed: "Forbear, my dear mother!"

The countess gave a cry of delight, as she recog-nized her son. The young man hastened from her to

kiss the hand of his aunt. Next to his mother, there
was scarcely anyone in the world for whom he cherished such an unbounded respect and affection as for
the angelic and pious Countess Ebba.

Charles Victor resolved not to leave a favorable
occasion unimproved, and accordingly, when the first
greetings were past, he turned to his aunt, and asked
for the intercession of her kind heart for a young and
unhappy being, who asked the sheltering favor of his
mother.

"What?" said Countess Ebba astonished. "My
intercession? Foolish boy! When did your mother ever
refuse her aid to unmerited misfortune?"

"Never, it is true," replied the youth, somewhat
embarrassed; "but my mother will judge, perhaps
more severely than my aunt, a person who has been
guilty of a youthful error."

Countess Eva regarded her son with searching and
somewhat clouded eyes. "Explain yourself," said
she; "who is it that has been guilty of a youthful
error?"

Charles Victor clasped her hand, and looked her
fearlessly and frankly in the eyes. "I bring with me
a young girl, whom I wish to place under my mother's
protection," said he, in a pleading tone.

The face of the countess darkened still more. "My
son," said she, severely, "you come from a frivolous
court, where it is said that that which in my youth
passed for virtue and honor, has now become a myth.
Must I endure the disgrace that you too. . . . . But
no! Tell me that I misunderstood your words. Your
father's son cannot forget his knightly honor, cannot
forget the respect due himself and his old mother."

"Of course he cannot; let him explain himself,"
pleaded, gently as ever, the Countess Ebba.

The young man now related, openly and simply,
his first accidental meeting with Esther Larsson at the
ramparts of Korsholm, at the tumult at old Larsson's,

and afterward in Lillkyro forest. He did not forget
to tell how she had saved his life on the ice at Danvik ; how he had offered her lessons in music ; how,
in childlike rashness, she had intruded, disguised, at
the unhappy masquerade at Count Tessin's, and how
that indiscretion had cost her her reputation and been
attended with the affront at the Hôtel d'Espagne. He
did not conceal the faults of Esther, but he depicted
.her training as the motherless and spoiled youngest
child of the wealthiest family in her native province ;
all the weakness of her father, and all his inexorable
severity, which she feared worse than death. He did
not forget to mention her uncommon qualities of both
mind and heart ; and closed with a prayer that his
mother would take that young, unhappy, and persecuted girl under her protection, until in some way her
father's pardon had been obtained.

The two ladies heard him with patience, merely
exchanging questioning glances now and then, when
the story became too pitiful to be explained except on
the ground of sympathy. When he had concluded, a
kind of family consultation took place.

"Have you reflected," said Countess Bertelsköld,
"that the law must adjudge you to be in the wrong, yes,
even threaten you with strict accountability? What
have you done, my son? You have snatched a daughter
from her father!"

"Mother, there are higher obligations than those of
the law."

"That is true. But if the letter of the law protects
the most sacred of all earthly obligations, do you
nevertheless venture to defy it? What do you ask of
me? You ask that a mother shall help you to rend a
father's heart!"

"Alas, you do not know that cruel father! He is
capable of killing her ; but he will not do that. He
will treat her more cruelly—he will sell her as a. wife
to a man whom she abhors."

"If it is a decent man, she must esteem herself fortunate to find that deliverance out of a scandal in which she does not seem to be altogether innocent. Your heart, my son, has in this case spoken more loudly than your judgment. But let us consult that which ought to speak more loudly than both judgment and heart—our conscience. Ask yourself if your sympathy for this young girl is so utterly free from selfish hopes that you could frankly look her mother in the eye—in case she had a mother—and say : 'What I do for Esther is solely for her sake.'"

The young man was silent.

"Well," continued the countess, "if on so delicate a question you cannot appear perfectly disinterested, so that your conscience does not smite you with the least upbraiding, then let us immediately send this imprudent child back to her father in Stockholm."

"Pardon me, Eva," interposed Countess Liewen, as her beautiful eyes filled with tears. "I have never been able to distinguish between the voices of the heart and of conscience ; and my heart tells me that we would be acting cruelly if we thrust from us an unhappy being who appeals to our protection, without even hearing and knowing her own self. Allow Charles Victor to present her to you. Be kind to the poor child ; lonely and forsaken as she now is, she needs comfort even more than she needs advice."

"God bless you, my beloved aunt !" exclaimed the young man, warmly kissing her hand.

The sternness in Countess Bertelsköld's countenance gave way before this irresistible sunshine. "Ebba," said she, tenderly, " when you shall be removed to the mansions of the blest, even the lost will choose you for their advocate; for your goodness is enough to melt the very gates of Heaven. Well, my son, your aunt did not think out that justice—she felt it; and that signifies more. Go, bring the young girl hither. This evening we will only think of my happiness in

having at my side all that is dearest to me on earth . . . .
But what? Your arm is bandaged? You are wounded?
How did it happen?"

Charles Victor could not lie. He was forced to
tell of the duel, which he had hitherto kept to himself.
His wounded arm was not yet healed.

"A duel! Great Heavens! And you killed your
opponent! Why did you not tell that immediately?
We must now think of your safety. Wait; I have had
some experience in dressing wounds; I had good practice in 1716, at the siege of Kajana castle." And with
these words the young man was obliged to throw off
his coat, and permit an examination of the wounded
arm.

"The bandage is well applied," said she. "Who
put it on?"

"My traveling companion," replied the young man,
smiling. "You see, mother, she perhaps might not be
unworthy of becoming your pupil."

"It is doing well, and is not dangerous, if not
neglected," continued the countess, as with skillful
hand she applied a new bandage. "But what is this!
A scar on the cheek! Where did you get that scar?
You blush! Not in any dishonorable strife, I hope?"

"Ah, you embarrass Charles Victor. A mother
ought not to ask too much," again interposed Countess Ebba, with a kindly smile.

"Perhaps my mother will permit me to bring
hither my traveling companion?" said Charles Victor,
in order to escape this examination.

"Can she not be sent?"

"No; she would not come then."

"What? Not come?"

"Certainly not."

"Well—go, then; but do not stay long."
Bertelsköld went.

"Does he love her?" asked Countess Ebba, after
he had gone.

"Alas! I can scarcely doubt it," replied the afflicted mother. "What a misfortune! But he must be saved!"

"Eva—what do you intend to do? Never forget that we, too, have been young—that we, too, have loved and suffered!"

Countess Eva pressed her friend's hand. A chord had been touched which had never ceased to vibrate.

Before they had left these recollections, the door once more opened, and Charles Victor entered, this time very pale.

"Well!"

"Esther has fled. She is not to be found. She regarded her long waiting as a refusal from my mother!"

CHAPTER XXXI.

THE MINE SPRINGS.

WE now advance over two months of time, to January, 1739. The long and intricate threads of the political intrigue were now well spun; the net had been paid out, and drawn so near shore that the large fishes were thought to be secure. The largest whale had, moreover, been harpooned, and drawn on dry land, where he had not since moved a fin. The Finnish unicorn—according to the eloquent metaphors of the time—had ceased to gore. Count Horn had descended from the pinnacle of power; and when this bugbear had fallen, the Hats felt little need to observe many ceremonies with the little bugbears.

The council of the kingdom was then accused, before the privy committee, of all sorts of errors: for instance, that, contrary to the instruction of the privy committee, since the last diet it had neglected the French and Turkish alliances, renewed the treaty with Russia, taken measures for the appointment of three vice-admirals at one time, contrary to the statute of titles, etc., etc. Their excellencies had defended themselves valiantly and worthily, but without effect.

This first success of the Hats came very near resulting in defeat at the outset. The other houses, of which they believed themselves secure, began to resist. The parties were of almost equal power in the palace of nobles, but in the other departments the Caps preponderated. The peasants were hesitating; the clergy and the burghers were defending the councilors, on the ground that they did not understand wherein these gentlemen had particularly erred. The Hats, foaming with rage, were exerting their utmost powers, and succeeded in prevailing upon the house of burghers to share their views.

Thus matters stood at the point where the individual threads of this story were once more knit together with the common skein of that noted revolution.

All Stockholm was in a ferment, all departments of government were in session, and the parties were contesting with the utmost passion for the supremacy. The house of burghers had divided into two factions. Plomgren and his adherents were doing everything to draw the plurality over to the side of the Hats. But on the opposite side stood Larsson, the burgher king, firm as iron and inflexible as a pine from the barrens of his homeland; and behind him a mass of citizens from the provincial towns, whose opposition was considerably sharpened by the general grudge against the privileges of the burghers of Stockholm. The principal argument was still that they wanted to know wherein the council had erred. The Hats replied, according to their instructions, that it could not be revealed; that it was a state secret. The Caps then stubbornly responded, that since the error was invisible the punishment ought to be the same. The Hats objected that it was enough that the privy committee knew the errors. The Caps replied that justice was more than all state secrets. It was impossible to drive them from this position.

The same hot battle was fought out within that fiery forge of all diet intrigues, the privy committee, where the resolution was to be taken. By eighteen votes plurality, the nobility there pronounced the word "guilty." But the clergy could not be persuaded to coincide. The burghers were divided here as in their full session; and yet everything now depended upon them, for if they kept with the nobility there would be two departments against one, as the peasants had no deputies in the privy committee, and this body voted by departments. In this decisive moment, when victory already seemed to lean toward the side of the Caps, and the burgher king stood like a rock, impregnable to all assaults, a note was placed in his hand, with the request that he should read it immediately, as the contents were extremely pressing. He mechanically opened it, and read the following short lines:

" A person who can give you information concerning your lost daughter is awaiting you in the corridor. If the welfare of your daughter is dear to you, come instantly."

There was no signature. The expedient had been well planned. The argument which Larsson held in readiness to confute the opposition and encourage his adherents died on his lips. He passed his hand across his high forehead, furrowed by care, and strode silently out.

Confusion and dismay arose among the Caps. What could induce their leader to leave them, in so important a moment, in the power of the plurality of the nobility ? Plomgren was not slow to answer that question. It was evident, he claimed, that the honorable member of the diet had nothing further to add;

14*

he was convinced, and regarded the cause he had defended as lost before God and man.

Meantime, Larsson found in the corridor the good and worthy wedded half of the butcher woman from Örebro, the same that a few weeks before had offered the two fugitives a night's lodging in her house. This estimable burgher declared himself moved to tell Larsson all he knew about the fugitives, who were supposed to be the same young persons who had pretended to be traveling to the Nora mining region. His story was so important that Larrson's pursuit was very naturally led in the wrong direction, and thus by means of the civil authorities and his own messengers, he had caused the track of the fugitives to be followed as far as Malmö, but of course without success.

The burgher king heard him, with frowning brow and compressed lips. At this moment he had forgotten everything—the diet, the council of the kingdom, Hats and Caps, friends and enemies ; everything was indifferent to him, if he could only get some intelligence concerning his lost child. But to his eager questions the butcher could only confess what was the truth, that he had no idea whatever as to where the two young persons had gone when they left Örebro.

The minutes passed, and Larsson had not yet finished his inquiries, when one of his most ardent adherents rushed out of the committee-room and besought him by all means to return, for their party was going down. The old man awakened as from a dream. " Yes, yes," said he, and returned abstractedly. It was too late. The Hats had won the victory with the burghers also, by a plurality of four votes ; and five councilors were declared guilty.

Larsson was silent ; in that moment of dissension, he was rent in twain. The father and the citizen were contending for his soul ; the one had taken possession of his heart, the other still retained mastery in his head.

The Hats in the committee now hastened to report the resolutions concerning the dismissal of the five most eminent councilors, Counts Bonde, Hård, Bjelke, Barck and Creutz, who were allowed to retain their former titles and four thousand dollars annual pension. But the political *coup* was not yet finished. The resolution of the privy committee was further to be approved by the estates of the realm in their full assembly.

And now the song, in all its changes, was begun over again. The debates of the estates became more and more stormy. It lacked but little of a pitched battle in the house of lords. The reason of this was again the obstinacy of the house of burghers.

Vanquished in the committee, Larsson had once more, with the whole power of his influence and inflexible character, appeared in the house of burghers in the defence of the arraigned councilors. Never had his voice sounded so effectively; never had his simple, practical argumentation been so well adapted to the comprehension of his audience, for the very reason that he who hit the nail so squarely on the head was himself a man from their own ranks. In short, vigorous, thrilling words, Larsson showed how the kingdom under the system of Horn had worked itself up out of its impotence into prosperity; how peace would be a vital question to the land ; how it was now sought to depose the councilors in order to bring another party into power; and how, if that was successful, there would soon infallibly be war, poverty, loss of men, civil hatred and threatening destruction. He therefore conjured his colleagues to listen to neither bribes nor threats from the opposite side. Like free Swedes they should stand by the good cause, and the right would at last triumph, while the unrighteous would be scattered like chaff to the four winds of heaven.

" Take care, Larsson ! " whispered from close behind him one of the hired adherents of the Hats. "Take care! Do you not know that outside there are crowds of blue-coats who are asking all comers and goers as to their resolution?"

"Men of Sweden, do you hear!" cried Larsson, in thunder tones that re-echoed through the hall. "They threaten us with the blue-coats! I ask whether the country has clothed its soldiers to defend us from violence, or to suppress the honest, lawful, free speech of the estates of the kingdom!"

At these words an indescribable tumult arose, and the greater portion of the house gathered around the burgher king, shouting aloud that no one should presume to deny them their lawful right.

Meanwhile Plomgren had slipped out and hastened to the palace of nobles, with the information that the cause of the Hats would be lost in the house of burghers if a deputation was not sent thither without delay, "which silenced the daring and encouraged the faint-hearted." The correction of the protocol was immediately discontinued. A large number of the nobility crowded around the bar with the cry, "*Pro patria et libertate*," and nominated themselves as deputies, with Lewenhaupt as leader. On the other side, Judge Hammarberg obtained a hearing, and represented how unbecoming it was for the one house to wish to force its opinion upon the other; and that if the deputation went to the burghers, he would immediately follow, with the other half of the nobility, and declare the deputation illegal, as sent without due vote. The confusion exceeded all bounds; seven or eight members sprang toward Hammarberg, shouting that he ought to be thrown out of the window; others drew their swords, and the Caps placed themselves with their backs against the wall to defend their lives. In vain did General Wrangel entreat them to remember that they were Swedish and not Polish noblemen. Count Tessin, speaker of the upper house, who had been "indisposed," appeared during the tumult in his dressing gown, and, after long rapping, obtained a hearing, when the uproar was by degrees quieted by the assurance that the deputation should retire, which also occurred with much clamor.

Its arrival at the house of burghers renewed the tumult and uncertainty there. The shopkeepers of the large towns became greatly alarmed. In vain did Larsson seek to inspire them with courage. He gained only delay. They wanted to consider more carefully. The burgher king was furious. "Consider," he exclaimed, "consider, when a righteous cause and the welfare of the kingdom hang upon our words? Are you burghers? Are you free men? And these whelps of nobility, who, if we were not the representatives of the realm, and thus just as good as they, would trample us under foot,—you let them, unpunished, deprive us of speech!"

Again some one behind him whispered: "Larsson, come out! Your daughter is a prisoner at the house of Countess Bertelsköld, at Falkby, in East Gothland."

Larsson did not even turn around. He passed his hand across his forehead; but only for a moment. The next minute he was again absorbed in his subject, unconcerned as to the noise, which from all points was outvoicing him. Such obstinacy and firmness made an impression on the faint-hearted, and they once more began to gather around the tall, powerful, white-haired old man, who so fearlessly led the cause of free speech and justice against the power of the nobility which threatened to grind them all. And again victory leaned to the side of the Caps. They at least carried through a mitigating resolution declaring that milder measures should be taken toward the councilors.

A message received a few days afterward changed everything. Four of the accused councilors had declared that in order to save the kingdom from civil feud, they would voluntarily resign their office.

Consternation, astonishment, triumph, and malicious delight alternated among friends and enemies. The burgher king had lost his highest stake. The Hats had won the victory.

CHAPTER XXXII.

Letter from Countess Eva Bertelsköld, née Falkenberg, to her son, lieutenant of engineers, Count Charles Victor Bertelsköld.

FALKBY, Jan. 20, 1739.

MY BELOVED CHARLES:—It was with the greatest relief that I received your note from Bergen, thanking God every day that in such dangers he helped you happily over the border to Norway; hoping also that you further find yourself *sain et sauf*, which, to your poor mother, is, next to God, the greatest comfort in this sad separation. That you propose, in the spring, to go thence to England, I have nothing against, provided, dear son, that you do not run in debt for the costly journey, and will take good heed that in London, which to many a youth is a bottomless gulf, you, God willing, do not receive harm. And there is said to be now-a-days frequent duelling among the youth of *société*. Dear son, I persuade you nothing concerning this that you have not already known and considered; reflecting that your *malheur* in Stockholm is to you a reminder that God and the king have given you a noble sword, to be used with valor against the enemies of the kingdom, and not in *avéntures* and strange *rencontres*. Take no offense at my maternal candor. God knows that it is well meant, and that I sufficiently know your noble character. But I think of your deceased father, how he so faithfully and manfully fought, even unto death, for king and country, constant amidst all adversities to the one end of fearing God and fighting for that which ought to be regarded the highest and holiest in this world, without heeding the foolishness of youth, and such sport as is now-a-days in fashion. For that reason he also left to you a glorious name, which is your only inheritance, and which, with God's help, you are to preserve honorably, and leave to your posterity.

Dear son, concerning your *affaire,* I have taken the liberty to write to her majesty, and have lately received a gracious and courteous reply, through Countess Tessin. Her majesty has been pleased to remember your late father, and also spoke of you, yourself, with praise, promising, *à tout possible,* to grant you her gracious protection. Your aunt—who, *particulierement* for that matter, has gone to Stockholm—writes that your uncle, the president, acquires greater influence every day, and has every probability of succeeding Count Horn in the council. He can thus, thank God, prevent his name from being drawn before the courts of justice in your person. But Ebba has not yet had the submissiveness to seek him; you know that none of the family has had the fortune to profit by his favor and affection—if, indeed, it may be called fortune. I may furthermore add that Baron Von Krauser, whom you had the misfortune to kill, is said to have been a *horreur* to all good people, and Count Hård is reported to have given as his opinion that you ought to have a reward, and no censure, for having freed Stockholm from that scourge, who had caused the death of seven or eight young persons in duels. Which, dear son, does not lessen your fault before the omniscient God, for so unfortunately bringing a guilty man prematurely before that judge who does not relent.

My beloved Charles, I earnestly entreat you not to

allow any despondency to gain control over you. Your pardon and return cannot be delayed longer than next spring. I need not say with what emotions you shall then be received at Falkby.

The unhappy young person who ran away from Flinta, and whom, the day afterwards, we found half dead with cold in the cottage on the other side of the lake, is still under my care, and is well. I confess that she has caused me much disquietude—not, however, through her conduct, which has from the beginning been more modest and submissive than I could have expected of her. That her education proved to be greatly neglected, was to have been foreseen. She has imposed upon herself the strictest care not to let me observe this; and whenever anything unreasonable has entered her mind she has always become angry, and afterward begged me, with tears, not to send her away. These excesses have, however, seldom occurred during the last week; and she has a tender heart and a firm character, on which I ' place much value. I have selected for her the best books in my library, which she reads with diligence and understanding; and every evening she reads to me out of your late father's bible, to my great comfort, particularly since my eyes do not permit me to read by artificial light.

What troubles and disturbs me is, as you can imagine, the arrival of her father, which I am dreading daily. God help us, dear Charles—what are we to answer, when that harsh man comes, to demand back what by right belongs to him, his own child? And it cannot be presumed that he will long remain in ignorance of that protection she has found at Falkby, although the duties of the diet, in which he is said to be much involved, have hitherto prevented him from seeking her. I proposed to the young person to go back to Stockholm, under the care of your aunt, promising her all possible protection and intercession, by so tender a *protectrice* as Countess Liewen, which had no other result than tears and prayers, which I was too weak to resist, though it might have been my duty. Give yourself no uneasiness,˙ my dear son, on account of the poor child. Everything will probably turn out well, especially since she does not seem to look unfavorably upon a very decent young man, Bergflygt, the gardener, who lives in the lodge. So it may chance that her father will allow himself to be persuaded, when his daughter's good name is saved by an advantageous match.

Last week I had a pleasant visit. Countess Stenbock, who spent Christmas in West Gothland, showed me the *gracieuse* courtesy, during the journey up to Stockholm, to visit Falkby. She was accompanied by Miss Malin, whom I had not seen for eight years : a *singulière hasard vis à vis* young Larsson, as it was the costume of this same Miss Malin that she used at that unfortunate masquerade which afterward became so sad an event for her. The countess related that anecdote to me, which I pretended to regard as incredible. She would not believe that you were mixed up in that affair, although malice asserted it, and she had dismissed her servant for her *escamotage* with the costume. Neither of the young persons, fortunately, could know the other, from the fact that Larsson, at her own request, remained in the kitchen chamber. Yet I will not conceal, my dear Charles, although little you may give heed thereto, that my god-daughter, Miss Malin, has improved in these eight years, and surpassed all my expectations. It surprises me that you have not spoken with more distinction of so amiable a person, with so excellent an education. In my youth, her talents would not have been looked upon with such indifference. She also spoke about you with a certain regard.

My dear Charles, when this sorrowful time is well past, we will talk more freely of your *carrière* in the fortifications. If, in this *embarras*, your uncle will

W   15

help you, I shall no longer remember his former harshness; but one cannot depend upon him; he himself depends upon his own wisdom, and on that sinful amulet, the king's ring, which bids fair ere long to lift him to the highest place of honor in the kingdom. God preserve you, my dear son, from ever receiving that hellish illusion into your hands, and being tempted by it, as the hearts of many of your kindred have been petrified by it harder than a rock. But stand fast by your father's faith, and by your father's honor; and your father's faith was that God alone can help us, but idols of copper are like the gods of Babylon, and change to ashes, with all who rely on them before the living God. Think upon this, my dear Charles, and write soon, that I may know it is well with you. Night and day this is the prayer of

Your faithful mother,

Eva Bertelskold.

P. S.   In the hurry of your departure, I did not have time to equip you sufficiently with stockings and shirts.   I now send you by a herring merchant, a half dozen of each, and, if it gives them any value, be assured it has been my delight both to knit and sew them.   But as the messenger is just about to depart, I do not know whether Esther has got them all marked. I see that in the haste she has on some of them turned the coronet upside down.   Farewell! I will send your compliments to the countess and Malin. *En toute hâte.*

E. B.

CHAPTER XXXIII.

AN EVENING AT FALKBY.

ONE day, in the beginning of February, a furious snow-storm arose, which covered plains, roads, and ice in East Gothland, with drifts almost as high as a man's head. The little by-road to Falkby was completely filled with snow, so that only the top of the picket-fence rose above the drifts, and the flag on the high pole which Charles Victor Bertelsköld had long ago erected opposite the gable of the red-painted house creaked as it swayed unquietly to and fro, like a sentinel who perceives the approach of a distant enemy.

Twilight had begun, and the Countess of Falkby was sitting, with her knitting-work, in the handsome morocco-covered arm-chair which her son had once sent her from Stockholm, and which comprised the only article of luxury in the otherwise plainly furnished room. A little distance from her, nearer the door, sat Esther Larsson, carding wool; and in the middle of the floor stood Bergflygt, the gardener, who had been called in to consult as to the construction of new hot-beds in the garden. He was a man about thirty years of age, with smoothly-combed light hair, and of very orderly, honest, and respectable appearance; ardent in service—that was his reputation—but whatever exceeded that, seemed to pass beyond his horizon.

When they had arranged as to the hot-beds, the countess skillfully introduced another theme of conversation. The garden lodge, she said, needed repairs before spring, and that could just as well be done now. It would be no more than fair for Bergflygt to have comfortable quarters. He could not be doomed to perpetual solitude. In the pleasant time of the year, he had his flowers ; but on such an evening as this, every human being felt the need of some one whose friendship and confidence could be depended upon . . . .

"One has to look after his window jars then," innocently responded the gardener.

"It cannot take a great while to look after them," resumed the countess, "and afterward, Bergflygt you again feel yourself alone."

"I beg pardon, but it takes a good while to attend to the jars, especially if they get mossy, and caterpillars show themselves on the leaves," continued the young man, without allowing himself to be drawn a hairsbreadth aside from the main matter.

"Esther, my child, see to the tea-water. There is a dreadful storm out-doors, and we need something to warm us."

Esther went out. The countess then thought best to go straight to the business; and without circumlocution she gave him to understand that a sensible and well-to-do man like Bergflygt ought to find himself a good wife.

That was intelligible. The honest young man blushed a little, and conceded that it might not be a bad idea, for while he was out in the garden the housekeeping went loosely, and while he was looking after the beans the sparrows were eating up his peas.

"Well, what hinders you, my friend, from marrying when you please ?"

"Well—well, but there is a little hindrance to everything," asserted the gardener. This hindrance he would not reveal; but enough was inferred, to show that he was musing on the matter, and entertained fears as to the possibility of a "mitten."

"But you know you might be mistaken," objected the countess. "What generous girl would disdain the hand of so fine a fellow ?"

"It might be," replied Bergflygt, with a sigh. "The one I want is said to be very rich."

"I hardly think you need to fear it," observed the countess, smiling. "Would you rather she were a poor girl?"

"That I would, surely," replied the gardener, with a comic expression of hopeless resignation.

"Indeed! To speak plainly, my dear Bergflygt, do you want Esther Larsson for your wife?"

The gardener thumbed his sealskin cap, and bravely answered that he would.

The countess continued: "It is not for me, but for Esther's father, to consent or refuse in this matter. I can only tell you, my friend, that I approve your choice, and wish the blessing of God upon it. You already know the reason why Esther came hither, and what was said about her in Stockholm—a trifling part of it truth, but the most part slander. So, my dear Bergflygt, you must never upbraid her for it, or say that in that, or anything else, you have been deceived. You know, too, how Esther every day becomes more submissive, judicious, and self-controlled—yes, I can say that she has every day become dearer to me, and I am inclined to believe that God sent her that trial in order to humble and bow her stubborn heart. What do you say to going immediately—to-morrow—to Stockholm, to ask her father's consent in person? It is reasonable that a father should be acquainted with the man to whom he gives his child. I shall take care that he learns through others also, that you are a good, honest fellow."

"I am most humbly thankful that your grace is so kind as to put in a good word; otherwise the rich man, who is said to be very like a king, might answer me that sweet-willow and lavender do not thrive together in the same jar. And, as to the journey, you see I would be smart, and get ready to start this evening. . . . . "

" That is impossible.   In such shocking weather I would not put my cat out-doors."

" Not on account of the weather, your grace, when the gaining of such a rare rose as Miss Esther is concerned—but I must be frank enough to say that I truly do not know what she herself has to say about such a rustic as I."

The observation was just, and the countess delayed answering until Esther shortly afterward came in with the tea.   She then motioned the girl to her, took her hand, and spoke to her with tenderness.   " Esther," said she, " as far back as you can remember, you have never had any mother.   Imagine that I am your mother ! "

The girl kissed her hand.

" Yes, child," continued the countess, " and neither have you at this moment a father, of whom to ask advice; and yet it is an important moment to you, for it concerns the restoring of your reputation and the union of yourself with a good man who asks your hand, and with whom, if God wills, you shall become a happy, esteemed and beloved wife.   Answer me now as you would answer your mother : What do you say about it ?   Will you extend your hand to Bergflygt, and become his wife ? "

Esther melted into tears, but answered nothing. The countess, while her own dark eyes gradually acquired that humid lustre which once rendered them so charming, resumed:

" Do not think that I wish to persuade you, child, far less compel you to a consent which you might some day regret, in case it was not given voluntarily. I read your heart.   I know what is passing there.   I have been young, like you; I know those dreams which play before the eyes in the spring-time of life.   Alas, my child, there comes a winter, when everything which does not have a firm root freezes to death; and next to faith in God, that root is respect for one's self and a consciousness of duties fulfilled. You owe yourself a reparation for your youthful error. You have an old father, whom you have deeply grieved and offended; to him also you owe the reparation of being able to walk before him, with head erect, and saying, ' Father, here you have your daughter back again, without blemish in the eyes of the world. Grant her your forgiveness, and all is again well, and your venerable white head shall not be laid with sorrow in the grave ! ' "

Esther was deeply affected. She threw herself on her knees before the countess, and whispered: " Your grace—my benefactress—do with me as you wish— you know best—I am ready to obey you ! "

The countess kissed her forehead, and kindly lifted her up. " Weep no more," said she. " I desire a renunciation, but I demand no obedience. Heaven preserve me from wishing to bind you by a rash promise. Fix for yourself the time you need, in order to be able calmly to consider the resolve you ought to make."

" No, your grace, no ! No consideration ! I will immediately obey," exclaimed Esther, with a touch of her former impetuosity.

The countess, dissatisfied, shook her head. " Remember," she cautioned, " that a promise once given ought to be unalterable. I admit it would be a pleasure to me if your determination did not take much time, as events may occur which—in a word, your father may come when we least expect it. But I entreat you, my child, reflect at least until to-morrow ! "

" No, no ! " continued Esther, in the same tone. " Who can say that to-morrow I shall be the same as I am to-day ? " and, leaning toward the countess's ear she whispered, "I fear . . . . myself ! "

The countess looked her sternly in the eye, almost with amazement, and a long painful pause ensued. The hitherto faint-hearted suitor began to lose patience, and stammered forth something to the effect that he would by no means compel the highly-estimable young woman against her will; she should say plainly yes or no.

"Well," said the countess, more severely, even harshly, and continuing the dark, searching look, "act in such way as you can answer for to God and to your conscience!"

Esther looked her straight in the eye. Her cheeks were dyed a bright red. She drew herself up with a dignity scarcely beneath the countess's own, and which was worthy of her father in his stately moments. "Your grace," said she, "I pardon you that in your heart you have increased the burden of my fault by adding one of which I am not guilty. If I extend my hand to this man, I do so without blushing before God or my conscience. What I have done wrong, he knows; and I have nothing to add, since I am neither better nor worse than I believe myself to be. Like him, I am of humble burgher origin; we may therefore prove suitable for each other. But neither your birth and rank, your grace, nor your kindness, which while I live I shall never forget, can permit you to affront me beyond what I have justly deserved. You perhaps do not think that we people of burgher rank have also hearts that feel, when they are trampled upon and wounded; but you are mistaken, your grace; we can be as proud as you!"

It was the daughter of the burgher king who spoke. But before the countess found time to reply, the jingle of bells was unexpectedly heard out in the yard.

CHAPTER XXXIV.

A GUEST AT FALKBY.

IT is a common experience that the very noblest characters, who otherwise view life from elevated points of vision, are often more open than others to the prejudices of their time. At the period of this story it was still half a century to that remarkable year, 1789. Who can wonder that as early as the year 1739, when the aristocracy was governing Sweden in the name of freedom, a noble lady like Countess Bertelsköld believed herself doing a good deed, when she made a suitable match for the slandered daughter of a burgher! This happy chance was in her eyes so plainly a providence from heaven for Esther's own good, that she probably was not aware how closely her own maternal plans for her son were connected with this union. The severe trials through which the countess had passed had not been without influence on her active and energetic soul, whose surface had become hardened by them; and it was therefore with no less surprise than anger that she heard Esther Larsson speak in her father's spirit, with a pride which the countess had not expected of a young person who in her view occupied an intermediate position between a waiting-maid and an adopted daughter.

She therefore found in the noise of the bells in the yard a welcome occasion to send Bergflygt out to see who could have ventured thither in this dreadful storm. She then turned to Esther, who was still standing before her, flushed and erect, with the daring words on her lips, and addressed her with the commanding tone of a mistress. "What does this mean?"

she asked. "Has my trouble with you been so entirely in vain that you forget to whom you speak?"

But Esther was now once more in her wild mood, and without lowering her glance replied: "It is not I who have forgotten it; it is your grace who has forgotten that the worm writhes when trampled under foot. I am eternally thankful for your protection; but it does not give your grace a right to insult me with unworthy suspicions. Your grace fears that I have some claim upon Count Charles. But I tell your grace, and it ought not to be forgotten, that sooner than debase myself by seeking to force myself into your family, I would die alone in a drift by the roadside."

While she was speaking there entered, accompanied by the gardener, a tall, white-haired, fur-clad old man, completely covered with snow, which he had not troubled himself in the least to shake off; he paused some seconds at the door, and answered Esther's last words with a deep sigh, as he said, half aloud: "I thank Thee, God of Jacob, that I have re-found my last-born in the land of Egypt, and that she is still worthy to be called my child!"

Esther started and turned around. "My father!" she exclaimed, and hid her face in her hands.

The countess, who had never seen the burgher king, understood in a moment whom she had before her. But she controlled herself, and went with dignity to meet him.

"I suppose," said she, "that it is Representative Larsson who is honoring me with a visit? I beg you be welcome in my house; and I esteem myself happy in being able to give you back your lost child. Esther, embrace your father, and beg him to forgive you for all the sorrow you have brought upon his gray head."

Esther stood immovable, and did not venture to raise her eyes. Perhaps she was just then thinking how her cousin, Marie Larsson, had once been received

on an occasion like this. But, whether it was years
and sorrow or those words he had just now heard his
daughter speak that had broken the stern anger of the
father, suffice it to say, the old man stretched out his
arms, and, with trembling voice, said: "Esther! My
child! My beloved child!"

And Esther flew into his arms. She had no words
with which to plead; she had only tears—such childlike, such passionately flowing tears, out of the inmost
deep of her heart, that they choked her voice, and with
that eloquent prayer she lay sobbing on her father's
breast.

It was as though an awful spell had in a moment
been broken. Old Larsson suddenly forgot all the
bitterness, all the threatening condemnations, on which
he had brooded during the long and difficult journey
through snow and tempest to find his daughter. Before Esther, the past disappeared like an evil dream, in
the over-happy feeling of possessing her father's love;
and the anger of the countess melted away like a
snow-drift in the spring sunshine, at the sight of such
an unexpected reconciliation between an erring child
and a harsh and deeply wounded father. The noble
lady understood it well—she was herself a mother.

But Bergflygt, the gardener, who had always
been accustomed to tread the room of his strict
mistress with the most profound respect, could not
comprehend the incivility of the stranger in entering
this sanctuary clad in a snowy fur-coat, and ·it was
with undisguised astonishment that he regarded the
scene between father and daughter, which in his eyes
had the noteworthy consequence that the snow began
to melt and run down from the fur coat upon Esther's
hair and shoulders. When, after the first moment of
the meeting, a silence ensued, the discreet man felt
obliged to entreat Miss Larsson to take care or she
would certainly be wet through.

That innocent observation operated on the agitated

feelings of the company like a wholesome cold shower-
bath. With a sunshine of smiles, Esther freed herself
from the arms of her father, loosened his belt, and
helped him off with his wet coat. The countess
ordered a warm meal, and bade her guest take
the seat of honor — the arm-chair — a distinction she was not in the habit of bestowing on
everybody. And Larsson accepted it without compliment; it was not at all his custom to make use of
compliments before people of quality. But it was
seen that he did as much as his harsh nature would
allow, not to fail in due deference toward the hostess.
Perhaps he feared to call forth new storms, which
might disturb his dearly-bought paternal joy.

Esther, occupied by the same fear, divided her
tenderest attention between the two old people. Now
she sought to read in the looks of the countess her
least wish, and anticipated it, while her pleading eyes
expressed a silent remorse for her lately unrestrained
passion. Now she again turned to her father with a
conciliatory caress, and as she furtively watched him
while she seemed to busy herself in spreading the
supper-table, her eyes were again obscured by tears.
She found her father much aged since she had last
seen him. The inflexible neck had acquired a bend,
the high forehead had become furrowed by deep
wrinkles, and it seemed to her as though the commanding look in those penetrating eyes had grown weak.
But she tried to persuade herself that it was from the
weariness of the journey. Indeed, the last mile he
had been obliged to wade on foot through the drifts,
as the horses sunk so deep in the snow that they were
hardly able to draw the empty sledge.

The countess, equally careful not to awaken the
storms before everything was prepared, led the
conversation from the journey and the snow-
storm to the farming at Falkby: and, quite unob-
trusively, allowed the services of her gardener to

stand forth in the most favorable light. Among other things, she described how Bergflygt had ordered half a peck of potatoes from Germany, and succeeded finely in cultivating that new vegetable, still very rare in Sweden, and in Finland almost unknown, and which ought to become very useful. Bergflygt, who had received a signal to remain, and had hitherto kept himself bashfully near the door, was now made to describe his attempt to the member of the diet, which he did plainly and clearly, as was his habit where he was in his proper domain. To the secret delight of the countess, Larsson seemed to follow this description with much attention. His ingenious head immediately designed a plan to introduce the new vegetable at Bertila, in Storkyro, and therefore he wished to under- stand the method exactly. Upon this the countess not only offered him a few of the roots for seed, but also took care that at the supper-table he himself had an opportunity to test the excellent qualities of the Amer- ican tuber.

Thus far all was well, and the three persons most interested seemed to have made a silent compact not to touch upon the delicate subject that evening, when, unfortunately, Bergflygt, who felt extremely encour- aged and flattered by the unwonted honor of sitting at the countess's own table, began innocently to speak about the apple-tree which was injured last autumn by frost, and how he covered the roots with straw, " the very same day that the young count came hither with Miss Esther."

If Falkby had fallen in ruins, it could hardly have called forth greater consternation than that innocent recollection awakened in two of those present. The countess sent the servant one of those flashing glances which kill the word on bolder lips than his, and the honest gardener was instantly stricken dumb, without himself knowing why. Esther blushed to the very tips of her ears and contemplated the little blue roses on the English plate before her as closely as though she had wished to look straight through it. The hostess hardly ventured to steal a glance at her gray-haired guest.

But this evening Larsson was not himself. A single time his forehead was wrinkled in the well-known creases, after which he turned to the gardener and said quite calmly : " When you have young trees you ought to tend them better. If they come to harm, it is most frequently the fault of the one who reared them. But it is likely, if God gives spring and sunshine, that they will again come to life and bear blessed fruits."

" Yes," said the countess, with emotion, " I know such a young tree. The storm had broken a branch, and the frost had blanched its leaves ; but, thank God, root and pith were sound. You have spoken truly : this tree needs tending and warm sunshine, and, if God will, it shall yet bear rich fruit."

They arose from the table. Larsson kissed his daughter on the forehead, thanked the hostess, and as he went to his room, said : " To-morrow I will thank you for my daughter."

CHAPTER XXXV.

THE INHERITANCE OF THE CENTURIES.

THE following morning, the snow-storm had given place to mild weather. At eight o'clock Larsson, stiff and stately, entered the room at Falkby where the countess was awaiting him at the breakfast-table. Early in the morning Esther had had a long private conversation with her father.

The salutations were made with a certain gravity,

some commonplace words were exchanged about the night's rest and the change in the weather, and the company sat down to the table. The old man ate with a fair appetite, but Esther's plate remained untouched, and her eyes were swollen with weeping.

When the meal was over, Larsson arose, bowed politely to the hostess, and thanked her for himself and his daughter. They were now about to go. The horses had been ordered.

All this seemed to the countess somewhat cold. She wasted no empty objections, but her heart softened at the thought of Esther's coming fate. Not until now, when they were to be separated forever, was she aware that this unfortunate child had become dearer to her than she herself had suspected. There was an affinity of soul between the two, which now, for the first time, became apparent to her : the same ardent temperament, the same energetic will, the same decided, proud, independent character. The difference lay in unlike ages, unlike trainings, unlike social positions. The foundation was the same—the rest depended on the chances of life.

The countess deliberated with herself whether she ought to be silent or speak. But when the hour of leave-taking had come, and Esther was resting on her bosom, it seemed to her as though her words yesterday had become a truth, and that she was a mother who was sending her child out to unknown scenes in the dreary cold of winter. She resolved to speak, and solicited a conversation alone with her esteemed guest.

Larsson accompanied her into an adjoining room, and the countess, with that caution which she thought ought to be observed, said that she owed to him an account of his daughter's sojourn at Falkby. She had received Esther as an erring child, whose precipitate flight had its reason in the disgrace she had suffered and the taunts she feared in Stockholm. Esther was that young tree, which had perhaps not been tended with sufficient care, and which had been injured by the frost, but which would again flourish and bear fruit under kind nurture. Her father could be at rest; the countess returned his daughter to him improved and purified by that hard trial. She hoped, therefore, that all missteps were forgotten, and that the forgiveness was complete.

Larsson laconically replied that he was grateful for the protection of the countess, and would no further bear his daughter's fault in mind, if she only thenceforth showed him that perfect obedience which was her filial duty.

"Well," continued the countess, warmed by the thought that she could still do something for Esther's happiness, "if you now possessed a proof that your daughter's reputation had not suffered—if, for example, an honest man, who is worthy of her, should ask you for her hand, what answer would you give?"

Larsson was silent for some moments. A suspicion flashed through his proud soul; and with a frown, he asked what her grace wished to say in this connection.

"Only this," replied the countess, unintimidated, "that there is a good young man in my house, who would esteem himself happy if you would give him Esther as a wife. You have only to consent, and Esther will become an esteemed, an honest, and a happy wife."

Larsson interpreted these words as a confirmation of his suspicion. He arose, and his glance darkened ominously.

"My consent!" he exclaimed. "That is enough! I now see through it all. I now know why you sent your son to Finland; why he insinuated himself into my kinsman's house in Stockholm; why Esther was disgraced, enticed to flight, and found an asylum with you. Do you want me to tell you why? Because your son was poor, and needed my money! Yes, your

grace, that is how it was! My money, in the end, out-
weighed all your titled pride, and you were not ashamed
to lower yourself so deeply as to call a burgher girl
your daughter, in order that your son should have a
chance to revel in luxury and gild his decayed escutcheon with the hard earned possessions of a simple
merchant. Such you are, high illustrious gentlemen
and ladies, who now-a-days rule the realm of Sweden.
You look haughtily down upon us, and consider us
convenient, and just worthy to brush your shoes and
carry the train of your skirts; but when you need our
gold, you are gracious enough to put up with it, and
our children in the bargain. My consent! To what
purpose should it be needed? I am no longer rich; I
am poor, your ladyship, poorer than yourself. So take
back your words! What do you care about my daugh
ter, when she can no longer be balanced with gold?"

"You utterly misunderstand my meaning," responded the countess, surprised and vexed, in her turn,
over so unexpected an interpretation of her well-meant
proposal.

But, without hearing her, Larsson continued:

"I will tell you something which you perhaps do
not know, or have by this time forgotten. My family
also has a long lineage. It dates as far back as the
family of the Bertelskölds. And between our families
there has been an hostility from the beginning, because
the one stood on the side of the oppressor and the
other on the side of the oppressed. I still recall the
time when your husband's father begged as a favor to
buy a few barrels of grain of my father, as all his
people were starving. I also remember the day when
six Larssons, all splendid young men, placed themselves under the command of your husband, and none
of them came back, for that honor cost them their
heart's blood. Lastly, I remember your brother-in-
law, the miserable intriguer who has now set himself
up to govern the kingdom. It is he who has destroyed

X　　15*

peace and concord in the land, who has twice disgraced daughters of my race, and will bring me to the beggar's staff. And you ask my consent for your son to wed my daughter!"

The countess, although herself wounded at her tenderest point, had found time to regain her composure.

"Representative Larsson," said she, with noble dignity, "you can be assured that I perfectly share your opinion concerning a connection between my son and your daughter. Moreover, that matter has never been in question. My design was to ask the hand of Esther for my gardener; a match which on both sides I regard as suitable. And now that you know my meaning, I trust you will look upon your other suppositions as at least quite precipitate."

Larsson continued: "Your ladyship is right in explaining her meaning. I have perhaps thought too much on old memories. But since I am poor now, as I said, I cannot be of service even in providing for your ladyship's gardener; and it might thus be best to close this conversation. Though—one word yet: Since I find that we are of the same opinion about our children, and it might possibly happen that they themselves had opinions of their own, ... indeed, who knows?—a count can also sometimes fall into follies, ... then let us here, in the presence of the all-seeing God, promise, you to me and I to you, never by word or deed to consent to the union of our children with each other! May none of us shrink from our destiny. May our families in all future time continue to stand in two distinct encampments, hand against hand and heart against heart, so that no cowardly reconciliation between us shall take place before the times have attained their consummation, and the verdict of posterity has been rendered in the cause about which we are contesting!"

The high-toned soul of Countess Bertelsköld perfectly comprehended the greatness of the thought which lay concealed in the hereditary hatred of the old burgher king. By birth and disposition an aristocrat in the better signification of the word, she was just as much convinced of the right of the nobility as Larsson of that of the people; and on this point her individual wishes coincided with what she regarded as the weal of her native country. She was therefore upon the point of unconditionally giving the promise demanded of her, when she was startled by a sight very unexpected to both.

Through the open door of the large room she saw her own son—whom she thought was far away in Norway—standing by the side of Esther Larsson, whose hand he had taken, while by some inaudible words he seemed trying to inspire her with courage and hope.

"You here!" exclaimed the countess, forgetting everything at this sight, which seemed an illusion of her excited fancy.

"Yes, my mother, and in the nick of time—thanks to your story about a certain rival!" joyfully exclaimed Charles Victor Bertelsköld, as he entered the room. "Not until the Norse Alps reared their high walls between us, and I stood on the unknown snowy grave of my father, not until then did it become clear to me that life was valueless without Esther's love. Representative Larsson, I sue, humbly, and in all honor, for the hand of your daughter. Mother! I beg that you will call Esther Larsson your daughter!"

Larsson and the countess exchanged glances. Higher walls than the Norse Alps now arose between the two young people—double unyielding walls of hatred and the inherited prejudices of centuries. The countess was silent; she knew the answer from the other side, and it did not fail to come.

The inflexible, severe, white-haired old man took his daughter firmly by the arm, and drew her with him.

"Come!" said he. "I thank the count for the proposal, and it may perhaps not be very badly meant. But fire and water can never agree. A Larsson and a Bertelsköld can never belong to each other. Know my answer, sir count; and I need not say that it is my last. Farewell, lady countess. Come, Esther, the horses are ready."

Esther obeyed. She did not weep; she did not entreat. She knew too well that the inheritance of centuries had separated them. But a gloomy fire burned in her eyes, and she whispered to the astonished youth, who vainly sought to detain her: "Do not follow me! My father is right. We can not belong to each other. But love each other, Charles— that we can do, even though sea and Alps divide us, for our whole life."

And she tore herself loose from her father, threw her arms around the young man's neck, and kissed him. "Farewell!" said she. "And now, father, I belong to you. Command me!"

A few moments later the sledge sped away from Falkby, and Countess Bertelsköld was alone with her returned son.

CHAPTER XXXVI.

THE KING'S RING.

ONCE more we enter the cabinet of President Count Torsten Bertelsköld. The ante-chamber is filled with foreign diplomats, courtiers, military men and higher officers, awaiting audience. All turn toward the rising sun. All vie in begging a glance of favor from the man who is now to take the reins of the kingdom, and, lifted on triumphing Hat-crowns, steer the fate of Sweden toward new paths, in the name of the estates and of freedom.

It is indeed in the midst of Sweden's so-called time of freedom. Within sits the soon-to-be omnipotent man, the real king of Sweden, although another bears the name. He has perhaps grown old somewhat, and withered, under the burden of all those intrigues which have conducted him to power; but no one observes it. The embroidered velvet coat skillfully conceals his leanness; the extremely well-dressed peruke hides the gray hair; a delicately-applied almost imperceptible paint gives the color of health and youth to the furrowed brow and shriveled cheeks. But a green shade over the eyes somewhat obscures the once keen glance, which penetrates all, yet can itself be penetrated by but few. That signifies but little, however; a casual weakness in the sight, induced by hard night-work. The count sits erect and vigilant as a youth, in the easy-chair inlaid with ivory and mother-of-pearl, and suns himself in the splendor of his approaching power. He stands at the goal of his whole life's endeavor. What incredible toils, what long-continued tension of mind, has it not cost him to reach this point! But the game is now won; he is now to occupy that place from which he has hurled his great master, Count Horn. What does it concern him, the successor, that this throne is built on the fluctuating wave of popular party favor? Has he not grown gray in the art of directing these unstable elements? And shall he not now, more than ever before, know how to control them?

The private secretary had not yet finished the report of the many and important communications of the morning, when the *valet* announced, in succession, the newly-fledged councilors Count Posse and Baron Löven, councilor of the superior court Ehrenpreuss, and secretary of state Cederström, together with ambassador Count de Lynar.

" Beg their excellencies to have the goodness to go up into the little *salon*," was the reply.

"Chamberlain Monsieur de Broman."

" Tell him to wait in the ante-chamber."

" Fiscal Spolin . . . ."

" Drive the impudent scoundrel out of doors ! "

The private secretary continued : " Humble memorial from the officers of the crown in Storkyro parish, Finland ; probate suit touching Bertila farm, continued by reason of the absence of the defendant under lawful excuse as member of the diet."

" Nevertheless will go thither.   Continue."

" Petition for grace respecting manslaughter and wounds from single combat; his majesty, from reasons which have appeared, has thought best, in chancery, to mitigate the sentence of the court-martial concerning Lieutenant Honorable Count Charles Victor . . . ."

" Stop !   I know already: One year's suspension from service, and a half year's exile.   One must do something for his good-for-nothing nephews. .. . . Go on ! "

" The board of chancellors is filled, agreeable to the proposal of your excellency.   Lord chancellor Baron Von Kochen and chancery councilors Nerés and Bahr hint of resigning . . . ."

" Add Count Bonde and others.   Continue."

" Count Tessin petitions for the office of ambassador to Paris."

" Indeed !   He petitions?   Well, when one has played out his farce in Stockholm, it is time to begin a comedy in Paris.   He shall have the position.   Go on ! "

" His majesty, through Monsieur de Broman, hints of increased pension for Councilor Count Taube . . . ."

" Refused.   His majesty has not always been pleased to adapt himself to the needs of the realm and the wishes of the patriots.   And as her majesty is said to be of a different opinion, the increase might be an indiscretion."

"Her majesty, through gentleman-of-the-bed-chamber Baron Höök, mentions the German waiting-women. They might be removed as superfluous, and the expense saved to increase the income of the other court ladies."

"Her majesty professes a praiseworthy frugality for the waiting-women; but as his majesty will probably have a different opinion, note down that the pay of the German ladies will be increased. Is there anything further?"

"Nothing, except renewed entreaty for support for the widow of the soldier Flinta. She says your excel-lency bound himself by oath to do this, when her husband took your excellency safe and sound to and from the late king Charles, at the siege of Stralsund."

"Flinta? Lives at Falkby, does she not?"

"At Falkby."

"Refused. You can now conclude."

"I will then have to reply that your **excellency** does not recollect the oath."

"You will answer nothing. Have I time to concern myself with old women's artifices, and oaths which I have never sworn? Enough. You can go."

With a low bow the secretary departed.

The count remained a moment alone. He was right. Who at this time could demand of him a thought of poor widows and long-forgotten oaths? He reveled in triumph to see the king and queen of Sweden, amidst the swarm of other supplicants, implore him, and implore in vain, for interpositions which related intimately to their personal sympathies and antipathies. With what delight would he not now behold that mimic king who once so deeply scorned and humiliated him, scorned and humiliated in his turn, and writhing beneath his overruling influence! And not only they, but all his enemies, high and low, should feel the

weight of his arm, should be themselves obliged to
bear him on their shoulders to power. The Hats
themselves, who thought to find in him a tool for their
plans, should learn their mistake. He should hold
them in check with the Cap party, the same as the
Caps with them. True to his habit, he should found
his inaccessible empire upon the very dissension which
was sundering the kingdom. And with all this he
would now for the first time carry out that idea which
he had received as an inheritance from his father, but
carry it beyond what his father had even ventured to
dream: he would place the nobility far above both
king and people, and when he had accomplished this
he would transfer Sweden into a republic, after the
Polish model, with arbitrary masters, and serfs; but
the founder of all this happiness reserved to himself to
be the most powerful, before whom the other mighty
ones should humbly bow.

At these proud, selfish, aspiring thoughts, which
caused him to forget the whole crowd of people waiting without, the count mechanically stretched out his
clenched hand, as though at once to embrace and
crush Sweden. He then felt on his finger the pressure
of that ring, which he had regained in a singular manner, and from which he had afterwards never more
wished to part. It was the king's ring.

A demoniac thought flashed through his soul.
" What despicable creatures are men ! " said he to himself. " They talk about a God, a Providence ; and this
miserable bit of copper is enough to put them to
shame. What has God, what has Providence, done
for me ? Nothing ! But this ring—it is ridiculous, but
it is nevertheless so—this ring carries irresistible fortune with it. When I had lost it, everything went
against me : work, wisdom, art—everything was in
vain. But since I have regained it, I succeed in everything. Yes, everything ! There is nothing any longer
impossible for me. I might ask a crown, if crowns in

this country were not now-a-days at a discount. But, if I gave them back their value? . . . "

Bertelsköld smiled, as he thoughtfully twisted the closely fitting ring. "Why not a crown?" he murmured.

Unconsciously he had the ring loose in his hand— that ring which, during eighteen years, had almost grown fast to his finger. A wonderful feeling, half scorn, half trembling, took possession of him. He held the ring toward the light, to see if he could still distinguish its mystical letters, R. R. R.—*Rex Regi Rebellis*. "Tell me," said he, "tell me—shall I ask a crown?"

Perhaps his hand trembled when he pronounced those words, for the ring slipped out of his fingers, and rang against the floor with a peculiar foreign sound; —at least, in the ears of the count it sounded like a lute-string suddenly severed.

Count Bertelsköld sprang up from the *fauteuil* to pick up the ring; but it grew strangely dark before his eyes. With difficulty he found the bell. "Light!" cried he to the *valet*. "Bring in light! You see it is dark!"

The servant looked with astonishment at his master, for it was ten o'clock in the forenoon, and the room was illuminated by broad daylight.

But the count continued to grope on the floor, as though in the deepest darkness, and constantly called for light, for he had lost something, he said, but what it was, he could not prevail upon himself to say. He probably feared that some one might again rob him of his most precious treasure.

The *valet* obeyed his command, and brought two lighted wax candles. Useless care! the count, in an irritated tone, complained that he was left alone in the darkness. The officers came out in confusion, and whispers soon reached the many who were waiting, and whose patience was about giving out, in the ante-

16

chamber and little *salon*. The rumor spread that Count Bértelsköld had suddenly become insane.

His physician was sent for, and the visitors crowded curiously about the door. They wanted to see the man who so recently was to govern a kingdom, and now was not able to govern himself.

The physician came, and found the count sitting in the *fauteuil*. A cold sweat had deluged forehead and cheeks, washed away the paint, and exposed to the eyes of all a pale, withered, and emaciated face. But they were mistaken—he was not insane—not yet.

"Is that you, my dear doctor?" said he, with a remnant of his former courteous tone. "Tell me, what signify these infamous whisperings around me, and what is the meaning of this thick darkness which envelopes me?"

The physician looked at him searchingly, examined his eyes, and replied seriously: "It means, sir count, that you are blind!"

"What? Blind? Are you mad? My eyes have been weak, it is true, but an hour ago I saw tolerably well."

"It is no common weakness, sir count; it is *amaurosis*. It has been slowly developing, and I have long feared something like this. But you must have experienced some violent emotion just now which hastened the attack of the malady."

"Yes—that is true," said the count, confused and brokenly. "You see, my dear doctor, I chanced to lose something—a bagatelle—not worth a copper farthing—a souvenir of my deceased father. One does not lose such things, you know, without chagrin, and—but tell me, it will not be long before I regain my sight? Listen, doctor! I must have my sight back, and that soon, I tell you! As though I had time to wait! Do you think my enemies will wait for me?"

"Sir count, I should deceive you if I gave you a hope which art is unable to fulfill. Everything indicates that you are, alas! for your whole remaining life irremediably blind."

"What! miserable charlatan! And you venture to tell me that, and do not know that you put your head at stake! Doctor, you must give me back my sight, do you hear? Dear doctor—you know that I can reward you royally. Say, what do you wish? Honors? Titles? Gold? All are yours; you have only to choose, for you know that Sweden awaits but my word. But then you must also promise to give me back the use of my eyes. *Grand ciel!* Govern the kingdom, and be blind! Why! that is absurd, is it not? But do laugh, doctor! Admit that it would be a *bêtise*, a *sottise!*"

"Once more, your excellency, I am at your service; but your sight I cannot restore."

The count sprung up from the *fauteuil*. "Ah!" he exclaimed, "I am imposed upon, I am imposed upon! These wretches venture to defy me, and it is not in my power to punish them. Where is my ring? Give me back my ring!—No—away! All, away! You might steal my fortune. *Malheur! Quel malheur!* My meanest servant can attain a crown! My bitterest enemy can conquer the world! And I am blind—impotent and blind! I now remember it was so: the king's ring was never to be lost éxcept by broken oaths! And such a miserable oath! Have I not broken more sacred oaths? Listen, my friends—if I have yet one single friend, then go to the widow Flinta, at Falkby, and offer her all my wealth, if she will get me back the ring! But she must do it soon, or I am lost, for there is no prosperity for me, in Heaven or on earth, without the king's ring!"

And thus the unhappy man continued to grope and rave, while those present drew timidly back; and the leaders of the Hats were already whispering among themselves that there was nothing here to be done, and that they must hasten to offer the power to Gyllen-borg.

Then, with the gentleness of an angel, a black-clad figure entered, approached the fallen statesman, drew him with mild force to the arm-chair, and whispered, " Torsten, do you know me ? "

" Ebba ! " exclaimed he, tightly pressing her hand. " Can you once more give me back my ring ? "

" No," said she ; " but let us pray that I can give you back your God ! ' What does it profit a man if he gain the whole world and lose his own soul ? ' "

CHAPTER XXXVII.

EIGHTEEN MONTHS AFTER.

ONE day in September of the year 1740, the first frosty night of autumn had been succeeded by a beautiful sunny morning, when a young girl was returning with a quick step to town from the vegetable gardens outside of Wasa. In each hand she carried a basket, the one filled with turnips, the other with cabbages, and on her head she wore a checkered woolen cloth, somewhat drawn forward over the forehead, as though to conceal a pair of handsome dark eyes and her black hair. When she passed by Korsholm she threw, as though from old habit, a transient glance up toward the ramparts, but continued walking, and turned from the main street into an obscure lane, where she went into a low and humble old house. She there set down her basket in the main room, which was also kitchen, and said to an older woman who was placing an iron pot over the fire :

" I have had good luc. to-day. Where will you

find more beautiful turnips or finer cabbages, Veronica?
The magistrate himself cannot show better ones. . . .
Do you think I can speak with father?"

"He is in the other room with Grenman, planning
business. I think he intends to open a store here in
the alley. Oh, Esther! Esther! To think that father
does not rather move to the house of brother-in-law
Blom, who bought father's large farm last spring, when
we were obliged to sell almost everything we possessed
and move hither into this old hut! Instead of struggling with poverty and care, father might still be able
to live in wealth as in old times, and you, my poor
Esther, would not have to go a mile a day for market-
ing in the villages."

"Live on charity, do you mean?" replied Esther
Larsson, a little warmly. "No, sister. Sooner than
beg our bread of our avaricious brother-in-law, who
bid in father's best possession for a song, we could go
to Storkyro, and ask a roof over our heads at the house
of our Hungarian cousin who took that pasture from
us. That could easily enough be done," added Esther,
good-naturedly; "he has just proposed to me."

"But you certainly never mean to accept a man
who is half Turk?" objected Veronica, with undisguised astonishment.

"Yes, when I have well forgotten that other one;
but as that is not likely to happen in my time, Istvan
—or Penna, as they now call him—will have to seek
where he pleases for a housewife for Bertila farm. Let
us see: I will open the door of father's room a little."

At these words, Esther softly opened the door of
the only side-room in the house and peeped in. In the
room, on an unpainted bench and by a table as mean,
sat the old burgher king, now cast down from his
prosperity and power, busied with his inseparable confidential assistant, Grenman (who had been faithful to
him in days of distress), in designing plans to make a
new fortune.

Larsson had grown old, and his stiff neck was bent by trouble ; but while his sharp eyes seemed to discern the times, his inventive head continued, as before, to spy out the best means of drawing advantage from conjectures.

" I tell you, Grenman," said he, " any one who wants to profit when it rains porridge must have the ladle ready in time. That we are going to have war before next year's grain is harvested, is as sure as ' morning flush foul weather brings.' But Blom and the others are making their calculations on the supposition of fine weather. I tell you, Grenman, there is going to be shocking weather. Within two years, a barrel of salt will cost two barrels of rye, and Russian hemp will be found only in the gallows. We must have money and lay in a supply."

With a sigh, the bookkeeper shook his gray head. He did not want to reveal the truth, that credit was at an end.

Animated by his speculation, Larsson continued : " I will write to Stockholm ; the Hollanders will sometime be obliged to hand over damages for our plundered ships. My old peasants will deliver me tar on credit, and Wasa rye for export. If that does not succeed, I will dress wounds, you split planks, my sons chop wood, and my daughters knit stockings. Money, Grenman, money we must have for salt and hemp. Next summer we will cut the window of the room out for a door, and make us a store."

" Yes, that looks likely," nodded Esther, in the door ; " you dress wounds ! No, father, I will tell you a better speculation. To-morrow you will be a member of the diet, and a member of the diet has credit."

" That depends," said the old man, smiling. Notwithstanding all changes and vicissitudes, there was still a glimpse left of the indulgent father and the spoiled favorite.

"Rely upon it," continued Esther. "I heard it said that there is a large party here which will vote for you, because the other is going to vote for brother-in-law Blom."

"Go away! No; come first and let me hug you, my little bother, but my last delight in this world! There, now you can go. And therefore it is my opinion, Grenman, that we should draw on Merlades & Sons, in Cadiz, for three thousand dollars, and order salt through Friberg & Winkelman, of Stockholm."

"But it will not do, it will not do," bewailed the bookkeeper, in a kind of desperation; for it was probably the first time in his life that he had ventured to oppose his patron and master.

"Will not do? Why will it not do?"

"Because," stammered Grenman, now driven to extremity; "because we have no credit. Tar, grain, everything goes to Blom past our door; and if I ask what it costs per barrel, behold they put on an insolent air and answer, 'Money!' Three thousand dollars! And we have not thirty!"

Larsson made no reply, and sunk into a gloomy meditation. Without money, the merchant is often obliged to extricate himself; but without credit, he is ruined.

"Perhaps it would not be impossible to find a way out," resumed Grenman, mischievously snapping his fingers at an indescribable article of birch-bark, representing a snuff-box.

"What do you mean, man? Do you presume once more to speak of partnership with Blom?"

"I mean," innocently responded the bookkeeper, "that now, since President Bertelsköld has become insane, and his nephew inherits the whole property, which is said to amount to five or six barrels of gold, it only devolves upon dear father to . . . ."

Larsson gave him a pair of eyes like three-inch spikes. But Grenman, observing his goddaughter

Esther in the door, gained a new transport of unprecedented courage, and boldly continued:

"So it only devolves upon dear father to satisfy all, and at the same time strengthen the credit of the house. In May, Merlades & Sons send a cargo of salt to Friberg & Winkelman; in June, Friberg & Winkelman send the cargo to Larsson & Co.; the following January, Larsson & Co. accept a bill of exchange on Merlades & Sons; net balance, one hundred per cent."

The old merchant snapped his fingers and walked a few turns to and fro in the room. The temptation was strong, but not strong enough to break his iron will. "Bertelsköld & Larsson!" he muttered. "No, that is a firm with which our Lord has no business to transact."

"But you have yourself said that terrible weather is coming," continued Grenman, who, like a slow horse, having once got in motion, jogged on. "Who is to be your daughter's support when you fail her?"

"Esther has brothers."

"And will she all her life eat their bread? No, master, there is a good deal of your own disposition in her. You will not go into partnership with your own son-in-law; Esther will not go into company with her brothers or her sisters-in-law. It is all yarn from the same hank, father Larsson; and for that reason you might untangle the skein."

"There is some truth in what you say," responded Larsson, struck by the justice of the remark. "I still hope to see the day when the storm breaks loose. I will then have a chance to see on which side the young man has placed himself. Esther, does he still write to you as he did the first year?"

"Yes, father. You have allowed it."

"Write him, then, to espouse the cause of his people, and I will think of your union."

"Father," replied Esther, "Charles Bertelsköld is

a man like yourself, and does not sell his principles. I can not write him what you ask."

"Well, let us say no more about it. . . . . What can Grönberg and Salovius want of me?"

The two honorable Wasa burghers entered, somewhat embarrassed, it seemed, over the poverty which reigned in the house, and after many circumlocutions stated their business, which was that the party opposing Blom intended to reëlect the former highly esteemed representative of the town, which duty they hoped he would not decline; but to this they would, however, add a little stipulation, namely, not to forfeit for the city the favor of those in power.

The burgher king arose, with head erect, and pointed out through the open window, which commanded a view of the ramparts of Korsholm. "Go," said he, "go to the ramparts over there and command them to become seats of green turf, in order that the high and mighty may be able to sit comfortably on them. What, think you, would the ramparts answer? They would say to you: 'We were not measured according to the standard of to-day, and were not made as a support for the arrogance of this hour. We were laid out in such a way that we could last through ages, and we were erected here to defend our country.' That is also my answer to your terms. You would never persuade me to be a Hat, brother, though I should hold out for twenty diets. And if Wasa is so concerned about the favor of those in power, she must send more pliable men than I. But then, Wasa may also consider what it will afterwards have left of itself."

Grenman and the two burghers exchanged glances. The one did not understand how a man could be poor, without friends, without credit, without the possibility of again beginning an active life, and still disdain connection with a rich and noble house, which could prepare the way for everything desirable. The others

Y

did not understand how one could be a fallen greatness, humiliated, slighted, yes, scorned by near
relations, and still thrust from him a brilliant reparation, merely to hold fast obstinately to old prejudices.
All three were, however, silent; the tall, white-haired
old man, with his old-time earnestness and firm bearing, overawed them into silence.

But Esther Larsson understood her father. She
approached him, threw her arms around his neck, and
whispered: " Father, you are a man, and I am proud
to be your daughter."

Lightning Source UK Ltd.
Milton Keynes UK
UKHW040618231118
332756UK00011B/1252/P